PRAISE FOR MARY STRAND

For *Driving with the Top Down*:

"*Driving with the Top Down* is like a margarita: tart, refreshing, and utterly intoxicating. At times funny, at times poignant, but always exhilarating, this is a novel you'll consume in lusty gulps. It's a journey full of twists and turns and surprising detours. The trip is a joy from beginning to end." —JUDITH ARNOLD, *USA TODAY* Bestselling Author

For *Sunsets on Catfish Bar*:

"Emotionally complex and deeply involving, this is the story of a woman dealing with impossible challenges—and finding grace and humanity in the journey." —SUSAN WIGGS, #1 New York Times Bestselling Author

For *Pride, Prejudice, and Push-Up Bras*:

Listed among "the best indie *Pride and Prejudice* books the IP staff has seen..." —*Independent Publisher*

"This Minnesota-set rom-com hits the ground running and never draws breath until its satisfyingly foregone conclusion." —*Jane Austen's Regency World* magazine

DRIVING WITH THE TOP DOWN

A PENDULUM NOVEL

MARY STRAND

Triple Berry Press P.O. Box 24733 Minneapolis, Minnesota 55424

Cover Credits
Cover & Logo design: LB Hayden
Lake and forest @ Pietus;
Feet hanging out of convertible @ pikselstock
Back view of convertible yellow car @ arastorguev

Ebook ISBN: ISBN-13: 978-1-944949-12-9
Print ISBN: ISBN-13: 978-1-944949-17-4

Printed in the United States of America

For all of the amazing women in Romex,
who've given me friendship and book help and occasionally
wine.

With all my thanks to:

Dina Curran, M.D., and Brian Strand, M.D., who gave me advice on the medical issues in this book, likely while wondering what on earth I was doing.

Dave Schouweiler, who helped me brainstorm the types of cool things an 11-year-old boy might be doing on his computer all day long, even though I bugged Dave about this on a Tuesday night at the Driftwood Char Bar, when Dave probably would've rather been listening to St. Dominic's Trio.

The Driftwood Char Bar and St. Dominic's Trio, which have made so many Tuesday nights so excellent.

Various other bars and restaurants in Uptown and downtown Minneapolis, which provided inspiration for the bars and restaurants in this book, although I *usually* didn't name them because, well, Things Sometimes Happened in my book.

Michael Bodine, who likes to say "I told you so." Quite cheerfully.

All of my friends who've provided critiques, edits, beta reads, blurb help, or brainstorming help on this book, including Jenny Crusie's Maui writers group, Just Cherry Writers, Romex, Ann Barry Burns, Tom Fraser, and Barbara Keiler.

Laura Hayden and Pam McCutcheon, collectively also known as Parker Hayden Media, LLC, who are quite simply there for me.

CHAPTER 1

With her eyes scrunched shut against the blinding late-afternoon sun, Gwen Stanhope walked out of the Medical Arts Building in downtown Minneapolis and told herself that turning forty was no big deal. Just another adventure in that glorious journey called life.

A moment later, she tripped on the sidewalk.

Her eyes, freshly dilated from a visit to her eye doctor, stung and kept tearing up. And she'd forgotten to bring sunglasses. Nearly blind in the sunlight, she used one hand to shade her eyes and took several tentative steps, finally turning the corner from 9th Street onto Nicollet. She kept picturing herself careening off the sidewalk and straight into some bus hurtling down the Nicollet Mall. The driver likely wouldn't stop. Maybe wouldn't hear the thud as he creamed her. She'd end her life impaled on some dental office's "Get a Brighter Smile TODAY!" sign on the front of the bus.

But who cared? In three months, three days, and—her watery, blurry eyes squinted to make out the time on her watch—just under seven hours, she'd be forty.

As if the looming milestone didn't already annoy her, Dr. Renfrew had added insult to injury when he prescribed reading glasses. Reading glasses! She might as well tattoo the words "Shoot Me Now" on her forehead.

Remembering another tattoo, another time, she felt her lips curve into a silly, daydreamy smile . . . before she jerked herself back to reality.

A block later, she squinted at one of the display windows at Dayton's—and it really *was* Dayton's again, at least in some small way, after they'd changed the name to Marshall Field's the year she graduated from high school and to Macy's five years after that. Several huge yellow butterflies fluttered around a couple of waxy bridesmaid-looking mannequins dolled up in rainbow colors. She sighed, wishing the butter-flies in the window didn't remind her of *his* tattoo. Wishing the waxy bridesmaids didn't make her think of stupid what-ifs.

Lately, almost everything reminded her of him.

No wonder she was so depressed.

A boy who couldn't be more than seven or eight gawked up at Gwen through tousled blond bangs. Maybe he'd never seen a woman with alien-size pupils who breathed a little hard as she stood like yet another mannequin in front of the display window. Gwen ignored the boy; it was just the sunshine hitting her dilated eyes that made her look like a train wreck. It couldn't be the wedding-like display, or the butterflies, or a few pathetic memories of a man she thought she'd long since forgotten.

The boy continued to stare, drawing onlookers. Really? Today of all days? If only someone would cart the kid away, she could pretend that the thought of some silly tattoo hadn't just unnerved the hell out of her. Who did this kid belong to?

"What'sa matter? Are you crying?" The boy took a step closer, forcing Gwen to back into an elderly woman, who slugged her with a purse the size of a microwave.

"Sorry!" Gwen held up her hands, trying to calm the woman and shield herself, then turned back to the boy and shook her head. Pointing at her eyes, she forced a smile. "I'm not crying. My eyes just hurt a little bit."

"You look like you're crying."

"Cody!" A woman grabbed the boy's arm and shot Gwen a nasty look as she yanked him away. "What have I told you about talking to strangers?"

"But Mom, she looks so—"

As heat crept up her neck and fanned across her cheeks, Gwen declared defeat and hurried away. Head down, blindly seeking refuge from the boy and his mom, from a Dayton's that wasn't what it used to be, from butterflies and tattoos. From being foolish and self-pitying and almost forty.

In her rush, she didn't see the man until she plowed head-first into his chest.

When Gwen stumbled backward, the man reached out to grab her hand with a firm grip that felt almost familiar.

"Gwen. It's you. After all these years." The crinkles at the corners of his eyes told her that he was a friend, not foe, but she didn't recognize—

Oh, God. Tucker Preston. Seriously.

Her visions of butterfly tattoos had conjured the original, the real thing. Tucker. In the flesh.

But his flesh, and everything else about him, didn't look at all like the Tucker she remembered. Blinking, Gwen gave her wet eyes a surreptitious swipe with the tips of her fingers, trying not to lose or smear whatever was left of her mascara. Trying not to stare. Trying even harder not to drool.

The skinny biker with shaggy, dark-blond hair had grown up, trading his ragged jeans for a shiny Italian suit and looking like he'd just stepped off the pages of *GQ*. She recognized his eyes and voice, but everything else had changed.

She wondered, not so idly, if he still had the tattoo.

"Tucker?"

He laughed full-throttle, his teeth gleaming in the bright sunlight, but both his laugh and his smile felt almost artificial. Or was she imagining things? Probably. "I can't believe I'm seeing you again after, what is it, sixteen, seventeen years? You haven't changed a bit."

She ignored his polite lie, knowing she looked like death warmed over and feeling closer to fifty than forty. She felt the color drain from her face as memories and embarrassed regrets rushed up and slapped her. "I . . . I never got a chance to explain what happened. It was just—"

Tucker slashed a hand through the air, and his smile lost some of its charm. "No need. Just so you're happy. That's what matters, right?"

If only. "Um, sure. Look, do you want to—"

"Oh, geez." Tucker interrupted her as he pushed up his sleeve to glance at the Rolex on his right wrist. "Sorry. I have to run, Gwen. I'm late as it is." Reaching out, he grabbed her hand, the one he'd dropped as soon as she'd regained her balance. "Great seeing you."

"Uh, you too, Tucker. Maybe we could—"

He never heard the rest of her sentence, which floated in the air as he whirled and almost jogged across the Nicollet Mall, disappearing into a door halfway down the next block. She'd been wrong about everything changing. He still had great legs and a cute butt.

Tucker Preston. Her first love. The man she'd left a lifetime ago for the man who, ultimately, had left her.

Stumbling, Gwen made it to her Honda Civic, a secondhand rust bucket she'd picked up for a song, and opened the driver's-side door just as the first fat teardrop slid down her cheek.

"You look like something they rejected at the gates of hell. On recruitment day."

As she turned her key in the lock on the front door of her house, Gwen glanced in the direction of the sharp voice cackling at her across the hedge. And looked back at her key. She wasn't up to it today.

Thirty-five, widowed at a young age, with money to spare and a flair for wacky clothes that seemed to be designed expressly for her slim frame, Leila Merrick stood out. She also had a riotous laugh that started with a rumble deep in her diaphragm and quivered to the blunt ends of her stylish blond bob.

"Yo! Hey, you in the little-old-lady slacks and mismatched socks. Gw-e-en!" Undaunted by Gwen's attempt to ignore her, Leila didn't give up easily. Or ever, come to think of it.

And Gwen loved her for it. Even on a day like today.

Glancing down, she disputed Leila's assessment of the charcoal-gray slacks she'd worn to work today but was horrified to finally notice the aqua and green socks on her feet. Aqua on one, green on the other. The way Tucker, the newly minted fashion plate, had seen her. No wonder he ran like hell to get away.

"How could you see my socks from over there?" Puzzled, she almost forgot her plan to escape from everyone and sink into the bathtub with an extremely large glass of wine. She turned to face her next-door neighbor, who was pushing her way through the small but growing hole that Gwen's kids had carved in the hedge between their adjoining yards.

"Lucky guess." Free of the hedge, Leila stepped around the baseball gear heaped in Gwen's front yard and skipped up the steps. She'd chosen a bizarre aviator look today, the yellow silk scarf that accompanied her hot-pink outfit floating behind her. "It'd be more of a shock lately if they'd matched."

Gwen shrugged. "So now I'm pathetic?"

"I'm just teasing." Leila's arm came around Gwen's shoulders, and a sparkle lit her eyes. "You know I'd rather focus my efforts on tormenting men."

"And you do a brilliant job of it." Gwen felt a smile threaten for the first time that day.

Her key still in the front door, she eased herself down on the front steps, and Leila joined her. Neither spoke for a long moment as they leaned back on their hands, serenaded by a symphony of lawnmowers, shouts from a kickball game down the street, and some teenager's music turned up to deafening.

Come to think of it, the teenager in question might be her own daughter.

Finally, Leila tilted her head to study Gwen. "Something's wrong."

"I have no idea what you mean." Her gaze averted, Gwen spoke by rote. "I went to work, saw my eye doctor, and came home at my usual time. Typical Monday."

Leila snorted. "Typical? Girl, you hate Mondays. What happened? The eye doctor? A killer deadline? Or did Ted-baby make another move?"

Gwen choked at the unwanted thought of Ted Harrison, a senior partner at Pembroke and McFarley, the law firm where she'd worked as a corporate paralegal for the last two years. The fifty-something, self-proclaimed silver fox was no fox. And who wanted to be called a silver fox in their fifties, anyway?

"Ted? No, I dodged that bullet today. He was in client meetings all day, and for once he couldn't think of an excuse to make me sit in."

"Okay, so it wasn't Ted. But it was something."

Gwen ran a hand through her hair—which, as of this morning, had sported a whopping three silvery-white hairs. She'd yanked them out, cursed at her mirror, and considered getting rid of every mirror in the house.

But that seemed a little dramatic.

She also knew that Leila would only laugh about the silvery-white hairs and everything else. Five years from now, she'd probably laugh at the thought of turning forty, too. "Just another Monday. My eye doctor says I need reading glasses."

"There are loads of cute reading glasses, and no one I know reads more than you do, so it can't exactly be a surprise." Leila frowned at her. "That can't be everything. Honestly, you look like a ghost."

Gwen blew out the breath she felt like she'd been holding ever since she ran into Tucker. Literally, unfortunately. "No, but I just saw one."

Leila's eyebrows rose. "Your ex? Rob?"

Gwen shook her head. "An . . . old boyfriend."

"Oh?" When Gwen didn't explain—and she'd probably already said too much—Leila patted her arm. "Listen. Sight unseen, if it's not Rob or Ted, he can't be all bad. You're trending upward."

"What makes you think that?"

"Simple. You always look hurt with Rob and annoyed with Ted. This one has you bugged. You do the math."

Gwen pushed a stray hair off her forehead. Not a silvery-white one, thank God. She didn't want to explore whether Tucker left her bugged, let alone surprisingly hot and bothered. "I was never too good at math."

"Like I said. Bugged."

"I just want something good to happen. I'm tired of

everything being so . . ." Gwen searched for the word but couldn't come up with it.

"Discouraging." Leila gave Gwen a quick hug. "I know. You've felt this way for the last two years, and it's time to move on. I thought you were starting to pick up the pieces, but you're on another downhill slide. Don't let him do that to you."

Gwen wrinkled her nose. "Tucker? I just saw him."

Leila's answering smirk made Gwen cringe. "Aha! *Tucker* is the old boyfriend. I usually have to work a lot harder to worm your dirty little secrets out of you. You're weakening under my constant assault."

"That must be it."

"Listen, you can spill all the Tucker details later." She waved her hand at Gwen's sputtered reply. "I don't have the time right now, as much as I'm sure you're dying to tell me everything. But you need something new. Something fun. I have just the thing."

Rolling her eyes, Gwen tried not to think about all the suggestions Leila had made in the two years they'd been neighbors and, quickly, friends. Ways to make her forget her ex-husband, to meet other neighbors and new friends—and now, undoubtedly, to find a man. Gwen didn't need another man. She just wanted to be happy.

She sighed. "Don't tell me. A blind date."

"Better." Leila's eyes danced. "Piano lessons."

"I don't—"

"Yes, you do. Or you did. In a weak moment, you confessed you used to love piano. Not that you had to say anything, considering that beautiful baby grand parked in your living room." Leila rubbed her hands in anticipation. "It's time for you to start again at the beginning."

Gwen almost said no, automatically, without another

thought. Her job, her kids, and her old house in south Minneapolis—in sad need of even routine repairs, most of which she couldn't afford—already consumed most of her time and energy.

The piano. Hmmm. Rob had laughed when she'd insisted on keeping it in the divorce. She'd kept almost nothing else to remind her of their life together, but she'd gotten sole custody of their beautiful kids, Sarah and Nick, and the baby grand. It cost more than most of the rest of the furniture in her house combined.

Her resolve weakened. An hour a week? Could she fit that into her schedule? Could she afford the small luxury?

Hmm. "I wouldn't actually have to start back at the beginning, you know. It's not like I've forgotten everything."

"You've forgotten more than you realize." Leila's serious gaze told Gwen she wasn't talking about piano lessons. "But we'll fix that. I know just the guy. Adam Flynn. He's younger, he's cute, and my friends all rave about him. He happens to teach piano, but that's just a side benefit." Leila's wink told the rest of the story.

Gwen groaned.

Before she could protest that she didn't want *that* kind of lesson, her cell phone rang. Fluttering her fingers, Leila hopped to her feet and sashayed back through the break in the hedge. "More later!"

Her phone kept ringing as Gwen opened the door and trudged inside. The phone screen told her it was someone from her law firm, and she hated it when they called her at home with yet another made-up crisis.

Especially when Ted did it.

Gritting her teeth, she finally answered the phone and barked a hello.

"Gwen?" The man chuckled, for reasons she couldn't fathom.

"Yes." She drew out the word, hoping it wasn't Ted, but she knew that voice only too well, and her luck wasn't that good. Especially today. "Who's calling, please?"

"Why, Ted, of course. I missed you today."

The perfect ending to a Monday.

"Did you need something tonight?" Please God, no. "I'll be in the office by eight tomorrow."

He cleared his throat, which Gwen had long suspected he did only to draw attention to himself. "The Treadman deal kept Danny and me locked up all day, and I couldn't break free to see you. Ask how your reunion went."

Damn. Last week, in a moment of panic when Ted asked her out again, she'd blurted that she had her twentieth high-school reunion all weekend. The one she'd had, in reality, a year ago. Except for a few fervent prayers not to run into him on her errands, she hadn't given it another thought.

She aimed for breezy. "Oh, you know, the usual. Saw my old friends. I still keep in touch with most of them."

Or the few who hadn't dumped her, like last week's garbage, the minute Rob left her. Like all of Rob's friends, and all the friends they'd made as a couple. Like her own parents had likely wanted to but couldn't, realistically, since they'd lose the only person in the family capable of stuffing and basting the Thanksgiving turkey.

"That's nice." Ted couldn't care less about her friends or her fake reunion or anything other than, probably, a tumble in bed. And why he wanted that, Gwen couldn't imagine. Rob hadn't been impressed, and no one else was pounding on her door.

"Um-hmm." She couldn't think of anything to build upon her lie and wanted to keep it simple. She also wanted her cell phone to go dead, but she should've thought of that before charging it last night.

Another throat clearing. "I have front-row tickets to the Eagles concert Friday night at the Xcel and hoped you could go."

Double damn. She'd spent entire nights listening to their *Greatest Hits* album, over and over and over, feeling —*knowing*—that they'd written "Desperado" and "Peaceful Easy Feeling" and, yes, even "Witchy Woman" especially for her, despite the braces she'd worn at the time. She'd felt their music to the depths of her soul.

A few years later, she and Tucker had spent hours wrapped around each other, exploring the nuances of first love against a backdrop of Glenn Frey, Don Henley, a twin bed, and cheap Chianti wine. Heaven. While it lasted. Then she'd said goodbye to Tucker, hello to Rob, and hidden her love affair with the Eagles from a man who relaxed to Puccini, Verdi, and Pavarotti. Gwen had tried hard to appreciate opera or at least fake it. To her, though, Italian meant pizza and spaghetti and, on a steamy day in July, chocolate or banana gelato.

A steamy day like today. The thought brought her back to Ted and his amazing concert tickets. But the concert would be with Ted. The slimy, annoying, condescending silver fox.

She'd rather listen to Pavarotti.

She ground her teeth in frustration. "I'm sorry. I just can't."

"Why?"

Her mind scrambled for an excuse she hadn't used on him yet. "Uh, piano lessons. I have piano lessons. Friday night."

With Adam Flynn or 1-800-PIANIST, she didn't care. But she wouldn't spend Friday night with Ted.

Hell hadn't frozen over yet.

———

"THANKS FOR LETTING me book a lesson on such short notice. I've heard great things about you."

Gwen gulped as she said the words. Leila's gushing about Adam, which had continued when she'd dropped by with a chilled bottle of pinot grigio and Adam's business card a few hours after she first mentioned him, had been Leila's first understatement in their acquaintance.

The man gave new meaning to the word gorgeous.

Thirty or thirty-one, to believe Leila. The blond streaks in Adam's untamed, light-brown hair made him look like he hadn't yet seen twenty-five, let alone thirty.

She felt overdressed in her long cotton skirt, billowy top, and flat sandals, which had seemed so casual when she'd debated—much longer than she'd ever admit to Leila—what to wear. His faded jeans, snug T-shirt, and bare feet completed the picture of a surfer boy taking a break from the beach. Lanky and five-ten or so, he had dimples that wouldn't quit and a body that probably wouldn't, either.

No wonder Leila had whistled when she tucked his card into Gwen's hand. The only question was why she hadn't kept it for herself. Of course, knowing Leila, maybe she had more cards where that came from.

Adam smiled, taking her hand as he led her into his apartment, a musty little studio on the top floor of a three-story building on the west side of Lake Harriet. "Come on in. Let's get acquainted before we start, okay?"

He didn't drop her hand immediately, and Gwen debated whether to retrieve it or let him borrow it for the evening. He'd soon decide for himself, since she could feel her hand start to get clammy. Cheeks flaming, she imagined it growing increasingly slick, eventually sliding right out of his grasp.

Their hands dropped naturally, despite her rich world of mortified imagination, and Adam nodded at his plaid, hand-me-down couch. He stretched out in the worn leather recliner next to it and propped his bare feet on a low glass coffee table.

Gwen struggled not to count the hairs on his toes.

She hadn't felt so tongue-tied since the day she'd asked the cutest boy in ninth grade to the Sadie Hawkins dance, only to be interrupted moments later by the shrill fire-drill siren. Racing down the stairs with the rest of her class, she'd tripped and fallen dead-center into the boy's back. He went with someone else to the dance.

Adam cleared his throat in a way that didn't sound the least bit like Ted Harrison.

"What's the scoop? Do you just want to get out of the house once in a while, or are we looking at concert pianist material?" His disarming smile made the contrast less harsh, but Gwen watched him size her up, almost like a slab of beef at the Lunds meat counter.

She didn't think "get out of a date with a toad" qualified as a suitable answer. "Are those my choices? Do you have anything in between?"

He smiled. "Fair point. Okay, tell me about yourself. Play any piano? Take any lessons? Ever?"

"A few." Gwen glanced down at her sandals, catching another peek at his toes as she did. "Actually, I took quite a few lessons when I was younger. I played from fourth grade through high school."

"What happened then?"

"Um, boys. Or men. And friends and parties. And college and work. And sports. At least, for a while. Then marriage and kids and . . ." Waving one hand in the air, Gwen tried to show the universe of excuses she'd had for leaving the piano behind.

She'd left so much of herself behind in the last twenty years, she hadn't given it another thought until she caught herself staring into Adam's warm, chocolate-brown eyes. She shivered. On a muggy July evening in a cramped little apartment that desperately needed air-conditioning.

Leila was right. She had to get out more.

"Bummer that you had to quit." As Adam studied her, his expression older and somehow wiser than she would've expected, Gwen tried not to flinch. Finally, he slapped his thighs and sprang to his feet, then walked over to what looked like a brand-new upright piano against the far wall. "Okay, let's see what you've still got."

Gwen followed more slowly, taking a seat on the smooth ebony bench and running a hand lightly over the keys. She didn't press down enough to make a sound, content with the touch of her skin on the ivory. She sometimes did the same thing at home, pretending to dust her baby grand only to feel its smoothness beneath her fingers.

Adam sat down on a small, padded stool next to the bench but somehow managed to press his shin lightly against hers. She didn't even think about pulling away. The warmth of him flooded right through his jeans and into the skin of her bare leg. It felt wonderful. Of course, pretty much anything rubbed up against a lonely thirty-nine-year-old woman with limited dating prospects would feel pretty damn good. Anything not attached to Ted or Rob.

"Whenever you're ready, play anything you'd like."

Gwen gazed blankly at him, having all but forgotten the piano lesson in the thrill of having a red-hot tamale flush up against her and not picking her pocket.

He touched her right hand. "Do you remember any particular pieces, or do you want sheet music? I need to get a feel for where we should begin."

And she was trying to get a feel of him. Or from him. Talk about different needs.

Despite her vow to call the music department at the University of Minnesota for *proper* lessons, she'd been more than a little turned on by the thought of being touched again by a man, especially one like Adam. A young, anonymous walk on the wild side for a woman who hadn't peeked past the curtain in more than fifteen years.

She felt like an idiot.

She'd nearly wet the skimpy cotton underwear she wore under her gauzy cotton skirt, the underwear she'd run out and bought today when she realized that too much of hers looked more military than Victoria's Secret. Adam's reaction? He wanted to know if she could play Beethoven, or maybe hum a few bars.

Without answering him, Gwen floated through an easy version of Beethoven's "Moonlight Sonata" before tapping out the opening notes to a Scott Joplin ragtime tune she'd memorized for a grade-school recital. She could do better, she knew. How much better, she didn't know. Her music books had gathered dust in the upstairs hall closet for the last two years and at her parents' house for the fifteen years before that.

After stabbing the final key, she looked at Adam, awaiting his comment. She hoped even this level of play beat all the silly women he *did* hit on during their lessons. The ones whose hair wasn't fading to gray—or, okay, silvery-white, and just a few strands so far, which was more than enough—and whose eyes weren't fading to nothing.

"Cute." Adam's gaze narrowed. His mouth opened as if

to say more, but he apparently thought better of it. Surprised, Gwen tilted her head at him. Her teachers had always praised her. Sure, she'd been a kid and her parents had paid them to praise her, but she'd expected to impress Adam, even if she didn't work too hard to do it.

"Why? What was so bad about that?"

He shook his head. "Sorry. I had you figured wrong."

"Wrong? Better than I am? Worse? How could you know what to expect?" All thoughts of having Adam touch her fled, leaving in their place the little girl who'd sought the approval of her teachers and the possibility of a career in music.

"No, no, nothing like that." Adam kept shaking his head, looking embarrassed.

She should've checked into his background instead of relying on Leila's gushing about attributes that bore little connection to piano. Maybe he worked only with more highly skilled pianists, and the women Leila mentioned were a figment of someone's oversexed imagination. Blushing to the roots of her hair, she tried to think of an excuse to slink away, her tail between her legs, without him noticing.

No. She didn't have to slink, and she sure didn't have to wait for the door to hit her butt on the way out. She eased back the bench and walked on stiff but proud legs to his old couch, where she reached into her purse, grabbing her billfold.

This had been a mistake. Not the first or by far the worst one she'd ever made, but she didn't need to compound it. "I'm sorry I took up your time. And on a Friday night, no less. I must've been mistaken about the required skill level, and I must owe you something for this."

"Put your money away. Please." Shaking his head as he stood up, Adam walked over to Gwen, waving away her cash.

"Not that I don't like money, don't get me wrong. But I'm the one who made the mistake."

"Oh?" Her brows furrowed in bemusement.

"When you called to make the appointment and gave your friend's name, I thought you were just another . . . groupie."

"Groupie?" She had to do better than one-word responses, but it didn't seem likely to happen anytime soon.

"Yeah." He didn't quite meet her gaze, but he also didn't blush. But then, men seldom had the decency to know when they should be turning bright red. "I seem to get more than my share of women who want to be my students but don't exactly have musical aptitude."

She might have musical aptitude, but she also had other needs. She choked on an embarrassed giggle provoked by Adam's opinion of women like her—desperate women who spent too many nights cuddled up with stuffed animals for companionship—while he awkwardly patted her on the shoulder.

Suddenly, she realized he didn't see her as he saw the others, and she wasn't completely comforted.

"If I'm not a groupie, what am I?" Stung, she ended the question on a squeak, but she knew the answer. A dull, almost-forty nothing without enough sex appeal even to merit a tumble on a dateless Friday night.

Her shoulders slumped, but he grinned and wagged a finger at her. "You're a pianist. Yeah, you're rusty, and you like to hide what you can do, but I'll just bet you've got some serious talent. Let's pull it out of you. Come on."

CHAPTER 2

Her first piano lesson in twenty years. She hadn't felt this nervous since her first date, at sixteen, with a clumsy, stammering, forgettable boy who pretty clearly wanted to lose his virginity and didn't have a chance in hell.

At almost forty, she looked a bit differently on Adam.

Like a silly bird, Gwen felt herself flutter and twitter, her hands a whirlwind of activity. Adam had to notice it. The thought brought crimson to her cheeks but didn't halt the constant movement of her fingers—on the ivories, in her purse, even hovering in the air with no place to go. She couldn't help it. It'd been a while since a man had paid attention.

Adam might not play Carnegie Hall, but he paid attention.

He did that awfully well.

If she could believe him, she was a rare treat among the hordes of women who camped out in his living room, paying for piano lessons and hoping he'd either turn them into a pianist or, more likely, consider them too intoxicating to refuse.

No, she wasn't like them at all.

With almost a decade on Adam, and this week's rogue traces of silvery-white mixed in with her longish auburn hair, she didn't have a prayer of intoxicating him without the assistance of at least a fifth of good scotch. Motherhood hadn't changed her trim, boyish hips or made her breasts droop onto her stomach, but she was too skinny and didn't have enough curves to excite a man. Rob had made that very clear. Oh, boy, had he.

But Adam's gaze kept pulling back to her, which bewildered her. Her own gaze was drawn to the floor, half hoping it might open up and swallow her whole. She liked the way Adam paid attention. She just didn't know what to do with it.

"Gwen."

She finally met his warm gaze, then blinked a few times before her own skittish gaze roved again to the floor, the wall, the piano, and every other old, worn, broken, inanimate object she could see. He actually didn't have much in his living room. Adam traveled light.

He grabbed her hand. "Let's hit the bench again, but this time show me more music and fewer show tunes." At her raised eyebrows, he laughed, tugging her back to the piano. "Yeah, even Beethoven can be a show tune, the way you were playing him. What was that . . . fifth-grade recital? Sixth? And you played through high school?"

Startled, she pulled her hand away and floated onto the bench. "Fourth grade."

When a tiny giggle escaped her, a shadow of a smile crossed his face.

"Gunner, huh? So do you need sheet music to get past fourth grade, or can you make it back up to eighth or ninth on your own?"

At his smirk, she stuck out her tongue—and cringed when she realized what she'd done. "As you can see, I'm permanently stuck in eighth grade, so maybe I can play something from then." She chewed on her lip. "Actually, I'm not sure. I played a little before I came over tonight, but it's been a while."

"Give it a shot."

Her fingers floated over the keys, and Rachmaninoff flowed into her ears and head. Excited despite her misgivings about the piano lessons—and about sharing a small space with a man hotter than the night outside—she couldn't wait to show him high school. Then maybe he could take her to college.

Half an hour later, with the help of some sheet music and little else, Gwen had brought her fingertips out of retirement and recaptured a fraction of the pride she'd once had. She blushed and stammered at his praise, which rang a little false at first but became more spontaneous and genuine the more she played.

She needed lessons, practice, and time to let it seep back into her fingers and her soul. To feel it to her toes again. Already, though, she felt herself buzz like an open wire of electric current. And it was only the beginning.

Finally. She'd found something that brought back part of her old self but also hinted at the promise of something new. It'd been too long. Longer than the two years since her divorce. Maybe since the day she'd married Rob.

"Okay, superstar." Adam flinched when his unexpected nickname for her slipped out, but she didn't bat an eyelash. It sounded kind of . . . cute. "Let's call it a day."

———

"What do you mean he didn't touch you?" Leila skimmed her gaze from Gwen's head to her toes, as if seeking the answer in the grungy gardening shorts and sleeveless T-shirt she sported the next morning, appropriately enough, in her garden.

"No, I didn't wear this to the lesson, if that's what you're wondering." Gwen pushed a stray lock of hair out of her eyes, but it clung to her sweat-soaked forehead. "Not that a man wouldn't go wild over this hot little outfit."

"Not at all." Dressed, improbably enough, in what looked like red silk pajamas, Leila would've sparkled even if it hadn't been such a sunny day. "But—"

"He didn't touch me. No hugs, no kisses, no Kama Sutra before or after. Although . . ."

"Yes?" Leila almost gasped.

"He *did* shake hands with me." Grinning, Gwen squatted in the dirt and gripped a large, thick weed that would probably be a tree by next week. She pulled. Nothing.

"I don't understand." Frowning, Leila tapped her matching red slippers on the ground. "You're a lot more— I mean, this doesn't sound like Adam."

Still tickled by the praise she'd received from him for how well she'd played, Gwen had almost forgotten the sting of Adam's initial apparent rejection.

She bristled. "Exactly how well do you know Adam?"

"Whoa. Hardly at all." Leila held up both hands. "After a friend gushed about her so-called 'lessons,' I sent several more women his way. I only met him one time, on the rooftop at Amore, when a few of us were having drinks."

Gwen pulled again at the weed. It wiggled but held its ground, so to speak. She considered grabbing the full-length dandelion digger, but she loved going head to head with a tough one. Another yank. The weed won.

Smiling, Leila gazed up into the ancient apple tree. She'd climbed it last week on a dare from both of Gwen's kids. "I was with two women who are both taking lessons with him. Or were, at least. I thought for a moment they'd claw each other's eyes out."

"And Adam?" Head down, Gwen pulled again at the weed. It unexpectedly gave way, and she flew backward, landing on her surprised butt.

Leila waved a hand in the air. "Oh, you know. Typical guy. Didn't seem to notice and wouldn't admit it if he did. They never apologize for anything, in case you've never noticed."

"I've noticed." From her sitting position, Gwen brandished the errant weed, then took aim and sent it sailing toward her weed bucket. Score. "I just thought that was an ex-husband sort of thing, not universal to men generally."

The tsk-tsking coming from Leila's mouth could've been heard a block away. "You need to get out more."

Not if Leila was right about all men being jerks who never apologized. "I'm already out there. I'm taking piano lessons."

"Mom!" The shrill wail echoing out the back door of Gwen's house belonged to Sarah. Her fourteen-year-old, who'd be starting her freshman year in high school this fall, usually sounded these days like a cross between a banshee and a flock of birds.

She wasn't sure what eleven-year-old Nick sounded like. He rarely spoke, seldom leaving the video games he played on the computer in his bedroom to join polite society.

Sarah waved the sheet of paper clutched in her hand. "Mom!"

Groaning to her feet, Gwen brushed the dirt off the back of her shorts and started toward Sarah. "Gotta run, Leila. Duty calls."

"Well, if anything other than duty calls, for God's sake

answer the phone." Waving at Sarah, Leila headed back toward her own yard.

Laughing softly, Gwen shook her head. Leila never gave up. She was also the best neighbor and friend Gwen could've dreamed of when she returned to her old neighborhood in south Minneapolis after her bitter divorce from Rob. When Gwen actually managed to buy her childhood home on a nostalgic whim, much to her mother's horror, Leila had appeared on her doorstep within thirty seconds, armed with brownies and a cold bottle of champagne.

If only Leila would stop the matchmaking. Or, more accurately, her relentless campaign to get Gwen laid.

"What is it, sweetie?" In another year or so, Gwen wouldn't get away with calling Sarah "sweetie." As it was, the five-four pixie wrinkled her cute little freckled nose.

"Basketball, Mom. Camp starts next week, and I need this doctor's form filled out before I go."

After prying the crumpled form out of Sarah's hands, Gwen quickly skimmed it. "But this says you need a checkup. You never mentioned that. It's Saturday, and camp starts Monday morning. How are we going to—"

"Oh, Mom." Chomping on a wad of bubblegum that would choke a horse, Sarah rolled her gorgeous green eyes. They matched Gwen's but somehow seemed more vivid, more alive. "We just give it to Dad, okay? Duh."

Sarah had a talent for making the word "duh" sound like a whole sentence, if not a paragraph.

"Your father is a plastic surgeon." Gwen read the form again, wondering why this was the first time she'd seen it. Oh, right. Because Sarah had announced when she signed up for basketball camp that she was in high school now and could handle everything herself. "Unless your basketball coach wants to make sure you haven't had a facelift this summer, I don't see how that's going to help."

"Funny." Chomp, chomp. It was a marvel that Sarah could speak at all around the blob in her mouth.

Pursing her lips, Gwen tried to think. She wished Sarah would get her act together and not always expect her mom to pull a last-minute miracle out of her hat. Like she said, she was in high school now. Ha.

Sarah jammed her hands on her nonexistent hips. "Just call Dad. He'll get it done. He always does."

"Oh?" Her kids sure exalted the man who never bothered to help out unless absolutely forced. She'd always tried never to complain about his thoughtless, self-absorbed behavior in front of Sarah and Nick, but maybe she should at least quit covering for him. It'd be an eye-opener for both kids. "Tell you what. *You* call your father. Let me know what he says."

Sarah's gaze dropped to the dirt at Gwen's feet, her bravado gone. "I, uh, tried already. Tiffany said he was busy."

"Tiffany? Is that his latest?" Why were Rob's little girl-friends always named after lamps or circus animals?

"Yeah, and she's nice, she really is. But . . ." As Sarah trailed off, her fingers twisted themselves into a pretzel and she stared blindly at Gwen's half-full weed bucket, even though the concept of helping her mom with gardening would never occur to her.

"But he never seems to have time for you." She got a brief nod and the faintest glimmer of a tear in response. Gwen ached for Sarah. "But maybe this time he will."

"Really?" Sarah's head shot up again, and sunshine bathed a face suddenly dry of tears.

Gwen tapped her on the nose. "I said maybe. I can't make promises for your dad. But please don't do this again."

Grinning, Sarah sprinted back toward the house.

"And stay off the phone." The scampering feet slowed. "If you and your friends waste the next three hours on this gorgeous day rehashing the finer nuances of every boy you know, I can't imagine why I should call your dad. You promised to mow the lawn today."

A high-pitched giggle confirmed her guess. "Oh, Mom!"

———

"She's your daughter, too. No, she shouldn't wait until the last minute, but if you spent two seconds with your kids, you'd know that kids do this. All the time."

Rob Stanhope wouldn't care what kids did or didn't do, but he'd usually do anything to get Gwen off the phone. She counted on that. She twisted a lock of hair around her finger as she kept talking.

"You know you don't do a damned thing for her. I'm sure you can't sign the form, but you know someone who can. Or someone who'd be willing to have her drop into the office on a Saturday afternoon just to do you a favor. You—"

"All right, all right." Rob gave in more quickly than she'd hoped, letting her save her breath and release her finger. "I need to make a call or two. I'll let you know."

"Let me know? What's that supposed to mean?" Gwen felt the beginnings of another copout by Rob. He wouldn't call, and when Gwen finally called back, a giggling Tiffany would say he wasn't available.

"Calm down." Rob's patronizing tone made her clench her fist. He'd used exactly that tone the day he explained why a hotshot plastic surgeon couldn't be married to a dull, going-nowhere nothing like her. "I said I'd do it. I just don't understand why she has to play basketball. She should be cheerleading or something. Dance line. Nick wouldn't touch a basketball if it smacked him in the face."

She counted to ten. Sarah needed the doctor's form signed more than Gwen needed to educate a neanderthal. "It's what she loves, and Nick doesn't happen to like sports. They're individuals, Rob. You'd actually enjoy them if you got to know them better. And they'd be thrilled to spend time with you."

Rob choked on something. "Uh, sure. Maybe sometime. I'll take care of Sarah's form. Let her know I will." So the absentee father could garner a few brownie points.

"Whatever you say." She gripped the phone in her hand so tightly, she thought her knuckles would crack. "And . . . thanks. Sarah appreciates it."

The phone clicked in her ear.

"Are you sure you don't mind?" Gwen held her breath, hoping Adam had time again on a Friday night. It wasn't that she couldn't take lessons some other night of the week in the summer, when she didn't have to hound one or both of the kids about their homework. But it locked Ted Harrison out of a Friday-night date, leaving her to find an excuse only for Saturday.

Come to think of it, it was already Wednesday afternoon. Ted had been conspicuously silent and in his office all week. Maybe he had real client work to do for a change.

As she clutched the phone to her ear, Ted hurried past the open door of her office, nodding at her but not stopping for his usual chat. Whew.

Adam's voice flowed over the telephone line like bourbon over rocks. "No prob. My schedule is wide open on Friday."

"Great." She heard herself chirp into the phone. "See you at seven?"

"Seven it is." Adam then mentioned a few pieces of new music she might want to try in addition to the old piano books she wanted to revisit. She hoped to draw out the conversation, but he brought it to a speedy close.

She hung up just as Ted appeared at her door.

"Got a moment?"

Too late to spread out enough files to make herself look busy. Damn. Gwen wished today's securities filings weren't already done and gone. "Sure."

He propped his bony butt on the corner of Gwen's desk, his cologne wafting too close to her nostrils.

As she peered at him over the top of her new, bright-blue reading glasses, she gave him the same wary look she'd offer most lawyers bringing work her way. Unintentionally, she probably terrified half the associates.

"So." He leaned in. Gwen fought the urge to lean backward. "Treadman Electronics needs a special shareholder meeting to approve the merger with Aertronix. Can you take care of the proxy materials, maybe work with Danny on that?"

She swallowed hard. "Uh . . ."

"Or will that be a problem with your workload?"

Since when he ever cared about her workload? As Gwen's mind scrambled in vain for the right answer to give him, whatever that was, Ted crossed his arms over his mildly sunken chest. The memory of him in a swimsuit and shirtless at the firm's summer party on Lake Minnetonka last year still made Gwen want to bleach her eyes, which didn't help her figure out what to do. But Ted hadn't asked her out for Friday or Saturday night or even Sunday afternoon.

She'd call it a win. It even made her feel almost generous toward him.

"Er, no. No problem." Caught off guard, Gwen forgot to ask about deadlines or even what the work entailed.

But as she gave it more thought, she realized that proxy materials for a public merger were typically handled by a lawyer—a senior associate or junior partner, even, and not a paralegal. Not her. She'd worked on some big transactions, sure, but she'd never done more than routine securities filings on something like the Treadman deal, which was worth several hundred million dollars.

She must be missing something. "Ted?"

He'd already left her desk and started toward the door. Turning, he spared her a quick glance. "Ask Danny any questions. Have to run. Three o'clock conference call. Thanks."

She didn't have to look for Danny Fitzsimmons. Five minutes later, he rapped his knuckles on her open door. "Got a minute?"

"That seems to be the popular question today." She waved him inside her office. "Join the party. I hear we're doing a deal together."

He sauntered in and landed casually in a chair. One leg swung over the side of it.

Having made partner last fall after only seven years at the firm, Danny hadn't lost his boyish charm or the bangs that often hung in his eyes. Despite his expensive suits, he wore ties that—like right now—were flamboyant and wildly askew.

Danny coughed. "No offense, Gwen, but I don't know what Ted's thinking. Treadman and Aertronix both need shareholder meetings. We have to do a registration statement for the deal, a full-blown proxy statement and prospectus. I would've had one of the associates draft it with me, maybe

George or Phil. It's not something a paralegal would typically do."

"So ask one of them. I heard George was light." Leaning back, she pointed at all the files neatly stacked on her credenza. "It's not like I'm dying for work."

"Sorry. Ted's orders." Danny grimaced. "What'd you do, piss him off? Or is he still trying, in his usual twisted way, to hit on you?"

Sputtering, Gwen tried to formulate a response. Tried not to blush. Failed at both.

Danny held up a hand. "Don't bother. Claudia and I saw it coming. Have you actually gone out with the guy, or are you torturing him? The shot to Ted's pride would probably drop him to his knees."

"I don't—"

"Oh, come on. You can tell Uncle Danny." Reaching out, he grabbed the edge of the door, swinging it closed. "Every disgusting tidbit. I might need it for the proxy materials."

"In your dreams." Gwen shot him a wicked grin, glad to have someone to unload on, even if Danny was a partner. It'd been too long since they'd had drinks. Unwilling to risk the possibility that Ted would show up at Pendulum, everyone's favorite downtown watering hole, Gwen had turned down all of Danny's and Claudia's recent happy-hour invitations. Pendulum was just down the block from their firm, and Ted had a way of finding out when anyone in the securities department was headed there after work.

Or at least when Gwen was.

"Seriously, tell me you haven't gone out with him. Ted practically foams when he sees you, but I can't believe you would." Danny bounced his leg in time to some unknown melody, but his gaze never left hers.

"How could I? I'm so crushed that you and Claudia never

want to have drinks with me anymore, I can't stand the thought of going out with someone else and running into you." Since the opposite was true, she struggled to keep a straight face.

Peering at her over the top of his funky glasses, Danny tried impersonating a senior partner. "Right. Like I'm the one coming up with all these lame-ass excuses. I'd almost think you *were* busy with Ted. Too busy for old friends like Claudia and me. The last time you turned us down, you made Claudia cry."

The door edged open, but no one knocked. Gwen prayed it wasn't Ted. "And ruin her mascara? I don't think so."

"Hey. I heard that." The door swung open the rest of the way, nearly slamming into Danny's bobbing leg. Claudia Burns, blond and waiflike, with long straight hair and sunken eyes, strode into Gwen's small office and shut the door behind her.

Danny glanced up, but his leg didn't miss a beat. "What makes you think we were talking about you? Your ears burning?"

The two had started at the firm a year apart, Claudia ahead of Danny, and were nearly inseparable. Claudia worked ungodly hours, even in the summer, when most people sneaked off to lakes and cabins. Danny craved a more balanced life and usually managed to get away with it. He scored big points on big deals and had an unlisted phone number.

"Not last time I checked." With Danny occupying the only chair not filled with stacks of files, Claudia leaned against the wall. "I figured you two were holed up in here, plotting a happy hour without me, even if your loyal secretary *assured* me you were hard at work on the Treadman deal. And here you're dissing me."

Gwen's laugh got stuck in her throat. "The Treadman deal? How would Becky already know I was working on it? I just found out myself."

"She's my secretary, too." As if Danny needed to remind her. When Gwen's last secretary turned into a flake, Danny had talked Becky into adding Gwen to her workload. "Ted told me he was having you draft the proxy materials when I was out at her desk."

Claudia's brows furrowed. "What do you mean, Gwen's drafting the proxy materials? Isn't Treadman a public deal?"

"Yes and yes. And Ted Harrison, in answer to your next question." Danny raised his hands, as if it were all out of his control and realm of blame.

"Ted? Why would he— Oh. But seriously?" Turning from Danny, Claudia shrugged an apology at Gwen. "Sorry, but Ted has to realize a paralegal wouldn't—"

Danny shook his head. "Ted makes the big bucks. He doesn't have to realize a damn thing."

"Look." Gwen's gaze went from Danny to Claudia and back again. "I'm not offended. I'd be relieved if someone else took over. Have George draft the proxy materials like we talked about, Danny, and I can help out enough so we can say I'm working on them, too."

"I'm not sure . . ." Trailing off, Danny appeared to weigh the pros and cons. He probably didn't relish the extra work he'd need to do if Gwen tried to handle the proxy materials, and she couldn't blame him.

Claudia rolled her eyes. "Oh, do it. Ted's out to lunch on this, and you know better. So does Gwen."

"Yeah, you're right." He turned to Gwen, flashing his trademark grin. "But this means we'll have to plot strategy. Over drinks, I think. Whaddaya say?"

She hesitated, glancing at her watch. She really did have

a lot of work on her plate right now, and she needed to avoid Ted. "Anywhere but Pendulum."

"Sounds good to me." Claudia looked at her watch. "Is five o'clock too early to blow out of here?"

"Why, Claudia, you're turning into a regular slug." Danny jumped up from his chair and headed for the door. "There's hope for you yet."

When he whipped open the door, Ted Harrison—his ear flat against it—stumbled into Danny's arms.

CHAPTER 3

"I'll never understand why you need to live here. In this particular house." Wrinkling her nose, the Chanel-clad Vivian Withers struck a Vanna White pose as she waved her hand at the living room of Gwen's house. Even now, two years after Gwen bought the house on Newton, which by sheer luck had been for sale when she'd become a single parent, her mother kept bringing it up.

"Stop. Please." She wished Vivian would get over it. "I've always loved this house and never wanted to move. Edina seemed like a foreign country. It still does."

Her parents had bought the house as a young couple, years before her dad's business leaped almost overnight from an insignificant tool shop into a multimillion-dollar electronics company. Vivien, who'd grown up in a family of considerable wealth, had hated every moment she'd lived here. After she'd finally talked Dad into leaving south Minneapolis for Edina, she'd never looked back.

Gwen loved looking back, where her best memories still lived. Before she married Rob. Before he dumped her for an unending string of flavors of the week.

"You were fourteen. You didn't know better." Her mother

pursed her lips, almost as if the conversation pained her. Gwen knew the feeling. "I was thrilled to leave this behind. The house, the neighborhood—" She sniffed, but that could be her allergies. "The people."

"But you don't live here. I do."

"I still wish you'd stayed in North Oaks." Glancing around, Vivian tapped her Ferragamos against the hardwood floor but didn't set down her Fendi purse. Her hand rested on her back, and she looked like she'd sucked on a particularly sour lemon.

"Look." Gwen waited until Vivian's pale blue eyes met her gaze. "You know perfectly well I couldn't afford to stay there. I didn't have a job when Rob left. Even now, I couldn't afford it on a paralegal's salary."

"That's not what I meant."

Gwen knew exactly what she meant. "I didn't leave Rob. He left me. You know that."

"Yes, but—"

"Don't even think about suggesting *again* that it was my fault. Rob started sleeping with a parade of bimbos practically as soon as we returned from our honeymoon." It still hurt. It hurt less when she didn't talk about it, but her mother refused to stop talking about it. As if constantly mentioning Rob might bring him back.

God forbid.

Vivian didn't notice Gwen's clenched jaw or her white knuckles gripping the back of Dad's old leather recliner. She never noticed. "Some men are like that, dear. It doesn't mean they don't love you, in their own way."

She could talk. Vivian had married the perfect man.

Gwen mumbled a profanity that made her mother's head snap back. Obscenities were off-limits in the Withers household. It might explain why no one in her family ever said much of anything.

She padded quietly to the kitchen, grabbing a glass of water and a moment's composure. She called out to Vivian. "Can I get you anything?"

"No, thank you, dear." Her mother's soft, modulated voice floated to her from the living room.

Returning, Gwen glanced at the grandfather clock in the corner, a treasured wedding present from her grandparents, one of the few things Rob hadn't had the chutzpah to grab in the divorce. Ten after six. She still had to shower and change and make it to Adam's apartment by seven for her second lesson.

Somehow, Vivian wouldn't approve of that, either.

"Aren't you meeting Dad at the club for dinner? I don't want to make you late."

She thought she heard her mother snort. Impossible. "How thoughtful. No, your father is out of town on business. He didn't expect to return until later this evening."

"Oh?"

At sixty-seven, her dad should be thinking about retirement rather than drumming up more sales for his electronics firm, but they'd probably carry him out of the place in a casket some day. Gwen couldn't imagine any other way he'd give up his corner office or let someone else be CEO.

Vivian sighed. "Successful men don't always have time for dinner at the club with their wives. That's why I have my golf league."

Her mother enjoyed golf as much as Gwen enjoyed Verdi. She played only for the sake of friends and good manners. Just like how she did everything in life.

A peek at the clock showed six-fifteen. Even with a ten- or fifteen-minute drive, assuming minimal traffic and being able to luck into a parking place anywhere near Adam's apartment, she'd soon have to skip the shower.

Vivian walked over to the stairs leading to the second floor. "Where are Sarah and Nicholas? I'd hoped I could treat the three of you to dinner tonight."

Dinner at the club. Even if she didn't have a piano lesson, Gwen would rank time spent at her parents' snooty country club right up there with the sound of nails on a chalkboard.

"Um, well, Nick's in his room—"

"Playing those ridiculous video games." Her mother gazed upward. "Really, Gwen, he'll never amount to anything if you don't do something about that."

Gwen laughed, even though she worried about Nick, too. "I don't know many eleven-year-old boys who want to do anything else. Maybe he'll be the next Bill Gates. Wouldn't that be sufficient?"

"Hmpf." Vivian probably thought Bill Gates was less than ideal, too, but didn't say it. "Is my sweet little Sarah in her room?"

"Only if there's a basketball hoop and enough space for a half-court game in there." Gwen shook her head at her mother's puzzled look. "Your sweet little Sarah hasn't gotten home from basketball camp yet. She's probably hip-checking other sweet little girls as we speak."

"Is that . . . safe?" Surprisingly, Vivian never objected to Sarah's love of sports, even if the thought of smelly uniforms on girls left her nose in a permanent wrinkle.

Gwen tried to picture her little slugger, who wouldn't be caught dead in a dress, doing anything safer than most of the sports she loved. "I'm not sure it's safe for the *other* girls, whether Sarah's on offense or defense. She doesn't take prisoners."

In her teens, Gwen had shared the same passion for

sports. Vivian hadn't understood it then, either, but she'd attended all of Gwen's tennis matches and ballgames. In heels and pearls. She hadn't looked or acted like the other girls' moms, which had always made Gwen cringe. She'd never known why Vivian even bothered.

A gleam lit Vivian's face before she replaced it with her usual society mask. "You and I could still have dinner. I'm sorry to ask on such short notice, but your father had originally thought he'd be back by now."

And Vivian wouldn't dream of insulting her friends with a last-minute invitation.

Six-twenty. Luckily or not, Adam cared more about how well she played than how she looked. Or smelled. Not that she needed the reminder.

"I wish I could." Pausing, Gwen sucked in a breath. "I have a piano lesson. At seven."

Vivian's eyebrows almost merged with her hairline. "Piano? I don't understand."

"I've had one lesson already. So far, so good."

"But you— You quit piano. Quite defiantly, as I recall, in the spring of your senior year. Just before your recital." Vivian touched her back again, as if the memory made it ache.

Gwen bit her lip, even though her mother's memory wasn't wrong. But she didn't need or want to discuss it, especially right now, or she'd never make it to Adam's place by seven. "I remember. But that was twenty years ago, and a lot has changed since then."

"Not all for the better." Her mother murmured it under her breath, but raising two kids had given Gwen excellent hearing.

She shrugged, no longer even remotely sorry she had to turn down the dinner invitation. "I agree, for what it's worth, but I'm trying to fix that now. Sorry, but I really have to run. I'm going to be late."

She sprinted over Sarah's shoes and sports paraphernalia spread out on the stairs, leaving her mother to either stay in the living room or make a silent exit. Another disappointment from Vivian's only daughter.

She peeled off her clothes and cranked the shower faucet to cool. Ninety degrees outside, and the conversation with Vivian had only heated her further.

Twenty minutes later, she opened the front door, running into Leila just as she reached out to knock.

"Can't talk. Sorry. Piano." Stopping only long enough to lock the door, Gwen whirled and nearly hit Leila again as she raced to her Honda Civic in the driveway.

Leila called out to Gwen as she unlocked the driver's door. "Did I see your mom leave just now?"

"Vivian hadn't yet reminded me enough about all the mistakes I made with Rob, so she made a special trip."

"Why do you always call your mom Vivian?"

The question hung in the air as Gwen shifted into reverse and backed out.

———

As she drove around part of Lake Harriet to Adam's apartment building on the west side of the lake, Gwen wished again she still had the Saab convertible that Rob had given her for her thirtieth birthday. She'd squealed, forgetting for a moment the sheer impracticality of having that car when she had one kid in pre-school and one in diapers.

They'd also bought a BMW SUV for driving the kids everywhere, but she'd kept the convertible for herself. For Gwen.

Nearly seven years later, she'd sold them both and bought the Civic because it didn't remind her of her spoiled, rich, elegant, hideous life with Rob. But sometimes, like on a clear, steamy night in July with the slightest whisper of a breeze, she pined for the Saab.

Pulling into an open parking space on the street, two buildings down from Adam's place, she set the brake and climbed out. As she ran a hand through her hair, she wished she'd had time to dry it properly. A convertible would've taken care of that, too.

Two minutes to seven. She hurried along the sidewalk, struggled with the heavy door to Adam's building, and opted for the stairs instead of the elevator, which had grumbled and burped the last time she'd come, almost as if it had eaten a small child and found it hard to digest.

She told herself her legs needed the workout of climbing to the third floor, even though Adam wouldn't notice. He viewed women either as pianists or . . . something else. Period. And she was a pianist. So she'd skipped last week's gauzy skirt and opted for capris and a cotton top. Simple and relaxed. Suitable for a lesson in a hot apartment on a night when the only thing getting touched would be piano keys. Despite Leila's promises.

Rapping on the door, she sighed.

Adam didn't answer immediately, and Gwen knocked again. He probably couldn't hear anything over the jazz CD blasting through speakers the size of a Volkswagen Beetle.

The music abruptly ended. A moment later, the door swung open to the sight of freshly washed, tousled hair, khakis, and a Hawaiian shirt buttoned halfway up. A few stray hairs peeked out from his otherwise smooth chest.

Gwen's stomach rumbled, and her fist shot up, shoving itself in her mouth.

Adam grinned. "I think I've got crackers in the cupboard, and too many green foreign objects in the fridge, but maybe we could grab a bite to eat after your lesson. If you can wait that long without gnawing on my piano."

Gwen's only thought, which repeated itself over and over, was that her bright-red face probably clashed with her yellow top. "My mother stopped by unexpectedly, and I forgot to eat. But I'm not really . . . hungry."

She could eat an elephant. He didn't need to watch.

"Naaa." His gaze skimmed her from head to toe, deepening the intensity of her blush, if that was even possible. "A skinny thing like you needs to eat. Unless you have other plans?"

"Um, no. No plans." Except for making sure Nick turned off his computer by a respectable hour and that Sarah had survived her week-long basketball camp. She could call her kids, after the lesson and before dinner, and be home by ten.

Knowing Adam's age and lack of interest in her, she'd be home by eight-thirty, her stomach full from roast beef sandwiches they'd scarf down at Arby's.

Adam had already walked over to the piano, retrieving from a tall cabinet next to it a stack of books and sheet music. "I wasn't sure what to start with. Maybe more of the stuff you played last week. Maybe something new. Or both?"

Gwen held up the black leather case she'd brought. "This might help. I can show you what I've done, although I'll need more practice on some of it. It's been a while."

"You practiced this week, right?" As he flipped through her music, he nodded appreciatively.

"Um-hmm." She'd played at least an hour every night and two hours each day last weekend. Nick had complained that he'd need a soundproof room if she kept it up, but at least he'd left his room to say something to her. During Sarah's rare breaks from shooting hoops in the driveway, she'd paused by the side of the piano, giving Gwen strange looks as she chomped her bubblegum in time to the music.

But Gwen couldn't admit how much she'd practiced, or how intensely, until she saw what Adam thought of the results.

"Okay, show me what you've got."

She did. With scales and routine exercises and longer pieces, she gave it everything she had. When she turned pages from time to time, she glanced up to see his bemused, far-off expression. Sometimes he gave a quick nod, but his clamped lips didn't smile. She wondered but kept playing.

His cell phone rang. She didn't think he'd answer it, but they both glanced at the clock high on the wall above the piano. Seven-thirty already.

Finally, he snatched up his cell phone and murmured a quiet hello. He probably wanted to spare Gwen the humiliation of having some young woman show up here if he didn't answer, breathlessly asking him—giggle—if they could get together. Like, tonight. Like, now. He'd come up with some pathetic excuse for Gwen, leaving her to handle the Arby's drive-through window on her own.

She suddenly realized that Adam was no longer talking on the phone. He stared at her as if she'd grown two antennae.

"Time's up." He pointed at the clock. "Still wanna grab a bite to eat? I'm starved."

"But your phone call. Don't you have to be somewhere else?"

"Huh?" Adam frowned, staring at Gwen and then down at his phone. "Oh, my sister just called for her usual Friday-night chat. I told her I was busy. No biggie."

Sure it was his sister. He'd spoken so low into the phone,

Gwen couldn't have caught a word if she'd tried. Not that she'd tried. Much.

When she didn't say anything, Adam stood up and grabbed his key ring off a hook on the wall, then headed for the door. "Gwen?"

"But you didn't say anything about my lesson. How did I do? And what should I practice for next time?"

"I wanted to hear you play. I figured we could talk about details over dinner."

———

"Two kids, huh?"

Adam had nearly choked on his chips and guacamole as he asked, but he recovered quickly. Most of the other women he saw for lessons probably had kids, too, but didn't mention it if they wanted to appear younger than they were to their youthful piano teacher. As if he couldn't see the crow's feet edging their eyes or the extra inches around their waist.

He stuffed another chip loaded with guac in his mouth— at least his twentieth—while Gwen put her cell phone back in her purse and nodded a response. She might not have extra inches around her waist, but she was practically forty. No point hiding it.

He swallowed hard. "What does your husband think about you playing piano again?"

As she thought of Rob, the guacamole suddenly looked unappetizing, even though Tinto made some of the best in town. "He'd be surprised. I never did anything he didn't expect."

"Surprised? Doesn't he know?"

She flushed, then fumbled around in her purse, seeking

any excuse to keep her head down. "*Ex*-husband. We've been divorced two years. And, no, he wouldn't know."

No reaction. "How old are your kids? They live with you, right?"

Gwen hung her purse over the back of her chair at the corner table. Not that any table at Tinto would've given them privacy. She'd already run into two neighbors at the bar, who looked at her curiously, and glimpsed a few more walking on the sidewalk past the huge windows that hid nothing and no one from sight. She wasn't embarrassed to be with Adam, or not exactly, but choosing a restaurant halfway between his apartment and her house might've been a mistake.

She took a long sip of her mojito before answering. "Yes. Sarah's fourteen, Nick's eleven. Old enough to stay home by themselves, but I feel better checking in with them. Sarah wasn't home yet when I left."

The cylinder lights above their heads glinted off his hair, dusting it with golden sparkles. She wished the light could work the same magic on her own hair, but that would probably take a blowtorch.

Okay, her hair probably didn't look bad, but she was tired of it. Tired of everything lately. Work. Life. Her only glimmers of happiness came from her kids, and, lately, with their normal teenage and pre-teen struggles, even that wasn't a given.

While they'd waited on the patio for a table, she'd learned more about Adam than she had in two full lessons. He'd accepted a full scholarship to Oberlin's music program, graduating with honors. After that, he turned down a position in his dad's hardware business and sacrificed a few material comforts—as she already knew from looking around his living room—for the chance to teach piano and sometimes perform.

From what she'd heard, he performed pretty well.

The intense look in his deep brown eyes penetrated her thoughts. Blushing, she spoke as he brought the bottle of Corona to his lips. "So what's the verdict? How'd I do tonight?"

As he touched his tongue to his wet upper lip, he caught her gaze and held it. "Hmmm?"

She felt herself tingle. "On the piano? The lesson?"

"Fine."

"Oh." She clutched the napkin in her lap, kneading it like a slab of dough. She didn't need to pay good money to hear someone say "fine." Especially when that someone didn't provide the fringe benefits he gave his other students.

"Much better than fine, actually. I haven't had many students like you, and I'm trying to figure you out. That's why I let you keep playing."

"Figure me out?" She wrinkled her nose. "I don't know what you mean."

The waiter arrived with their dinner. Lomo saltado—flank steak—for him and shrimp tacos for her. She'd eaten here a few times with Leila, who always ordered the lomo saltado, and had almost ordered it until Adam did. She didn't want to be one of those silly women who ordered whatever the man did.

So, instead, she'd ordered the opposite of whatever he did. Like the mojito, even though she would've loved a Corona.

Apparently, Sarah wasn't the only fourteen-year-old who lived at her house.

Adam took a long swig of his beer, then glanced around the restaurant before answering. "The dark smudges under your eyes. The way your fingers take command of the piano keys. The way your pulse beats on your throat when you bubble over with excitement. The way you grip your water glass when you're nervous. Like now."

The man noticed everything. She let go of her glass.

He grinned. "And, yeah, your skill level. It's tough to figure after two lessons."

She'd hoped for more advice from Adam. Tonight, she'd sailed over some passages, trembled a bit with others. She had her favorite composers, like he undoubtedly did, the ones who made her fingers dance. She knew she hunched too often over the keys, feeling unsure every moment and fidgeting when she paused. But when she closed her eyes and played, just played, the melodies flowed, haunting her sweetly.

She wanted to make that happen more often.

"Your fingers sure fly on the up-tempo pieces, but you still make it look graceful. Helps to have such long fingers."

She peered at them, holding them out like foreign objects. "I suppose so. My mother always said that."

"Did she play?"

"Bridge, mostly." Winking at him, she felt like a naughty little girl. "No. Vivian never does much of anything herself, but it doesn't stop her from offering her opinions."

"She was right about your fingers."

"I'll let her know." She stared at the opposite wall a moment, wishing he'd comment on something other than her fingers. "But what else? I'm not sure what needs the most work."

Adam picked up his knife and fork, cutting into his steak. "That's our wonderful dilemma. What you should do next."

They discussed what she'd played tonight, the music she needed to practice more to bring out its richness, the pieces she should work to master by the following week. Moments slid into longer ones, until Gwen glanced at her watch and jumped.

"Yikes! It's almost ten. I'm so sorry, but I need to get home." She'd forgotten her kids. In the last two years, that had never happened. She flew from her chair.

Adam stretched, rising to his feet more slowly. "Let me catch the check and walk you to your car."

"Oh, but—" She nibbled on her bottom lip.

Pulling out his wallet, Adam grabbed a few bills and laid them on the table. "My treat. For my favorite student."

She laughed nervously. "I won't tell anyone."

"Feel free." He tugged lightly on a lock of her hair, then—too soon—released it and turned to leave. "Come on. Somebody needs to get tucked in."

Her kids probably did, too.

———

"Don't 'oh, Mom' me, young lady. It's not the end of the world." While she strained to button the back of her own dress, Gwen tried to get Sarah into something other than shorts and a jersey. She called out periodically for Nick, who was missing in action.

"What if someone sees me?" Sarah made a face at the sleeveless dress that Gwen had pulled from the back of Sarah's closet after making sure it had no bows, ruffles, or lace.

"I think that's the point." She called Nick's name again and heard a hopeful scraping sound coming from his room. "Your grandparents will see you, and your aunts and uncles. I've told them all that I have a cute daughter. Don't make a liar out of me."

"Oh, Mom." Sarah rolled her eyes, but she slipped the

dress off the hanger. "I don't even know who's getting married. Some cousin? What's the point?"

Nick's room had again become silent. Gwen hadn't seen him since breakfast, and it was almost eleven-thirty. "There's your answer. You don't even know my cousin Greta, after all the hours she sacrificed to babysit you when you were little. The utter shame of it almost makes me weep."

"Spare me." Grinning in spite of herself, Sarah slammed her bedroom door.

The closed door didn't stop Gwen from calling after her. "And stay off your phone. We have to leave in fifteen minutes, or we'll be late."

Sarah's door peeked open a crack. "Now, there's a tragedy." It closed again, more softly this time.

Inspired, Gwen marched down the hall to Nick's room, rapped sharply, and waited a moment before flinging open the door. Her son, still in his pajamas, sat at his computer, his face two inches from the screen. "Nick! Don't you know what time it is? We're leaving for Greta's wedding in fifteen minutes."

"Uh-huh." Not one muscle twitched.

Digging through his closet, Gwen retrieved a pair of khakis and a striped, button-down Oxford. He didn't really have a decent sportcoat, and the odds of getting a tie around his neck in this lifetime were currently slim to none.

"Nick." His eyes flickered. "Let's go, sport. Put these clothes on and run a comb through your hair. You could use a haircut, but I didn't think of that until now."

"Huh."

"Not that I would've seen you to notice how long your hair has gotten, since you're practically growing roots in this room." No movement. "Nick. Get dressed, or I'll make sure my cousin Helen's cute little Rosemary dances with you at the reception."

She didn't think Nick could move that fast. By God, her son could be a track star. "See you downstairs."

———

THREE HOURS and fourteen glasses of punch later, Gwen wandered around the Nicollet Island Pavilion, gazing out the windows at the Mississippi River while trying to avoid a sneak attack by her mother and most of her female relatives. Her cousin Greta's wedding to Riley, held outdoors with the happy couple married under a wooden arch covered with flowers, had been simple and honestly joyful.

But at this point, she just wanted to escape. Her kids probably did, too.

As she glanced at her diamond-and-gold watch—her college graduation gift from her parents and her most expensive piece of jewelry, since she'd long since sold everything Rob had ever given her—she felt someone's gaze boring into her back. She slowly turned, plastering a cautious but hopeful smile on her face.

Okay, maybe just a cautious smile.

She'd scoped out the crowd when she first arrived for the wedding, and it hadn't changed much when everyone had moved inside for the reception. Too many of her relatives, echoing Vivian, viewed Greta's wedding as just another chance to quiz her about why she "let Rob get away." Aside from Greta, no one she still counted as a friend was here. And the only available men over thirty-five were bald, wildly unattractive, or wearing plaid. Sometimes, all three.

The man grinning at her right now was none of those.

Stepping closer, Andrew Smythe Withers III, known to

his friends as Skip and to Gwen as Dad, gave her a quick hug. Since the dawn of time, the Withers family didn't hug. Vivian had easily adapted to that tradition, never giving Gwen or her brother Mac more than a rare peck on the cheek, but Dad was a closet hugger. As kids, Gwen and Mac hugged and even wrestled with him—but only if they had no witnesses.

Right now, her dad's eyebrows waggled a few times.

Gwen laughed. "Hi, Dad. How long were you standing there? Getting up the nerve to talk to your favorite daughter again?"

"My favorite *oldest* daughter." As he'd confided to Gwen the day Sarah was born, Dad had always wanted more kids. Not that he didn't love Gwen and Mac—and oh, boy, he did—but Vivian had quit after producing Mac, three years after Gwen. If Gwen had been a boy, she might've even quit then, believing that her husband would be content just to have a son. No. And when he'd suggested they adopt, Vivien had given that a hard pass, too.

It wasn't the only thing they'd disagreed on, even though Dad had usually let her run the show. She'd put "Andrew Smythe Withers IV" on Mac's birth certificate without even asking her husband. In a rare moment, Gwen's dad had apparently shouted at Vivian, announcing that the kid deserved his own damned name, not the name of "some jackass great-grandfather."

As far as Gwen knew, it was the only time her dad had ever sworn. Or lost his temper. It was also how MacAllister Kendall Withers got his own damned name.

"How's my baby girl? Busy dodging relatives at the punch bowl?" He made an uncharacteristic face, tilting his head toward the crystal glass in Gwen's hand. "You know, that stuff can kill you. It doesn't have any alcohol to save it."

"Say it isn't so." She rolled her eyes. "But since I'm almost forty, I'm not exactly your little girl anymore."

"Always and forever." Her dad had always said that when he tucked her in at night. Warmth spread through her at the words.

She swirled the red liquid in her glass until it almost splashed over the side. "You'd think the relatives would forget about Rob. It's not like I'm the only person who ever got divorced. And it's been two years."

Her dad looked thoughtful. "There haven't been a lot of divorces in your mother's family. Or in mine. Maybe they don't understand. Or maybe they're jealous."

"They're not jealous." She snorted. "And what's to understand? I wasn't enough for Rob. Too bad he had to let everyone in the world know."

"Maybe you're *not* good enough for him. Rob's a plastic surgeon, after all."

The words stung, leaving a sharp pain in her side. Looking down at the floor—Dad was actually wearing beat-up boat shoes with his suit—she felt tears shimmer, but she'd shed too many for Rob already. Too many for what she'd given up.

A hand tapped the bottom of her chin, tilting her gaze upward to her dad's sheepish face. "I'm sorry, honey. You and I used to make fun of the same things. I keep forgetting that the idiot took that away from you, too."

Gwen blinked. "The idiot? Rob? You always acted as if he was a second son to you."

Despite his earlier complaints, her dad accepted a glass of punch from the tall woman behind the table in the floppy floral silk hat. "I already have a son. And a daughter. For once in my life, I'd say that's enough."

"I don't understand."

"Rob was fine. For a while." He shook his head. "I had him pegged, though, even before your wedding. I'll always regret that I never said anything to you. Your mother—"

"She was thrilled. I know." Gwen leaned one hip against the punch table. "But I thought you were, too. You always spoke highly of Rob. I heard you."

Glancing around the large room, her dad spied Vivian on the opposite side of it and exchanged a small wave. "If you think about it, you didn't hear me say much at all. As the years went on, I said even less. I couldn't stand Rob. Even more, I couldn't stand how he treated my little girl."

"I'm not a little girl."

"So I hear." The corners of his eyes crinkled. "I know too many men like him. Too full of themselves. But your mother thought . . ." He shook his head. "From the start, she thought Rob was the man for you. I figured she must know you better than I did."

"You're kidding, right? Vivian and I have never agreed on anything. I think she hates how I'm raising my kids, too."

"You're doing a wonderful job." He glanced around the room again. Gwen's gaze followed his to Nick, who was barely tolerating the effusive hugs of the two talkative aunts who had trapped him, and to Sarah—

Who had somehow smuggled a pair of jeans into the reception and was now wearing them.

Gwen's dad burst into laughter. "Sarah's a little pistol, just like her mom at the same age. How's her jump shot coming along?"

Gwen and her dad traded stories about Sarah's basketball career, which she'd soon put on hold for volleyball season. Gwen then caught her son's bugged-out eyes, which pleaded for help escaping the killer aunts.

She started toward Nick, her dad at her side. "I'm not

always so sure about Nick, Dad. Rob doesn't see him much, and maybe Nick needs more male attention. He sits in his room all day playing computer games."

"Hmmm." Her dad studied Nick, a shorter version of Rob but with sandy brown hair. "Depends. Are his computer games pretty masculine or too, er, girly-girl?"

"Girly-girl" was Sarah's term for the clothes and toys Vivian insisted on buying her, despite the fact that they all landed in the far corner of her closet floor.

Did Vivian know? "You've been talking to Sarah?"

Her father's eyes twinkled. "Don't worry. Her secret is safe with me. Besides, she needed an accomplice for smuggling in her reception attire today, and, well . . ."

Gwen shook a finger at him. "Dad!"

Grabbing her hand, he pulled her into another hug. A moment later, he headed toward Nick. "Sorry. Have to save my grandson." In a lower voice, he spoke again as Gwen kept pace with him. "He'll be fine. Probably better off not spending much time with Rob, anyway." He winked at Gwen. "Loser."

Gwen laughed until tears bubbled in the corners of her eyes. Her dad rescued Nick, then rushed to protect a smug Sarah from any scold Gwen might've even thought about giving her. Greta's wedding hadn't been such a bust, after all.

Until Adam walked in, a gorgeous young woman draped on his arm.

CHAPTER 4

"Small world." Gwen mumbled under her breath, wishing she'd escaped sooner.

"Hmm?" Her dad, ruffling Nick's hair with one hand and draping his other arm around Sarah's narrow shoulders, glanced around the large room.

"Nothing."

But then "nothing" walked over to Gwen, smiled, and said hi. Without looking the slightest bit mortified that he'd brought one woman too many to the reception. Basically, Leila was right about men.

At Gwen's greeting, which she hissed between her teeth, Adam looked expectantly at her dad and kids. She didn't look expectantly at Adam's date. She tried not to look at her at all.

It was difficult, of course, since the young woman was almost Adam's height, weighed twelve pounds—all of which were in her breasts—and had such stunningly blond hair, it was obviously dyed. Okay, her eyebrows were blond, too, and she looked like she'd just gotten off a boat from Norway. She also looked young enough to still have issues with acne.

Not that Gwen could see any. It was probably at her hairline.

Adam offered his hand to Gwen's dad, who shook it and introduced himself, Sarah, and Nick. Traitor. And just a moment ago, she'd actually liked her dad.

"I'm Adam Flynn. Gwen's piano teacher."

Her dad's eyebrows rose. "You don't look old enough to be one of Gwen's old piano teachers."

"I've taken good care of myself." Everyone other than Gwen laughed. Especially the blonde clinging to Adam's arm as if she owned it. Grinning, Adam explained. "I'm her *new* piano teacher. Hasn't Gwen mentioned her lessons?"

"No, but she seldom speaks to me." Her dad sighed loudly.

"Give it up, Dad." True, she hadn't gotten around to mentioning it to him yet, but she was more than a little surprised that Vivian hadn't told him, either. "I've just taken two lessons so far. It's easier to play my piano than dust it."

"You always were practical." Amusement glinted in her dad's eyes, and Sarah and Nick suddenly seemed extremely interested in their mom's piano lessons. Or at least her teacher.

The blonde yawned. Maybe Adam had kept her up late. Since he'd been out with Gwen last night until ten, it must've been much later than she wanted to think about.

Adam tugged on the blonde's arm, drawing her into the conversation. "Sorry, I forgot. This is Katie."

Gwen hadn't minded not being introduced to Goldilocks —er, Katie. She hadn't minded not staring into her huge brown eyes. Chocolate-brown eyes. A little like Adam's, but more syrupy.

Katie fluttered her eyelashes and tittered. Figured. She looked about sixteen and definitely acted like it.

"Hi." The meek voice was both unexpected and nervous.

Adam put his arm around her. "Katie's my bratty little

sister who somehow knows whenever I'm in the middle of a lesson, because that's when she always calls."

Katie giggled again. It didn't seem as annoying now. In fact, she seemed like a sweet girl. Despite her fifteen-inch waist and forty-inch bust, Gwen could grow to like her.

Gwen turned to Adam, possibly starting to like him again, too. "What brings you here? I didn't see you outside at the ceremony."

"Riley and I go way back. He even threatened to make me one of his groomsmen, but he knows I avoid tuxedos whenever I can." He coughed. "Especially when they coincide with weddings."

"Can't say I blame you." Gwen's father chuckled.

"I love weddings. They're so magical." Spoken by sixteen-year-old Katie, who seemed genuinely sweet, but Gwen still couldn't fathom having a conversation with her.

Had Greta's wedding to Riley today been magical? They were a cute couple, but weren't they too young for such a huge step? At twenty-five, Gwen had been way too young. Greta, the youngest daughter of Vivian's sister Roxanne, was almost thirty. Shouldn't she have waited at least another ten years?

"I guess magical depends on your perspective. How old are you?" Jesus. Talk about rude. The question had simply popped out of Gwen's mouth before she could stuff it back in, as if she were sixteen, too.

Katie didn't seem to notice. "I turned twenty-six last Tuesday. My girlfriends threw a party for me." She giggled again.

Sarah, who giggled a lot with her girlfriends but not when she thought her mom might be listening, rolled her eyes.

Katie was either shy or—Gwen feared—had heard something hilarious about Gwen from Adam.

She hoped Katie was just shy.

"Happy belated, and good to meet you, Katie. We were actually just leaving." Despite the bone-crushing boredom of the reception—until Adam walked in—Gwen suddenly wanted to linger and talk to Adam about something other than chords and scales. But she didn't need an audience, and she'd already made enough of a fool of herself for one day.

"Were you?"

"Uh, yeah, Dad. I promised Sarah and Nick I'd get them out of here as soon as I could."

"Since when?" Sarah, who probably assumed she'd be facing execution by firing squad for wearing the jeans, wasn't rushing for the door. Only Nick looked thrilled. But he was probably still terrified of dancing with Rosemary and hadn't blown up any aliens in a few hours.

Right this moment, Nick was Gwen's favorite child.

"Since now. Gotta go. Bye." Lacking a good reason to leave and the grace to stay, Gwen nudged both kids toward the door.

She could've sworn she saw Adam smile.

———

"How ARE you doing on the proxy materials?" Ted Harrison had changed tactics, from constantly asking her out to constantly asking her about the Treadman deal. Danny was handling the proxy materials with George Kravitz's help. At least, she assumed so. Except for including her on a few emails, Danny hadn't kept her up to speed.

Gwen clutched her can of Diet Coke as if it offered a lifeline.

"For the Treadman deal?" Playing dumb wouldn't buy

much time in the absence of a miracle, but a miracle would be nice.

Ted frowned, blowing air loudly out his nose. "Of course the Treadman deal. Where are they?"

She contemplated knocking over the Diet Coke. Diversion. She took a sip instead, her sixth or seventh since Ted had walked in. "They're either in word processing or on Danny's desk, I think. We should have a first draft by Friday."

"Friday?" Ted ground his teeth. "You've had the assignment for a week, and you need four more days?"

His voice dropped an octave on each of the last few words.

Danny. Danny. Danny. Help. Help. Help.

Positive affirmations didn't bring Danny any closer to her office. So much for all those New Age books Leila had dropped on her doorstep along with wine. At least the wine had been good.

She straightened her spine. "Actually, you asked me to do the proxy materials—with Danny—last Wednesday afternoon. It's only Monday morning. Treadman's CFO—" What was her name? No clue. "Er, she won't be able to pull all of the necessary information together until Wednesday, at least. The Aertronix lawyers said they'd try to send us their sections on Thursday. It'll be a push to send out a decent draft by Friday."

At least, that's what Danny had guessed last Thursday. With her luck, the what's-her-name CFO had dropped everything else and sent her portion of the proxy materials already, and the lawyers representing Aertronix had finished their work over the weekend.

Ted jammed his hands in his pockets—or tried to. His expensive but tight pants would have trouble accommodating paper clips, let alone his bony fists.

"Okay. Tina Michaels—" The CFO. Bingo. "And the Aertronix people need more time." He cleared his throat. "You didn't say how you're doing on the portions we're preparing. We need to be ahead of the game, not just keeping up."

The dreaded Y chromosome never ceased to amaze her.

Danny Fitzsimmons poked his head in the door. "They're just doing a few sections. We're preparing eighty percent of the registration statement. Don't worry, Ted. We're on it." He nodded at Gwen. "And Gwen is leading the charge."

Veins throbbing on his temples, Ted didn't appear to appreciate the cavalry's sudden appearance.

"If you don't mind, Danny, I was asking Gwen about the proxy materials. We don't need three people billing their time for the conversation."

"That's a first." Danny grinned, pretending not to notice Gwen, who squirmed and did everything short of raising her hands in surrender. "Actually, I need to bring Gwen up to date on a few things. She's working with *me* on the proxy materials, if you recall."

Relieved, Gwen felt the air whoosh out of her lungs. Ted looked so deflated, she almost laughed. Trying to avoid his gaze and Danny's, she pulled out the bottom drawer of her desk. Five pairs of black and navy-blue pumps stared back at her.

"I recall." With his voice chilled to something near freezing, Ted turned his back on Danny, dismissing him. "How far have you gotten on the proxy materials? Did you work over the weekend? Or did social obligations distract you?"

Finally. Ted's typical Monday-morning question for the last several weeks. He just hadn't had witnesses before.

Danny smirked at her from behind Ted. "Yeah, any hot dates this weekend? Inquiring minds want to know."

A twist of Ted's head wiped the smile off Danny's face until Ted turned back to face Gwen. Danny then made goo-goo eyes at Gwen and hung his head from an imaginary noose.

Feeling anger bubble in her stomach, Gwen ignored Danny. "Social obligations have never stopped me from getting my work done, Ted. I can't believe you'd even suggest that. You asked me to work with Danny on the Treadman deal, and I've done everything Danny has asked of me."

In other words, nothing. She frowned at Danny, wishing he'd just admit to Ted that he'd asked George to prepare the first draft. Danny hadn't made partner by being gutless.

Ted looked from Danny to Gwen, then walked out of Gwen's office without another word.

After shutting the door, then whipping it open again to make sure Ted wasn't pressed against it, Danny slouched in the only free chair in Gwen's office. "Hey, at least you never went out with the guy." His eyebrows rose, as if making sure, and she shook her head. Emphatically. "Good. Ted is really acting weird, though. I guess that's what happens when your wife walks out and takes the kids."

Gwen blinked.

Despite Ted's recent date requests, she didn't know much about his private life. No one did. Unlike most lawyers, who had family pictures on their desks or occasionally mentioned their spouses or kids, Ted kept all aspects of his personal life on a need-to know basis.

And he didn't think anyone needed to know them.

But knowing about his divorce actually made Gwen empathize, at least a little. She understood only too well how a divorce could scar someone. Rob had left two years ago, and she still hadn't gotten over it.

"When did she leave him?"

"Two weeks ago."

————

"Two weeks ago?" Practically shouting the question, Leila slammed shut the book she'd been reading—something about sexual mating styles, as if she needed more knowledge—and slid it back on the shelf. Shock etched itself across a face famous for taking everything in stride.

Gwen cringed. "Could you speak up? I don't think the woman in the far corner heard you." She glanced at the older woman with the improbable beehive hairdo and cat-eye reading glasses, who glanced up from the book she perused. "Or maybe I was wrong."

Tuesday was book lovers' night at Leila's new favorite haunt, Books and Ab's. Knowing Leila, she'd come for the promise of abs. After a furtive glance at the other customers, Gwen suspected Leila was out of luck. The store hosted a wide variety of book clubs and readings, and it offered lots of cozy nooks for curling up with the right book. There were far more women than men, though, and no one looked as if they'd spent quality time working on their abs.

Not that it mattered. Tonight, Gwen just wanted a sympathetic ear.

"You *wish* someone was listening." But Leila dropped her voice a few decibels. "But at least you have bragging rights, for once in your life. All my hard work is paying off."

"Paying off? What hard work?" Gwen grabbed a book off the shelf before scanning the title. *Sex You Wouldn't Mention to Your Mother*. Wasn't that redundant?

Maybe she'd quit blushing by the time she turned forty. In the meantime, if she didn't drag Leila to a different section of the bookstore—and quickly—she'd need a paper bag for her head.

Leila flipped open Gwen's book to a page filled with anatomically improbable illustrations. "Hmm. I haven't tried that. Do you think—"

"No. Please." Gwen scanned the crowd again, certain her mother had somehow entered the store. "Could we return to what I was telling you? Obnoxious married men—and someone I actually work for—actually bugging me to go out with them?"

Leila chewed thoughtfully on the wad of gum she'd stuffed in her mouth before blowing a bubble. "I don't see why you're upset. Like Danny told you, Ted scammed every-one. Why a married guy is twisted enough to make the whole world think he's divorced is beyond me, but it's not like you went out with the guy."

"But what if I had?"

With a tap of Leila's finger, the bubble popped. "I'd throw a party. The whole city would celebrate."

"Funny." Out of the corner of her eye, Gwen watched a man with glasses and shaggy brown hair approach them. She spoke more softly. "It's not like I'm hopeless. I'm taking piano lessons."

"Yes, but to play piano. That's not why I sent you to Adam." Leila paused to hug the man, who gazed from Leila to Gwen and back again. "Jon! I dragged another innocent woman into your lair. Meet Gwen Stanhope, who by the way is perfectly available."

The heat of Gwen's blush felt like a volcano. She'd kill Leila. Tonight, if possible. "Hi."

The man shook her hand, very businesslike, as if he hadn't heard Leila's comment, or had heard enough similar comments from Leila to make him immune. His bright blue eyes pierced Gwen. "I'm Jon Abelard. Thanks for coming in."

"You work here?"

"Even worse. I own the place." His smile was sheepish and accented by a shrug. "We've been open almost a year."

Books and *Ab's*. Abelard. Duh, as Sarah would say.

Leila broke in. "Jon is the best. He always has exactly the book I need, whether or not I know it." Smiling at him, she ran her fingers up his arm. "And he's available, too."

"I'm not as sure of that as you are." A shadow crossed his face, replaced immediately by something else. Graciousness. "But I'm happy to meet your friend."

Absolutely ecstatic, from the looks of it. Not.

Gwen smiled at him anyway. "Nice to meet you, too. I'm sorry it's taken me so long to visit your store. Leila raves about it."

She bit her lip, wishing someone would rave about *her*. After two years on her own, having a man to flirt with—who wasn't married, engaged, living with someone, or otherwise depressed or depressing—would be a nice change of pace. She'd love to have someone to practice on for when she was ready.

Jon didn't look like he wanted to practice. He wasn't even sure he was available, which told her to run, not walk, as far and as fast as she could. And hidden inside baggy clothes, he drooped in ways that weren't physical—as if too many burdens overwhelmed him. Only his twinkling blue eyes hinted at life.

Leila glanced at her Mickey Mouse watch, which did wonders for her slash-cut Versace dress. "You'll have to get to know each other better later." Her eyebrows danced. "I promised Gwen I'd introduce her to my book lovers' group. Tonight we're discussing 'Diamonds for a Woman's Soul.' I like the concept. Chocolate is too fattening and chicken soup's too soupy."

She skimmed a hand along her slim hip, as if she had something to worry about. Gwen glanced down at herself, questioning her own choice of baggy jeans and tie-dyed tank top.

Jon didn't appear to notice. Gazing at the wall, he spoke more to himself than the two women. "She loved emeralds and pearls. Diamonds were too cold."

His odd chuckle left Gwen shivering.

———

"THIS IS GETTING to be a regular Friday-night date."

Fifteen minutes into her third piano lesson, Gwen looked up to find Adam's face contemplative. "Sorry. I didn't mean to cramp your social life. Would you like to find a different evening or something on a weekend day?"

Brushing against her, Adam reached for the piano book propped in front of Gwen and closed it. "Fridays are fine. And you don't need to apologize."

"I didn't mean—" She faltered, not exactly sure what she meant. "Sorry."

He dropped the book on a pile and set some new sheet music on the stand. "It must be exhausting, carrying the weight of the world on those skinny shoulders."

"They're not so—"

Adam tapped the music, not looking at her. "Skinny? Yeah, they are, like the rest of you. Nothing wrong with that, but you feed everyone except you and take care of everyone but you. And you're always saying you're sorry. Man, that ex must've done a number on you."

She bristled. "You don't know what you're talking about."

"Sorry. Oops—now I'm sounding like you." He touched a hand to her shoulder. Her skinny, pathetic shoulder. "Seriously, you have a lot of talent, but I'm not sure you have the level of desire it takes to pull it off."

First she was skinny, and now she didn't have enough desire? It was like being with Rob all over again.

Finally realizing what else he'd said, she frowned. "Pull what off?"

His eyes focused on a spot above her head. "There's a little competition coming up. Like a recital, but, like, different."

Now he sounded like her fourteen-year-old daughter.

She rolled her eyes, also like her daughter. "Could you put that into language I might understand? Details?"

Straightening the already straight music on the stand, Adam's fingers fluttered the way hers did when she was nervous. She didn't know surfer boys ever got nervous.

"End of September at the U of M. It's a competition for piano students and teachers. Except for some scholarships, there's not much of a prize, but it brings you recognition."

She sputtered. "But it's already August. I'm on my third lesson after more than twenty years. You're kidding, right?"

Grabbing her hand, his own felt warm and tempting. "Just think about it. You don't need to decide today."

"I'm not sure I want the recognition." She laughed, nearly choking on it. "I don't even recognize myself."

"Yeah. I know." Whatever that meant.

She played and he listened, interrupting her from time to time with suggestions or gentle corrections. Neither one mentioned the piano competition again. Ending the final piece with a flourish, Gwen sat back and smiled, a not-so-secret part of her waiting for and wanting his applause.

She got a peck on the cheek instead.

"What's that for?" Turning to face him, Gwen found Adam's lips still hovering. Too close. He leaned in and kissed her again, a light brush of lips on lips.

Fire on ice.

Masculine assurance on ineptitude.

"Sorry." Flushing, she felt the sting of rejection as he pulled away. "I'm not—"

"Nice lips, Gwen Stanhope." He touched them again, this time with his fingertip. Softly. "I'm the one who should be sorry, but I'm not. I've been dying to know how you taste."

Her lips tingled, and she wanted to run screaming out of his apartment.

She didn't budge. "I probably have apple breath, since that's what I ate before I came over here."

"Gross." Disgust tinged the word.

"I know. It reeks for hours, I swear. I don't know why I eat them. Sorry." She looked down, not sure whether the apple breath or her inane, high-pitched explanation of it might be more humiliating. Probably a tie.

He nudged her chin back up with a touch of his finger. "Now you're apologizing for eating apples, for God's sake. Can't you believe I'd want to kiss you?"

Not really. "It's not that."

"No? So you don't mind if I kiss you again?" He leaned closer. "Just to get beyond your apple complex?"

"Yes. I mean, no. I don't mind. I mean—" She sounded twelve and wanted to slap herself senseless, even though she was already there.

"Good."

He didn't wait for more, brushing their lips together once, twice, then settling his firmly against hers. He tasted tangy, like mint and chocolate and pineapple all jumbled together in an explosion. And she'd worried about apples.

Then he took it deeper.

His tongue touched her lips, gently, before sweeping inside her mouth. She felt her own tongue do a happy-dance with his, twirling and gliding and exploring this strange new being inside her.

Disappointment tugged at her when she realized the assault was limited to her mouth. Adam's arms just held her, although his hands etched little circles on her back. Her own arms were tucked tightly against his chest. She had no idea what to do with them. For now, she didn't do anything except feel a little stupid.

His breathing became harsh, harder . . . then stilled. His fingers stilled. His lips planted a final, soft, savoring kiss on hers before pulling away.

"You're sweet." He tapped her chin again.

Sweet.

In other words, undesirable. Skinny, apologetic, and far from sexy. Adam had taken her lips for a spin because he felt sorry for her, but it ended there. If Leila could be believed, the guy slept with more than a few of his piano students. But not Gwen. The apple-breath loser.

She'd been humiliated before. With Rob, plenty of times. She'd just never forked over cold, hard cash for it.

"I have to go."

A frown marred the smooth skin of his face. "See you next Friday?"

"Sure." If hell froze over. She'd send a text, canceling. She couldn't handle it right now.

Standing up, Adam held out his hand. Gwen avoided it by jumping to her feet in a jerky movement that couldn't be called graceful.

"Are you all right?" He grasped one of her arms but

stopped short of shaking her. He probably thought she'd break.

"Perfect."

"Okay." After tucking a few stray hairs behind her ear, Adam tilted his head to really look at her. "Promise me you'll think about the piano competition. Or recital, really. It's not that big a deal."

Just another opportunity for humiliation. "If it's not a big deal, why should I bother?"

"Because I asked?"

CHAPTER 5

"You don't need him or his piano competition, and you can do better." Leila offered her quick take on Gwen's latest dilemma as she stuffed a deviled egg in her mouth. "But you actually *make* these? Unbelievable."

Gwen rearranged the unused silverware for the neighborhood picnic, held in her backyard every year on the first Sunday in August, and pulled another carton of lemonade from a cooler. An ant was crawling on the lid.

Frowning, she swatted at another ant scurrying across the card table next to the cooler. "You don't like the eggs? Sarah always begs me for them."

"Love 'em." Proving her love, Leila swallowed the deviled egg in one bite and snared another. That made at least five. "I just can't believe you *make* them. You can buy them by the dozen at the grocery store, and no one would ever know."

"I would." Gwen wrinkled her nose, then sampled her first deviled egg. Mmm. "It's not hard to do, and it makes Sarah happy."

"Sarah? What makes Gwen happy?" Leila's wave took in the whole backyard, where twenty adults milled around, with or without their kids. "You organize everything, you cook damn near everything, and you clean up. You probably clean the coffee pots at work."

"I don't drink coffee."

And Leila was starting to sound like Adam, which was starting to annoy her.

Shaking her head, Leila steered Gwen over to a lawn chair. Her feet ached from a day of constant motion, and the scorching midafternoon sun burned like a toaster on fire.

After dragging another chair next to Gwen's, Leila fanned herself. "You need to put yourself first for a change. You don't need to survive turning forty. Forty isn't a big deal. But you do need to focus on being happy. At any age."

She meant well. She just didn't understand.

Spying some picnic debris on an empty chair, Gwen automatically jumped up to clear it. Before she could, Leila nudged her back into her chair and snagged the tail of Nick's shirt as he walked by. "Nick, honey, go pick up that plate before your mom has a heart attack."

"I'm busy." His face was pink, the result of either his first ascertainable day in the sun this summer or the halter top and minuscule shorts that Leila wore. Her outfit had flushed the faces of several men at the picnic, whose wives looked ready to hose them down, but Nick was only eleven. Gwen's baby.

Leila's hearty laugh drew more stares. "Busy destroying more cities on your computer? Try another one. Pick it up, cutie, or Aunt Leila is going to hug you until she squeezes your brains right out of your head."

Gwen closed her eyes. When she found the strength to open them again, Nick was dropping the offending trash in a wastebasket. He then made a beeline for the house, Leila hooting as he did.

"He's not a toy."

"No, he's practically a teenager, and he doesn't need his

mama picking up after him." Shifting her sunglasses from the top of her head to her nose, Leila sank into her lawn chair.

"It's not that."

"Yes, it is."

"No, it's—" "Yes." "No. "Yes." "No." "Yes." Trading retorts at split-second intervals, the two women stopped only when both collapsed in laughter.

"I won! Naa naa na na naa." As she jabbed the index finger of each hand in the air and bounced in her chair, Leila hummed a victory tune.

Gwen wished she lived her own life with such gusto, right down to Leila's bright-red toenails, Mickey Mouse watch, and wicked smile.

"I wish . . ."

Leila studied her over the tops of her sunglasses. "I wish a million things for you, but don't wish for what you don't want or can't handle. Believe me. You're not ready." She pushed the glasses back to the bridge of her nose.

A soccer ball slammed into the back of Gwen's chair, stunning her, and Sarah tiptoed up to retrieve it. Gwen snagged her daughter's arm. "Nice try, kiddo. Should I be grateful it wasn't a basketball?"

Sarah shrugged sheepishly and returned to her friends.

After a long stretch of blessed but awkward silence, since Leila had apparently run out of unhelpful advice to offer, Gwen finally stood up to finish clearing the mess. Relaxing meant thinking about Adam and too many other aspects of her life, all of them frustrating. Leila didn't bother to either stop her or help. No one else did, either.

Why did she host this picnic every year?

Bustling around despite her exhaustion, Gwen snapped lids and wiped up spills, rethinking the interrupted conversation. Her wishes felt vague and elusive, but Leila's words deflated her. She dropped back into her lawn chair. "I'm practically forty and my kids are growing up. When do you think I'll be ready for whatever it is you think I can't handle?"

A sly grin lit up Leila's face. "Baby steps. Maybe things haven't worked out with Adam yet, and maybe they never will." Her face wore a dreamy look, though, as if she still had a hope that Gwen didn't share, even though she'd already admitted that Gwen didn't need him. "But I haven't given up. We just need to take more baby steps."

"We? And what baby steps? I seem to fall down the stairs every time I take them." She had the bruises on her heart to prove it.

"So don't go near stairs." Leila's gaze flickered from Gwen's toes to the top of her head, making her want to squirm. "But you don't take enough time for yourself. We all need self-care, and it's time we got you waxed, buffed, and polished."

"I hope you're talking about my car."

"No, you." She rolled her eyes. "That piece of garbage you drive isn't worth the effort."

———

"I can't believe you talked me into this." As her feet soaked in warm, soapy water, Gwen leaned back and tried not to utterly lose herself in the vibrations from her massage chair—or listen to Leila's moans of pleasure from the next chair. "The massage felt wonderful, but why would anyone take time off from work to have hot wax smeared on her forehead and stripped off until she screams? I'd love to know."

Her friend didn't open her eyes, but one brow arched. "Because you'll look gorgeous. Even more gorgeous. You're practically forty, as you love to remind me, and you've never had your brows waxed. Wait 'til I talk you into a bikini wax. It's time to grow up, little girl."

A bikini wax? No way. "I never knew growing up could be so painful."

"Not true. Your brow wax must've been a picnic compared to Rob."

"Ouch." The feeling of bliss evaporated, replaced by a niggling concern that she'd left something undone at work. "I'm also not sure that red toenails are me."

"So get blue ones. Or gold. You'd look wonderful in gold."

The spandex-clad young woman giving her a pedicure—whose name was Christine, or Chrissie, or something like that—handed Gwen several color wheels. There had to be over a hundred choices, ninety of them a variation on red or pink. The gold dazzled. "Hmmm." She touched every color before picking . . . blue.

Vivian would die if she saw her with blue toenails.

A soft bubble of laughter escaped. Christine or Chrissie Spandex stared at Gwen as if she'd grown three eyes. She couldn't blame her. She probably had second-degree burns on her forehead from the hot wax, and now she was giggling. Acting like someone Christine's age. Actually, no. She didn't have blue-streaked hair or a pierced nose.

"Are you okay?" Christine frowned as she wrapped a hot towel around Gwen's foot.

A little embarrassed, she waved a hand. "Sure."

Observing the lithe bodies and smooth skin on Christine and her counterparts was enough to strip the giggles right out of her. The massage had felt fantastic, but the afternoon had mostly gone downhill from there. Right now, she just wanted to go home.

She half-listened to the lively patter of conversation between Leila and the bleached blonde doing her pedicure, who sounded far more knowledgeable, and nice, than she would've imagined someone with large breasts and a tiny butt could be.

The young woman sounded like she had a sugar-daddy boyfriend. Some rich older guy—probably bald and insecure—who pampered her. The world hadn't changed entirely.

Leila finally opened her eyes and twisted to face Gwen. "You seeing Adam tomorrow?"

"Oh, no!" She'd forgotten to cancel her piano lesson. Texting him on Thursday afternoon wasn't enough notice, and texting to cancel—permanently—was probably rude anyway. She blew out a breath. "I guess so, but I'm seeing him for my piano lesson, and only because I forgot to cancel. I'm not 'seeing' him in the way you think."

Unfortunately.

"Just so you're seeing him. And he's seeing you." Leila looked too smug, as usual. "He'll love it."

"Love what?" Scrunching her nose, Gwen had a good guess what Leila meant. "This isn't for Adam. It's for me."

"Now *there's* something we can agree on." Leila shimmied her shoulders as the blonde massaged her foot and calf. "Ooh. That feels so good." She turned again to Gwen. "You're right. But when you look good for yourself, the guys all notice."

Gwen snorted. "I don't care who notices."

Christine slathered another mound of goop on Gwen's foot. It felt ridiculously good, but she didn't have to admit it to Leila.

"Whatever you say." Leila fiddled with the buttons on her chair, and the vibrations grew louder. "I hate it when a spa afternoon ends. Lucky thing we have time for one more treatment."

"Time?" Gwen looked at her watch. Five-fifteen already. Yikes. "I thought the pedicures were the last thing."

"And go out in public with your hair greased up from the massage? I don't think so." Leila cringed as she ran a hand through her own messy hair.

The nail techs started applying polish to their toenails at the same time. Fidgeting, Gwen couldn't believe that the usually high-energy Leila could sit still that long.

"I'm not going out in public. I'm going home, and I can wash my hair there." Her eyebrows still felt a little strange, this was costing her a small fortune, and she wasn't sure how many more gorgeous, fit, spandexed young women could work on her before she started crying.

Leila was only thirty-five. She didn't understand.

Proving it, Leila shook her head. "You may be *stopping* at home, but you can't park yourself on a ratty sofa in a dark corner of your living room when you look this stunning. We're going out."

"My sofa isn't that ratty, and you seem to forget that I have two kids to take care of. And a piano lesson."

"Your piano lesson isn't until tomorrow night. Nick won't notice that you're not there, and Sarah will be relieved. She won't have to stop shooting hoops to eat a healthy dinner when she'd rather shove a bagel in her mouth and run back outside."

"That's not the point."

Leila waved her hand in the air. "It's exactly my point. You're in the prime of your life, and you don't even realize it. It doesn't get much better than sex at forty. We need to get you some."

Gwen could've sworn Leila's nail tech had been about to send Leila to the floor dryer, but she applied another coat of polish. Time to short-circuit the conversation before the four women exchanged phone numbers.

"I don't need anyone's charity. If it's going to happen, it will." Gwen felt three pairs of eyes gazing at her. Despite her words, she also felt like the lowest form of charity.

Leila waved off her nail tech and eased herself out of her pedicure chair, then slowly padded to the dryer. "It'll happen. Especially when we get all that gray out of your hair."

"There isn't *that* much gray."

"Finally. You admit it."

GWEN'S HAIR was a richer hue of auburn than she remembered, and the blunt cut swished against her shoulders every time she turned her head. Like now, as she caught her reflection in the former—and current—Dayton's show window.

As she glanced down, her sapphire-blue toenails peeked out from the three-inch sandals that hurt like hell but made her look like a model. Or a sea nymph, as Leila had said. A sea nymph in sandals? Whatever.

"Nice." The wolf whistle couldn't possibly be meant for her. "I don't see you all those years, then twice in a month. And looking different each time."

Tucker Preston circled Gwen as she stood, planted in the middle of the sidewalk, the wind knocked out of her. She tried to picture the scruffy young man in ragged jeans who used to tinker with motorcycles. The grown-up version looked too good for her peace of mind.

He wasn't wearing a suit this time, but his black silk shirt and charcoal slacks had an easy—and sexy—elegance. The men in her firm didn't dress this well for Friday casual.

Friday. Gwen nearly fell off her sandals. For a long and far too starstruck moment, she'd actually forgotten her lunch date with Vivian. Her mother probably wouldn't recognize Tucker after so many years and how much he'd changed, but she'd rather not take any chances. Vivian and Tucker had never been a good combination.

"Hi, but sorry. I actually have to run." She'd agreed to meet Vivian here, in front of Dayton's instead of at Hell's Kitchen, which was two blocks away and an unusual-for-Vivian choice for lunch. With any luck, Tucker had somewhere else he had to be. Soon.

"Too bad." Tucker's gaze still took her in. All of her. He'd once touched and kissed every inch of her as she'd shuddered and sighed, but never on a public sidewalk.

Okay, maybe once.

But she'd been twenty-two, not approaching forty, and today she felt both exposed and unsure of herself. Had he ever gotten married? Had he gotten over her?

Had she ever really gotten over him?

"Why don't you stop by my place sometime? We can catch up and talk about old times. What do you say?"

Was that a date? "Um, sure. Where's your . . . place?"

"Right down the street. One of them, at least." He laughed, maybe a little too hard, when he saw her bug-eyed expression. "My restaurants. I figured you must know. Melba Toast is a block down Nicollet on the other side of the street."

Gwen gulped, the name sticking in her throat. Melba Toast. One of Tucker's quirky nicknames for her all those years ago. She'd always thought it was odd that someone would give a restaurant that name. "That's your place? Wow. It has great food."

Her stomach rumbled as her vocabulary took a sudden leave of absence. She'd actually suggested it to Vivian for lunch today. Thank God Vivian had picked Hell's Kitchen.

"You've been in and I missed you?" He glanced at her hips the way he used to moments before waging a deliciously full-frontal assault on them.

Remembering only too well, Gwen shivered. "Just once, but I loved it."

The heat in Tucker's gaze told her that he'd noticed the shiver. He'd always noticed everything. "Damn. But now that you know, I hope you don't sneak in again. I also own a couple of places in the 'burbs. Tootie Fruitie and Hazel Nut."

"I've heard of them." Everyone had.

Three of the hippest restaurants in the Twin Cities. Tucker had used the weird nicknames he'd given *her* while they'd explored sex and lacked money in the macaroni-and-cheese days of young adulthood. Now he'd struck oil with restaurants offering weird names, funky food, and throbbing salsa music.

She'd eaten at Melba Toast and Hazel Nut. Leila was a regular. All this time, she'd just thought the names were an extremely bizarre coincidence. Like how the radio played an Eagles song every time depression got the best of her and she needed a fix of instant happiness.

Tucker suddenly looked past her, down the block, which reminded Gwen that Vivian could appear any moment. She slid a glance to either side. No sign of her mother, thank God.

He grabbed her hand, sending tingles up her arm. "You said you had to go, and I should get back to work." He grinned, almost looking like the biker she'd once loved. But hadn't loved enough. "Not that they miss me or anything."

"It's good seeing you—"

"Seriously. Stop in sometime so we can catch up. You

look great, Gwen." Backing up, he bumped into someone, prompting both of them to tangle in a quick two-step to avoid falling.

Perfect. Vivian had arrived.

"Sorry!" "Excuse me!"

Their mingled voices made the perfunctory apologies. Taking Vivian's arm, Tucker flashed his usual grin, which hadn't lost its dazzle. "I'm so sorry, ma'am. This is why they don't let me out much."

Vivian patted him on the forearm. "No, no, dear. My fault entirely. I was too focused on my daughter, wondering who her handsome friend was."

"Tucker—" He broke off, a flash of recognition crossing his face before he covered it with a polite mask. Seventeen years ago, he wouldn't have bothered.

Vivian didn't notice Tucker's hesitation. She also would never expect such a well-dressed man to be the scruffy love of Gwen's misspent youth. "Tucker, I'm Vivian Withers."

"Yes, Mrs. Withers. I'm Tucker Preston." A horrified light dawned on Vivian's face. "I believe we've met."

———

"I suppose you just *happened* to run into that man, now, after all these years." Vivian sniffed, then picked up her napkin from her lap and dabbed it on the corners of her mouth, even though she hadn't touched a single bite of food yet.

Gwen took another sip of water. "Yes. I did."

"And you haven't kept in touch with him all these years." She narrowed her gaze. "He cleaned up nicely. A person couldn't really blame you."

Gwen considered dumping the rest of her water in

Vivian's lap. It probably didn't happen often at Hell's Kitchen.

"It's just that—" Vivian gave her an awkward wink, which had to be the first wink of her life. "Isn't that the concept I've read about, where women keep a so-called 'boy toy' on the side? No wonder Rob had issues."

Why Gwen hadn't ordered a Bloody Mary with her lunch, she had no idea.

She reached instead for another roll. Her third. "You're unbelievable."

"Why, thank you, dear." A shadow crossed Vivian's face, and she pressed one hand against her stomach, the other behind her back. She grimaced when their waiter set a salad in front of her. "But I'm not quite sure what you mean."

"It wasn't a compliment." Gwen dug into her hamburger with gusto. She'd normally get a salad, too, but it drove Vivian nuts when she ordered a burger and fries in a restaurant. Bonus. "I've seen Tucker twice now in the last seventeen years. I ran into him in front of Dayton's a few weeks ago, and again just now."

"It's not really Dayton's anymore."

"Whatever. That's what they're calling it again." Sort of.

Vivian touched her back again, wincing slightly. "It's not 'whatever,' dear, and I wish you wouldn't talk like your teenage daughter. You need to stop living in the past."

"*I'm* the one who's living in the past?" Her mother arched one brow in response. "You have two feet planted in ancient history. You're convinced I'm still seeing Tucker and still married to Rob. We're talking delusional."

Too late to retrieve her words, even if they were true, Gwen sucked in a breath.

Vivian touched a fork to her salad but still didn't eat anything. Even though she'd insisted on eating here, and

Hell's Kitchen had fantastic food. Not to mention Bloody Marys. "I know you're no longer married to Rob. It's a shame, but there's nothing I can do about it."

Gwen shook her head without responding.

Her food untouched, Vivian set her napkin on the table. Gwen was halfway through her burger and hunched over her fries as if the waiter might steal them from her at any moment. Until today, Vivian had never failed to correct her manners or posture.

Vivian waved to the waiter, who removed her salad. "And what does your *friend* Tucker do, dear? Still play with greasy motorcycles? His attire would suggest otherwise."

Gwen gobbled the last fry, smearing it in her ketchup for added effect. "Tucker owns a few restaurants. He's done pretty well for himself."

Vivian's face looked a little peaked, perhaps from too little sunshine or too little food. Gwen couldn't believe Tucker, or his choice of employment, would matter to her mother, let alone upset her. Not after seventeen years.

The moment passed. Vivian ran a hand through her perfectly-coiffed hair, leaving it slightly mussed. "Most restaurants fail. I hope for his sake that Tucker has savings of some sort."

Gwen laughed. "I hate to disappoint you, but he happens to own some of the most spectacular restaurants in town."

"I'm sure that pleases you, dear." Vivian's pained expression was nothing new.

Tipping her head to the waiter, Gwen sat back in her chair. "It's just a fact. Of course I'm happy for him, as I would be for anyone. But that's all. Nothing more."

"Whatever you say." Vivian blinked, and the waiter brought the check. "Let's go, shall we? You undoubtedly must get back—" Another grimace, the one Vivian usually gave when contemplating Gwen's employment. "To your job."

———

"Mom? It's Sarah." News flash.

"Hi, sweetie. What's up?"

Gwen pressed her cell phone to her ear as she glanced at the clock on her desk. Quarter after four. She wished she'd played hooky again this afternoon, since she'd accomplished nothing after that awful lunch with Vivian. Ted Harrison had chewed her out for an hour about the Treadman proxy materials, which apparently still hadn't gone out, and Danny was nowhere in sight. She had a feeling, though, that Ted's temper tantrum had more to do with her new hairdo and the skirt Leila had insisted she buy during their quick stopping trip to Southdale last night. Everything was shorter.

But Rob should've picked up the kids by now for his once-a-month weekend. If Sarah had forgotten to take one of her many items of sporting goods, too bad. It probably wouldn't fit in Rob's latest miniature sports car, and Gwen couldn't and wouldn't drive all the way to North Oaks to drop it off. Even if she didn't have tonight's dreaded piano lesson, she wasn't up to seeing Tiffany or Bambi or whoever else Rob was probably also entertaining.

"Oh, Mom." Sarah's voice didn't have its usual chirpiness.

"What's wrong? Aren't you guys having fun with Dad? You've been talking about him nonstop all week." Even Nick had made a few appearances outside of his bedroom, bragging about the "cool" and "fun" stuff he could do with his "cool" and "fun" dad.

Gwen had gritted her teeth but kept her opinions to herself. She did everything for those two kids, sacrificed everything for them, and she always would. In a heartbeat. But she might as well be invisible. All they ever cared about was precious Rob.

A tiny whimper filtered through. "Oh, Mom."

"You already said that. What are you guys doing?"

A sniffle. "Nothing. Dad never came to pick us up. And I called him, you know, just to see when he'd be coming. I swear I didn't try to bug him."

"I'm sure you didn't, sweetie." Sarah had a trigger-happy dial finger, but at fourteen she already knew better than to use it on her always-too-busy father. Nick still didn't. Gwen bore the brunt of Rob's angry phone calls every time the boy acted like a boy and called his dad.

The sniffle turned into a high-pitched wail. Gwen held the phone a little farther from her ear, then spoke again. "So? When is your dad picking you up?"

"He's n-n-not." Sarah's gulp sounded like she was swallowing a large steak, whole. "Tiffany told me he's busy and can't come and maybe can't see me at all this weekend. Or Nick either. She sounded kinda mean."

She'd kill Tiffany. First Rob, then Tiffany. "I'm sure she must be mistaken. You've had this weekend planned for a while. Did you talk to your dad?"

"I asked for him, just like you told me to. He wasn't really mean, but he said he couldn't come, and then he got off the phone real fast, like he was busy."

"Or something." Sarah didn't need to grow up any faster than she already was, so Gwen would save her views on Rob's sex life for Leila. "Don't worry, sweetie. I'm sure your dad will call back when he's less busy. He wants to see you."

And pigs could fly.

"Mom, do you have to go to your piano lesson tonight?"

Sarah was genuinely upset, true, but the girl also had a mile-wide manipulative streak in her.

She'd gotten that from her father.

"I'm sorry, but I do. I promised the teacher I'd be there." Sarah had to learn responsibility, and she wouldn't get it from Rob. "But I'll be home for dinner before I go."

"Okay." The phone clicked in Gwen's ear.

Half an hour later, her cell phone rang again. Ted had left early, thank God, and she was about to sneak out. After Sarah called, she'd asked Danny for a rain check on happy hour.

Her screen displayed her favorite photo of her dad's smiling face. "Hi, Dad."

He didn't offer his usual greeting. "It's your mother, Gwen." The low rumble of his voice, which had always soothed Gwen as a child, washed over her, making her feel guilty in a way that Vivian never could.

"Hey, I'm sorry. Yes, I told her she was delusional about Rob and Tucker, but I don't think she—"

"No, honey. It's not that." His voice broke. "She's . . . she's in the hospital."

CHAPTER 6

"We don't want you to worry." As he moved restlessly around Vivian's private hospital room, Gwen's dad gazed everywhere but at the maze of wires and tubes attached to every nook and cranny of her body. He also didn't look at Gwen.

He'd never been a good liar.

Despite the fact that her heart was still in her throat after her frantic drive to Kendall South in rush-hour traffic, Gwen couldn't help rolling her eyes. "My mother is dying and you don't want me to worry. That's priceless."

"I'm not dying." Reaching behind her head, Vivian fluffed the king-size pillow she'd brought from home, snug in its silk pillowcase. "Don't be melodramatic, dear."

"So you're saying I shouldn't have skipped my piano lesson. Because this is no big deal?" She'd texted Adam with shaking hands right after getting the call from her dad. Thanks to stress and her guilt over getting out of the lesson so easily, after wanting to cancel all week, she'd typed a string of nonsensical gibberish, most of it misspelled.

Adam's reply five minutes later: "Ok."

"I can't imagine why you did. Your father told me all

about about your handsome *young* teacher." Leaning back on her pillow, Vivian struck a pose worthy of Greta Garbo.

Gwen's dad flinched. "All I said was that I'd met Gwen's piano teacher. And I might've mentioned that nobody tells me anything anymore."

"Poor dear." Vivian reached out and patted his hand. "I saw the young man across the room at the reception, with that sweet young thing on his arm—"

"That was his sister."

Vivian waved a hand at Gwen's interruption. "And I don't believe I've ever seen our little Gwen sprint so fast to get away from someone. Even when she used to play all those sports." She fluffed her hair. "First the boyfriend, now this."

"Boyfriend? Gwen has a boyfriend?" Her dad's bushy eyebrows knit together.

"I don't have a boyfriend, Dad. I'll keep you posted."

"Not a *new* boyfriend, perhaps. I'm talking about your *old* boyfriend. The one you still see." The ringless hand pressed to her mother's stomach didn't diminish the smug expression in her eyes.

Gwen heard her dad sputter, but she fixed her gaze on Vivian. "I thought you were here for cancer. No one mentioned anything about the psych ward."

"Gwen!"

Vivian spared her husband a glance. "It's all right, Skip." She moaned slightly, which probably had zero connection to her health. "I find that I'm virtually the last to know about Gwen and her young man. I had to see them together in the street."

Gwen's dad darted frantic looks between his wife and daughter. Shrugging, Gwen reached into her purse for some gum. Gum-chewing repulsed her mother.

She popped a piece in her mouth. "You're quite the drama queen, you know."

"Really?" Vivian's eyebrows rose. "I'm just stating the facts to your father, whom you've left in the dark. I'm surprised, Gwen. You usually tell him everything."

"Where's Mac?" As a diversionary tactic, it was pathetic, but Gwen wasn't ready for explanations, especially when she had nothing to explain. About Tucker *or* Adam.

"Oh, sure. Just when it's getting interesting, she asks about me." Her grinning brother, with newly spiked and streaked blond hair, poked his head into Vivian's room.

Gwen hurried over and hugged him. It'd been too long. It was always too long.

Her dad took a step forward, as if he wanted to hug Mac, too, but retreated when Vivian pursed her lips.

"Lurking again?" Gwen laughed, almost choking on her forgotten gum. "You could've saved me a lot sooner."

"And miss the fireworks?" Crossing the room, Mac leaned over his mother's bedside and pecked her on the cheek. Vivian flushed at the reckless display of affection, but she put up with anything from Mac. Even at thirty-six, he was still her baby.

Actually, it wasn't much different from how Gwen felt about Nick. But Nick was eleven.

Mac whistled. "So you've got some hunk stashed away? I can't believe you haven't brought him by to meet the family. Man, I'm totally bummed."

"You sound like either a Valley girl or Sarah. Take your pick." Reaching up, Gwen ruffled his hair—or what was left of it after his latest haircut. "Speaking of psychos, who mowed your hair and dumped all that bleach in it? You could sue, you know. Maybe you should talk to one of Dad's lawyers."

He ran a hand through his hair, driving the multicolored spikes even higher. "I *am* a lawyer, sister dear, in case you've forgotten."

"A lawyer without a job, if you keep your hair like that."

She grinned at Mac, who thrived on change as much as she clung to the status quo. After skating through college, then partying hard for another five years, he'd surprised everyone the day he abandoned surfing off Malibu for Columbia Law School. Now he worked for a nonprofit in Duluth, giving legal advice to people who couldn't afford it.

Vivian never mentioned what he did or, if pressed, lied about it. Mac's clients appalled her.

"Everyone loves my hair. They only wish they had the balls to do it." Too late to retract the offending word, Mac lifted his shoulders slightly. "Uh, sorry, Mom."

Vivian didn't so much as lift an eyebrow. Wow. The pain medication must really be kicking in, because she'd normally swat even her precious Mac for language like that. He got swatted a lot.

"I think your mother needs her rest, guys." Tilting his head toward the door, Dad shuffled out of the room.

Vivian closed her eyes and didn't object.

Mac leaned in for another kiss on the cheek. "Catch ya later, Mom." Vivian nodded slightly, her lips pursed.

Gwen moved toward the bed, but she stepped backward when she reached the side rail. She couldn't do it. Couldn't drop the same casual kiss on Vivian's cheek that Mac did freely, easily, even when Vivian threatened to swat him for it. Gwen couldn't remember the last time she'd shared even that trace of affection with her mother.

She waved before realizing that Vivian couldn't see her. "Bye."

Outside, she and Mac caught up to their dad at the elevator. As he looked away from them, at nothing, his normally square shoulders drooped. Gwen wasn't sure how she felt about Vivian, her sudden illness, or the possibility of losing a mother she'd somehow—long ago—already lost. But she felt awful for her dad.

"How bad is it, Dad? Mom doesn't look so hot." Mac held out his arms, offering their dad a belated hug.

"It's not good." He ran a shaking hand through his hair. Somehow, when Gwen wasn't looking, it had turned silvery white, and she felt as if he'd aged ten years since Greta's wedding. "I don't know what to do."

Skip Withers always knew exactly what to do. And did it.

Gwen patted his arm, feeling useless. "Oh, Dad. That's what doctors are for. You know she'll get the absolute best care here."

Kendall South Regional Medical Center had facilities, technology, and physicians to rival those of the Mayo Clinic. Vivian's father, Jack Kendall, had funded a sizable portion of its endowment. According to Gwen's dad—although he'd never said anything in front of Vivian—Jack had spent the last few years of his life trying to make up for a lifetime of questionable but lucrative business dealings by throwing gobs of money at every charity he could find.

Kendall South would spare no expense to give Vivian the medical miracle she needed. At least, if it possibly could.

But from the little that Dad had already shared about Vivian's condition, it would definitely have to be a medical miracle.

He shook his head, agreeing with Gwen's unspoken assessment. "I'm sure she will, honey, but there may not be much they can do. The cancer has already advanced so far."

"How could that happen?" Mac jammed his hands in the

pockets of his jeans. "I saw you guys a month ago. Mom looked great, like always."

"She hasn't been feeling well, and she's had terrible back pain, but you know your mother. She doesn't like to complain."

If so, Gwen didn't know her at all. Vivian spent every moment of her existence complaining. Usually about Gwen and the "dreadful" choices she'd made.

Even Mac, Vivian's golden child, raised an eyebrow. A perfect impression of Vivian. "Uh, yeah. So she's been a little off. But her lousy golf swing could cause the back pain. She's not really dying, right?"

"How long *were* you standing outside that door?"

"Long enough to know better than to come inside. Gwen was getting her butt whupped." Mac shot Gwen a quick grin, then turned back to their dad. "I heard you guys talking about dying, but Mom said she wasn't. Which is it?"

"They don't have all the test results yet, but the prognosis isn't optimistic." Dad, who'd always been so strong and hearty, looked ready to crumple. Mac and Gwen both put their arms around him, an impromptu group hug that lasted forever.

"Do they have any sense of . . . time?" Gwen heard the sharp edge in her own voice and didn't know where it came from.

Her dad stared at her, his jaw dropping. When Mac elbowed her, hard, Dad waved him off. "No, it's okay. You two have the right to know. Vivian didn't want to tell you, and you startled me by thinking to ask."

Gwen hugged him again. In a golf shirt, her dad's arms were ice cold. "You raise a couple of National Merit Scholars and then tell them not to ask questions. As if."

"As if. Now *you're* the one sounding like Sarah." The

corners of her dad's eyes crinkled. "You're right, as always. My two little idiot savants."

"Hey!" Mac puffed out his chest. "I'm not little."

As usual, in times of stress, Mac and Gwen and their dad traded insults and teasing along with hugs. Vivian had never joined the trio, instead staring at them as though she questioned their gene pool.

After more bantering, though, Gwen wanted an honest answer. "When, Dad? What have the doctors said?"

"You get that serious look from your mother." Her dad chucked her under the chin, then gazed down the hall. A cluster of doctors and nurses had gathered outside Vivian's room. "It's too soon for them to know. At this point it's more an educated guess, but the oncologist looked grim when we asked her to share her thoughts. She knows her stuff."

"But why so sudden? I just saw her at lunch."

"It's not as sudden as you think. Your mother has amazing fortitude. The back and stomach pain she's been trying to ignore became too much for her this afternoon, and she called me on the golf course. I drove her to the hospital, and she returned from a series of tests just before you arrived." He met Mac's gaze, offering a small smile. "Both of you, apparently."

Mac shook his head. "I don't get it. They just ran some tests, so they can't know anything yet. And some quack doctor already makes her diagnosis?"

Gwen had watched the slim, black-haired woman leave the group outside of Vivian's room and approach them. She now tapped Mac on the shoulder. "Monica Lauren. I'm your mom's oncologist. Or the quack doctor, if you prefer." She held out her hand to Mac.

He grasped it with obvious reluctance. "No wonder. Mom probably thought you were related to Ralph."

The doctor looked puzzled a moment, then laughed softly, exposing her straight, brilliantly white teeth. "That's good. I like it when my patients and their families have a sense of humor. It comes in handy."

Gwen offered her own hand to the oncologist. "Then you're at least partly out of luck. Vivian isn't exactly known for her sense of humor."

Dr. Lauren's eyes widened slightly, but she didn't respond. Small wonder. She didn't know Vivian yet. She didn't know any of them.

She turned to Mac. "Anyway, you're right. It's too early to make a diagnosis with a high degree of certainty. We'll know much more by Monday or Tuesday. It's tough to get test results late on a Friday."

"Then who says it's cancer?" Mac looked defiant, but his lower lip trembled. "Who the hell goes around getting their kicks scaring the shit out of us?"

"Mac—"

Dr. Lauren held up a hand, cutting off Gwen's dad. "It's okay."

"No, it's not." Mac crossed his arms and looked ready to stomp his feet, much like he'd done when he was ten.

"You're right. I meant your dad didn't have to protect me, not that I don't appreciate the effort." She smiled at Dad before gazing first at Gwen, then Mac. "Your mother was anxious to know something. Anything. Between the information she provided, my physical exam of her, and the preliminary results of the MRI and one of the blood tests, I wasn't encouraged. It does look like cancer. But as I said, we'll know more soon."

"Then why'd you say anything, if you don't know for sure?" Spitting out the words, Mac stopped just short of spitting on the floor. Gwen wanted to comfort him somehow, but she knew he'd blow her off right now.

"Your mother insisted that I tell her what I thought, even after I told her I needed more test results." Dr. Lauren smiled gently at Mac. "I suspect you know she's a formidable woman."

———

"You DON'T KNOW the definition of the word."

Gwen wasn't quite sure which word, exactly, Ted was talking about. All the four-letter words he'd spewed in the ten minutes since he'd returned from lunch, during what had become his daily tirade, left her head spinning. She'd kill for a glass of wine. Or someone to save her. Or someone to save her who could also offer her a glass of wine.

She wasn't picky.

She also wasn't hopeful. In the two weeks since Danny had told her about about Ted's marriage issues, and for a while before that, everyone from senior partners to paralegals and secretaries had steered clear of Ted. Gwen hadn't been that lucky. He kept finding her.

Danny's team had filed the proxy materials for the Treadman deal with the SEC on Friday, and they wouldn't hear anything for at least a week. If the SEC decided to review, it'd be at least a month. In any case, nothing would happen this week.

Waving his hands in the air like a couple of pinwheels, Ted seemed to think otherwise.

"I don't know what you're talking about, Ted."

"You never do, do you?" His glare ordinarily could make Gwen and everyone else in the office cower, or want to run shrieking down the hall. Not today.

Ted's mood was nothing compared to hers.

Leaning back in her chair, Gwen crossed her arms, shivering slightly in the frosty air-conditioning. "I don't have time for this today. If you have a problem with the Treadman deal, talk to Danny. I'm not working on any other deals for you right now. So spare me."

She flinched inwardly as she spoke the words, but she maintained her composure. What a perfect time to acquire a spine. Her life, and her job, flashed before her eyes. Ted was a pain in the ass, and her work here wasn't exactly rocket science, but she needed the paycheck. She'd rejected her own lawyer's demands for alimony from Rob and accepted only minimal child support, preferring to brave the cold, harsh world rather than beg for every crumb that Rob might throw her way.

"Well, well." Ted's cold smile didn't reach his oddly glittering eyes. "Our scared little rabbit is turning into a lion. I like it. I like the change."

Anything Ted liked, Gwen didn't. Especially when it sounded like an insult.

"Oh?"

"I've always liked the quiet types. You know, good looking—although you're a little skinny—and docile and eager, if you get my drift." The man was a pig. A toad. Or as Nick would say, a turd. "I figured I could mold you into something. But I like the spark even better. You'd be wild in bed."

"Unless Gwen has had a lobotomy in the past few days, Ted, I think she'd offer you a simple 'no' and send your obnoxious butt on its way." Danny. With or without wine in hand, her savior had arrived. Steam practically whistled out of his ears, and his balled fists looked ready to punch something. Like, say, Ted.

"I don't believe I was talking to you, Danny." Ted's lip curled, and he didn't look even remotely embarrassed, let alone apologize. "You'll have to excuse us."

"I don't think so." Danny's hands went to his hips, and he looked like he planned to stay as long as it took. Twenty years junior to Ted, Danny might have more guts than brains standing up to a senior partner, but Gwen could kiss him for it.

"You might want to consider bringing your résumé up to date, Danny boy." Ted's claws came out, and Danny flinched wordlessly at the sound of his detested nickname. "We might have an opening in your office quite soon."

"Yeah, well, résumés sound like a good idea all around, big guy. After all, your *wife* wouldn't want you to be unemployed, would she?" Danny looked pointedly at Ted, who darted a furtive glance at Gwen.

She'd never actually seen a bullfight. Danny, the matador, was about to get gored.

She threw herself in front of the matador. "It's no secret, Ted. I wish I'd known earlier, when you kept asking me out, so I wouldn't have had to waste all that time thinking up excuses. At the moment, 'no' sounds good enough to me."

"Have it your way." Ted's gaze swung back and forth from Gwen to Danny, ultimately landing on Gwen. She forced herself not to show fear. "I could've helped you, Gwen. Made your life more comfortable. Given you money and prestige. With the best boarding schools, you could've had a break from your kids."

"The break I want isn't from my kids." Listening to Ted was like an ugly replay of Rob, and she wished Ted had been this clear about his intentions sooner. She could've slapped him and been done with it. "But what did you want from me, Ted? I don't see the connection."

"You're a lot smarter than my wife, but you don't know it. I can't stand a big ego on a woman. Women should know their place."

Danny snorted. "Yeah, well, your place isn't in Gwen's office. And once the management committee gets an earful of this, it might not be in your own."

"Don't underestimate me, Danny boy. And don't stick your nose where it doesn't belong, or you can hit the pavement." Without glancing back, Ted stormed out the door.

Sending Gwen a silent apology, Danny followed him.

———

"They didn't fire that bastard?" Monday evening, Gwen had barely gotten home from the hospital after work when Leila appeared at her front door with a pitcher of daiquiris. After hearing Gwen's blow-by-blow of her day, Leila had been both shocked and sympathetic. But her vicarious thrill at what she called Gwen's takedown of Ted made her squeal and clap her hands.

Gwen shook her head. "Ted wasn't kidding about his power in the firm. After Danny told the management committee what Ted had said to me, Ted pulled every string available to a senior partner with a huge practice. The firm can't afford to fire him."

"What happened to Danny?"

"He's okay, I think." Danny had been shaken, but he'd stood up to the firm's top brass, and several of them privately—very privately—applauded him. "The management committee apparently knew enough about Ted's recent behavior not to dispute Danny's word. They just won't do anything about it, even if I file a sexual harassment complaint."

"You haven't filed one yet?"

Shrugging, Gwen took a sip of her strawberry-banana daiquiri and shivered. It was so icy, it made her toes curl.

But in a good way.

Already finished with her first one, Leila reached for the pitcher. "I don't understand. It was bad enough when he hounded you for a date, but he practically stripped you bare —with his words, at least—in front of Danny today. Hasn't your firm heard of #MeToo?"

"He didn't know Danny was there, and he claimed it was consensual." The thought made Gwen's stomach churn. And maybe she sounded like she was defending Ted, but she definitely wasn't. She was trying to hang onto her job.

The rest of her daiquiri went down in a gulp.

"So now what?" Squinting at her glass, Leila picked a stray green strawberry leaf out of her drink and tossed it in the bushes.

Gwen's stomach rumbled. After only one daiquiri, she thought she saw birds dancing on the hood of her Honda. She'd never handled Leila's alcoholic concoctions too well. "Bottom line, if I file a complaint, I might make things ugly for myself. And I need this job."

"If you ask me, you need it like a hole in the head, with Ted operating the drill."

Leila could talk. In her late twenties, she'd married a seventy-something lifelong bachelor with no kids and a lot of money. He'd suffered a fatal heart attack on their honeymoon, and the young widow hadn't had a moment's financial worry ever since. Actually, Gwen didn't completely understand Leila's money situation. Inexplicably, she'd moved out of her dead husband's mansion and bought the cozy three-bedroom next to Gwen.

She also didn't work, but she treated Gwen to high-priced dinners and dropped "anonymous" gifts on her doorstep from time to time, and Gwen organized the neighborhood and made Leila a part of her life. Leila called it a fair trade.

Gwen wouldn't argue with her. She'd never win, anyway.

"I can't say I'll drink to that." But she held out her glass for another daiquiri. Any moment now, she might start dancing on her car, too. "I have a lot on my mind. Ted is just one stress among many."

After refilling Gwen's glass, Leila topped off her own again. "How's your mom?"

"Good. Bad. I don't know."

Gwen had recapped the official medical diagnosis with Leila on Sunday night, after her second full day spent pacing back and forth in Vivian's room and the hospital's corridors, grounds, and cafeteria. The bright, cheerful cafeteria contained some of the lousiest food she'd ever had the bad luck to eat.

In the parking ramp next to the hospital, she'd also smoked her first cigarette since college, and probably her twentieth. Mac had joined her, chomping on Cuban cigars that earned the siblings some ugly looks from passersby.

Mac had gotten rid of his cigar only once, when Dr. Lauren joined them on a break. Monica. Vivian's oncologist had quickly overcome her shaky beginning with the family, especially Mac, and was fast becoming a friend. A friend they needed right now.

The prognosis didn't look good, but Monica had run more tests and told them not to lose hope. Gwen wasn't sure she had any hope to lose.

"I guess that pretty much covers it." Leila lit a cigarette, watching the smoke curl from her lips, and nearly fell backward when Gwen held out a hand. "You don't smoke."

"Didn't." Taking a menthol light, which wouldn't be her first choice, Gwen made a face. "Things change."

Leila gazed thoughtfully at her for a long moment. "Apparently." Sarah ran up to the front steps just then, hot in pursuit of an errant basketball, and Leila swatted her on the butt. "Go get 'em, girl. But aren't you supposed to aim for that little hoop attached to the garage?"

Sarah rolled her eyes before stopping to frown at the cigarette in Gwen's hand. With a shake of her head, she raced away, whooping as she dribbled in for a layup. Gwen had dragged Sarah and Nick to the hospital for a couple of hours each day this weekend. Less activity than usual for on-the-go Sarah. More than usual for Nick.

They'd both gotten a reprieve today. Gwen had stopped by the hospital on the way home from work, but she'd spared the kids the trip down all those ammonia-smelling halls. Lord knew there'd be more of them to come.

She coughed slightly, the taste of tobacco not as good as she remembered it. Maybe it had never been. Maybe nothing was quite as good as she remembered it, but that was a thought for another day.

"So." Leila's voice interrupted her musings. "Is there any actual news about your mom? Unless you finally get some encouraging test results or ask for a second opinion, things don't sound too good. Do they still think it's pancreatic cancer?"

Gwen blew out a final puff of smoke in a whoosh, then crushed the cigarette under her heel. She didn't smoke. Some things really *should* be left in the past. "They won't have one key test result until tomorrow, but it's their best guess. With so much stuff going on in and around the stomach area, it's amazing that they even have an opinion already. When I got an ulcer five years ago, it took my doctor a month to diagnose it."

"Then she'd never met Rob." Leila laughed at her own joke. "How's your dad holding up?"

"Okay, I guess. Mac was able to take a few days off from work, so he's spending most of his time at the hospital with Dad. It means I don't have to." Gwen shrugged. Maybe she sounded selfish, but it was complicated. Her entire life with Vivian had been complicated. "It doesn't hurt that Mac seems to be attracted to Vivian's oncologist. Not that the woman notices Mac—or not too much. She's probably scared off by his crazy new haircut."

Whistling, Leila ran a hand through her short blond bob. "I caught a glimpse of it when he stopped by on Saturday to pick you up. He should sue his hairdresser for malpractice."

"I can't believe you're not attracted to my brother. Should I be insulted or relieved?" After thinking she'd just seen a squirrel dance an Irish jig on the fence across the street, Gwen set down her drink and groaned to her feet, then headed over toward Sarah in the driveway. She waved to Leila. "Come on. Let's show Sarah how it's done."

Despite her loud protests, Leila got up and joined them. Gwen already had the ball, spinning it on her finger. "Great. I'm being punished for offering my opinion of your darling brother's awful hair."

Giggling, Sarah stole the ball out of Gwen's hands and flipped it through the hoop before running back to Leila. "You like Uncle Mac? Ooh, I'm gonna tell him."

Leila's dramatic sigh could be heard two blocks away. "Like mother, like daughter."

God, I hope not.

Gwen thought of Vivian, who'd always been imperious, cold, and the exact opposite of understanding when it came to Gwen, although she admittedly hadn't been so bad with Mac and their dad. Now, her mother might be dying. How was she even supposed to react to that, let alone handle it?

By comparison, it almost made dealing with an ass like Ted Harrison seem like a picnic.

Almost.

CHAPTER 7

"It's not the end of the world, dear. Mac is here." Vivian's voice floated over the phone, brushing off Gwen's guilt at not being able to stop by the hospital today. And, at the same time, adding to it.

Ted—who was speaking to her again and dumping more work on her, neither of which filled her with joy—had kept her chained to her desk long after she'd planned to leave for the day. He'd finally left five minutes ago, at six-fifteen, and she had a piano lesson with Adam at seven. His only opening was today, Wednesday. Feeling a surge of guilt for cancelling on him at the last minute on Friday, she'd said yes, even though she really didn't have the time.

Guilt was chewing her up and spitting her out this week.

But enough about Vivian. "I'll stop by after work tomorrow." Sarah had a softball game at seven, but she could leave work by five—no matter what Ted wanted—and visit Vivian before the game. Maybe she could even drag Mac to the game. Sarah would be thrilled.

"Only if it's convenient." Vivian's voice took on a whiny edge of tragic proportions even if she just had a head cold. "Mac has time for me. He's so attentive, aren't you, dear?"

Gwen could hear low murmurs, probably from Mac. She flinched involuntarily. Mac had always sucked up to Vivian and had his mother's simpering adoration to show for it.

Vivian had trouble remembering Gwen's birthday.

"I need to run. See you tomorrow." Ending the call, she felt tears bubble up in her eyes. She swiped at them with her sleeve, shut down her computer, grabbed her purse, and hurried out the door.

———

"You're not yourself tonight. Timing's a bit off."

Gwen glanced up at Adam, seeing concern in his eyes. She'd played like a seasoned pro at her last lesson, when he'd pushed so hard to try to get her to enter the competition. Tonight she hacked at the keys like a third grader.

Now he was probably trying to figure out how to tell her politely that the competition would be way over her head.

She hunched over the keys. She didn't even *want* to enter the damned competition.

Or, at least, probably not.

Biting down on her lip, she worked to regain her composure. "Sorry. I haven't practiced much." When Adam pursed his lips, she swallowed hard on a sniffle. "I haven't had any time. Between work and my mother . . ."

"No excuses." His words slapped her, and she jumped. Grabbing a tissue, Adam dabbed at her eyes with gentle hands. "That's not what I meant."

Her lips still trembled, but the faint glimmer lighting his eyes steadied her. "Thanks. My mother is . . ."

"I'm sorry to hear that." Standing up, he shuffled through a stack of sheet music. Men. They never waited for a woman to complete a sentence, especially if the sentence involved her feelings. Swiveling on the bench, she turned away, only to be stopped by Adam's hand on her shoulder. "Hey, I really am sorry, but we don't have a ton of time. Let's work on getting your concentration back."

"I don't think I can today." Her shoulders drooped along with the rest of her.

"Sure you can. Let's try something." He tapped a finger on the piano, squinting at nothing while he thought. "Close your eyes. Take a few deep breaths, in and out. Focus."

Her eyelids softly closed. "On what?"

"On me, of course." They flew open again, and Adam laughed. He touched the tip of her nose. "Just kidding, you goof. Close your eyes again. Don't say anything."

She followed his instructions this time and even put a finger to her lips to prove they were closed. He talked her through a simple meditation he used whenever he needed to calm himself. Startled when he pulled her finger away from her lips, Gwen's eyelids fluttered open.

He'd moved closer. Too close, if her staccato heartbeat was any judge. When he licked his lips, her gaze flew to them.

Good grief. The sight of his lips regressed her back to age sixteen, when almost any pair of lips seemed too hot to handle. Adam didn't have sixteen-year-old lips. His were a wild mix of sweet, sexy, and utterly tempting. She struggled to look away, even though she wouldn't mind a repeat of their kiss during her last lesson. Just to make sure she hadn't imagined it, of course.

Adam pulled back, his lips now a flat line of concentration.

No kiss tonight, apparently.

He was probably focused on working a miracle with her fingers, while she focused on doing the same thing with his lips. Talk about feeling sixteen again. Sighing inwardly, she wished for a moment she'd chosen a piano teacher who wasn't quite so . . . focused. But the competition was at the end of September, and it was already the middle of August. If she ever actually agreed to enter it, they didn't have much time.

Turning back to her sheet music, she started playing again, amazingly improved. Hmm. Maybe she could play now and—she hoped—kiss later?

In life as in music, timing was everything.

———

"I don't want to, and you can't make me." The pout curling Nick's lower lip almost made Gwen smile, but it wouldn't help the situation if she did.

She jangled her key fob in the air. "I'm not sure if that sounded more like a toddler or a teenager, but you're not in either camp, kiddo. Let's get moving. Sarah's game starts in just over half an hour, and she has to warm up."

The softball field was only a mile away, but Sarah's cleats were tapping impatient new grooves in the hallway floor. "Sarah Stanhope, what have I told you about wearing cleats in the house?" As she turned to face her bubblegum-blowing daughter, she saw Nick tiptoe in the other direction, trying to escape.

Gwen whirled on him. "Nice try. Now get in the car, both of you. Uncle Mac is going to be there."

"Ooh!" Squealing, Sarah jumped in the air, landing with a clatter that meant more pockmarks in the floor.

The news didn't improve Nick's attitude: his pout turned into a sneer. Definitely approaching the teenage years. "Dad wouldn't make me go."

"Your dad wouldn't go himself." Gwen flushed, wishing she could call back her words. She'd caught herself making digs about Rob in front of the kids too many times lately, which told her how stressed she was. Still, it was no excuse. "But Sarah wants you to go, and so do I. And Mac has to go back to Duluth this weekend, and he said you haven't even shown him your computer yet."

"Like he'd want to see a stupid PC. Nobody does." Nick hung his head, looking genuinely upset, but Gwen had hoped to be able to wait until Christmas to spring for a laptop. "Nobody except Dad."

Right. Rob hadn't ever set foot in Gwen's house, so he'd have a tough time seeing Nick's computer. Not that he'd want to, or would even bother to talk to Nick about their son's pride and joy. If a computer didn't have two big breasts and a tiny waist, Rob wouldn't give it the time of day.

Gwen pulled Nick into a hug, even though he struggled in her arms. The joys of motherhood. "Honey, we're all proud of how talented you are with your computer."

"I'm not, and I'm gonna be late for my game." Sarah slammed the door and stomped outside.

"Yes, even Sarah is, but she's your sister, so she'd rather die than admit it." That drew a rare smile from Nick. "But you spend too much time in your room. School is going to start in a couple of weeks, and I want you to spend some time outside. Computers are great, but there's more in life."

Nick grumbled, but his feet finally shuffled toward the door.

Ten minutes later, Gwen sat down next to Mac in the bleachers as Sarah ran onto the field and Nick sulked at the far end of the bleachers, very much alone.

"What's up with him?" Mac jabbed his thumb at Nick, his eyebrows raised.

Gwen leaned back against the empty row behind her. "Oh, you know. Eleven going on sixteen." She turned to Mac. "Why do you suppose Nick is so enamored of Rob? The way he gushes about him all the time, you'd think Rob walked on water."

"A psychiatrist would say he just wants to grow up and learn to be a man, and his father is the most obvious man to emulate."

"And also the worst."

"True." Mac stared out at the field, where Sarah scooped up a hard grounder at shortstop and fired the ball like a cannon at the girl playing first base, who nearly fainted at the impact. "Damn, she's good. Just like you were."

She didn't think he'd even been aware that she used to play sports. "Me? I was just joking around. Sarah's a lot more serious."

"I might've been three years younger than you, but I wasn't blind." Mac's disbelief covered his face. "But you're right about Sarah. If that kid gets much more serious, she'll kill one of her teammates with that arm."

"You should see the bruise she put on a girl's thigh from the line drive she hit last week. The girl actually collapsed in the dirt." Gwen laughed. "I tried not to cheer too wildly, but, wow, did she connect. I thought the other girl's mom was going to kill me."

He smiled. "Mom was just like that."

"What? Getting mad at other moms whose kids hurt her precious daughter? I don't think so." Gwen shook her head. Vivian would've never made a public display that bordered on human.

Mac leaned forward, watching Sarah as he spoke. "You were so intent on the game, you never saw her up in the stands, waving and screaming. Dad would try to hold her back, but she'd be wild with glee at every damn thing you did."

"You're joking. She would've soiled her white gloves."

Mac held out his hands, staring at the back of them. "Yeah, those white gloves are pretty funny, especially nowadays. You think any of those other country-club women still wear them like Mom does?"

"Hard to say. Dinosaurs seem to be enjoying a new era at that club." Gwen tipped her nose up, imitating the snooty women she'd met there. "Like Mom—er, Vivian."

Mac tweaked her nose, pulling it back down from the stratospheres. "You may be my big sister, but you don't know Mom as well as you think. Give her a chance, Gwen. Yeah, she has a few old-fashioned ideas, and you guys haven't always gotten along. But she's dying."

"At least she has her precious son to comfort her." She looked away, pretending interest in the argument breaking out between two moms and the third-base coach. "She never liked me. She never even tried."

Mac drew his arm around Gwen, smothering her in a hug the way he'd done since college, when embracing his sister stopped embarrassing him. "You'd be surprised, kid."

He held her a moment, then hopped to his feet and stepped gingerly between the spectators scattered along the bleachers below them. He nodded over at Nick, still sitting by himself and pouting for everyone to see. "Gotta talk to my nephew. Maybe I'll take him back to Duluth with me and have him fix all of our office computers."

"Did I mention he's only eleven?"

"Thanks for coming downtown for lunch." Gwen glanced over the top of her menu at Leila, who ran an orange fingernail down the list of entrées.

She'd run into Tucker a week ago today. Was it too soon to make an appearance at Melba Toast, his downtown restaurant? She hoped not. Just in case, she'd brought Leila for backup. Leila probably spent almost as much time in Tucker's restaurants as he did.

"It's such a sacrifice in my busy day." Leila's eyes twinkled. "Ooh." Touching her tongue to her bright-red lips, Leila brought even more male attention to their table than she had when she'd strutted into the restaurant in four-inch stilettos and a clingy miniskirt. "Mango shrimp with pineapple salsa. To die for."

"Please don't. I have enough death in my life right now." Gwen frowned at the menu, not really seeing the words printed on it.

"How's your mom?"

The words came into focus, and Gwen spied the Caribbean chicken in the right-hand column. Her favorite. "The same. Barely eating, looking horribly thin, and clinging to the sweet delusion that Mac is her only child."

"So the cancer hasn't changed anything."

"What?" Gwen's gaze flew to Leila's face.

Her friend's lips twitched. "Face it. That's no different from how she's always been. Birdlike appetite, skinny like you, and treats you like shit."

The waitress chose that moment to appear. Despite all the work facing her that afternoon at the office, Gwen asked for a glass of wine to accompany the lemonade already in front of her. Leila ordered a second mai tai, even though she'd hardly made a dent in her first one.

Gwen touched her napkin to one corner of her mouth

before remembering that Vivian always did that. She set it back in her lap. "At least I can count on you to cut to the chase, but I never actually said she treats me like, um, shit."

"Don't worry. You can swear in front of me, little girl." Leila's low chuckle drew another round of interested looks. "No, you've never put it exactly that way, but I'm pretty good at connecting the dots."

"Talk about connecting." At the sound of the deep male voice, both women's gazes flew up, even though Gwen knew without looking who owned that voice. Tucker grabbed her hand, holding it for a moment instead of shaking it. "Gwen, I'm so glad you came. This is becoming a great habit, seeing each other like this."

Something that felt like excitement bubbled up her throat, making Gwen choke on her words. "You too, Tucker. Uh, this is—"

Her mind went blank.

"Leila Merrick." Leila offered her hand to him, batting her eyelashes at what she probably considered fresh meat. "Don't you love this place? Do you come here often, too?"

Tucker laughed, his rich baritone tingling through Gwen. "You might say that. I'm Tucker Preston. I own the place."

Except for spilling his first name to Leila a month ago, right after suddenly seeing him again after seventeen years, Gwen had never told her about Tucker. She realized her mistake as she watched her best friend devour him with her gaze. The two women didn't poach on each other's turf—or wouldn't, at least, if Gwen *had* a turf. And despite all these years, Tucker was Gwen's turf. She almost growled.

Leila's eyelashes fluttered. "My. Gwen hasn't told me about you." Gwen kicked her under the table. Flinching, Leila sucked in a breath but smiled brightly. "I'm sure she wanted to keep you all to herself. Not that I blame her."

Tucker's white teeth gleamed. "Oh, Gwen and I are old friends. I'm happy to make new ones."

He hadn't flirted with such ease—or at all—when they used to be together. Gwen seethed, both remembering and preferring the younger, rougher Tucker. She didn't know how to handle this version of him.

"I know the feeling." Leila slid her an inscrutable look before turning back to smile up at Tucker, who leaned over their table. "It's sweet of you to stop by and make me feel welcome. It's *so* hard for me to meet new friends."

"I can imagine."

In another moment, Gwen expected Tucker to pull up a chair and join them. Or maybe he'd just sit on Leila's lap. Or ask Gwen to leave. At this point, she didn't care.

Her best friend was making moves on the love of her life, who also didn't seem to care that Gwen was here. But she wouldn't make a scene. After Rob, she'd sworn she wouldn't let another man humiliate her. Even if she had to avoid all men in order to make that happen.

Right this moment, it wasn't what she'd call a sacrifice.

Leila patted Tucker on the back of his hand, which lay flat on the table. "Thanks for stopping by. Now, if you'll excuse us, we need to finish some fascinating girl talk."

At Leila's abrupt dismissal of him, Tucker looked stunned, but he made a smooth recovery. "Of course. Great to meet you, Leila." He turned to Gwen as if he'd suddenly remembered her existence. "We still need to catch up. Can you stop in again sometime?"

After listening to his conversation with Leila, she hadn't expected the question. "I'm pretty busy these days."

"Please?"

For better or worse, she'd always been a sucker for that

wide-eyed, pleading look of his. "Um, maybe next week? I don't know."

He straightened, adjusting his tie. "Wonderful. I hope to see you then." With a last backward glance at them, he strode from their table, stopping briefly at a few more tables before he disappeared from sight.

"That's some man you're hiding from me." Leila smacked her lips in appreciation. "Here I've been breaking my back to set you up with Adam, and you've already found yourself a *man*."

"I found him a long time ago." Gwen still hadn't quite forgiven Leila for hitting on Tucker. She glanced down at her chicken, which had arrived just as Tucker walked away. Its aroma was lost on her.

"I know." At Gwen's startled look, Leila shrugged. "Okay, I didn't *know*, but you mentioned a guy named Tucker." She placed her hand over Gwen's, squeezing it. "I may be the world's biggest flirt, but I don't steal your men. You need someone to trust. You're stuck with me."

"It doesn't matter." Gwen brushed back a stray hair. "He obviously isn't interested in me anymore."

"Don't kid yourself." Choosing a red pair of chopsticks from the tall glass on their table, Leila plucked a shrimp from her plate, swishing it around in the salsa. "Men are like that. Most of them, anyway."

The dreamy look on Leila's face told Gwen that her friend had found some man she considered the exception to the rule. She didn't ask who he was. She wasn't sure she wanted to know.

Gwen's food sat untouched. "They're like what? They think some women are attractive and others aren't? Women are like that, too. I can't blame him."

"Rob really took you for a ride." Leila jabbed her chopsticks in the air, nearly taking out the fresh flowers on their table. "Your friend scoped you out the whole time he was talking to me."

"Flirting with you."

Leila kept waving the chopsticks with reckless abandon, apparently forgetting the shrimp still clutched between them. "Okay, flirting. Most men do that. They like the attention, and they like to make other women jealous. It's their version of multitasking."

"Tucker didn't used to be like that." Gwen still felt a twinge of embarrassment—or regret?—about parading Leila in front of Tucker, but the spices wafting up from her plate finally became too great a temptation. She stabbed a small piece of chicken with her fork.

"How old was he? Twelve?" Leila dipped a finger in her salsa and licked it, rolling her eyes in delight.

"Early twenties." Gwen paused between bites. "We met in college and were together for a while."

"No wonder you kicked me so hard. I'll have battle scars for weeks." Leila wagged her finger at Gwen, but her eyes twinkled.

"I barely nudged you." Gwen couldn't help smirking. "People will just think you got too exuberant in bed."

"Mmm." Another shrimp landed in Leila's mouth, surprisingly enough, considering the spastic way she handled her chopsticks. "So apparently my reputation is safe."

"Such as it is."

Leila scrunched her nose. "Good to know. But how long has Tucker been back in the picture? I wouldn't suspect you of keeping a secret like that."

"That's where you'd differ with Vivian." Gwen said it casually, giving her friend time to let the meaning sink in.

Leila's chopsticks clattered to her plate. She whistled,

drawing more looks. The woman could snap her fingers and attract men like flies. "No. She didn't."

"Oh, yes. She accused me at lunch last week of keeping something going with Tucker the whole time I was married to Rob. Then she insisted on sharing her theory with my dad. I don't think he knew what she was talking about."

"She didn't, either." Leila gave Gwen an assessing look. "After surviving both your mom and Rob, it's amazing that you're not more screwed up than you are."

Gwen shrugged. "I'm not sure I survived them. The jury's still out."

"Sure, you're still picking up a few pieces . . ." Making her point, Leila snared a piece of Gwen's chicken. "But you survived all right. Now you just have to move forward. And triumph."

———

"Mac. Dear Mac. What will I do without you?" With her head cushioned against the large pillow, Vivian rested the back of her hand on her forehead.

Gwen felt like throwing up. As she watched all of Vivian's constant dramatics, she couldn't tell when the pain was real or fake. She questioned most of it.

Mac took Vivian's hand. "You know I have to get back to work, Mom. I'll return as soon as I can, and Dad and Gwen are still here. They'll take good care of you."

Vivian made a face but didn't respond. She addressed her hospital tray as if it were afternoon tea at the Ritz. Minus her white gloves.

Dad jumped into the void. "He's right, Viv." No one else was allowed to use that nickname. Gwen wasn't sure even her dad had permission. "Mac will be back, and Gwen and I are always here for you. You know that."

She ignored him. "If that's how you feel, Mac. I'm sure I can't stop you from leaving, no matter how soon my death may come." Her sigh hung in the air.

"You got that right, kid." Mac ruffled his mother's hair. Despite her wan smile, she quickly smoothed it again. "You're a pain in the butt, you know that? Dad and Gwen will have their hands full." He turned to them. "Tough job, guys."

Vivian's chin came up, but the oxygen tube in her nose made it difficult for her to look haughty. "To think I spent twelve hours in labor only to produce such an ungrateful wretch."

"Last I heard, it was ten. It keeps climbing."

Feeling invisible in the corner of the flower-strewn hospital room, Gwen piped up. "I've got you beat. I'm at fifteen and holding."

As usual, Vivian didn't acknowledge her. She reached for Mac's hand, straining against the tube protruding from her right wrist. "It was worth it. You've been such a comfort to me in my old age."

Mac turned her grasp into something resembling a high-five. "Right. Like sixty-three is real old."

"Or like you're much comfort." Gwen couldn't resist, even though no one seemed to remember that she was in the room.

Except Mac, who gave her a teasing glare. "I comforted Sarah the other night when she banged herself up sliding into home."

"Oh, dear." Vivian, who'd closed her eyes, now reopened them. "I hope she didn't get injured the way she does so often. I wish you'd take better care of her, Gwen."

At least Vivian finally realized that Gwen was alive and right here in her hospital room.

Mac barked a laugh. "Gwen doesn't stand a chance keeping that kid safe any more than you did with Gwen, Mom." Both Vivian and Gwen raised their eyebrows. "Man, you should've seen Sarah. She came in so fast, she took out the catcher *and* the ump. I haven't laughed so hard in ages. Even Nick looked up from his book."

"Damn." Dad rubbed his hands in glee, stopping only when he caught Vivian's withering stare. No one swore in front of her. "Wish I'd seen it. Does Sarah have any more games coming up?"

Even before Vivian got sick, his work schedule kept him from most of Sarah's games. On the rare occasions he was able to see a game, he more than made up for it, yelling loudly and often from the bleachers.

"The league championship is next weekend. Maybe you can stop by for one of the games?" But her mother would still be in the hospital, most likely. Besides, she'd faint at all the tumbles in the dirt that Sarah would inevitably take.

"We'll have to see, honey. If I can. You know." He nodded at Vivian.

He'd probably be right here at Vivian's side. Even if Gwen and Rob were still married, even if he hadn't had all those other women, she couldn't imagine Rob doing that for hours on end. "I understand. We'll play it by ear."

"You act as if I'm an invalid." Vivian hated to be left out, even though the powerful pain medication didn't stop her from clutching her back every few minutes. "Of course you can go to Sarah's game, dear." She nodded at Gwen's dad. "One of the girls from the club could visit me."

A string of country-club friends had called and visited

Vivian in the last week, forcing hospital staff to assign a ward clerk to act like a concierge. The flowers she'd received could fill every church in the city. No, Vivian wouldn't lack for visitors.

Mac and Gwen exchanged glances at Vivian's drawn-out sigh. Dad clutched her hand. "I can stay, Viv. I don't have to go to Sarah's game. I just thought—"

"It doesn't matter, dear." She patted his hand through the railing on her bed. "I'm sure Mac will be back by then. He can stay with me."

Mac winced. "Sorry, Mom. No can do. I'm in trial the following Monday, and I'll have to work next weekend." He turned to his father, ignoring Vivian's furrowed brow. "But you should take a break, Dad, and go to Sarah's game. You'd love it, and you could give Mom the play-by-play afterward."

"I don't think he needs to go quite that far, dear." Vivian gave her head a slight shake, careful of the tube connected to her nose. "You know I've never understood sports."

Snorting, Mac ruffled her hair again. Vivian tried to swat him, but her hand couldn't reach. "Tell that to the pope, Mom. I used to catch you reading rule books on the sly when Gwen was in school. You couldn't bear not knowing everything that was going on."

"No!" Gwen and her dad shouted their disbelief in unison.

"Yes." Mac nodded. Vivian closed her eyes, but her lips twitched. "You guys should've seen it. She'd sneak into the living room and pull out whichever book she was reading—depending on which sport it was—from under a sofa cushion."

"That's enough, Mac." Vivian pushed the button for more pain medication, making a big show of it. "I'm sure your father and Gwen enjoy your droll, make-believe stories, but I never did any such thing. I know nothing about sports."

Her three visitors shared a smile.

"You know best, Mom." Mac chuckled. "Hey, maybe you'll have time to learn a few sports facts before I come back. Gwen can help you out on that, even without dragging Sarah in for reinforcements. Besides, it's about time you guys talked. And got to know each other."

"We can't—"

"I don't—"

Mac waved off their sputtered protests. "You guys have more in common than you realize." Gwen felt sick at the thought. They had nothing in common. Nothing whatsoever. "If you'd break down and talk, you'd find out."

Gwen's dad nodded his agreement. "Mac's right. I'll leave you two alone more." He turned to Gwen, an apology in his eyes. "I should have done that a long time ago."

Mac clapped his dad on the back. "No time like the present, I always say." The two men grinned at each other.

The two women—

Each looked away.

CHAPTER 8

A car door slammed, tires squealed, and a high-pitched whine filtered through the haze produced by the deepening dusk and Gwen's second glass of albariño. She leaned back in the rocking chair in the living room, flexing her feet to keep the chair in constant motion, and willed the intrusive noises to stop.

She pondered her late-afternoon visit with Vivian, ended on a reprieve when Mac had to go. Gwen had slunk out the door at the same time, brushing a kiss on her dad's cheek and touching Vivian's cold hand. The slight contact had been more than enough for both women.

Or at least for her. If Dad and Mac could be believed, she'd never known Vivian at all. That wasn't likely to change any day soon, cancer or no cancer.

The whining grew louder, and a sharp bark punctuated it. A dog. The day was ending on a high note.

"Mom! Guess what!" The front door banged open, and her taciturn little Nick was jumping up and down, matching the wiggling movements of the black and white bundle of fur that he barely restrained on the end of a leash.

No. God, no.

"Don't tell me." As her breath caught in her throat, she stopped rocking and fixed Nick with her worst maternal glare. "Better yet, turn around *right now*, walk back out that door, and come in again without a dog. A mangy, flea-ridden, godforsaken, howling, scratching, biting dog."

"I told you." Sarah followed Nick inside, a mixture of smugness and outright fear on her face. The smugness won, and she kept nodding like one of those sports-figure bobbleheads she collected. "Mom hates dogs. Or all animals, but she really hates dogs."

"That's not true. I've been terrified of them since I was a little girl." Gwen's spine went rigid when Nick took a timid step closer to her. She tried to breathe normally. "I'm not even remotely kidding, and you both know that. Keep that thing away from me, and get it out of the house. Now."

His lower lip quivering, Nick reached down and patted the scruffy little dog at his feet. It bared its teeth and growled. At Gwen.

Her lips quivered, too. She wasn't safe in her own living room anymore.

"Nick, where did you get that thing? You know better, and you need to return it." Keeping one eye on the dog, which drooled as it eyed her lower leg, Gwen looked at her son. When she'd tried all these months to find something for him to do besides computer games, she hadn't been thinking of four-legged animals.

Her terror had begun early, the day her parents brought home a yapping little dachshund that bit everything in sight. Everyone knew it, including her kids. Gwen didn't allow dogs anywhere near her, let alone in her own house. Her friends kept theirs in another room when she visited. Had Nick really failed, after all these years, to get the message? Impossible.

But Rob definitely knew, and this was beyond cruel even by his standards.

She'd kill him.

Nick's mouth opened, but only the word "Fluffy" came out—as if a mutt that hadn't seen the inside of a bathtub in at least a month could possibly be called "Fluffy." Frozen in place, Nick stared at Gwen, his eyes wide.

Hers were even wider. Keeping her gaze locked on the dog, she slowly eased out of the rocking chair and side-stepped across the room to the edge of the kitchen.

Sarah moved to stand between Gwen and the dog. She'd always been good on defense, bless her. "Dad bought Fluffy at the animal shelter. He said he felt bad about missing last weekend, and he wanted to make it up to us. Or to Nick. Whatever."

Her shoulders sagged, and Gwen saw the stab of hurt in her eyes. Clearly, Sarah hadn't gotten anything out of the bargain. The few presents Rob ever bought "for the kids" always seemed to match Nick's interests, never Sarah's. Her daughter didn't share Gwen's holy terror when it came to animals, but they also weren't a big deal to her.

Having Rob come to one of her games would be a big deal.

Both kids needed a hug. Sarah, because she'd never get any attention or foolish gifts from her father. Nick, because he wouldn't own that dog longer than the time it took Gwen to drive to North Oaks and dump it on Rob's doorstep.

But Gwen couldn't hug either of her kids right this moment. Her knees locked in frozen horror as she mentally prepared herself to make a mad leap onto the kitchen counter if the dog broke loose of Nick's hold. If she made any sudden moves toward her kids, that little killer might chew her to pieces, then lick its chops as it waited for more.

"Nick. Seriously, you know I can't have an animal in this house." Gwen held up her hands. She'd be as gentle as possible, but she wouldn't negotiate on something that was a matter of life and death to her. Just the thought of having that dog in her car for the trip to Rob's house made her want to vomit.

Trails of tears rolled down Nick's cheeks. "I-I-I didn't know. I want Fluffy. You never let me have anything." His pitiful wail filled the living room and Gwen's eardrums.

"Let you have anything? That computer of yours is fast enough to strip paint. Tell me about it."

Nick choked out more words between wails. "B-but it's not a laptop. And you hate it when I use it, and you always say I'm just playing games. Y-you hate me."

The dog stood on all four stubby legs, growling even louder as it fixated on Gwen. She badly needed to go to Nick. She literally couldn't. The dog scared the hell out of her.

Sarah avoided the whole situation by slinking off to her room.

Trying to keep her shaking from turning into convulsions, Gwen wrapped her arms around herself. "Nick. I love you, sweetie. I'm not trying to be the bad guy, and I'm not mad at you. But your dad knows I'm terrified of dogs, and he bought that . . . Fluffy anyway."

Screaming and stomping his feet, Nick almost landed a foot on the yipping dog. "He told me you'd say that. Dad loves me. I want to live with him!"

Gwen counted to ten, then blew a breath upward, hitting her bangs. "Have you asked your dad?" Nick stared at her, not answering. "I'm not sure his . . . lifestyle would allow him to have you all the time."

In the divorce, Rob hadn't even asked for visitation or parenting time.

"Dad wants me, and Tiffany's nice, and I'd have the best time. And I wouldn't have to sit all by myself at Sarah's stupid games. Or nothin'."

"Then it's settled." Gwen got the expected response to her immediate capitulation. Nick's eyes bugged out. "When we take Fluffy back to your dad, we'll take you, too. I really hope you'll visit Sarah and me, though. I'll miss you to the moon and back."

"Uh, yeah." The stark fear in Nick's eyes matched what Gwen felt every time she looked at Fluffy.

"I won't miss you!" Sarah hadn't gone as far as Gwen thought, and her sisterly reaction carried all the way down the stairs.

At Gwen's tense urging, Nick trudged upstairs to his room to pack the clothes he'd need for a longer stay with Rob. Fluffy's tail wagged as the dog trotted beside the glum boy. Gwen prayed that the damned thing wouldn't pee on her floor.

———

"It's just for dinner, Gwen. You can break away that long." Leila's pleading voice whispered into the phone. Her date, or someone else she didn't want to include in the conversation, must be five feet away.

Gwen closed her eyes. They flew back open when she realized that, with her luck, Ted Harrison would walk by her office and chew her out for sleeping on the job. Or for not sleeping with him, as the case may be. "Sorry. I'm up past my eyeballs in work, and Vivian whines if I don't stop by the hospital every day." Remembering a routine SEC filing she needed to make today, she tucked the phone against her shoulder and started digging through the files on her desk. "But who are you trying to set me up with this time?"

"Oh, no one." Leila laughed, but it sounded forced. "I'm trying to set myself up with someone. Jon at the bookstore has this gorgeous friend, and I was thinking—"

"I am *not* going out with the so-called gorgeous friend while you sink your claws into that poor man. Didn't you hear him? He's not on the market."

Gwen had visited Books and Ab's again, once, since Leila introduced her to Jon Abelard on book lovers' night three weeks ago. The quiet, friendly man remembered Gwen, greeting her like an old friend and asking after Leila. Of course. Men—available or not—always wanted Leila.

"Wrong." Leila's hushed whisper was almost unintelligible. Gwen quit searching for the file and strained to listen. "I want the gorgeous friend. You're the excuse for me to invite him. And don't worry about Jon. He's fun, and he really doesn't feel sorry for himself, no matter what you might think."

Gwen could understand feeling sorry for yourself. In the first few months after Rob left, she'd allowed herself an occasional day in bed with chocolate and a box of Kleenex. Part of her missed those days. "But why would he feel sorry for himself?"

"His wife died two years ago." Leila's voice dropped even lower. "He still hasn't gotten over it. As if it doesn't happen to everyone eventually."

Stunned, Gwen couldn't imagine how awful that must be. "Maybe everyone's not as resilient as you are."

"Hey, I'm just asking him to have dinner with us." Leila's voice rose. Whoever she'd been avoiding must've moved away from the phone. "Friday? Can you make it? Please?"

"Friday?" Gwen almost relented, but she had another

piano lesson on Friday, for reasons that eluded her. "I can't. I already booked a lesson with Adam."

"You're still not getting laid." It wasn't a question. "But you're still taking lessons from the guy. When I mentioned baby steps, this wasn't what I had in mind."

Gwen walked over to the door of her office, shutting it against eavesdroppers. Like, say, Ted. "Maybe it wasn't what I had in mind, either, but it gets me out of the house."

"So does taking out the trash, but is it making you happy?"

Sometimes yes. Sometimes not so much.

She glanced at the clock on her desk. She'd promised Vivian a visit after work. "I can't help it if I don't move fast enough for you, but I do like playing piano. And I'm trying."

"I know you are. You're seeing Adam, you got all dolled up at the spa—and I nearly died when you let Nick bring that dog home." Leila whistled. "Talk about changes."

Gwen had taken the dog back to Rob three nights ago over Nick's shrieking protests. When no one answered the door, Gwen had tied the mutt's leash to the front door and left with Nick, who'd decided to stay with Gwen "a little while longer." Five minutes later, a long string of expletives greeted Gwen on her cell phone. Just as she figured. Rob had probably cowered behind the front door when he saw her roar up the long driveway.

"Keeping that dog wouldn't be a mere change. It would require a lobotomy." Gwen shuddered, still remembering only too well her frantic drive to North Oaks while she'd wondered every moment if the dog would break loose and jump on her from the backseat. "The dog was yet another little gift from Rob. And since you were busy watching the neighborhood out your front window, you saw me take the dog away. Back to its rightful owner."

"So I guessed right." Leila voice dropped again, this time to the soothing sound that always, somehow, made Gwen feel better. "I'm so sorry. Just when you try to make some changes in your life, all these horrible things keep taking a swing at you."

Gwen sighed. "Tell me about it."

———

"Good news, dear. They're letting me out of here on Friday. I must be cured." Vivian ran a hand through her hair, which her hairdresser had washed and styled in a visit earlier that day.

A glance at her dad told Gwen a different story.

Perched on the edge of a chair on the far side of Vivian's bed, he hunched forward, shoulders stooped, seemingly mesmerized by the plastic cup he rolled back and forth between his hands.

Gwen set her purse on the end of Vivian's bed and stood on the other side of it. "Why so soon? Has Monica changed her diagnosis?"

"Dr. Lauren. Physicians like to be addressed more properly, dear." Vivian glanced at her freshly manicured nails. "After all that time they spend in medical school and residencies, I think they deserve it."

This wouldn't be a quick visit. Gwen grabbed a chair and dragged it closer to the bed. "I think you're confusing physicians generally with Rob. They're not all egocentric."

"Just plain 'Monica' works for me." Gwen released an embarrassed breath as the physician in question strolled into the room, wearing a long white lab coat over jeans and a red silk blouse. After quickly checking Vivian's computerized chart, she smiled at Gwen. "I wouldn't want to be called egocentric, even if all my siblings think so."

"That's just a lucky bonus of having siblings." Gwen stood up, greeting Monica with a quick grasp of her hand.

Her dad did, too. Propped up by more pillows than usual, Vivian sat forward. Not that she'd shake hands. Gwen and Mac had grown up with her constant warning that strangers carried too many germs easily passed through handshakes and hugs. It didn't explain why she also never touched friends or relatives.

Monica's wry grin didn't hide a slight blush. "If my bratty younger brothers were even remotely like your brother Mac, I wouldn't have to complain so much."

"Ahem." Vivian tapped her nails against the metal bedrail until Monica looked at her. "How soon can I leave on Friday?"

Monica's gaze narrowed as she again scanned the chart. She turned to Gwen's dad, then Gwen, before addressing her patient. "Anytime, I suppose, since you're checking out against medical advice."

Vivian swished her hand through the air. "Oh, pooh. You doctors always get so technical." Her studied nonchalance didn't seem to move Monica. "You said this can be done on an outpatient basis."

Brows furrowed, Gwen's dad spoke up. "That *is* safe, isn't it, Doctor? Even though it's not your first choice? It's just that Vivian would be so much more comfortable at home."

"I don't see how that's possible." Monica laughed at the three quizzical looks she received. "Everyone and their sister has visited, all your meals are catered, and someone seems to be running a beauty salon in this wing of the hospital. Next thing I know, you'll be getting a pedicure."

Vivian suddenly gazed out the window. "She'd, er, agreed

to come in tomorrow, but I rescheduled when you said I could leave."

"Good." Monica shared a grin with Gwen. "I'd hate to have my other patients think you're getting special treatment."

"Speaking of treatment—" As Gwen spoke, Vivian closed her eyes, but her dad nodded at her to keep going. "What did you recommend, and what is my mother trying to do differently?"

Vivian's eyelids fluttered, but she didn't say anything.

Monica stepped up to one of the machines at the head of the bed, fiddled with a couple of knobs, then typed some notes into the computer. Gwen thought she might not answer.

When she finished typing, though, Monica turned back to her. "The cancer has a big jump on us, and it moves fast. I want your mom to undergo an aggressive therapy of radiation and chemo. With her in the hospital, I could monitor it and prescribe higher doses—with better results—than I'd feel comfortable doing on an outpatient basis." She kept talking despite Vivian's raised hand. "Even the best home nursing care can't match what we can do here."

Vivian sniffed. "That's not what you said."

"Yes, it is." Gwen's dad shrugged. "But maybe you didn't hear it that way."

The two exchanged a look that Gwen had seen many times over the years. Her dad rarely won on those occasions.

Monica clapped her hands to draw their attention. "Fine. Take a break from this place. I know you weren't prepared to come here when you did, Vivian, and it's not a bad idea to take a little time to . . . get things organized at home." Gwen heard a faint catch in the doctor's voice. "The important thing is not to get your mind set on staying there. If we need to make changes, I'll talk you into coming back here. I'm good at it."

"Thank you." Vivian beamed, another victory tidily won.

The oncologist shook her head. "Don't thank me. It's your decision. I'm just not stopping you."

———

"Stop!" As Ted Harrison's rasping voice barked out the command, Gwen flinched. She'd hoped to finish the assignment this morning so she could help her dad get Vivian settled at home this afternoon. "What are you doing with those?"

Becky Tercell, Gwen's secretary, kept stapling the forms while Gwen gave Ted the obvious answer. "Didn't Danny tell you? We received an SEC inquiry on stock trades made before Treadman announced the deal with Aertronix. Danny asked me to distribute it to everyone in the office who had any connection with the deal. On paper, not by email. Becky and I are doing that."

"No need. I'll have my secretary handle it." Ted wiped his palm against his forehead, which glistened with sweat.

He had to be joking.

Ted's secretary hadn't done any serious work in the whole time that Gwen had worked at Pembroke and McFarley. Gwen couldn't believe the woman would soil her hands with a fairly routine intraoffice distribution.

Gwen pointed at the short stack of papers. "Thanks, but we're almost done stapling, and Becky already printed the envelopes. No need to involve Karla."

"It's no trouble." Before Gwen could stop him, Ted swept the pile of papers off the credenza behind her desk, then grabbed the ones that Becky was still stapling. "Karla will take care of everything."

That would be a first. Gwen shrugged at Becky, who said nothing. SEC inquiries about insider trading weren't that unusual, but Gwen's knees always shook when she read the list of people who'd traded. Even though she didn't own any individual stocks, she didn't even want to *know* anyone on the list in case the Securities and Exchange Commission went after her in its investigation, too. Danny had once admitted he had the same irrational feeling, but Ted's reaction—to this and everything else lately—seemed wildly out of proportion.

Ted gave her a tight-lipped smile before he left her office, clutching the sheaf of papers.

———

SATURDAY DAWNED BRIGHT AND CLEAR, a perfect first day for Sarah's softball tournament. Hoping to win the league championship, Gwen's pumped-up teenager wasted no time waking everyone up, even dragging Nick out of bed over his howling protests.

By nine o'clock Sarah was on the field. Perched in the stands, Gwen checked her cooler and tote to make sure she'd remembered everything. Sunglasses. Sunscreen. Bottled water. Cell phone. Enough bagels and other snacks to last a week, which Sarah and her teammates would probably inhale by noon.

Nick huddled at the far end of the bleachers, his usual scowl plastered on his face. He hadn't mentioned the dog in a couple of days, but his anger still shimmered. Couldn't he stand leaving his computer for a few hours on a gorgeous day? Apparently not. But his temper might have more to do with the message Nick had left for Rob on Monday night, asking if he could live with him. Gwen had felt a sting of pain—for Nick, but also for herself—when she overhead her fragile son make the call.

Rob hadn't called back all week.

As she watched Nick, her dad showed up at the game, surprising her. He immediately walked over to Nick, taking a seat on the far side of him. He'd actually left Vivian to come here. Although Gwen would bet he wouldn't miss a single play that Sarah made, she also knew he'd focus his attention on Nick. She dabbed at a rogue tear in the corner of her eye.

Thank God for Dad.

Rob ignored his son and, as much as she tried, Gwen didn't understand this stage Nick was going through. Her dad, who lived and breathed electronics for work, would happily talk to Nick about coding and design and whatever games he played on his computer all day long.

But even if he hadn't known a thing about computers, Dad would've done the same.

She waved at him, and he waved back, then put his arm around Nick and spoke intently to him. The scowl eased from Nick's smooth young face, leaving a boy who sat a little straighter and even whistled when Sarah threw out a girl at home plate.

Gwen leaned back on her hands and angled her toes toward the sun. After two years of hating her life—and much longer, if she were honest—she'd finally started trying to fix things this summer. Nothing ever seemed to go right, sure, and the thought of her fortieth birthday still depressed her. But a sparkling clear day, a softball field, and three of the people she loved most in the world offered her a small respite. Right now, she'd take it.

Sarah's team came up to bat. The first girl hit a wobbly fly ball that somehow dropped between the other team's center fielder and shortstop. Then Sarah bunted, sprinting to first base while the pitcher, catcher, and girl playing third base nearly bumped heads scrambling for the ball.

Gwen wished for a moment that Vivian could see Sarah in action, then wondered why she'd even had the thought. By her own admission, Vivian didn't understand sports. They were dirty and dangerous and undignified. Everything Vivian wasn't.

Vivian didn't understand Gwen, either. And Gwen didn't understand her. Understatement. She never would, no matter how much Mac tried to shove them together.

Several minutes later, Sarah and her teammates jogged back onto the field after Sarah got nailed stealing home. Tilting her head back, Gwen basked in the warm sunshine of late summer. Two more weeks until Labor Day. Her eyes flew open at the crack of a bat, just in time to see the pitcher duck as the line drive rocketed over her head—and watch Sarah, ponytail bouncing, collide with the girl playing second base.

Lurching to her feet, Gwen was pushed gently back down by a hand on her shoulder. She gazed up into her dad's smiling face.

"She's fine. See?" As her dad pointed, Gwen watched Sarah brush some dirt off her butt and help her teammate to her feet.

The breath she'd been holding came out in a whoosh. "You're right. I just—"

"You're just a mom." Her dad's eyes twinkled as he sat down beside her, wearing a golf shirt with his company's logo and a somewhat ratty pair of old shorts that Vivian likely wouldn't approve. "I'm well aware of the affliction. I sometimes worried they'd have to carry your mother out of your games on a stretcher. She got so wound up. Even worse than you do." He nudged her shoulder in a playful gesture.

"I don't get wound up." Gwen sounded defensive even to her own ears. "Or not too wound up. But what do you mean about Vivian?"

"I don't know why you call her Vivian." Her dad stared at the field, but he didn't seem to be watching the game anymore. Something between reproach and remorse tinged his voice. "She's your mother, Gwen. She cares about you. She . . . loves you."

His voice caught on the L-word. No wonder. Gwen couldn't imagine it being used in connection with Vivian.

Appropriately enough, a cloud appeared, marring the perfect day. Gwen glanced over at Nick at the far end of the bleachers, totally absorbed in the book he was reading. "Right."

In Gwen's whole life, Vivian had never even told her she loved her.

No, she had. Once.

During her senior year in college, Gwen had spent a semester in Rome—missing Tucker, studying Italian, and absorbing the fine points of gelato and Chianti. She'd scribbled a few postcards to her parents and a longer letter to Mac. Her dad called several times, Vivian once. At the end of that strained conversation, Gwen had almost dropped the phone when Vivian told her, after a few awkward pauses, that she loved her. Startled, Gwen thanked her and hung up without saying she loved her, too. With Vivian, the concept seemed too foreign and too late.

Now, almost twenty years later, it was way too late.

Her dad didn't try to argue, but the smile left his face. Since Mac drove back to Duluth last Sunday, Dad had found a dozen excuses to leave Gwen and Vivian together during

Gwen's daily appearances at the hospital. Long silences followed, except for the times when Vivian had sufficient energy to remind Gwen of all the things she'd ever done wrong—with Rob, with her kids, with being alive.

Gwen wouldn't strike back at someone lying in a hospital bed—not even Vivian—but she didn't have to stand there and take it. She cut each visit shorter than the one before it. By Friday, when Vivian was released, her dad had conceded defeat.

He looked defeated now.

Feeling guilty, she tapped his shoulder. "How's she doing on her first morning free from bedpans?"

A dull smile barely curved his lips. "She's happier at home, but I don't think it'll last. Two of her friends are with her now, but she's already had a few run-ins with the nurse we hired."

Same old Vivian. "Can you hire someone else?"

He shrugged. "I suppose so, but Vivian's standards are not easily met."

"You don't have to tell me. I've never met them." At her dad's frown, Gwen put her arm around him. "It's okay. I guess I just never measured up." When he shook his head, she kept talking, but her voice choked up. "You and Mac want us to suddenly get all cozy, but I'm almost forty. If it hasn't happened yet, it's not going to."

His voice dropped to a husky whisper. "It's no time to stop trying."

"Oh, Dad. I don't think either of us ever *started* trying."

"That's not true." He gazed at her, then over at Nick, before looking back at the ballfield. "Your mother sometimes has trouble expressing her feelings, but—"

Gwen cut in. "On the contrary. She's never had trouble

telling me how badly I botched things with Rob. Or anything else I ever touched."

"Gwen. She's—" Her dad's voice broke, and he waited a minute before speaking again. "She's so proud of you. Of all those marvelous talents you had growing up. Believe it or not, your mother was your biggest fan. I think she's . . . she's disappointed in herself for encouraging you to marry Rob."

"Encouraging me?" Gwen almost shouted the words, then lowered her voice when she saw Nick's head pop up from his book. "She practically threatened to disown me unless I gave up the one true love of my life to marry a . . . a butthead." She'd been using Nick's vocabulary too much lately, but it fit.

Her dad locked his arms around his bent knees. "She meant well, but she made a mistake. Not, in her mind, because you married Rob—she still thinks doctors are created above the rest of us." He rolled his eyes. "But because you gave up the rest of yourself when you got married. Your sports, your music, all those things you did so well."

"It was time to grow up." Gwen waved at Sarah as she rounded the bases on a triple. "Besides, I can't believe that a woman who's spent her entire life on the golf course or in a hair salon would care. She'd rather have me at home, darning socks and taking care of my husband and kids."

"Your mother doesn't darn." Her dad's dry comment drew a reluctant laugh from Gwen. "No, that's not what she wants for you. That's her life, one that she chose. It doesn't make it right for you."

"It worked well enough for you, having her at home." Gwen couldn't keep a note of reproach out of her voice.

Her dad actually laughed. "At home? Vivian? Not working never kept her at home. You know perfectly well that we had cooks and maids and nannies and what-have-you, but

I didn't marry a homemaker. I married a strong woman who had other ideas. I also raised one."

"I'm not sure you did." Gwen's eyes filmed over with unshed tears. "I'm not strong. I didn't have the guts to stay with the man I loved, and I couldn't keep the one I married. I have a thankless job and spend my time organizing picnics and bake sales." She drew in a choked breath. "And no one even notices or cares. Or loves me. Even the kids treat Rob better than me. Nick wants to *live* with him. I'm a complete failure."

Nearly twenty years' worth of tears escaped, flooding her eyes and threatening to wash her away, and she tried to ignore the curious stares of half of the crowd of parents at the game. Her dad said nothing at first, wrapping her in a hug while he somehow produced a handkerchief from his pocket, as fathers have done since the dawn of time.

When the sobs slowed to a trickle, he tilted her chin up and gazed affectionately at her. "Your kids adore you. Mac and your mother and I love you. You're not a failure, although you might rethink the job, not to mention the bake sales. And I wish for your sake that you'll try a little harder with your mother."

Wow. Dad wasn't pulling any punches today.

They both watched the game in silence for a few minutes before he turned back to her. "Really, though, I can think of only a couple of things that you truly need to fix."

Flinching, she looked down at her feet. "What?"

"You lost yourself somewhere along the way." As his first words hit, she almost didn't hear the rest. "And I'm not too sure you love yourself as much as the rest of us love you. I think it's time to start."

CHAPTER 9

She'd expected Danny's scowling face ever since the moment she arrived at work and flipped through her mail. Rushing down the hall to Becky's desk, she'd found their secretary, who expected him at ten. He arrived in her office thirty seconds after ten.

"Good grief, Gwen. Can't you and Becky handle something as simple as distributing an SEC inquiry?" He tossed his copy of the botched papers on her desk. "It didn't even make it around to people until Saturday afternoon. I wanted everyone to get it before they left for the weekend. The response deadline is tomorrow."

"I know." Horrified, she looked again at her copy. Splotches covered some names, and others were cut off at the bottom of the page. She didn't understand. Becky had already made all the copies when Ted grabbed them Friday morning. Someone—like Ted's incompetent secretary, Karla—had just needed to finish stapling, stuff them in envelopes, and distribute the envelopes to twenty people on their floor. Even Karla could handle that.

"So explain." But he didn't let her. "Christ. First Ted goes nutso on us, and now you're messing up, and this isn't like you. Or Becky. She could've done it by herself, and the two of you together pulled up short."

He dropped into a chair and ran a hand through his shaggy bangs. "Sorry. I'm just pissed. Ted's going to come down my throat on this one, and it's the last thing I need."

At Gwen's tilted head, Danny swung her door closed and looked at her expectantly.

She wondered why everything kept going wrong. "Danny, it's my fault, and I'm sorry, but I can promise Ted won't come down your throat."

"You have a lot more faith in his stability than I do."

"Doubtful." A bubble of nervous laughter escaped her. "Becky finished making the copies—which didn't look at all like these—and was almost done stapling them Friday morning when Ted grabbed the whole pile and insisted that Karla would finish up. I tried to stop him but couldn't. I have no idea what went wrong."

Danny snorted. "Karla? She spends Fridays filing her nails. And she should, since she spends the rest of the week using them on everyone."

Karla was the office tattletale and backbiter. Danny's words were an exaggeration, but not by much.

Gazing at the stacks of files on Gwen's desk, Danny thought for a moment. "Okay, there's no point complaining to Ted or Karla. They'd just deny it, and Ted would send my butt to the management committee again. Actually, I almost wonder if that was his plan. Did you happen to keep the original inquiry that the SEC sent?"

She pulled it out of her top drawer and passed it across her desk. "I held onto it for filing."

"Good work." Jumping up, Danny looked like Christmas had come early. "I'll have Becky make a stealth mission to a copier on another floor and try it again. Without Ted's assistance this time."

"Seriously, I can't imagine how even Karla botched it this badly." Gwen ran a finger down the list of names on the copy Danny had thrown on her desk. "It's almost as if she spilled her lunch on some of these names. I can't read them."

After perusing the clean copy, then the botched one, Danny frowned. "I'm not so sure we can blame this on Karla, as much as we all appreciate her stellar efforts." He tapped his chin as he looked again at the clean copy. "A few names seem familiar. I need to study this anyway, but I'd better pay special attention to the ones that got 'missed' on the copying."

Gwen's jaw dropped. "You don't think Ted might've—"

"I'd like to say no." Danny shook his head. "Don't speculate, and don't mention this to anyone else, not even Becky. I'm probably just being paranoid, but the SEC doesn't fool around. We can't, either."

———

"Good for him." Leila settled into the lawn chair she'd dragged from her backyard to Gwen's garden, where Gwen was on the losing end of another tussle with weeds.

Another Monday. She'd come straight home after work, her head aching from the drama caused by Ted, who'd gone missing in action even before Danny recirculated the SEC inquiry. Her weed-filled garden offered a reprieve she wouldn't find at her parents' house. Despite her dad's best efforts, she hadn't visited Vivian since Friday.

Gwen's silence didn't dampen Leila's enthusiasm.

"Your dad is so sweet." She waved her hand at Gwen's raised eyebrows. "You're always saying it yourself. Now he's dropping everything to take care of your mom. And he's trying to patch things up between you two. Finally."

"He should save his breath." Tired of pulling with no success, Gwen whacked at one obstinate weed with her clippers.

Leila kept extolling the virtues of Gwen's dad—which, most days, Gwen wouldn't argue with—before moving on to Vivian. "You're a lot like her, you know."

Gwen eyed her clippers, considering whether to alter Leila's stylish bob. The thought alone improved her spirits. "Since you don't know Vivian, you'll forgive me if I find the comparison less than flattering."

"I try not to let facts get in the way of my opinions." Laughing at her own humor—as always—Leila bent down, almost as if she were suddenly interested in weeding. She came back up with a can of lemonade.

Gwen tried a change of topic. "How was your dinner with Jon Abelard's hunky friend? Did you go?"

"Wish I hadn't." A rare frown crossed Leila's face. "Jon brought his friend, and I invited a friend from book club to tag along. Some friend. She usually looks like a librarian, but she showed up wearing a leopard-print dress. First chance she got, she sank her teeth into the guy. She even went home with him."

"Jon?"

Leila's hands flew up. "His friend! Tony. I could rip her eyes out." Despite her threats, Leila looked as if she almost admired her former friend's chutzpah.

Sitting back in the dirt, Gwen laughed. It felt good after a tense day—or a tense few weeks. "I didn't think Jon looked like the type to pick someone up." She glanced sideways at her neighbor. "Or did you forget your crush on Tony and go home with that poor man?"

"Hardly." Leila sipped her lemonade, scrunching her nose. Why? Because it needed vodka or prosecco? "Not that I don't like Jon. I do. He's an old soul and a dear man, and I could talk to him for hours."

"Old soul?" Gwen rolled her eyes. Lately, everyone claimed to be an old soul.

"You can see it in the eyes." Leila pointed to her own, which were a stunning shade of violet. "As if he's already lived a million years and remembers every minute of them."

"Poor man."

"Why do you keep calling him that?" As usual, Leila didn't wait for a response. "Jon's great. Maybe he's not interested in dating right now, but he doesn't need pity."

Gwen started pulling weeds again, wondering why she bothered. "He just seems so sad. No wonder he looks a million years old."

"Jon doesn't look a million years old; his eyes do. There's a difference. Believe me." Leila practically purred.

The itch to throw a clod of dirt at her was overwhelming. Gwen resisted it. "I thought you two just talked."

"That's what I said." Leila gave her an arch look, as if she knew what Gwen had been plotting. Looking down, Gwen loosened her grip on a dirt-packed weed.

"Good." Standing up, Gwen brushed off her shorts and took a step toward the house. "Jon seems like a sweet man. You shouldn't toy with him the way you do with—"

"Most men?" Leila had stood up, too, and started to follow Gwen. She stopped. "Is that what you really think?"

Hearing the hurt in her voice, Gwen looked sharply at her friend, who looked away.

She drew in a breath. "No. I didn't mean anything. I just—"

Leila waved her hand to stop the denial. "I know how it

is. Everyone's suspicious of the rich, wicked young widow who breaks men's hearts and sends them to an early grave." She gazed over at the apple tree, maybe to avoid having to look at Gwen's face. "I just didn't think you were like everyone else."

She picked up her lawn chair and small cooler and headed back to her own yard.

"Leila, wait! You don't understand." Having almost reached the fence between their yards, her friend didn't turn back. Gwen went after her, stopping only when she heard Nick shout from inside the house. Even though he probably just wanted permission to drink another Coke, she trudged inside. She'd fix things with Leila later.

She tried, anyway. For the rest of the week, she rang Leila's doorbell, called, and texted a dozen times. No answer. She almost thought Leila had left town until Thursday, when she caught a glimpse of her backing out of her garage. By the time Gwen raced outside, Leila was gone.

———

"What's a nice girl like you—"

"—doing slumming in a place like this?" Gwen tried to stop her nervous laugh, but she'd told herself she could have lunch in Melba Toast, alone at the bar, and not run into its owner.

Tucker stood behind her, proof to the contrary.

She hadn't seen him in seventeen years. Now she kept running into him, always on Fridays. Sure, twice now in his restaurant, but she'd eaten here before without ever seeing him. Her luck was changing.

She hoped it was for the better.

"So. You came." His husky voice held no trace of doubt that she would.

She almost hadn't returned after two weeks ago, when he'd drooled over Leila and left Gwen feeling like the ugly stepsister. She didn't feel much better today, but she'd had a rough week. Melba Toast had great food and an atmosphere guaranteed to shake Gwen out of her worst mood. The fact that she might see Tucker had been almost incidental.

Almost.

Setting down her menu, Gwen twisted sideways on her barstool. Tucker took the empty stool next to her.

"Where's your friend? Leila?" Tucker glanced around as if he expected her to appear at any moment. Or maybe hoped she would.

Gwen's heart sank. Despite Leila's assurances, the woman Tucker wanted was Leila, not Leila's mousy little friend who'd lost her heart to him all those years ago.

This had been a stupid idea. "I just wanted to grab some lunch, so I stopped by alone. Hope that's okay."

"More than okay." Tucker's eyes lit up the way they once had, when he used to hang out with a mousy little girl who would some day be Leila's friend. "It gives us a chance to talk."

She waved a hand, hoping he didn't notice that it shook slightly. "I don't want to keep you from your other customers."

"That's why I hire waiters." How did his teeth gleam so brightly like that when he smiled? "They protect me from my other customers so I can concentrate on you."

Tucker touched her hand just as the host came up behind him, tapping him on the shoulder and asking about someone's misplaced reservation. His eyes flickered in mild annoyance, but he didn't withdraw his hand.

As Gwen listened to the two men talk, she thought about all the changes that seventeen years had brought. Her own star had burned out or faded, but Tucker's was still rising. He spoke and moved with assurance and finesse—and, okay, he looked almost too gorgeous. The young man she'd known so well had grown up into someone she hardly recognized.

She wondered if he recognized what she'd become.

He finally turned back to her, gazing steadily at her while he held her hand. Gwen felt herself blushing.

"Where were we?" Tucker's eyes were still the soft hazel she'd loved staring into for hours at a time. "Oh, yeah. You were about to tell me why you're suddenly back in my life. It's been forever."

"Am I? Back in your life?" She sounded meek and mystified to her own ears. Gwen prayed Tucker's ears heard something more sultry.

Laughing, he stood up. "Sure looks like it." He nodded at a waiter's unspoken question as his hand lightly caressed Gwen's forearm. "But maybe not right this minute. I might need to hire new waiters, since the ones I have seem to need my advice today."

She watched as he strolled away, stopping to greet a table of customers before meeting two waiters at the entrance to the kitchen. As they gestured at each other, he rested one hand on each waiter's shoulder. After a few minutes, they all nodded. Another problem solved.

Her order arrived, and Gwen nibbled while she watched the constantly shifting tableau around her. It reminded her of college, when Tucker had tended bar for extra cash. She'd shown up every night, half an hour before closing time, and watched the action from her spot at the end of the bar. It never failed to amuse her. Tucker had chatted, laughed, sympathized, and yelled with the best of them. And at the end of the night, she'd gone home with him.

She blinked. It was a little after noon, not midnight. These days, Tucker *hired* the bartenders, and a five-dollar tip no longer meant the world to him. And Gwen was thirty-nine with two kids, not young and childless and carefree.

She wouldn't be going home with Tucker tonight.

Sighing, she heard someone else sigh. In her ear.

Tucker, making her tingle in all the old places. "A lovely woman sighs, and my heart weeps." His grin told her *that* was a massive fib. "Okay, I was never too good at poetry, but didn't it sound a little like Lord Byron?"

A laugh rumbled through her. "Not even remotely." At his feigned hurt, she tapped his nose, just as she'd done in college whenever he teased her about how studious she was. "Not even like Lord Henley, for that matter."

"Don Henley." Tucker whistled, either in appreciation for the Eagle's drummer or shock that Gwen's tastes hadn't changed. She couldn't tell which. "You still like the Eagles?"

She felt herself flushing. "Um, yes. But I always liked Glenn Frey better."

"How could I forget?" Tucker's hoot drew several curious looks. "You threatened to run away with the guy if they ever came to town. I had to bribe him to stay away."

"Right. Like you would've had enough money—" Too late, she covered her mouth.

It wouldn't have taken Tucker long to figure out she'd left a penniless guy with an always-broken motorcycle for a plastic surgeon who could give her anything. Theoretically. Long after Gwen had followed Vivian's advice all the way to North Oaks, where her rich husband spent his time with other women, Tucker and Rob had both proven Gwen wrong.

If Tucker realized it, he didn't cram it down her throat. "No kidding. There wouldn't have been enough money in the world to keep you away from Glenn Frey."

Salsa music pounded from the speaker above the bar, even at lunchtime. "It sounds like you've moved on. You definitely don't play Eagles music here."

"Sure I do." He pointed at the ceiling. "But in my condo, which is right above us. The Eagles, Tom Petty, Bob Seger. Plus Minneapolis bands like the Melismatics or Semisonic or the Suburbs. You like them, too, don't you?"

She nodded. "My friend Leila also likes to drag me out to the Driftwood to listen to St. Dominic's Trio." Talking about local bands was smarter than thinking about his condo or the large bed it probably held. "So why do you play salsa music in the restaurant?"

"Market research. Salsa makes people want to eat, drink, dance—" Tucker's eyebrows danced, too. "And leave big tips." His hips swayed to the heavy beat. "It's not bad once you get used to it."

She could get used to him swaying like that more often. Or again. Gwen licked her upper lip, forgetting she had a full afternoon of work and a visit to Vivian before her piano lesson. She'd avoided Vivian all week, and her dad had finally called this morning, begging.

"Damn. Pesky waiters. I have to run." Tucker hopped off his barstool again, then wrapped an arm around her as he bent to whisper in her ear. "Come back sometime when I don't have to work so hard. Please?"

She nodded, her arm tingling where his fingertips had lingered. All he had to do was ask.

"How nice of you to visit." Insincerity dripping from her tongue, Vivian extended one hand toward Gwen, as if she should kiss her mother's ring or something.

Gwen touched her hand lightly, then released it. "Sorry I couldn't come all week." The guilt churning her stomach jumped a notch when she studied Vivian's face, which looked more pale every time she saw her. "I've been really busy."

"Oh. Well." One thin hand swished through the air. "I suppose that's how it is with children, but thank goodness Mac's trial ended so quickly. *He'll* be able to spend time with me."

And Gwen wouldn't. Or didn't. The message came through loud and clear.

She forced a smile. "It's not like you're hurting for visitors. Dad's going to run his business into the ground, the way he dotes on you, and I keep hearing about this large posse of friends who stop by."

Vivian beckoned to Gwen's dad, who hovered in the corner of the dining room, which he'd converted into Vivian's temporary bedroom. In a few long strides he reached her side. "Your father has been my salvation, dear. I wish you had someone like him to take care of you."

Same old, same old.

"But I don't. Rob is ancient history, and you know it as well as I do."

Her dad coughed into his hand, and Vivian closed her eyes, reclining on the hospital bed they'd set up in here.

Dad patted Gwen's shoulder, a little awkwardly. "I don't think your mother meant Rob, honey. She just wants you to be happy."

Gwen rolled her eyes at the blatant lie. Her mother's eyes remained closed, so she didn't force the issue.

"Anyway, I have Sarah and Nick. They'll take care of me

in my old age. Either that, or no one gets to inherit the piano." Gwen laughed, the hollow sound echoing in the room. No one laughed with her.

Vivian's eyelids fluttered open. "Do the children take piano lessons? Perhaps from the same teacher you've been seeing?"

The scorn in her measured, aristocratic voice might not be obvious to an outsider, but Gwen heard it. Just like she'd heard the subtle disappointment and scolding in Vivian's voice so many times over the years. It always nailed its target.

Even as she winced, Gwen almost laughed at the thought of Sarah or Nick taking lessons from the friendly neighborhood stud. Not that Adam couldn't teach. He offered a healthy dose of praise with his criticism and showed her new ways to express herself in the music.

She just hadn't expected it. She'd halfway expected to get laid. Or, okay, *Leila* had expected her to get laid. Instead, Gwen played classical, jazz, and a little rock on her Friday night "dates" with Adam. Then she went home alone to her small double bed.

"Gwen? Are you all right?" Her dad sounded concerned, but that wasn't a surprise. The puzzled frown wrinkling her mother's forehead was.

"Fine. I'm fine." She closed her eyes, remembering Vivian's original question. "But, no, the kids haven't taken piano. They're not interested."

"That doesn't mean they shouldn't play." The weak voice almost didn't sound like Vivian, but the words did.

Gwen blew out a breath she'd been holding for twenty-five years. "Yes, it does. You made me take lessons, and I swore I'd never do that to my own kid."

"But you play so well." Vivian's eyelashes fluttered. "And you're taking lessons again. Obviously, you enjoy them."

"That's not the point."

"Then what *is* the point?" Vivian tried to prop herself up on her elbows, but she sank back down, the strain obvious. Dad moved closer, grabbing an extra pillow to set behind her head. "Lord knows you always have a point, dear."

A glance at her watch told Gwen that her mother had managed to push her up against the wall in less than ten minutes. Not a world record, but efficient.

She inhaled a deep breath, trying to calm herself. She choked on it. "You're tired. Maybe I should let you rest."

Her dad looked from one to the other. "She's right, Viv. It's been a long day."

"It's been a long week, dear." Vivian smiled at Gwen's dad, her eyes shimmering with wetness. "A long few weeks. But Gwen has finally found time to visit, and I don't want to send her away."

No one spoke, and the blunt knife of guilt twisted in Gwen's gut. Another direct hit. Her piano lesson wasn't for another hour or so. She nudged an ottoman with her knee, moving it closer to Vivian's bed before she dropped onto it.

She searched for a safe topic. There weren't any.

Vivian spoke first. "Your father and Mac think we should get closer, dear. Tell me. Why aren't we close?"

Definitely not a safe topic. Vivian's eyes drifted shut again, but only after piercing Gwen with their dull blue intensity.

"I'm not sure I have that much time." Gwen checked her watch again, mostly for her dad's benefit. "This could take hours."

"Gwen." Her dad's voice held reproach. She flinched as if struck, but she felt a lifetime of hurts inside of her and brimming over. She'd always been wrong. Too messy. Too difficult. Too angry. Too imperfect.

Biting her lip, she glanced at Vivian, who watched her impassively, as if she were a frog being dissected in biology class. Vivian had always watched her like that. Without warmth. Without feeling. Without all the things Gwen had longed for. The things Vivian gave only to Mac and to Gwen's dad.

She'd never had enough left over for Gwen.

"It's all right, Skip." The thin hand waving in the air looked more feeble than before. "Leave her alone."

Gwen wiped her eyes on her sleeve. "That's the problem." She sniffed, trying to clear her throat so it wouldn't sound like she was drowning. "You always left me alone. I had to figure everything out for myself, and I always did it wrong."

"You were strong. You didn't need my help the way Mac and your father did." Vivian accepted another pillow from Gwen's dad, letting him wedge it behind her so she could sit up all the way. She patted his hand before turning back to Gwen. "I didn't have anything to give you."

Stunned, Gwen could only stare. After a moment, she found her voice. "You could have tried giving me some love. You used it all up on them."

"I always loved you."

"Right. As if that was apparent to anyone." Gwen lurched to her feet and started pacing, although she kept her gaze on her mother. "It was always about you. And Mac and Dad. And your country club. And your friends. Even your friends' kids, those marvelous fictional children you gushed over every chance you got, just so I'd know I wasn't like them. Suzy Perfect and Billy Fantastic and all the rest."

"I loved you most of all." Vivian lifted one slight shoulder, as if it were obvious. "You were my first, and my daughter. Once I had you, nothing was ever the same."

"No shit." Gwen's retort drew a quizzical brow from Vivian but no lecture about swearing. "From then on, you had a sloppy little brat to lug around, at least when you couldn't palm me off on babysitters. You hated it. Then Mac came along, and you cut me loose."

"Hardly." Vivian smiled as if remembering. "You were only three when Mac arrived. You'd begged for a playmate. He wasn't quite up to the task for a few years, especially since he was so sick at first, but then you two were inseparable."

"But you took care of Mac."

From the corner of her eye, Gwen saw her dad slither out of the room. Coward.

Vivian nodded. "Mac was a baby. A sick baby. I couldn't spend as much time with you as I wanted, but you didn't seem to mind. You could already read, even though you were so young, and you amused yourself for hours with your books. I was so proud."

"Proud? Of what?" Sitting back down on the ottoman, Gwen pulled her knees up and wrapped her arms around them. "I was lonely. Those books were the only thing I had."

"Don't be melodramatic, dear. You know I don't like it."

Gwen blew out a frustrated breath. "I know all the things you don't like. My clothes, my hair, my grades, my boyfriends, my jobs, my life. That pretty much sums it up."

"I always wanted the best for you. And your hair looks nice." Vivian ran a hand through her own, which was thinning from the radiation. "I'm envious."

Gwen laughed, the sound bitter in her ears. "You've never liked anything I had, let alone envied it. I may as well have been invisible."

"Sometimes I thought you were."

After all these years, Gwen hadn't expected the intensity

with which Vivian's words stung. She'd actually thought herself immune.

Tears swam in her eyes. "That's what I figured."

"You don't understand." The weak voice drew Gwen's gaze to Vivian, who clutched her bony hands together. "I never could make you understand."

Gwen rested her elbows on her knees, wishing Vivian still had time to help her understand and make all the hurts go away. But she didn't. "Nope. On top of all my other faults, it turns out I'm also stupid."

CHAPTER 10

"It's not like that." Sarah's lower lip trembled, but she didn't back down.

Labor Day weekend had come and gone in a blaze of picnics and family tantrums. Tuesday morning, sixth-grader Nick had already left for his first day of middle school after griping bitterly at having to leave his computer. Gwen thought she was home free until her fourteen-year-old appeared in the front hall, dressed for the first day of ninth grade in a miniskirt and knit top that left little to the imagination.

Actually, not true. It left quite a bit to a freshman boy's imagination, since Sarah didn't yet have the curves to go with the outfit. But telling her that wouldn't help.

What had happened to her cute little tomboy who refused to be associated with skirts and other vile trappings of the feminine world? Leila must've gone shopping with Sarah and drugged her into submission. Gwen couldn't imagine this happening any other way.

"Oh? How is it, then?" Gwen heard herself sounding more and more like Vivian every day.

"Um—" Blowing a bubble that threatened to pop all over

her face, Sarah looked more like her little girl. "It's, like, everybody dresses like this, Mom. I'm not trying to hook up with any dopey guys." She giggled and turned red, much as she had two years ago when she'd asked Gwen to buy her first bra.

"I thought you hated skirts. You didn't want to be caught dead in one at Greta's wedding a month ago."

Sarah just blew another bubble and turned an even brighter shade of red, if that was possible.

"So what prompted the sudden change?" Gwen blamed racing hormones and peer pressure. Another year of scruffy jeans and football jerseys would've been nice. Right now, she'd settle for another week of them.

Hanging her head, Sarah scuffed the toe of her black Converse high-top against the floor. At least she'd evidently opted for comfortable shoes over a more dramatic fashion statement. Or maybe she hadn't been quite ready to give up her tomboy days altogether.

Gwen smiled. "Okay." Bending slightly, she hugged Sarah. She remembered those years all too well. "Don't say I didn't warn you. After you spend a whole day tugging on your skirt and wondering how you're going to sit down, you'll wish you'd worn something more comfortable. Like jeans."

"Whatever."

As her daughter's long-suffering sigh hung in the air, a horn honked and Sarah sailed out the door.

For once in her life, going to work didn't sound too bad.

———

Fifteen minutes later, knuckles rapped on the front screen door as Gwen made a last visual sweep of the living room and kitchen before locking up. Damn. She usually left for work before any unwanted visitors tried to stop by. The excitement and trauma of another school year had delayed her usual quick exit.

Double damn. On top of everything else this morning, she'd forgotten to take back-to-school photos.

She started toward the door—only to have it open unassisted. Either solicitors were getting bolder or she had a housebreaker on her hands. Or a kid who'd forgotten something.

Or Leila.

Her best friend made her first appearance in a week. A week when all hell had broken loose at work, Adam again ignored her many charms, and her own mother basically told her she was too dumb to live. A typical week. She couldn't blame Leila for avoiding her.

She'd needed Leila's comfort and advice so badly last Friday, after her long-awaited conversation with Vivian dredged up bitter memories for both of them but resolved nothing.

She rushed forward, but a sharp look and raised hand from Leila brought her up short. Stopping, she didn't realize at first that she held her breath.

"What the hell did you think you were doing—"

The air whooshed out of her lungs.

"—letting me act like such a jerk?" Leila offered a sheepish grin and held both arms open. Like a kid presented with a brand-new toy, Gwen raced over to her. Laughing, crying, and hugging, they rocked together in a rhythm of friendship that Gwen hadn't known with anyone else in a long, long time. Maybe ever.

"I'm sorry." Pulling away, Leila held Gwen at arm's length. "Forgive me?"

Gwen shook her head. "I think it's the other way around.

You thought I accused you of toying with innocent men, and maybe that's what I sounded like."

Leila fluttered her eyelashes. "If the shoe fits?"

"I didn't mean it. Really. Everything has been going so wrong for so long, and I took it out on you." Grabbing Leila's hand, Gwen pulled her into the living room and pointed at the chintz-covered sofa she'd picked up for a song at an estate sale. "I'm late for work, but stop in for a minute. I've missed our chats. I've missed *you.*"

"Same." Leila propped on the edge of the sofa. "But I can't stay long. I'm having my nails done at nine-thirty. First day of school, you know." She shimmied her shoulders in pretend excitement.

"Tell me about it." Gwen sat on the yellow flowered armchair she'd inherited from her grandmother, which Nick always called the big ugly dandelion. "Speaking of which—"

Leila burst in. "Hey, didn't Sarah look fabulous in her back-to-school outfit? I can't believe you let her— I mean, she sure is growing up."

"Thanks to you."

"She promised she wouldn't tell you." Leila clapped a hand over her mouth. "Busted."

Gwen wagged a finger at her. "Someone should arrest you for contributing to the delinquency of a minor. But Sarah didn't spill your secret. I'm just familiar with the size of her allowance, and it can't handle much more than a pair of shoelaces."

Leila shook her head. "Thank goodness she couldn't afford more. You should've seen the stuff that kid picked out. I made her get something more tasteful."

"Tasteful?" Gwen's eyebrows rose. "If that hot-mama look is what you call tasteful, I'm not sure I want to know more."

"That's probably wise." Despite her manicure appointment, she scooted back on the sofa and demurely crossed her legs. "So what's been happening with you? Any progress with Adam the studmuffin?"

"Adam? You've got to be kidding." Her words drew a frown. "All he cares about is how well my fingers move on the piano keys. He must be saving himself for someone else."

"That's not what I hear." Leila tapped her fingers on her knee as she stared at the grandfather clock in the corner of the living room. "Maybe you're not sending out the right vibes, but I understand. You're a little out of practice."

"I'm not so sure about that." Feeling smug, Gwen flicked a cool glance at her fingernails. They needed a manicure, too.

"Oh?"

"Maybe Adam just isn't the right man to receive my vibes."

"*Oh?*"

For once in her life, Gwen was the one teasing Leila, not being teased. She loved the blank look on her friend's face. "Maybe someone else—"

"Stop!" Uncrossing her legs, Leila jumped to the edge of the sofa, both of her feet poised as if for flight. "Who is it? Tell me it's not Rob."

"Rob? You've got to be kidding." Gwen rolled her eyes. "Not if he were the last man on earth." As she shook her head, she realized—finally—that she believed it. She'd been over Rob for a long time. It had taken her only two years to admit it.

"That's good to hear." Leila sat back again, her sandals tapping the floor. "But I left you alone for just a week. How did you find a new man so quickly?"

"Must be the hairdo." Running a hand through it, Gwen got caught in a small tangle. "Or maybe not. But I never said he was new, even though *you* meet new men all the time. I don't see why I can't."

"Oh, stop pouting. You could if you wanted to. You're just not the type, which isn't necessarily a bad thing." Leila patted the empty space next to her on the sofa. "But tell me all the juicy little details. I've had a dry month."

Gwen didn't move. "It's only the third day of the month."

"No wonder." Leila moved farther down the sofa, closer to the chair where Gwen sat. "But could you speed this up? At this rate, I'll never make it to my manicure."

Gwen bubbled over with excitement, blurting out what had consumed her thoughts all weekend. "It's Tucker."

"Tucker?" Leila's eyebrows drew together. "Your old boyfriend? Like, from two decades ago? The one I met?"

"Exactly."

"Hmmm."

For once, Gwen couldn't read Leila's reaction. "What? What's wrong with that?"

Wordless, Leila stared at Gwen. In a sudden, awful moment, Gwen realized that Leila might be attracted to Tucker. With her luck, her gorgeous and bold neighbor might've already done something about it. Leila's week-long absence started to make more sense.

"You didn't." The words shot out of Leila's mouth like an accusation. Gwen had been on the verge of making the same one.

She flinched. "Didn't what?"

"Duh." Laughing, Leila lost her intense look. "Get laid. Resurrect your youthful folly. Have a cigarette afterward." She waved a hand in the air. "All that stuff."

"No, I didn't. Not yet, at least." Gwen sniffed. "But it wouldn't be some random thing. Tucker was my first love. Probably my only love, since Rob was obviously a mistake."

Standing up, Leila stretched her arms above her head, groaning as she did. "Hey, far be it from me to give you any advice."

"Since when?"

"Good point." Leila's hands dropped to her waist, and she bent her head from side to side. She never skipped her morning calisthenics. She just didn't usually do them in Gwen's living room. "First loves are a wonderful thing, but not usually something you can repeat. No man can live up to a woman's glorified image of him. Especially the first man she loved."

"He hasn't changed." At Leila's raised eyebrows, Gwen shrugged. "Okay, he's older. More polished. Dresses better. Has a great business and probably a boatload of money." She wanted to wipe the knowing smirk off Leila's face. "But he, uh, still listens to the Eagles."

"There you go." Leila's smirk widened. "I see you've already covered the important stuff."

Feeling deflated, Gwen clasped her hands in her lap as she stared at the floor. "Not yet. But I know enough about him to still want him. I never stopped wanting him. I guess that's probably stupid."

She felt Leila's fingertips under her chin, tilting it upward. Leila grinned at her. "Nothing about you is stupid, my friend. Just do me a favor. Go slow. Keep your eyes open."

Leila treated her like a kid who didn't know better. Gwen bristled. "They're open."

"Good." Leila glanced at her watch. Mickey Mouse continued to light up her wrist. "I really should run. If I keep Tiffany waiting, she'll split my nails or something."

"Tiffany?"

"My manicurist. You remember—she did my pedicure. She's the best."

Gwen remembered her. There were too many Tiffanys in the world. Rob had one. Now Leila had one—in a manner of speaking. From the limited impression Gwen had formed of the woman who did Leila's pedicure, they weren't *all* bubble-headed airbrains. This Tiffany could actually think and speak with intelligence and do nails at the same time.

"Has she worked long at that spa?"

"Forever. I've seen her for about a year, after being on her waiting list for ages before that." Leila headed for the front door. "Now she's taking business classes at night and planning to open her own spa. Just listening to the girl exhausts me."

Gwen grabbed her purse and followed Leila outside. While Leila had her nails buffed and polished, some people had to work. Unfortunately, she was one of them.

———

GWEN'S HONDA CIVIC chugged to a stop in her parking ramp, lurching forward when she accidentally released the clutch before turning off the ignition. Oops. In the rearview mirror, she saw a man walk by, shaking his head at her.

Some men were easily annoyed by women who drove stick shifts.

Or who drove, period.

She wished she still had her old convertible. She didn't miss any other trappings from her years with Rob—except all the years she'd lost—but very little in life gave her the same amount of sheer joy as the feel of the wind in her hair.

Even if driving with the top down on her convertible made her hair look as if a maniac had gone after her with an eggbeater, it had always been worth it.

She just hadn't realized she'd miss it so much. Now, with

a mortgage and a constant stream of bills, she couldn't return to those days. Climbing out of the Civic, she trudged to a new day. In the salt mines.

Danny grabbed her the minute she got off the elevator and practically dragged her down the hall to the nearest office. The office happened to belong to Claudia, the third member of their old happy-hour trio. Danny nudged Gwen inside, surprising Claudia, who sat at her desk. Staring out the window. Like a catatonic zombie.

Knowing Claudia, she'd probably spent all weekend in the office, billing more hours than any other two lawyers combined. The dark circles beneath her eyes had grown worse since the last time Gwen saw her. She looked terrible.

"Have you heard?" After slamming the door, Danny shouted the question, startling her. He buzzed with nervous energy, pacing back and forth around the stacks of files on the floor. "I still can't believe it."

Gwen looked from Danny to Claudia, who didn't appear to know any more than Gwen did what had happened. Her features remained frozen while a flood of emotions raced across Danny's flushed face. "What? What is it?"

He clenched and unclenched his shaking hands, then drew a deep breath. "Ted Harrison died by suicide. Sometime during the weekend. Karla found him in his office this morning, his brains splattered all over his chair."

Oh. My. God. "Wh-what?"

"Danny." Claudia's expression didn't change, but Gwen understood it now. She already knew and didn't want to hear Danny's graphic retelling of the details.

Gwen couldn't blame her. She felt faint. Sick. She covered her mouth, just in case. A scream wanted to erupt.

"Sorry, guys." Rueful, Danny jammed his hands in his

pockets. "It just seems like something out of a Grisham novel. A deal goes bad and, poof, some lawyer winds up dead."

Gwen shook her head, clearing it. "What deal? What deal went bad?"

Claudia met Gwen's gaze, her dull eyes still showing no signs of life. "Treadman. It didn't go bad, though. Danny's just a little caught up in his crime thrillers." Her wan smile brought a shrug from Danny. "Apparently, the SEC called Ted late Friday. They called Danny this morning to follow up, but by then Karla had, um, found Ted."

Claudia looked at Gwen as if the whole thing made sense. It didn't. "I don't get it."

Danny ran an agitated hand through his hair. "Gwen, remember how Ted insisted on handling the SEC inquiry, then screwed it all up? I was afraid he was trying to cover up names he knew, and it turned out that I was right. Ted apparently told a bunch of friends about the Treadman deal, and they bought stock on the inside information. So did a few sham entities that Ted had formed to do the same thing."

"Ted had friends?"

Danny and Claudia both stared at Gwen.

"Sorry." Mortified, she held up a hand. "That was horribly tasteless of me. I don't know what I was thinking."

Danny snorted. "I admit I had the same thought. But even more, I can't believe that Ted of all people did this, except that he'd been acting so weird for a while now."

Still, it made no sense. Ted harassed women, screamed at secretaries and paralegals, and thought way too highly of himself. But he didn't need money. He'd been born with it, and it must've grown to massive amounts by now. His houses, cars, boats, and a multitude of other expensive toys made that clear. More important, Ted had written the firm's insider-trading rules. He'd also enforced them, hounding everyone in the office about the many traps for the unwary.

It looked like he'd jumped into the traps, feet first.

"Ted, Ted, Ted." Danny's voice interrupted her thoughts. "They're still sorting out the details, but something made him get greedy, and I guess his pride wouldn't let him get caught." Shaking his head, Danny stared at the ceiling. "I don't get it. He was a piece of work, but he knew so much." His voice dropped to a whisper. "He taught me a lot."

Claudia nodded. "He just didn't take his own advice."

———

Gwen floated through the day in a grim stupor, never lingering in one spot, never remembering what she'd just done or where she'd been. A half hour after she heard the news, the firm closed for the day. The management committee acknowledged that no work would get done. They encouraged everyone to go home and spend time with their loved ones.

Gwen's loved ones were both in school. Sarah had volleyball practice in the afternoon, and one of her teammates had invited her for dinner at her house. Nick had computer club after school. Shuddering, Gwen imagined a bunch of kids all whining in unison about how their nasty parents made them leave their computers to eat dinner. To think she'd wanted Nick to get out more and meet other kids.

Leaving the sunlit day, she blinked at the sudden darkness. A clink of glasses filled the air, and chimes over the bar rang out three o'clock. Melba Toast. Gwen glanced around in a daze, not exactly sure how she'd gotten here. She remembered thinking she shouldn't drive until her head cleared. It had probably been her only rational thought since hearing about Ted.

She stood frozen, trying to focus. The lunch crowd had long since departed, and even by Minnesota standards it was too early for dinner. A few waiters with empty trays wandered through the room, looking almost as dazed as she felt. Happy-hour revelers crowded the bar area, some of them probably parents celebrating the new school year and the return of sanity.

An arm came around her. The smell of Polo cologne tickled her nose.

Tucker. She hadn't consciously known she needed salvation. Her savior appeared ready and more than willing to provide it.

"You look like you need a drink." He nodded to a passing waiter, who rushed to his side. "The lady would like something tall and intoxicating."

The lady was already standing next to something tall and intoxicating. A drink with those qualities might be too much.

Turning to Gwen, the waiter looked expectant. "Yes?"

She wasn't sure alcohol was the answer. "Oh, I don't know. Maybe a lemonade?"

Tucker put a finger on her lips, stilling her. "I know just the thing. Let's toast the good old days with a couple of Screaming Orgasms."

She couldn't believe he'd said it in front of the waiter. Blushing, she didn't think she'd had one in seventeen years. Rob always gave out long before then.

Tucker gave her a quick squeeze. "You'll love it. San Francisco style. The cognac makes all the difference."

San Francisco? Cognac?

The waiter hurried to the bar, leaving Tucker with his

finger still on Gwen's lips. She wanted to lick it. Take it into her mouth and . . . mmm. Her lips curled in pleasure.

"See? You can taste it already." Tucker withdrew his finger, leaving Gwen alone except for her imagination and Tucker's arm curled around her waist. "I'm so glad you came."

Not yet, but she sure seemed headed in that direction.

As his fingers danced along her spine, sending shivers from her head to her toes, a trickle of doubt assailed her. "I'm not sure this is smart."

"Best idea you've had in a long time." His voice deepened. "I've missed you, Gwen." His mouth hovered near her ear, brushing against it as he whispered. "I still want you."

Warm and tingly and more than a little bit woozy, she wished she had somewhere to sit down. Or lie down. With her head in Tucker's lap, gazing up at him. In all her fantasies, the clocks spun backward, returning her with Tucker to their early twenties and moments she hadn't dared hope might come again.

She still loved him. She always would.

Maybe, just once, the gods would be good to her.

Their waiter bustled back to them, retrieving from his tray a couple of drinks with silly little umbrellas and a basket of onion rings. Tucker must still love onion rings. In the old days, they'd gobbled half the world's supply of them.

Nothing had changed. He'd probably even kept his tattoo.

Her sudden desire to rip off his clothes must stem from wanting to satisfy her curiosity about the tattoo. Nothing more. It didn't explain why she kept wetting her lips.

It also didn't explain why his gaze bored into her lips. It looked as if his hunger went far beyond onion rings, too.

The waiter left. Tucker grabbed Gwen's hand, pulling

her to a corner table fifty feet from the nearest patron. Five minutes later, they'd both gulped down their Screaming Orgasms, and Gwen was ready for another. This time, she didn't want the bartender's version. She wanted Tucker's. Every inch of it.

He tilted his head, and Gwen heard herself answering yes to his unspoken question. Felt herself being tugged to her feet and led through the maze of tables, past the bar, into an unadorned back hallway, and up a flight of stairs. To Tucker's condo.

To heaven.

She wasn't sure whether he closed the door before, or after, her blouse unbuttoned itself and her skirt dropped to the floor. Her gaze followed the path of his shirt as he pulled it over his head, exposing a chest that looked so familiar. His slacks came undone. She couldn't take her eyes off his hands as they eased the zipper slowly downward, teasing her with a flash of red silk boxers, then with the real thing.

Nothing had changed. It had just gotten bigger.

She stood, shivering, in black stockings and the matching pink silk bra and panties she'd had the unbelievable good luck to wear. Today of all days. Despite Leila's constant nagging, Gwen still usually wore the simple cotton underwear she'd bought after Rob had left, figuring that silk brought vanity, and vanity brought trouble.

Right now, trouble stared her in the face. After sweeping through her mouth, taking no prisoners, Tucker's lips and tongue blazed a trail of red-hot kisses, followed by his exquisitely roving hands. They moved in tandem, sliding from her neck to her collarbone, then around and over her breasts again and again before taking a smooth glide down her stomach, and landing— Ooh. Right there.

Kneeling, Tucker paused for a moment, grinning up at

Gwen like a sixteen-year-old with his first set of wheels. Or his first girl. She felt giddy and numb and suddenly, very suddenly, unsure what she should do. Or whether she should be doing it with Tucker. She opened her mouth, but only a shudder escaped.

He didn't give her time to change her mind. Moving back to the business at hand, his teeth gripped the lace at the top of her bikini panties and tugged downward, burrowing his nose into her and provoking her startled gasp. Mission accomplished, his tongue gave a lazy lick to the tops of her thighs before taking a plunge inside, to a spot where more wetness seemed almost redundant.

She hadn't felt like this since— Since Tucker.

The hands moving over her hips went still, as if Tucker was entertaining the same thought. Back together, finally, after too many years apart. A sigh escaped her, but she smiled at his upturned face.

Moments later, she lost her bra and panties, retained her stockings, and was tumbling headlong into Tucker's king-size bed, rolling around in black satin sheets and experimenting with some wrestling holds they didn't show on TV. Laughing. Gasping. And somehow, all at the same time, feeling like twenty-two and sixteen and practically forty. Feeling wonderful.

Tucker's hands and lips continued their assault, giving Gwen the courage to mount her own attack. Her hands slid the length of him, bringing unexpected pleasure at the light that shone in his eyes. Joy bubbled inside, threatening to drown her.

She'd come home.

He brought her there, sweeping her beneath him, then finally moving his hips into position between her legs. A condom later, a single thrust took him inside. Her heart pulsed in rhythm to the pounding beat of their joined bodies. The tempo grew, faster and harder, until she felt something explode inside of her. Startled, she gasped as a second wave soon followed. A moment later, Tucker cried out her name.

Utterly spent, they curled around each other, Tucker's leg thrown casually over Gwen's hip, her head tucked into the curve of his shoulder. Perfection. She hadn't known it existed like this, for a woman in the middle of life, long past the carefree days of college. With a man she loved, who still loved her.

"Oh, hey, there's something I wanted to tell you." His voice rumbled, husky in the aftermath of their passion. Another moment of perfection. A man who actually shared his thoughts and feelings. "Gwen, I'm married."

CHAPTER 11

"Married!"

Expecting something more along the lines of "I told you so," Gwen blinked at Leila's incredulous response.

"Shit happens." Leaning against the yellow-and-black counter in Leila's art deco kitchen, she shrugged. "Unfortunately, it happens to me All. The. Time."

After Tucker's way-too-belated confession, she hadn't uttered another word. Mortified, she'd grabbed her scattered clothes off the floor, scrambled back into them in record time, and made a mad dash for the door.

But not before giving him the hardest slap on the face that she could possibly deliver.

Tucker hadn't tried to stop her, either from slapping him or rushing away, and he definitely hadn't bothered to explain himself. Maybe she'd been just another sexual escapade for him. Maybe it was revenge for leaving him all those years ago. Maybe—

Leila pulled Gwen into a breath-squeezing hug, as if by doing so she could also squeeze out all the heartache. Gwen had come straight here after the disaster, walking right in Leila's front door without knocking or ringing the bell. She'd startled Leila, but at least not in the arms—or any other body parts—of a man. Finding her in the kitchen baking cookies, she'd almost fainted.

She didn't think she'd ever caught Leila doing anything even remotely domestic.

"Oh, sweetie." Grabbing a tissue from a box on the counter, Leila dabbed at Gwen's eyes. "You didn't deserve that. You've had too many jerks in your life."

Gwen tried, and failed, to stop the surge of tears she'd held inside since the moment she'd fled from Tucker. Her mascara was probably halfway down her face. "Tucker's not a j-jerk. He's j-just m-m-married!"

As she stuttered the words, the hot, wrenching shame rushed back. Her stunned horror. Her empathy for Tucker's wife. Remembering only too well the stark pain that Rob's sexual escapades had brought her, she'd spent the last half hour blaming herself bitterly for not asking a single question before leaping into Tucker's bed. She'd now unknowingly inflicted the same pain on Tucker's wife, and she'd never forget it.

But she suddenly realized the truth. Tucker *had* known exactly what he was doing.

He *was* a jerk. No excuses.

She sucked in a deep breath and let it out slowly, then calmly walked over to the sink and ran cool water over her face, hopefully washing off the last of her mascara. "You're right. He's a jerk. Or worse."

"Of course he is, you poor thing." Leila handed her a few more tissues, then tilted Gwen's face upward to finish cleaning it and gently fuss over her. "He also just fucked my best friend for sport." She crumpled up a handful of used tissues and threw them hard at the wastebasket—or as hard as anyone could throw Kleenex. She missed. "Boy, that pisses me off."

Seeing Gwen's wide eyes, Leila picked up the tissues and dropped them gently in the wastebasket. "Don't worry. I'm not going to shoot him or anything. I'd just like to."

"It's tempting, I admit, but please don't." Gwen offered a shaky smile, then made her way on weak knees over to the center island and perched on a stool. "I've had a horrible day. I'd rather not have anyone else shot."

"I can't believe I forgot!" Leila took the stool next to hers. "Ted Harrison's death was all over the news. Isn't that the Ted who kept hitting on you?"

Nodding, Gwen felt like she'd been run over by a truck. Several times. "He'd been so strange lately. No one expected him to kill himself, though. I guess he must've thought he'd never live down the shame of what he'd done."

She'd never shoot herself, but she knew the feeling.

Ted had left a long, rambling, and mostly incoherent suicide note on his computer, which his secretary, Karla, had found and forwarded to several people in the office. Danny showed it to Gwen. They'd all been stunned—including by the fact that Karla actually knew how to use a computer. The rest of the note hadn't illuminated much except Ted's embarrassment and bitter anger. He hadn't left the world peacefully. Gwen supposed suicide victims seldom did.

"The news anchor said something about insider trading, but your firm's spokeswoman was pretty tight-lipped and the media hadn't learned much yet. Is it true?"

"I'm probably not allowed to say." But Gwen nodded as she spoke, then dropped her head. The effort to hold it all together exhausted her.

Leila patted her hand. "Where are the kids? Do you want me to help you out with them tonight?"

"Is that why you're baking cookies?" Gwen grinned, her first genuine smile since Tucker had dropped his bomb. She pointed at the steaming cookie sheet on top of the stove. "Should I be alarmed that you're turning into a domestic goddess?"

Leila reached over and grabbed a cookie, blowing on it to cool it off. "I'm a woman of many talents. Most of them are just hidden."

Gwen popped a cookie into her mouth. Triple—or quadruple—chocolate chunk. "Mmm." The chocolate sent her floating to the ceiling. "Delicious." She swallowed it in two bites and wanted another. "Thanks, but the kids are fine—despite their mom. Sarah is at a friend's house, and Nick probably took a frozen dinner up to his computer. Knowing him, without bothering to nuke it in the microwave."

Leila snatched another cookie, swallowing it whole. Glancing at the clock over the sink, she gave a sheepish grin. "I almost forgot—I can't help tonight anyway. I've got book club."

"At Jon's store?"

"Of course." Leila looked at the cookie sheet three times before giving in and taking another one. "Want to come? I'm not sure I should leave you alone tonight."

Gwen shook her head. "Sorry. I wouldn't be good company, and I should check on Nick, even if he doesn't think so. And Sarah will be home soon. I want to see how their first day went."

"That's right!" Leila talked through her constant munching. "They're really getting up there. Nick in middle school and Sarah in high school already. How time flies."

"When you're having fun." Gwen shrugged at her pathetic attempt at humor. "Or whatever it is I'm having."

"It's called a life." Leila wiped a crumb off her chin.

"Right now it's not the one you want, but at least you've finally climbed back into the saddle. You just have to remember how to ride."

————

"You're not concentrating." Adam glanced at his watch, prompting Gwen to peek at her own. Twenty after seven. She'd fumbled every piece so far tonight, and they had only ten more minutes left. "Start that one again, from the top."

Gwen's fingers stilled as she stared blindly at the sheet music in front of her. Three long days after they'd discovered Ted's body and she'd unfortunately rediscovered Tucker's, shock still clogged her pores. Adam, who noticed everything, hadn't commented. Yet.

Just once, she'd give anything for a hug—or even a compliment, even if it wasn't sincere. Right now, she'd rather have the personal attention he apparently gave his other students than his high aspirations for her.

But no one ever asked her what she wanted.

"Your hair looks great." Reaching forward, he brushed back a lock of hair that had fallen into her face. "But I'd rather see that cute little nose of yours. There. Much better." Tender. Sweet. She almost fell off the bench in shock. He must read minds.

Despite the dark circles under her eyes the last few days, which even Leila's outrageously expensive makeup couldn't hide, she felt her whole face light up.

"I've had a tough week." Understatement of the year. She glanced up at him shyly before dropping her head again. Unlike so many men, who bulldozed in with questions or instant solutions, Adam waited for her explanation. She dodged it anyway. "I can't believe it's already Friday. Or that Friday is finally here. I'm not sure which."

"Not a lot of time to practice this week?"

She squared her shoulders and, this time, looked directly at him. "You might say that. A senior partner at my law firm died by suicide, and that's just for starters."

Flinching, Adam drew back. It didn't surprise her, obviously, but she'd hoped for more. For comfort, if not understanding. For a masculine shoulder to cry on—the one thing Leila couldn't give her, and right now she couldn't ask it of her dad. Gazing at the wall, she felt something inside of herself shut down.

She'd always taken care of everyone else. Her kids, her friends, her neighbors, her co-workers. She'd even cared about Ted—not enough to date him, but as a human being, in those rare moments he'd acted like one.

She was tired of caring. It was someone else's turn.

"I'm sorry." His words lacked eloquence, but he'd made an effort. Gwen offered a slight smile.

She fluttered her fingers over the keys, imagining—as she had when she'd first played piano in grade school—a butterfly alighting on a field of flowers, one by one. Her childhood game. Time to play again. She ended the lesson with ten minutes of near-perfect play.

Closing her favorite book of Beethoven pieces, Gwen smiled again, this time feeling it inside of her. "Thanks."

"What did I do?" Standing, Adam pulled a different music book from a shelf and handed it to her. More complex pieces from Beethoven. She flipped through the pages, grimacing at how much she'd have to practice if she wanted to play them well.

Right now, she didn't exactly have extra time or reserves.

"You didn't make me tell you about my week." She

laughed, not easily, but more like herself than she'd felt since Tuesday. "Everyone else has. I dreaded another interrogation."

"I don't like to pry."

She tilted her head at him. "What *do* you like to do?"

His startled expression quickly relaxed—as if, for a split second, Adam thought she'd been flirting. Obviously, he'd decided just as quickly that she wasn't. She knew she was different. Or at least Adam thought so.

She both liked and hated that.

"I like to play piano. And, once in a while, saxophone and drums. And I like to teach piano—or I would if all my students were as good as you." She blushed. He was good at flattery, but she also knew he didn't relish giving lessons to a bunch of middle-aged women with too much time, and too little talent, on their hands.

"What else?"

"Exercise." She'd just bet. "Sports. I played rugby in college, and I still like to find a game when I can. And I ski. And sail. And, well, do pretty much anything."

And *anyone*, she suspected, but for some reason she'd been an exception. Would that change if she actually agreed to do the competition? And did well? She wouldn't hold her breath, and she definitely wouldn't ask him. She wasn't a charity case, even if Rob—and maybe Tucker—had treated her like one.

She knew Adam liked her. They usually ended her lessons with a discussion of music and a million other topics completely unrelated to music. She actually enjoyed talking to him. For a surfer boy with way too much sex appeal, Adam had intellect and wisdom beyond his years.

In return, he thought she was nice. Probably in a do-gooder, PTA-mom sort of way.

Nope. She wouldn't hold her breath.

"I used to play sports." She offered a shy smile. "Mostly softball and basketball, but I loved pretty much every other sport, too. My daughter is just like that."

He blinked. "Seriously?"

"It's been years since I've done much, but I've been thinking about picking it up again."

He frowned.

"What? Is something wrong with that?" She *had* been thinking that some serious exercise, and not just an occasional walk around Lake Harriet, might make her feel better. Adam's skeptical look made her feel like two cents. "My friend Leila thinks I should start doing what I used to love."

"Leila says that? Did she also tell you to say you love sports?"

His sudden hostility deepened the knot on her forehead. "I don't understand. Do you actually *know* Leila?"

"I've met her, and I hear her name a lot." He sighed, meaningfully, evidently lumping Leila and her in with all of his other women. She refused to be lumped with anyone, which was something else he didn't know about her. "So you like sports. Play any tennis?"

"Not in years." She tilted her head to one side, wondering if she should take it up again. It would give her something to do with Sarah. "I was thinking I should start off slow, not with tennis, where someone might expect me to have a decent serve or killer backhand. I used to, actually, but I left them behind on a court somewhere twenty years ago."

Standing up, Adam offered his hand to help her up, too. "Do you want a glass of wine?" At her tentative nod, he went to the kitchen, calling back for her to grab a seat on the couch. "I've got some white, if that's okay."

"Don't you have another lesson? Or other plans?"

"Nope." Returning to the living room with two glasses and a bottle, he poured the wine, then handed one glass to her and sat a foot away on the couch. "I don't usually make plans on Friday nights. But a glass of wine sounded good."

"Sounds good to me, too." She stifled an unexpected laugh with a hand over her mouth. "I have to admit, it's not the first glass of wine this week that did."

"I can imagine. You've had a crappy week."

"You don't know the half of it." Taking a sip, she leaned back against the cushions and closed her eyes. Peace.

She felt him move closer. That wouldn't be bad, either. "Then I suppose you wouldn't mind getting some good news for a change."

One eye opened. "Oh?"

"Yeah." Twisting sideways toward her, he grinned at her. One hand touched her thigh. Lightly. "You know that little piano competition I keep mentioning?"

"It's been cancelled?" Her other eye opened. After setting down her glass, she sat up straighter.

His smile dimmed. "No. It's three weeks from tomorrow. September twenty-eight. I took the, uh, liberty of signing you up, just to make sure we got in."

"We? Me and who else?" The wine was forgotten—or wasted on her now—and her toes tapped against the wooden floor. She clenched one fist, mentally giving herself space to slug him. The competition wasn't news, but she didn't want to discuss it tonight. Or think about it. Or do much of anything.

His hand moved on top of her clenched fist.

"Just you. Your proud teacher will be there, though, standing in the wings and cheering you on."

"Well, color me happy." She pulled her hand away. "Why did you do that? I wasn't ready the first time you mentioned it, and I don't see that changing in the next three weeks."

Reaching for her hand again, he wrapped both of his around it. "That's why I'm the teacher and you're the student. You're ready. I wouldn't say that if it weren't true."

"It's probably not the first line you've handed one of your students." She had him there. His startled face acknowledged the truth of her slam.

He drew a deep breath. "I've never lied to you." He hadn't had to. They'd stayed out of bed. "You're my best student by a long shot. You don't have to play in the competition, but I wish you would. You're good. I think you have a real shot."

"What's the point? I'm a little old for Juilliard." She shrugged. "I'm not sure I want to spend the next three weeks freaking out over it—practicing every minute, losing sleep, getting sweaty hands. You know, the whole shebang."

Shaking his head, he actually smiled. As if he'd already won. "You only need to practice for three weeks, and they'll fly by. But skip the lost sleep and sweaty hands. Especially the hands. I hate holding sweaty hands."

His eyebrows waggled, turning her scowl into a reluctant smile.

"Cute. Very cute." She batted her eyelashes. "I'd almost think you were flirting."

He grinned. "If it means you'll do the competition, absolutely."

———

"Why are you avoiding her?" The deep voice growled into Gwen's ear, too early in the morning for most people to call. Peering at the clock on the nightstand, she groaned. Twenty after seven on a Saturday.

"Mac. Good morning to you, too."

Her brother chuckled. "Yeah, mornin' yourself. But what's up with you and Mom? I hoped you guys would patch things up if I stayed away a while."

"Right." She rolled her eyes, wondering when someone—anyone—in her family would get a clue. "You stayed away because of work, or maybe your latest flavor-of-the-week girl-friend. Whatever. It's been only three weeks. Vivian and I have been working on this feud for forty years."

Silence greeted her. Mac wasn't known for it.

She sat up in bed, punching her pillow a few times for no good reason. "Besides, I talked to her. You and Dad are crazy if you think anything will change."

He sighed, the sound loud in her ear. "She's dying, Gwen."

"We don't know that." She felt the usual pinprick of guilt that accompanied any thought of Vivian's cancer. She hugged her pillow, crushing it. "Besides, it's not like I didn't try."

"A week ago. Yeah, I heard all about it."

"From Vivian?" It'd be just like her to go running to Mac. Her favorite child. Her only child.

"No, I didn't hear it from *Mom*." Mac hated it that she called Vivian by her first name. Too bad. "Dad told me. He was pretty shaken up."

"Dad's a big boy. He didn't say anything to me."

Still, the pinprick grew into a gaping knife wound. Unable to face another reopening of other old wounds, she'd avoided her mother—and therefore Dad—over Labor Day weekend. The week that followed had been beyond lousy, bringing her no closer to another dreaded visit. She couldn't stomach it.

"And you're a big girl." Mac's voice caught on something. "Mom and Dad aren't getting any younger, Gwen. It's time to quit blowing everything that ever hurt you completely out of proportion."

"Is that what they say?" Gwen fought the urge to throw her cell phone at the wall, especially since she couldn't afford a new one. She yelled instead. "What the hell do any of you know about me, or how I feel, or how much I've been hurt? I've taken care of myself my whole life, Mac, while *Mom*—" She sneered the word. "Spent all her time kissing your damned boo-boos. Give me a break."

"That's not how it was." Mac dropped his voice to something just short of a whisper. "Mom's reserved. Tough to get close to. Fine. You know what kind of family she grew up in, and they were all like that. If you'd worked at it, like I did—"

She clenched the phone in her hand, feeling the sting. "Tell me about it. Tell me how cozy I had it. I dare you."

Silence greeted her, then the rushing sound of an angry breath. Next came Mac's voice, low and controlled. "You don't know me any better than I know you, but I'm at Mom and Dad's. Get your butt over here. Let's talk."

She peered again at her clock. "It's seven-thirty in the morning."

"You're right. Wait until eight."

———

"Mom! I can't find my kneepads!"

The sleepy, high-pitched voice shrieking down the stairs at Gwen in short bursts belonged to none other than Washburn

High School's volleyball player of the week. From the commands she'd been receiving all week, Gwen could've sworn the honor should have been Imperial Duchess of the week.

"Look under your bed!" She shouted back at Sarah, a moment later realizing that Nick hadn't yet appeared. No surprise. These days, he often slept late on weekends. Gwen didn't completely miss the dawn wake-up visits he used to pay her, but she missed the little boy he'd once been. Sometime last spring, he'd engrossed himself in the world of computers, where Gwen was a few megabytes short of knowledgeable.

A few minutes later, Sarah stomped down the stairs in her practice uniform, complete with knee pads around her shins. As she burst into the kitchen, Gwen was grateful that volleyball didn't require cleats. Her floors wouldn't survive it.

"You have practice this morning? It's not even eight o'clock." Gwen had no intention of heading to her parents' house this early, despite Mac's guilt trip, but she'd have to leave sometime soon. The next phone call she got would be from Dad, using his Chairman of the Board voice.

"Oh, Mom." Grabbing an apple, Sarah chomped on it. Loudly. "We hafta be there by nine, but I thought I'd get in some extra work. You know, so I can—"

"—be player of the week next week, too?" Gwen poured Sarah a glass of orange juice. "Don't you think you should let another girl have the honor?"

Based on the drawn-out sigh and rolled eyes, Gwen suspected that Washburn's drama department could use Sarah's talents as much as its sports teams did.

"You just don't get it." Another chomp.

"Try me." The microwave dinged. Pulling her bagel out, Gwen slathered it with peanut butter.

Sarah's gaze followed the bagel all the way into Gwen's

mouth, but she shook her head—furiously—when Gwen held out the bagel to offer a taste. At five-four and one hundred ten pounds of hard-packed muscle, Sarah didn't need to lose weight. Lately, though, she'd shown signs of dieting. The glass of juice that Gwen had poured for her sat untouched.

"You don't need to lose weight." Gwen took another bite, hoping her obvious pleasure would tempt Sarah. It didn't. "With all the exercise you get, you need to take in some calories." Sarah made a face. "You already look perfect, but you won't if you get too skinny."

"You're pretty skinny." Sarah didn't give up easily, but she stared at the bagel the way vultures eye a fresh carcass.

"I know." Gwen scrunched her nose. "I'm too skinny. Just ask Leila. Why do you think I'm eating this?"

"'Cause you've always been a sucker for bagels and peanut butter?"

Gwen laughed. "Besides that."

"'Cause you wanna grow up to be big and strong." She recited, in a monotone, the mantra that Gwen had repeated so often to both of her kids since they'd been toddlers. "Give me a break, Mom. I'm practically fifteen."

"In eight more months."

That earned Gwen another eye roll. "Whatever."

"So." Before she screwed the cap on the jar of peanut butter, Gwen passed the open jar under Sarah's nose, teasing her. "Do you need a ride to practice, or did you want extra credit by running all the way there?"

Ignoring her, Sarah walked over to the cupboard and retrieved a low-fat granola bar. Gwen couldn't stand them, but she kept her mouth shut. It was a step in the right direction.

Sarah swallowed the bar in two large bites. "Umpf." She tried talking with her mouth full, but a look from Gwen made her finish chewing first. "A ride would be great, unless you're too busy with all your stuff you're always doing lately."

Hearing the sharp tone of Sarah's voice, Gwen glanced at her. "What does that mean?"

"Nothing."

"Sarah . . ."

Swinging one leg over the back of a chair, Sarah perched on the edge of the seat. "It's just, like, well, you know." Her teenager waved one hand in the air, indicating the magnitude of whatever she meant to say.

"I'm not sure I do." But she had a good idea.

Sarah glanced out the window, avoiding Gwen's sharp gaze. "You've got your piano lessons and stuff. And, like, nobody's making you take them."

Gwen couldn't really explain the piano lessons without forcing a mother-daughter chat on sex and turning forty and other catastrophes of life. Besides, although she loved playing piano again, she wasn't entirely sure she understood the piano lessons, either. Or why she'd agreed to play in the competition.

She'd fallen for too many men's lines lately. And never to her advantage.

Sarah didn't wait for a response. "You're always talking to Leila and doing stuff with her. And you, like, hang out with Gran and Gramps all the time. And Mac."

Vivian hated being called Gran. "You know your grandmother is very sick. She's probably going to die. I need to—" She didn't know what she needed to do about Vivian, but she hoped she'd figure it out before it was too late. "I need to spend some time with her. I'm not sure how much longer she'll be with us."

Her stomach rolled as she said it. She had to visit her parents and Mac. Today. Now.

"I get that, but you never take us along." Head down, Sarah rummaged in her backpack. She rearranged it at least three times a day.

"I didn't think you wanted to go." Cringing, Gwen watched as Sarah retrieved what looked like green sweatsocks from her backpack and tossed them on the floor. "And I haven't always gotten along too well with your grandmother. Sometimes we argue."

"No shit." Sarah's eyes flew open the moment she apparently realized what had just slipped out in front of her mother.

"Sarah Elizabeth." Gwen shook her finger at her. "Don't talk like that. Not until at least tenth grade." She winked at Sarah, whose jaw dropped. Keeping her daughter off balance was a job perk.

"Yeah, right." Sarah's ponytail bobbed as she nodded. "But I'd like to see Gran and Gramps, too. And Mac. You can go ahead and fight in front of me. It's not like I never saw you and Dad go at it."

The conversation was going from bad to worse. "We tried not to argue in front of you. I'm sorry. Things with your dad were sometimes hard for me."

"No sh—" She had the grace to blush. "Kidding. My other friends' parents fight. It's no big deal. And I've seen you and Gran fight. Lots."

"Then you're practically grown up." Getting out of her chair, Gwen tugged on Sarah's ponytail. "Come on. Let's go check on Nick and see if we can wake the dead. Then I'll give you a ride to practice."

"Do you hafta?"

"Give you a ride?" Gwen frowned, studying her daughter. "I thought you wanted one."

"Yeah. But I don't see why we have to get Nick. He never looks too good before noon."

———

FORTY-FIVE MINUTES LATER, after dropping Sarah at school and Nick at a computer-crazy friend's house, Gwen pulled into the driveway of her parents' home in Edina. The garage door stood open, her dad's Lexus was missing, and Mac's Jeep was nowhere in sight.

Her family's usual warm welcome.

She pushed down her automatic spurt of concern, convincing herself they'd probably all gone out for brunch. It didn't make sense, with Vivian mostly confined to her bed—but, then, her family had never made sense.

As she stood in the driveway, debating what to do, her cell phone rang. Mac. Maybe Vivian was fine and had just needed to get outside. Go somewhere. Maybe, after a lengthy debate, they'd even decided to invite Gwen to join them. She answered on the second ring.

"Hello?"

"Gwen? Sorry." She could barely understand the words racing out of her brother's mouth. "Everything's happening so fast, but I called as soon as I could."

"No problem." Calmer, Gwen felt less concerned, less upset by being excluded. They hadn't forgotten her. Or at least not completely. "I just got to their house. Should I wait here or meet you guys somewhere?"

"We're at the hospital. Mom's not doing so good."

CHAPTER 12

"It's all my fault."

Standing near the nurses' station in the intensive care unit, where Vivian had been taken, Gwen shook her head. She'd never forget her sharp words this morning with Mac, who'd probably repeated them to Vivian, who'd been rushed to Kendall South in an ambulance.

Mac's arm came around her. "There you go, taking all the credit again." He nodded at the glass window of Vivian's room. Their dad, Dr. Lauren, and two nurses hovered over Vivian, who lay with her eyes closed. "Dad's taking it pretty hard, but Monica says it's just a temporary setback. This time."

"What happened?"

"You said it was your fault. I figured you knew." Mac rubbed his knuckles on her head. "You dope." His faint grin quickly faded. "Actually, no idea. We'd just had breakfast, Dad and I were talking Mom through her piece of toast, and all of a sudden her face flushed, then got really white, and she closed her eyes. Dad grabbed the blood pressure monitor, and she was ninety over fifty. I was already dialing 9-1-1."

Gwen shivered, wondering how close they'd come. "Did you tell her what I said to you?"

"What? And spoil a nice piece of toast?" Rolling his eyes, Mac gave her a light punch on the arm. She'd probably get a bruise anyway. "No, I figured that was between you and me. And we still have to talk about it. Like it or not, you're stuck with me."

"I do like it." She gazed through the window at Vivian, not really seeing her. "And I'd like to talk. It's just that sometimes I feel a little sorry for myself."

"No shit."

She slugged him, not at all lightly. "Now I know where Sarah gets it."

———

Dragging after several hours at the hospital, Gwen arrived home at four to an empty house, a note from Sarah mentioning a pick-up basketball—*basketball?*—game, and no word from Nick.

She called his friend's house, where the boy's mom sounded ready to throw a hammer through her son's computer. Gwen could empathize. She even had a hammer. After confirming Nick's delivery home after dinner, she set down her phone.

It rang right back at her.

"Adam?" Calling to see if she'd been practicing for the competition? Seriously?

"Gwen? That you?"

"Sorry." But not really. "I've had a busy day. No time for piano."

"I wasn't calling about that." He breathed a little too hard into the phone, as if he'd been running. "It's a gorgeous day outside. I thought you might want to swing a tennis racquet around. You know, shake the dust off."

Was he kidding?

She'd promised herself that she'd get active again. She just hadn't planned on it happening so soon. "You sound like you've already run a marathon. What makes you think you can take on an old lady at tennis?"

"You're not that old."

Ouch. "Gee, thanks. Flattery will get you everywhere."

He paused. She imagined him beating himself senseless. "I mean, you're— Oh, hell. I just thought tennis sounded fun, and we were talking about sports last night, and . . ." His words trailed off as if he acknowledged defeat.

Laughing, Gwen dropped into the nearest chair. Adam had a great telephone voice. She didn't mind teasing him, either.

"Gee, I don't know. I've got this ruthless piano teacher who's always cracking the whip about practicing, so maybe I should check with him first. You know, get his permission."

He snorted. "I've already cleared it with him. He says all work and no play makes Gwen a dull girl."

Ouch again. "When did you want to play?"

"Now?" Adam laughed, the sound loud in her ear. "That way, you still have time to practice your piano tonight."

———

WITH THE WIND at her back and the sun in Adam's eyes, she really should be doing better. Of course, that assumed a decent forehand, a functional backhand, and actually hitting her serve when she tossed the ball in the air. So far, that hadn't happened too much.

Her tennis game sucked. But she loved every minute of it.

A secret place inside of Gwen envied Sarah every time she raced off to play her sport du jour. She didn't want to discourage her. She just wished Sarah would ask her to play.

She had an equal chance of going with Sarah to her first dance next Friday.

Adam didn't seem to mind her mistakes. His shouts of encouragement sailed over the net more often than her return volleys did. She clobbered another shot, sending it flying over Adam's head and the fence behind him. She just needed more practice.

He strolled to the net, motioning to Gwen to join him. His smile probably hid a latent desire to smash his racquet over her head, which would at least end the most horrendous game of tennis she'd ever played.

"You're doing well." Wiping the sweat off his forehead, he glanced at her racquet. She'd been wrong. He didn't want to break his own; he'd rather smash *hers* over her head. "Your racquet probably needs restringing if you haven't used it in years. Or you might even want a new one."

He almost implied that he'd play again with her. Gwen laughed. "It's hard to know if I need a new racquet, since this one has made so little contact with the ball today."

"Yeah, yeah, yeah." Adam rested his free hand on the net, a fraction of an inch from hers. As he gazed into her eyes, she felt herself blush. "You're looking a little flushed. Do you want to keep playing, or go grab a lemonade or something?"

Her current flush wouldn't be helped by lemonade, but any liquid sounded good on her throat. "I brought a thermos of water. Want to take a quick drink from it and keep playing?"

"I don't know." He slid her a sideways glance, but he was grinning. "I might have boy germs."

"I'll risk it."

———

"In my opinion, you're taking too big a risk." Vivian's oncologist, Dr. Lauren—or Monica, as everyone except Vivian called her—stood near the head of Vivian's bed in the ICU. Gwen's dad stood on the other side. Mac and Gwen huddled together at the foot of the bed.

The latest test results hadn't been good. After delivering the news to the family early Sunday afternoon, Monica offered various options, recommending some over others. The one Vivian chose—doing nothing—hadn't been among them.

"Maybe we should talk." The plea in her dad's voice made Gwen's heart constrict. "You haven't had a chance to think about it, Viv."

Vivian's voice had weakened. She swallowed a few times before croaking out an answer. "I've spent a month flat on my back. If I haven't been thinking, what do you think I've been doing?"

Monica held up a hand, looking at each of Gwen's parents in turn. "You're both right." She was good. "Even if you've spent a lifetime thinking about possibilities, none of us expected such a sudden turn for the worse. You should talk about it—all four of you. It's your decision, Vivian, but at times like this, families count."

Vivian flicked an oddly nervous glance at Gwen. The pain in her mother's eyes made Gwen's own eyes burn. "I'm well aware of that, Doctor." Vivian held out her hand to Monica. "Thank you for seeing us on a Sunday. And for your honesty. I think I'd like to be alone with Skip and my children now."

"Good." Monica touched Vivian's shoulder, shook hands with the other three, and offered Mac a small smile before turning back to Vivian. "And you're welcome. I've enjoyed getting to know all of you. You're a remarkable woman, Vivian. I envy your family."

It wasn't quite the way Gwen would've put it.

She looked at Monica but didn't catch her eye. The physician turned and left the room, closing the door behind her.

Alone with her family, Gwen felt the sterile emptiness of the ICU room, barren of flowers or other reminders of friends and loved ones. Now it lacked even the team of nurses who took turns fussing and fiddling with the mind-boggling array of monitors, wires, and tubes. The room was a far cry from the one they'd given Vivian on her last stay here, which had over-flowed with gifts, visitors, and a constant stream of activity.

Mac, silent since Monica had shared her diagnosis, moved closer to Vivian and took her hand. "I don't under-stand, Mom. Monica says they've already had some success with that drug in clinical trials. Why not do it? What do you lose?"

"Besides my hair?" Vivian struggled, weakly, pointing to her head, where her chic and always-perfect blond haircut had been replaced by thinning hair in an indistinct shade of her natural gray. A few bald patches dotted her scalp.

Gwen's dad ran a loving hand through Vivian's hair. "Your hair looks fine, Viv. I hope that's not what's troubling you."

"I didn't say it was. Not that dying doesn't . . . trouble me." She chewed her lower lip as Mac brushed the back of his hand against her cheek. "I didn't want to die so soon."

"But you don't have to." Mac patted Vivian's hand. "You heard Monica. The new drug therapy gives you a chance. You could—"

"—spend a few more weeks or months lying in this bed?

Or another bed?" Vivian motioned to the plastic water pitcher on the bedside table, and Gwen's dad refilled her cup, handing it to her. She sipped through the straw before speaking. "I can't do anything. I can't eat, I can't sleep, and the terrible pain and nausea exhaust me. I don't want to live like this."

No one spoke at first. Feeling her eyes fill, Gwen turned away to wipe them.

"If you need to leave, dear . . ." Vivian, her voice even weaker, had misinterpreted her momentary need to turn away from everyone.

"Uh, no, Mom." She hadn't willingly called Vivian "Mom" in at least twenty years, if not longer. Tears clogged her throat. "I was just—"

"—trying valiantly not to be another weepy female." His back to their parents, Mac walked up to Gwen and waved a hand at her wet eyes. She stuck her tongue out at him. "Now I find out. I've got a wimp for a sister."

"A wimp who can still take you down. I don't care how tall you've gotten." She clenched her fist, knowing his bicep was as hard as a rock. Thank God he'd never call her bluff.

"Now, children." Vivian spoke the words she'd uttered a thousand times in their childhood, when Mac kept trying to prove he wasn't three years younger than Gwen, and Gwen kept trying to remind him he was. They both grinned. "Please stop that."

Vivian briefly closed her eyes again, then opened them. "Your father is right. I suppose we should talk."

"I'm a selfish man, Viv." Gwen's dad held Vivian's hand, rubbing it in a soothing motion. "I want you with me—with all of us—for as long as possible."

"Yeah, Mom, me too. Stay here with us." Returning to the

head of the bed, Mac grabbed Vivian's other hand and chimed in. "Please?"

Gwen couldn't find any words. Despite the beseeching looks leveled at her by her brother and dad, nothing budged past the lump in her throat.

She met her mother's quiet, searching gaze. Nodding, Vivian acknowledged Gwen's silence, even though she couldn't possibly understand how Gwen felt. Gwen didn't understand it herself.

Vivian offered a slight smile. "Men are selfish, although quite wonderful in their own way. Women are more realistic about life. Isn't that right, Gwen?"

Three heads turned in her direction. Gwen looked at the floor, scraping the bottom of her sandal against it, much as Sarah might do in an awkward moment. "I'm not sure about that. I'd like you to stick around, too."

"Are you sure you want to come?" Pausing with her hand on the passenger door handle of Gwen's Honda, Leila looked across the roof at Gwen. "I mean, I obviously love having you tag along to book lovers' night, but you're finally patching things up with your mom. Maybe you want to spend the evening at the hospital."

"Please." Opening her door, Gwen slid behind the wheel and fastened her seatbelt. "We haven't patched things up. And I stopped in for a quick visit after work. I could use a break."

Leila fastened her own seatbelt and smoothed out her bright-red skirt. As usual, its hem was only slightly higher than Mount Everest. "But you've made a start. I'm proud of you. Really proud. I can't imagine your mom's reaction to being called 'Mom.' It must've blown her socks off."

"They were underneath a sheet at the time. You'll have to ask her yourself." Gwen waited for a group of neighborhood kids on bikes to pass before pulling into the street. Recognizing a couple of them, she waved. Nick used to hang out with them, in the days BC. Before Computer.

Ignoring the first blasts of air-conditioning, Leila rolled down her window and hung out an arm. "What I wouldn't give for a convertible on an evening like this." She pointed at the kids who'd biked past, now a hundred yards down the street and almost at the corner. "Then maybe we could pick up a couple of boys, although those ones look a little young."

"Just a little." Smiling, Gwen shook her head. "Don't you already have enough boys in your life? How do you keep them straight?"

Leila tilted her head toward the window, letting the breeze play with the ends of her hair. "The contact list on my phone and a good mind for details. How about you?"

"Me?" Gwen's eyebrows rose. "Are you kidding?"

Leila's smirk was almost bigger than her face. "Reliable sources tell me you were spotted playing tennis this weekend with a certain piano teacher we all know and love. And although I normally hate to bring up painful subjects, you had quite a romp in the sheets with—"

"Don't remind me. Please." Gwen drove slowly through the city streets, passing Lakewood Cemetery and turning onto Hennepin Avenue. They passed several groups of kids running, biking, and playing kickball. The recent return to school must leave them bursting with energy. Gwen couldn't remember what that felt like. "Tucker was, as you and I both now know, a one-time mistake. And Adam—"

Leila practically jumped in her seat. "Yes?"

"We talked a bit after my lesson on Friday, and I told him I wanted to start playing sports again." Gwen stared down Leila, daring her to contradict her. "So Adam called up on the spur of the moment Saturday, asking me to play. Tennis."

"Glad you clarified that." Leila hooted.

"Hmpf." Jon's bookstore was a few more blocks away, in Uptown. Gwen started scanning for open parking places. They usually had to walk a block or two. "I'd just spent several awful hours at the hospital, and I needed a break. The exercise felt good. That's all."

"If you say so." Leila smiled sweetly, which meant she didn't believe a word. There was no point trying to convince her. "But I still wish we were tooling around in a convertible. It'd be a kick."

Spotting a tight parking place a block from Jon's store, Gwen parallel parked, drawing an appreciative whistle from Leila.

She breathed a sigh of relief. All three cars still had unblemished fenders. "I used to have one when I was with Rob. It's not that big a deal."

Other than the fact that she remembered her old Saab every single day from April through October, it really wasn't a big deal. The Honda Civic took her where she needed to go. She didn't mind. Much.

"You've got to be kidding." From the scornful look on Leila's face, her friend didn't believe it any more than Gwen did.

Gwen opened her door. "Why would I kid about that? I had a Saab convertible. It wasn't practical."

"That's the whole point of convertibles." Stepping onto the sidewalk, Leila adjusted her skirt. Compared to her, Gwen felt a little plain in her sky-blue silk slacks and a matching top that had looked better in the mirror. "You're not looking for practical. You're looking for fresh air . . . and possibly men."

"I wasn't looking for men at the time. Not that I'd drive a convertible to chase after men." Ignoring Leila's knowing look, Gwen caught up to her on the sidewalk. They walked to the bookstore in relative silence, broken only by Leila's periodic exclamations over the displays she saw in almost every store window they passed.

Jon Abelard greeted them before they'd even made it to the door of Books and Ab's. Next, he'd have valet parking.

"Leila! And Gwen! I'm so glad you're joining us again." After hugging Leila, Jon started to offer a hug to Gwen before abruptly turning it into a two-handed handclasp.

Leila tucked her hand into the crook of his arm before marching him back inside the store. Gwen followed a few feet behind the dynamic duo.

"Have you read tonight's book?" Jon turned back to Gwen, smiling at her, probably trying to make her feel more included than in fact she did. She was used to skiing in Leila's wake. "The love scene in the church parking lot has to be one of the most inventive I've ever read."

She couldn't quite picture Jon analyzing love scenes.

"Uh, no." Gwen glanced quickly at Leila, hoping she wasn't offending Jon by not having read the book. "I had a hard week, and Leila talked me into coming at the last minute. I hope it's okay."

"Don't be silly." Leila paused a moment, forcing Jon to stop while she looped her free hand through Gwen's arm. "Jon and the gang are thrilled to have you." She turned to Jon. "Last week was Gwen's worst week on record. And, believe me, that's saying something."

"It's not like—"

"—like you don't have awful things happen to you all the

time?" Leila squeezed Gwen's arm. "But you're turning it around. It's just taking a little longer than I expected."

Jon peeked around Leila at Gwen. "Selfishly, I hope you'll take your time fixing whatever it is." He looked curious but must've considered it rude to ask questions. Unlike Leila. "I think I'm Leila's next project." He pretended to shudder.

"Oh, you." Leila picked up her pace, dragging Gwen and Jon along with her. "You'll love my help. In the meantime, let's tear into that book. I can't believe those three nuns didn't notice the car bouncing like that."

Wow. Gwen decided to pick up a copy of tonight's book, even though it'd be too late for book club. Maybe she could borrow Leila's copy if she hadn't drooled on it too much.

"Just don't go spiking the punch again, Leila." Jon greeted another customer, then ushered the two women into a brightly lit room at the side of the store, where ten women and a few men stood around munching on cookies. "Please. Carol O'Melveny needed a ride home last time."

Laughing, Leila patted her bulging purse. "Best thing to happen to that woman all year."

———

"Here are my comments on the Carruthers board minutes. Not many—nice job." Danny dropped the paperclipped pages on Gwen's desk. She scanned the few red marks on the top page without looking up.

"Thanks. I'll have Becky turn it around this morning."

"No rush." He dropped into the chair across from her, drawing her gaze. "I don't expect to get much done today. Becky would rather have us focus on celebrating her birthday. Are you still up for lunch? The three of us?"

Gwen looked at her calendar, her eyes wide. "I can't believe I forgot."

"I can."

She'd been sleepwalking through her job since last Tuesday, when they'd found Ted. And maybe for a while longer than that. Gwen had hoped no one had noticed, since she'd worked hard to keep up with her workload.

"Don't get me wrong." Danny brushed a hand through his hair, which—as always—looked like it needed a haircut. Or at least a comb. "There's nothing wrong with your work." He pointed at the board minutes he'd handed her. "Everything's great. But you're . . . I don't know. Not really here lately."

Gwen felt herself go numb. She couldn't afford to lose her job. Danny was a good friend, but he also happened to be a partner. A suddenly powerful partner. With Ted's death, Danny had inherited a million-dollar practice overnight.

"I-I—" She calmed herself, working not to stammer. "I've been here. I've left a little early a few times to visit my mother in the hospital, but I took work home or came in early to make up for it."

"No question. Taking care of things with your mom is your highest priority." Danny picked at a piece of lint on his knee. He'd been going after that same piece of lint since he sat down. Gwen hoped he nailed it soon. "I ought to know, since I took a few weeks off after my sister's accident last year. If anything, you should take *more* time, not less."

"But you said I haven't been here lately."

"I wasn't talking about your mom." He swiped at the piece of lint, apparently giving up. Finally, he looked at Gwen. "I mean that your head hasn't been here. I know it's been tough about Ted—"

Grateful for an excuse, Gwen broke in. "Yes. It has."

Danny pursed his lips. "But I don't think that's it. Or, at least, it's not the whole story."

He didn't have enough hours in the day for her whole story. Divorced, with an ex who'd convinced her she was a loser and two kids who thought the jackass shot the moon. Her mother, with whom she'd fought since the dawn of time, was dying, and now they'd never have a chance to resolve things. Her old—married—boyfriend had slept with her for kicks. Her piano teacher, who slept with everyone else, wouldn't come near her with a ten-foot piano.

And she was practically forty. Half dead.

That was just for starters.

She ran a shaky hand through her hair. "You can't blame me for being upset about Ted. It's not just his death. He was so weird before he killed himself. And now it can't be fixed."

"Insider trading can be fixed with enough money. That's being taken care of." Danny's gaze bored a hole into her. "Ted had issues. They weren't completely unusual, though, considering the type of guy he was. Asking you out all those times was obnoxious, but it wasn't weird. You're great, Gwen. Everyone thinks so."

"They think so only because I'm the one who bakes a fucking cake for practically every goddamned person's birthday around here." Appalled, she covered her mouth. It hadn't bugged her—not really—until a secretary two floors down had called Gwen yesterday, requesting a birthday cake in a way that sounded like a demand. She didn't even know the woman.

But today she'd forgotten to bake a cake for her own secretary.

She'd have to stop by Wuollet's Bakery the moment Danny left her office.

Blinking, Danny stared hard at her. "See? It's not just Ted. What's happening, Gwen? What's eating you up?"

"Nothing." Nothing she'd share with a partner—even a young partner she considered a friend. She didn't whine, and she liked the thought of keeping her job. It paid the bills, even if it didn't always thrill her.

He stood up. "Fine. I'd ply you with liquor and worm it out of you with Claudia's help, but we got SEC comments today on the Treadman deal. The sooner we turn them around, the sooner we can call the shareholder meetings." Pausing at the door, he poked his head into the hall before turning back to her. "The market hasn't been kind to the deal, especially with the allegations against Ted, and Tina Michaels at Treadman wants it to happen. Fast."

"Do you need my help?"

Her shoulders sagged, the weight of the world feeling especially heavy today. She'd hoped to cut out early so she could spend some time with Nick after school. His home-room teacher had called first thing this morning, asking why Nick had missed two days of school last week. It'd been news to Gwen. Still, she felt obligated to make the offer to Danny.

"Thanks, but George and I have it handled." He rapped his knuckles on the doorjamb, drawing her attention. "Take care of yourself. It's been too long since I've seen you smile."

Normally, Danny was the one person in the office she could count on to make her smile. And after a few drinks, laugh.

She tried to smile. Her face felt like it cracked.

"Nice try." He looked at Gwen with kind but sad eyes, older than his years. "Life's short, Gwen. If this place isn't making you happy, do something about it."

Right. Quit. And lose her house and her kids in the

bargain, since she wouldn't have the money to support herself or them. "No, thanks. I'll stick it out."

Danny snapped his fingers, as if he'd just thought of something. Gwen suspected he hadn't. "I almost forgot. You know the firm has that tuition reimbursement program. You're eligible for it after two years. By my calculation, that was sometime this summer."

"July twelfth." She groaned. Danny was trying to be thoughtful, but he had no idea. "It's a little late for fall semester, though, and I'm not exactly eager to take on even more burdens than I already have. I'd rather go in the opposite direction."

"I'm not talking about a basket-weaving class." Frowning, Danny patted his pockets, as if searching for something. His hands came up empty. "Or even a seminar on securities filings. You don't need more of that crap."

"Then what do I need?"

He smiled. "Law school. I've been thinking about this for a while. The LSATs are in a few weeks. You could start school next fall." Seeing her blank stare, he kept talking. "You're the brightest paralegal we've got, and you're bored here." He waved his hand at her. "Don't even try to deny it to old Danny. I know you better than you think."

Gwen sucked in a breath, stunned at the unexpected turn in the conversation. Law school. Danny had obviously started using illegal drugs. He was hallucinating right here in her office.

"If you know me so well, it won't surprise you that I'll be forty next month." She crossed her arms, smirking at him.

"So?" Frowning, he didn't look even remotely impressed by her logic. Or by her upcoming birthday. "Will the LSAT exam interfere with your birthday party or something?"

"Not likely. I'll be hiding under a rock somewhere that

day." Hard to believe that Danny had graduated from Harvard. She had to explain everything to him. "Danny, law school takes three years. By the time I'm done, I'd be forty-three, almost forty-four."

He shook his head. "Like they say—how old will you be in three years if you *don't* go to law school?" He didn't wait for her to answer. "Think about it, Gwen. You could go to the University of Minnesota or one of the other local law schools, working part-time. The firm will cover your tuition. Or at least part of it."

"You're crazy, Danny. Ted's weirdness got to you."

"Yeah." His lips quirked. "Does that mean I'll have to start pestering you for dates? I'm not sure I'm up for that."

She threw her legal pad at him.

CHAPTER 13

"I thought you *liked* skirts now."

Trudging inside the house after a tough day at work—highlighted by the delivery of an LSAT application from the irrepressible Danny—and a short but difficult visit with Vivian, Gwen felt and probably looked as crumpled as the black skirt she'd bought Sarah for tonight's dance. The skirt lay in a heap at the foot of the stairs.

"Oh, Mom." Sarah's voice called from upstairs. "Like, I don't *think* so."

Had it really been so long since Gwen had been a teenager?

"But you wore one to school last week. It looked cute." In a virginal hooker sort of way. But Sarah obviously needed encouragement.

"Cute?" Sarah followed her rejected skirt down the stairs. "No wonder everyone practically barfed all over it."

If true, the school cafeteria might actually be the culprit, but it was more likely that her daughter was exaggerating. "You just felt different. I'm sure everyone liked it, even if the shock of seeing your knees in a skirt instead of gym shorts sent a couple of them off to the hospital on a stretcher."

Sarah didn't laugh. She gave Gwen a high-school-sized glare that was mostly undone by the freckles scattered across her pert little nose. "Oh, Mom. It was totally gross."

"We both know that Leila doesn't buy gross clothes, and wearing skirts is part of growing up for a lot of girls. Like it or not, you looked cute—" She shrugged at Sarah's raised eyebrows. "Sorry. I meant good looking. The fact is, boys are going to notice you more now. They probably already check you out, even in your gym shorts, but I'm sure it feels safer when you're wearing gym shorts or jeans."

"Oh, Mom." Sarah cringed, probably disgusted at Gwen's reference to anyone checking out her daughter—as if her mom would even know about such things. "This isn't gonna turn into one of your birds-and-bees talks, is it? I already know all that stuff."

"I'm sure you do. I don't even want to think about it."

"I'm gonna wear jeans." Sarah's fists rested where her hips might someday exist. "So quit bugging me."

"Me?" Gwen smiled. "I wouldn't dream of it."

Sarah blinked, looking as if she hadn't expected to win the war without at least a minor skirmish. "Hey, don't you have another dopey piano lesson tonight?"

"Sure do." Gwen glanced at the clock, wondering if she had time to change. Maybe. If Nick was safely occupied—for a change—and Sarah didn't need a ride to the dance. "Who are you going to the dance with?"

Squinting at Gwen, Sarah answered carefully. "Um, Diana and Kelly?"

Sounded safe enough. "Do you need a ride? Or is one of their parents picking you up?"

"I . . . don't need a ride." Still in her shorts from volleyball practice, Sarah scuffed the toe of one sock against the floor, staring down at it. "Aren't you, uh, heading out soon? I thought you had piano."

"I do." Gwen frowned. She still needed to check on Nick and, if possible, change into something more comfortable. "But I can give you a ride. How are you getting to the dance? I don't mind you girls walking together on the way over to school, but you need a ride home. It'll be dark by then."

At the rate she was going, Sarah's toe would soon peek through her sock. "No problem. We've got a ride."

"With Diana's parents? Or Kelly's?"

"Uh, I guess I asked Dad for a ride. Him and Tiffany."

Gwen couldn't close her open jaw if she tried. "Your dad? Tiffany? That—"

"It's not like that, Mom. Tiffany's cool. I wanted the girls to meet her. She, like, wears the coolest clothes and just sorta knows what it's like."

Being approximately fourteen herself, Tiffany would.

"I don't understand. And I can't believe your father agreed. Are you *sure* he'll give you a ride?" Memories of the weekend he'd cancelled on the kids without warning came crashing back. Gwen had gotten a dog—briefly—in the bargain.

Rob would probably send her a Doberman this time.

"Oh, yeah. It's totally cool. Dad'll be great."

———

"Not so great." At Adam's words, Gwen glanced up sharply. Standing behind her, he peered over her shoulder at the sheet music and the position of her hands on the keys. He shrugged. "Sorry. You just seem distracted tonight. Another rough week?"

Other than learning her daughter preferred Rob and his

little girlfriend over her, it hadn't been bad. Not if she compared it to Ted's suicide and the fiasco with Tucker the week before.

She'd avoided stupid sex and dead bodies all week. She just hadn't expected Sarah to slam her in the solar plexus.

"I've had worse." She rubbed her hands, then fluttered them over the keys. Tchaikovsky led her list of favorite composers, and the music of *Swan Lake* might be her favorite. At least, it had been until she'd heard herself play it just now. Adam's assessment had been kind. "I'll try again. In between work and trips to the hospital, I haven't had as much time to practice as I'd like, but I can do better."

Adam nodded. "I'm counting on it. The competition is two weeks from tomorrow."

"Don't remind me."

"Two weeks from tomorrow. Two weeks from tomorrow." Laughing, he squeezed her shoulders, then gave them an impromptu massage.

Adam's hands were wasted on a piano.

"It's hard to complain about your constant reminders when your hands work such magic on me." She blushed but went in deeper, wishing she could be more like Leila when she grew up. "I didn't know how badly I needed it."

"Stick with me, kid." Nudging her to one side, Adam sat down next to her on the bench. "If you play your cards right, there's more where that came from."

She probably wouldn't know what to do with it.

The moment passed. Adam was again serious. He probably hadn't even intended any sexual innuendo in his words and wanted only her best performance for the competition. Sighing, Gwen realized that she should be grateful he saw so much promise in her. It felt like a lifetime since anyone else had.

Twenty minutes later, as Gwen hit the last note with a flourish, Adam clapped. Loudly. Sticking his thumb and one finger between his teeth, he even whistled in ear-splitting Leila style.

"It wasn't *that* good." She blushed, peeking through her bangs at Adam, who still crowded her on the piano bench. He usually alternated between sitting on the padded stool next to the bench and pacing behind her while she played.

He wrapped his arm around her waist, deepening her blush. "All I ask is that you play your heart out. And you did. We've got some work to do before the competition, but you're in good shape." Grabbing her side, he squeezed. "Yep, very good shape."

That provoked a flurry of mindless stuttering, interrupted by Adam's other arm, which snaked around her stomach, catching her in a sweet but awkward hug. He topped it off with a kiss on her cheek, ending on a loud smack.

Brotherly stuff. Younger brotherly stuff. He didn't mean anything by it.

His hands lingered, holding her a little tighter, and his lips hovered near her ear. As Adam's breath fanned her cheek, she felt her temperature rise several degrees. It was a little early for hot flashes.

Utter mortification had never felt so good.

Then it was over. Just like that, Adam released her and hopped off the bench, striding across the room. Halfway to the far wall, he halted mid-stride and spoke without looking back at her. "Can I, uh, get you a glass of wine? Or a beer?"

She'd promised Nick she'd be home by eight, and she half expected a teary phone call from Sarah, begging for a ride home from the dance after Rob and Bimbo bagged out again.

Regret and relief warred within her. She wished she could stay, maybe see if Adam's hands might work some more magic, but she wasn't sure she was up to it. Just when she'd hoped she was ready again to play with grown-ups, Tucker had really thrown her for a loop.

Lurching to her feet, she gathered her music and found her purse. "Sorry, but I have to pass this time." Adam looked as disappointed as the dog she'd flung back at Rob. Somehow, it surprised her. "I wish I could stay. Rain check?"

He shrugged, offering a curiously sad smile. "Rain or shine, the offer stands."

"Good." On an impulse, she walked over and kissed his cheek, then headed for the door before she did anything else that would only embarrass her further. "I'll look forward to it."

———

The blank eyes staring through her and the pale, wan face didn't remotely resemble Vivian Withers. Seemingly overnight, her mother had become a hollow shadow of the vibrant woman she'd been only weeks ago. Or even days ago.

"Hello, dear." Her mother's weak voice mirrored her body, a hoarse whisper in a room where she could've heard a pin drop. Moved on Wednesday from the ICU to a large private room in the oncology wing of Kendall South, Vivian seemed dwarfed not only by the room but also by her bed.

"Hi . . . Mom." Gwen shivered, trying to hide her reaction from Vivian but unable to stop it. She flicked a glance at her dad and Mac, whose tired eyes stared almost as blankly.

For the past week, her dad had stood guard in Vivian's room at least fifteen hours a day—and sometimes twenty-four. It made Gwen feel guilty for stopping in only for an hour or so most nights after work.

Sarah, despite begging Gwen a week ago to let her see her

grandparents and Mac, kept making excuses not to go to the hospital.

Gwen couldn't really blame her.

Mac's schedule might account for the sheer exhaustion that left him on the verge of keeling over. He'd driven three hours to Duluth Monday morning after a long weekend at the hospital, then another three hours back here late last night after work. Despite a string of lengthy trials on his fall schedule, he'd almost cancelled his workload for the week. Vivian had talked him out of it, but she'd admitted she hoped she could see him again this weekend. He hadn't disappointed her.

Gwen, bringing up the rear, hadn't arrived at the hospital today until five minutes ago, just before noon. Guilt washed over her, but the frequency of its appearance lately made her almost not notice. Sarah had volleyball practice on Saturday mornings, and Gwen had gone to watch, dragging Nick along only by promising him he could play on his computer this afternoon. Rob had done his duty last night, to Sarah's overly enthusiastic pleasure, and Gwen half expected him to show up at practice.

Now that he was parent of the year.

He hadn't shown, but she'd seethed in anticipation the entire two hours she'd spent in the bleachers, one of only three parents there.

"How are the . . . children, dear?" Every word presented a challenge to Vivian, who struggled to smile.

At this point, her dad and Mac didn't bother trying.

"Uh, pretty good, Mom. Sarah's the star of the varsity volleyball team, even though she's only a freshman. I watched her practice this morning." Vivian nodded, the slightest movement of her head. "And Nick's, well, still interested in computers."

To say the least. After interrogating him for an hour on Wednesday, the day his homeroom teacher ratted him out to Gwen, he'd admitted that he'd wandered around the neighborhood until she left for work, then come back home to "work" on his computer. He'd snarled when she called it "play," stunning her with his blunt hostility.

Nick was turning into a problem child, and Gwen felt helpless to stop it. She'd hoped to pull Mac aside for a little advice on boys, but the sight that greeted her at the hospital shoved that issue onto the back burner.

She looked again at her mother, her remaining strands of gray hair matted against the pillow. Vivian had finally agreed, after much pleading from her husband and kids, to try the recommended drug therapy. For the first time, Gwen wondered if they'd been wrong. From this angle, prolonging her mother's life—and pain—didn't look like such a brilliant idea.

Vivian's body had shrunk by at least another ten pounds, resembling a skeleton under the sheet and blankets that didn't seem able to keep her warm. Gwen had missed Dr. Lauren's morning visit, but the looks on her dad's and brother's faces told her she hadn't missed any good news. She wouldn't make them repeat it in front of Vivian, but she hoped to catch Mac in the hall when he left to grab lunch.

Her mouth dry, Gwen couldn't stomach the thought of lunch. Or of losing Vivian, just when she had a hope—only a trace of a hope, maybe, but the first one in decades—of finding her.

After the difficult scene in the ICU last Sunday, when Gwen had choked out both the word "Mom" and her desire to keep Vivian in her life for as long as she could, the two women had forged a fragile truce in their decades-long war.

Gwen didn't know how to end the war. It was too early for either side—or both—to declare a victory. Or peace.

Her mother wouldn't be in the battle much longer.

No one made a move toward the basement cafeteria. Having just arrived, Gwen couldn't be the one to suggest it. Clearing his throat, her dad spoke. "Gwen, we had a visit from Monica this morning. And we've done some talking."

So much for sparing Vivian from depressing conversation.

She looked from her dad to Mac, avoiding her mother's gaze. "Without me?" She stared at the floor, hurt stabbing her. "So, uh, what did you guys decide?"

Her mother's eyelids fluttered open, her weak voice intruding. "We didn't . . . decide anything, dear." Her pale blue eyes searched Gwen's face. "We wouldn't do that without you."

Her struggle to form those words had an immediate effect. Grimacing in pain, Vivian closed her eyes again, her face paler than before. Gwen felt like a jerk for questioning her family. She'd always felt left out, left behind, and she figured . . . well, this time, wrong.

"Of course not, honey." Her dad clutched Vivian's hand, straining with the effort not to crush it. His eyes, close to unfamiliar tears, flashed at Gwen. "But Monica admits it's not going well for your mother. The drugs aren't helping, and you can—" He swiped his free hand at his wet eyes. "You can see that your mother is having a tough time of it."

Vivian's eyes didn't open, but she spoke. "It's not that bad, dear. Not really."

"You're a trouper, Mom." Mac brushed a hand across his face in the general direction of his own eyes. "No doubt about it."

Gwen moved closer to Vivian, leaving her customary

position at the foot of the bed, and reached for her hand. It felt ice cold. She patted it awkwardly, wishing she could show the same physical warmth to her mother that had always come easily with Sarah and Nick. Determined to try harder, she held her mother's hand in both her own, rubbing it lightly.

It felt pretty weird. Embarrassed, she looked only at her mother, not wanting to see the knowing grins her dad and brother were probably exchanging at that very moment.

"What do you want to do . . . Mom?" The word still stuck in her throat. "What else did Monica say?"

Her dad answered. "At this point, Monica doesn't think the drug therapy will do much more than perhaps extend your mother's life a short period. She can't predict how long. She also doesn't know how long your mother—" His voice broke, and Mac quickly put his arm around their dad, hugging him. "How long she has with us."

"Oh, Dad." Gwen squeezed her mother's hand. "Mom, I'm so sorry." The hollow in the pit of her stomach grew to gargantuan size, threatening to turn her inside out. "Mac, I—"

She broke down, tears rolling in waves down her cheeks. For her mom, her dad, for Mac. For herself. For all the years she hadn't tried harder to understand her mother or let her mother get closer. For all the years she hadn't bothered to try at all.

Head down, Gwen heard footsteps, felt someone's arm come around her. Mostly, she just felt numb. Sick.

A hand tugged her gently to the foot of Vivian's bed, where she collapsed into a chair. She looked up into Mac's face, where a trail of his own tears had left their mark. Their dad kept his vigil, holding Vivian's hand. Breathing softly, Vivian appeared to be sleeping. Or already gone? Gwen gasped, her quick cry caught by her hand over her mouth.

Vivian's eyelids fluttered open. Three heads leaned forward to catch her whispered words. "Don't be sad, dear. I'm . . . prepared for it now."

Silent, his eyes bright with unshed tears, Gwen's dad looked at the ceiling.

Gwen gazed around the room, at three people she'd never really gotten to know. Even her dad and Mac, close to her in many ways, seemed like strangers. "B-but I don't want you to go, Mom. I-I don't even know you yet."

Bitter tears flooded her eyes, leaving patches of wetness on the Eagles T-shirt she'd worn to Sarah's volleyball practice, even though the Eagles now annoyed her almost as much as Tucker did.

"I'm . . . sorry, dear." Closing her eyes again, Vivian faded into a peaceful sleep.

———

"Knock, knock." Late Sunday afternoon, Leila poked her head inside the open front door of Gwen's house. Looking around wildly, Gwen stuffed the papers she'd been reading underneath her on the sofa. Her neighbor, in black skinny jeans and a fluorescent yellow top, hooted. "Nice try, girl-friend, but your butt's not big enough." She slapped her own. "Try this one on for size."

"No, thanks." Gwen smiled, but she wasn't coughing up the papers unless Leila knocked her off the sofa. And she wouldn't put it past her. "What's new?"

Approaching, Leila looked to each side of Gwen, probably deciding which angle to attack from. "Not much with me. From the looks of it, though, whatever egg you're laying on that sofa is new. Spill."

"It's nothing." Gwen brushed back a wisp of her hair,

then tried crossing her legs until she realized the movement exposed more of the papers. She brought her leg back down on the papers just as Leila swooped in to make a grab for them.

"Ha! Got it!" Scanning the sheets, Leila's triumphant grin faded. "I don't understand. The LSAT? Isn't that an exam for law school or med school or something?"

"Law school." Avoiding Leila's penetrating gaze, Gwen glanced down at the coffee table. She really should dust it one of these days.

Leila kept reading. "So who's thinking about law school?" She dropped the papers on the coffee table.

"No one." Gwen's gaze moved to the rocking chair across the room. Its wooden arms probably needed dusting, too. Like everything else in this house. "Me. I don't know." Getting up, she walked to the back-hall closet, where she kept the dust wipes.

A hand grabbed Gwen, stopping her. "Hold it."

"I'll be right back." Leila's grip slowed Gwen's forward progress but didn't stop her altogether. "I need to dust the rocking chair."

One eyebrow went up. "Almost every time I see you, you're rocking a hole in the floor with that chair. When did it manage to gather dust?"

"Oh, you know." Slipping out of Leila's light grasp, Gwen went to the closet and found the dust wipes. On a mission, she headed for the rocking chair, stopping when she realized it didn't have any dust whatsoever. It gleamed. Sarah must've actually done her chores yesterday after practice. Next thing she knew, Nick would leave his computer and rejoin society.

"Don't you stay busy enough with work and piano and PTA and all those nutty neighborhood things you do? You're now stooping to housework?" Leila's mouth twisted in distaste.

"I'm not doing PTA this year." She ignored Leila, whose eyes popped open. "And Sally Knowles volunteered to be in charge of the next neighborhood party. I think it's Halloween."

"Did you claw Sally's eyes out? Isn't that your turf?"

"Of course not." Okay, it had been, but only for the last two years. She'd gone rigid when Sally had asked, right in the middle of Gwen's Labor Day barbecue, and had to remind herself to breathe. But lately the idea had grown on her. Someone else's turn. She'd resigned from the PTA board the same week.

Grabbing the wipes from Gwen, Leila held them at arm's length. "You're not getting these back until you explain. What's going on? Law school? Giving up all your activities? What happened to the Gwen we knew and loved?"

"I'm still here." Gwen feinted to one side, then snatched back the wipes. She needed something to do, and she couldn't go near the LSAT application until Leila left. "Look. You told me to take some baby steps. I changed my hair, I'm taking piano lessons. I played tennis."

"Once."

"It still counts." Gwen dropped onto the sofa, Leila following her. "Danny Fitzsimmons suggested law school. I'm just thinking about it. About a lot of things."

"Your mother's situation is hitting you pretty hard."

"She's dying, Leila. How else am I supposed to take it?"

"It's just that, I mean, you've never been close. I don't know—" Leila grimaced, for once in her life unable to express herself. "I wasn't completely sure you even cared."

She hadn't known she cared, either, about a mother

who'd seemed stiff and cold her whole life. Until now, when it was too late to do a damned thing about it.

Gwen closed her eyes. Her latest round of tears had ended only ten minutes before Leila had stopped by. God, she hated it. The whole damn thing. Her mother dying, crying, being weak. She hated anyone seeing her like this.

For once in her life, she wished Leila would leave.

Leila pressed a pillow into Gwen's arms until she hugged it. "I don't mean it badly, Gwen. It's often harder to lose someone you've had a less than ideal relationship with."

"Tell me about it." Gwen crossed her arms, willing herself not to cry. "You haven't lost anyone, have—" She broke off, remembering Leila's brief marriage, which had ended with her much-older husband's death on their honeymoon. She'd always figured Leila hadn't given it another thought. She never mentioned the man. Gwen didn't even know his name.

"Only my husband." A wry grin crossed Leila's face, but her eyes lacked their usual sparkle. "Patrick and I had an unusual relationship by most people's standards. We were still getting to know each other. I think I loved him, but I didn't know him. Not really. I didn't know how to handle his death." She brushed some imaginary dirt off her jeans. "I got a lot of helpful suggestions about how to spend his money, though."

Gwen sucked in a breath, thinking of the many crass jokes that neighbors had made over the years about Leila's "good fortune." While too loyal to echo their cutting words out loud, she'd wondered about the nature of Leila's marriage.

She didn't know her friend any better than she knew her mom. Sinking even lower, she shook her head.

Leila waved a hand. "Don't worry about it. Ancient history, right? I'm just saying I know it's hard. I haven't lost either of my parents yet, and I hope it doesn't happen anytime soon."

"I hope not, either." She kept praying, against the odds, that her mother would recover and become her mother again. Maybe for the first time.

"Hey, enough morbid stuff." Reaching for the LSAT materials on the table, Leila flipped through the pages. "So you're thinking about law school. This is what I get for telling you to take a few baby steps. Next thing I know, you're jumping into the deep end." She whistled. "Looks hard. And the deadline's coming up." She tapped her leg, calculating the dates out loud. "It's next Friday? You don't have much time."

"I know." Gwen shrugged. "My piano competition is in two weeks, my mom is close to dying, and now I have to decide about law school."

"Your piano competition?" Leila's eyebrows rose an inch.

"Oh, did I forget to mention that?"

CHAPTER 14

"I can't do it." Tossing the LSAT materials on Danny's desk, Gwen backed toward the door. "I can't afford it, and I don't have the time right now to deal with this. I have too much going on."

Danny leaned back in his beat-up leather chair, a treasured hand-me-down from a partner who'd retired the year he joined the partner ranks. He didn't spare a glance at the papers she'd dropped on his desk. In all the clutter, he might not find them if he tried.

"You don't say." He sounded more like a senior partner every day. Next thing she knew, he might even start combing his hair.

"I appreciate your thinking of me like this, Danny, I really do, but it just wouldn't work." She held up her hands, trying to explain with circles in the air what she couldn't with words. "My job, my kids, my mom . . ." She shook her head. "Not now."

He picked up the LSAT materials but still didn't look at them. "I'll have Becky fill out the application for you. It's all online anyway." He pushed a button on his phone, buzzing their secretary.

Stunned, Gwen stepped closer, then made an inelegant grab for the papers. He held them over his head and out of her reach, the way Mac used to do when they played keep-away as kids. And sometimes as adults. "Didn't you hear what I said? I can't do this."

Becky's voice floated through the intercom. "Yes?"

"Could you come here? I've got something for you. Thanks." Releasing the button, he grinned. "You didn't say you don't want to do it. You said you can't. I'll help you with that."

Gwen sputtered. With Ted Harrison no longer around to bully everyone, Danny was stepping neatly into his shoes. He'd even started wearing bowties and suspenders—which made an odd match with his shaggy hair.

She glared at him. "You can't just—"

He held up his hand, cutting her off. "If you really don't want to, no one is going to make you. Not even Becky." Their secretary, who'd walked in and stood waiting for her assignment, looked startled. "I know you're tough, Becky, but you can't force Gwen to go to law school if she doesn't want to. Even if she'd be the star of her class."

"Gwen's going to law school?" Becky looked back and forth from Gwen to Danny. "What did I miss?"

"I'm not going to law school." Gwen jabbed a finger at Danny. "You missed Danny doing his impersonation of Ted. You know, ordering people around until they tremble when he comes down the hall. He's getting pretty good at it."

"Thanks." Danny snapped one of his suspenders. "I didn't think you'd notice."

She rolled her eyes. "Everyone noticed, and you heard me, Danny. I said no. Now, if you'll excuse me, *some* people around here have to work."

Pausing at the door, she watched Becky, pen and notepad

in hand, approach Danny's desk. Her bright-blue glasses kept slipping down her nose. "What did you want me to do?"

Gwen started to walk out but stopped when she caught Danny's response. "Here's a paper copy of the LSAT materials, but the application is online. I want you to . . ."

She whirled, took two quick strides, and snatched the LSAT materials out of his hand. As Becky gasped, she shook the papers at Danny. "If anyone's filling out the application, it'll be me. If and when I decide."

Danny didn't miss a beat. "Don't take too long!"

Clutching the papers, she slammed the door behind her.

She hurried past the lobby area and the receptionist's desk, headed back to her office. The shrill squeak of Aurora, the firm's receptionist who had a thing for tie-dyed clothing and purple hair, stopped her. "Gwen! Yoo hoo!"

Almost noon. She wasn't expecting any packages or visitors, and she didn't have lunch plans with anyone. In her rush, she hadn't noticed any clients in the lobby, but she'd had her head down as she went by.

Maybe a client had stopped in to sign or drop off documents for a securities filing. Anxious about the pressing cash needs of their start-up companies, some of them tried to speed things along by showing up in person.

Or maybe Aurora was just being friendly. Gwen had been nice to her when others in the office rolled their eyes at Aurora's hair and flowing garments or laughed behind her back. And not from too far away.

Maybe Aurora wanted Gwen to bake her a birthday cake.

Groaning, she turned back, forcing a smile.

At the sight of Tucker, her breath caught.

His elegantly tailored gray flannel slacks and navy blazer hadn't been bought off a rack. His confident expression also didn't come cheap. Gwen had paid for it two weeks ago with a pound of flesh—so to speak—in what might've been the most humiliating moment of her life.

After all the humiliations Rob had handed her, that said something.

"Tucker?" As she spoke, he rose from the chrome-and-leather sofa and brushed out the creases in his slacks, sending her a hopeful smile. She'd love to send a fist sailing right through the bright enamel gleaming at her. The presence of Aurora and an older couple in the lobby saved his teeth. For now. "What do you want?"

"Can we talk?" He took a few steps toward her but stopped, probably because he finally noticed her scowl. "Somewhere private?"

A wide-eyed Aurora hung on his words as her gaze swept him from head to toe. Yes, Tucker made an impression. With foolish women who didn't know enough to run like hell in the opposite direction when they saw him coming.

Gwen stared at Aurora until she caught the receptionist's gaze. With raised eyebrows, she forced Aurora's attention back to the delivery packages on her desk.

She turned back to Tucker. "We don't have anything to discuss."

Aurora's head popped up again at Gwen's clipped words and maybe the strong hint of an approaching train wreck. The older couple in the lobby looked up, too.

Jesus. She didn't want Tucker here, let alone in her office. It was small enough without adding six feet of arrogant male to it. She wasn't up to this, no matter how much Leila had coached her to handle the inevitable confrontation with him.

She didn't *want* to have to handle this.

"Please?" His boyish charm had always made her melt—and appeared to be working with Aurora and the white-haired woman in the lobby—but she'd seen an entirely different man two weeks ago. A married man whose kisses had wound up slicing her in half.

"No." She escorted him through the glass door leading to the bank of elevators, then stood apart from him, far enough to avoid the hand that tried to take hers. He'd already taken enough. "Go away, Tucker. I gave my heart to you a long time ago. I didn't mean to give you my pride, too."

"It wasn't like that—"

She pushed a button for the elevator and left him standing there. "Yes, it was."

Head high, she turned away and walked through the door to the lobby without looking back.

She held it together until she reached her office and slammed another door. For the second time in five minutes.

———

"We're going to have a happy family dinner, and you're both going to like it." Gwen sat down at the chipped and scratched kitchen table, a glowering Sarah and zombie-like Nick on either side of her. Tonight, both kids obviously preferred the safety of their rooms over Gwen's forced good cheer.

Just once, she wanted a goddamned normal dinner. She'd raced home from the hospital, where Vivian looked the same as she had this weekend, to catch Sarah and Nick before they could escape—Sarah to a ballfield or a friend's house, Nick to his computer. Tucker's surprise appearance at work had been the sour icing on a cake layered with several clients' rants about bills and a partner's harangue about . . . she still wasn't sure what.

She needed to spend time with Nick. Mac had come over yesterday morning, spending a couple of hours locked up in

Nick's room with him. It hadn't improved Nick's attitude when he'd made a brief appearance for lunch. Later, he'd silently grabbed a frozen burrito and some of Gwen's pasta salad for dinner in his room. With his computer.

She didn't have Mac's patience. One of these days, she'd send a heavy object through the computer monitor.

"Is this the part where we hold hands and sing 'Kumbaya'?" Sarah smirked at Gwen's frown before offering a blithe wave of her hand. "It's okay, Mom." She bit into her corn on the cob. Along with hamburgers, it was both kids' favorite meal. "We learned about this in health class. I think it's called a midlife crisis."

After trying to rein in her temper, Gwen finally snapped. "You don't know everything, Sarah. Your dad's friend Tiffany is a midlife crisis. What I had was a bad day."

"You've had a lot of them lately."

Nick didn't say anything. For once, Gwen was grateful that he rarely spoke. It allowed her to go one-on-one with Sarah, which almost gave her even odds.

"So, Nick." She smiled brightly, ignoring Sarah. "What did you do in school today?" She hoped he *had* been in school, but that question probably wasn't the best way to start a conversation with a boy who was already glaring at her.

He almost didn't answer. "I went, okay?"

"That's a good start." As she bit into her burger, she remembered the ketchup and reached for it. "Do you like your teacher?"

This time, he didn't answer. His food sat untouched.

"He's in middle school now, Mom. He has a bunch of teachers, including grouchy old Halligan." Sarah couldn't resist the jab at her former math teacher, who'd once sent a note to Gwen asking if Sarah did any homework in between her various athletic events.

"That's *Mr.* Halligan, Sarah." Gwen smiled. The man *was* a grouch. "Nick, you're not eating anything. Aren't you hungry?"

Silence.

"He's s'posed to go somewhere with Dad and Tiff tonight." Without Sarah's inside scoops, Gwen would know nothing. That might be preferable. Both kids seemed to adore Rob and "Tiff" these days, but she didn't need to hear about it. "Aren't you, Nick? Huh?"

Nick didn't speak to Sarah much more than he did to Gwen. Girls were pretty low on his hit parade, and sisters seemed to be on a par with pond scum.

A horn honked, and Nick bolted from the table.

"Nick! Where are you going?" Sarah had already supplied part of the answer, but Nick hadn't cleared it with her. Neither had Rob.

Leaving the table, Gwen scrambled to the front door, blocking it when Nick tried to leave. "I asked you a question, young man. I assume that's your dad, but nobody asked me about this. Where are you going with him?"

He tugged at her arm, but she wasn't budging. She still had a few inches and almost thirty years on him.

Nick muttered something under his breath that didn't sound flattering.

"I asked where you're going. I'm your mother. You're not leaving this house without telling me, or without my permission."

"I'm going out with Dad. And Tiffany." He stared defiantly at Gwen through bangs that had grown too long without her noticing. Traces of spit flew at her as he shouted. "I don't hafta tell you where. Dad's the only one who cares about me. You don't want me!"

Stunned, Gwen stepped back from the door, letting him

leave without another word. Clutching her throat, she remembered a conversation she'd had a long time ago, when she hadn't been much older than Nick was now.

That day, she'd shouted the same angry words at Vivian.

———

"IT'S NOT A DATE."

"No, it's worse. It's a dinner date at my house, and you're making me cook." Pressing her cell phone to her ear as she stared out the window over the kitchen sink, Gwen blew upward at a wispy bang that had driven her nuts all afternoon. She wished she could blow off Leila's latest crazy adventure as easily.

"This might be the most scathingly brilliant idea I've had all week." After explaining the double date she'd dreamed up, Leila cackled, for reasons unknown to Gwen. Leila and Jon Abelard. Gwen and Adam.

Neither woman dated the men in question. A double *blind* date, in more ways than one. "It must be a slow week, but give yourself time. It's only Wednesday."

"Be grateful. I'm trying to give you two a nudge."

"What about you? Does Jon need a nudge?" As she spoke, Gwen loaded the dinner plates in the dishwasher, then turned on the kitchen faucet. Maybe Leila would take a hint.

"Jon?" Munching on what sounded like a carrot, Leila audibly swallowed before she spoke again. "He probably needs more of a kick in the pants, but not from me. I'm just helping him get back out there in the world."

"I forgot. He's your next project." Tempted to start the dishwasher, which would completely drown out their conversation and end the call, Gwen instead wiped the counter. "Does that mean you've declared me a success?"

"I'm not even close to done with you."

Leila had responded too quickly, the answer too obvious to her. After thinking she'd already made so much progress becoming herself again, Gwen felt a punch in the gut. "Lucky me."

"Oh, sweetie." Leila practically cooed into the phone. "You *are* making progress. You look good, you're getting out, and you're not letting everyone dump all over you." She paused to munch some more. "Or at least not as much as before."

"I don't let people dump on me."

"Girl, that big red 'X' on your back might be fading to pink, but, yeah, you do. You dropped PTA and the neighborhood stuff, but your kids manipulate the hell out of you." She cut off Gwen's automatic protest. "I love those guys, but they do. And don't get me started on the men in your life."

"Can I help it if my kids like Rob?" Gwen sniffed, feeling the sting a little too sharply. "They're supposed to. He's their dad."

"He's a lousy dad who's just trying to show his girlfriend what a great dad he'd be. For *her* kids." Leila snapped her fingers. "Once they're married and she gets pregnant, he'll drop back out of your kids' lives in a New York minute."

"I don't believe that."

Or she didn't want to.

Sure, he hadn't paid much attention to Nick or Sarah until a month ago, when he'd started doing a few things with them. Maybe he'd just waited until the kids had gotten old enough to become interesting to him—even though Gwen had considered them fascinating from the start.

Nick badly needed a father figure, and Sarah thought her dad and Tiffany were a lot cooler than her boring mom. If Leila was right, the kids would be crushed.

"I hope I'm wrong." Impossible. Leila never admitted being wrong. She certainly wouldn't hope for it. "But does Saturday night work? Sevenish?"

"Why is it at my house? And who's inviting Adam?"

"I've already invited Jon and Adam. I left a message on Adam's phone." Listening, Gwen rolled her eyes. Talk about people dumping on her. Leila was at the head of the line. "And you've seen my house. It's a mess, and you know I don't cook."

"How convenient that I do."

"A lucky thing for me." Leila actually laughed.

"What was it you said about people dumping on me?" Spying a dirty glass tucked behind the toaster, Gwen rinsed it and loaded it in the dishwasher. "Does that include you?"

"Of course it does. And after Saturday night, I really wish you'd do something about it."

———

"Just type in your name. It's an electronic signature, but I didn't feel comfortable doing it for you." Becky Tercell leaned over Gwen's shoulder the next morning, pointing at the signature line of some form on her computer screen. Glancing higher up the screen, Gwen thought it looked oddly familiar. She scrolled to the top.

Her LSAT application.

"Becky! I don't believe it." Gwen tried to push her chair away from the computer but didn't get far, since Becky kept hovering. Politely, unlike Danny, but still hovering. Gwen settled for crossing her arms. "You heard me tell Danny that I'd decide if and when I want to do this. I'm guessing he put you up to it."

"Of course he did." Becky shrugged. "You're both my

boss, but Danny pulled rank. I think it's the first time he ever has."

"See? I'm a nice guy." The culprit in question poked his head inside Gwen's office, ducking when she threw a pen at him. "You've really got to work on your aim, Gwen. You haven't hit me yet."

"You're giving me lots of target practice."

"You're welcome." Danny eased into the chair across from her. "And don't worry. You can still decide, but you need to do it fast in order to make the deadline. Take a look at the info on the screen, sign it if you want, and Becky will submit it."

Unwisely, Becky moved closer to Gwen's desk.

She grabbed another pen, although she'd much rather throw it at Danny than Becky. "I'm still deciding. I don't even have enough money for the application fee."

Or if she did, this wasn't how she wanted to spend it.

Danny shot her the sort of patronizing smile that reminded her of Ted. She sincerely hoped it wasn't his new look. "It's taken care of."

"How?"

Whistling tunelessly, he glanced at her framed Degas ballerina print on the wall. "Let's just call it the Ted Harrison scholarship fund."

"Let's not." Studying him, Gwen tried to figure out his angle. It wasn't readily apparent. "What gives, Danny? Why do you care so much about this?"

"I care about *you*. Like it or not, you have a lot of friends here." Danny caught Becky's eye, and they both nodded. "You've got talent. I hate to see it wasted."

"But what does Ted have to do with that?"

"Long story." Danny stared at the framed Walker Art Center poster on another wall as if seeing it for the first time. The poster had been on her wall for the last two years.

"Try me."

After examining every other piece of fairly cheap artwork in Gwen's office, Danny glanced at her, then bent down to tie his shoe. Gwen could've sworn she'd seen him wearing his usual loafers today, but she didn't peer over her desk to find out.

Finally, he sat up again. Gwen and Becky both leaned toward him, waiting for his explanation with equal fascination. "Did I ever mention my, uh, family to you guys?"

Two heads shook in tandem.

"It's no big deal. My dad ran out on us when I was twelve, and Mom worked a couple of jobs to make ends meet. I had two younger sisters. You know, the usual story." He waved his hand as if it were normal. In the world in which Gwen had grown up, it wasn't. "But it meant no college. I worked all the way through high school, but no dice. I figured I'd get some regular job after I graduated, even though I'd always wanted to be a lawyer."

"You probably watched too many legal shows on TV." Gwen smiled, even though Danny's story pained her. It also explained a lot about him.

"You got that right." Sharing her smile, Danny relaxed. "Anyway, spring of twelfth grade, I get called into the principal's office. Shittin' bricks. We'd had a party that weekend, and I figured I was busted." He grinned sheepishly. "But then I saw Ted. I mean, I didn't know him then. He'd called my high school, offering to pay some kid's way through college and law school if the kid had talent."

"And when they couldn't find anyone, they asked you?" Covering her laughter with her hand, Becky watched both of her bosses' jaws drop at her unexpected slam. With twenty years' experience at the firm, she was a great secretary—but not even remotely the type to throw out one-liners.

"What are you guys, a comedy act?" Danny pretended to be irritated, but his snicker gave him away. He slouched down in his chair, apparently done with his story.

Gwen thought it only raised more questions. "How come we've never heard this? You'd think Ted would've made sure everyone knew."

Danny studied his hands in his lap. "No idea. Ted told me not to mention it. He also put in a word for me with the hiring committee, or I'd probably still be out there looking for work."

"Now you're lying." Gwen made a tsking sound. "Nice try, but graduating at the top of your class from Harvard might've helped." She held her thumb and forefinger a millimeter apart, indicating how much it had helped. "Just a tad."

"Well . . ."

"Danny's so modest." Becky, in truth the most modest person Gwen had ever met, thought the sun rose and set on Danny. His ego probably *was* smaller than any other partner's in the firm. It didn't say much.

He gave an aw-shucks lift of his shoulders, the sort of thing Gwen had seen him do after winning most of the points in a tough negotiation. "I'm just here to serve the client."

"And me, apparently." Gwen glanced again at the application on her computer screen—including the application fee. "You still haven't explained the money. Ted was wealthy even before becoming a lawyer, and maybe he could afford to spread it around. No offense, but I wouldn't say that about you. I can't take your money, Danny."

"You're not." Danny waved off her objections. As usual. "Look. Even with your late registration, the test itself doesn't cost that much. Since the test is two weeks from Saturday, it's too late to take a preparation course. Money saved. See?" He held his hands out.

"Money saved and test flunked." Gwen shook her head. "That's what I mean. It's been almost twenty years since I took a test. I'm not prepared. And it's not just the LSAT fee, although even that is more than I can afford to throw away. It's the law school applications and law school itself. Like I said, I can't do it."

Danny nodded at each of her objections as if they were trivial, which was more than a little annoying.

"Yes, you can. With your experience here and a glance through the sample questions, the LSAT will be a breeze for you. Trust me." He nodded again when she frowned. "And I'm really not helping on the money. I wasn't kidding about Ted's scholarship. After he died, we found out that he'd set up a trust fund, to be given only to the next 'kid' he picked. Under the fund's provisions, the firm's management committee now gets to pick. And they picked you."

"B-but . . ." She could only sputter.

"There's no better choice." He leaned forward in his chair. "Just sign the application. It's all courtesy of Pembroke and McFarley—and the dearly departed Ted Harrison."

She looked at Becky, who nodded at her. On impulse, she signed her name on the screen.

———

"Sorry, honey. I have to practice." Gwen looked up at Sarah, whose chin rested on the raised top of the baby grand. Basketball in hand, Sarah had just asked for a ride to the public courts over at Lynnhurst Park, just a few blocks away.

Somehow, the concept of exercise never seemed to occur

to her daughter until she *arrived* at her field or court or gym of choice.

Cue the dramatic sigh. "You're always practicing. Or reading those dumb books for that test." Sarah tilted her head at Gwen. "You're not really gonna go to law school, are you? You're, like, too old."

"Thank you." Gwen studied the last few bars of the piece, which she'd just fumbled three times in a row. Sarah's check to her ego hadn't helped. "I suppose I'll have to get a facelift."

She smiled brightly at Sarah, whose eyes were saucers. "Nooooo."

"Bummer." Gwen gazed at the ceiling, pretending to consider the problem. Bad idea. There were an amazing number of cobwebs up there. "Then I don't have any choice. No law school. I'll resign myself to volunteering as assistant basketball coach for your team." Sarah looked horrified. "But what a perfect way for us to bond. I used to be pretty good at basketball, you know, back in the days before the earth's crust cooled. I should go call your coach now before I forget."

"Law school's not so dumb." The words rushed out of Sarah's mouth before Gwen could get up from the piano bench.

She seriously needed to spend at least an hour practicing tonight, if not more. Her next lesson was tomorrow night, and the competition a week from Saturday.

And the LSAT the week after that. Unbelievable. She had to quit letting everyone—including Leila—talk her into things. Slowly but surely, her life was becoming more interesting, but she was paying for it with exhaustion. And on top of work, piano, exam prep, and failing miserably at the mom-of-the-year award, she needed to clean the house and whip up some semblance of a dinner on Saturday night. Oh, yeah. And visit her mom.

Vivian's health declined more each day. Mac planned to arrive late tonight rather than tomorrow. He'd called this afternoon, telling Gwen that he'd had one of his hunches. Thinking about it, she shivered. Mac's "hunches" had a morbidly high accuracy rate.

She'd stopped by Kendall South, as usual, after work. If anything, Vivian had looked a little more cheerful, a little brighter, than the last several days. After staying forty-five minutes, Gwen had left the hospital feeling more hopeful than she had in a week.

Sarah lingered by the piano, her desperate need to show up for tonight's pick-up game apparently forgotten. Gwen studied her. Lately, between her schedule and Sarah's, they didn't get many chances to talk. "Didn't you do enough damage at volleyball practice this afternoon? Why do you need to play basketball tonight, too?"

"Oh, Mom." If Sarah's eyes rolled back any further in her head, she'd lose them. "Basketball tryouts are only two months away." To Gwen these days, two months would feel like a lifetime. "And I hafta get ready. Coach Plant doesn't like to pick freshmen for varsity."

"Imagine that." Returning her focus to the sheet music in front of her, Gwen stretched her fingers to try a difficult chord. "But I do need to practice now. I'll be in much better shape after the competition next week."

"No, then you'll be studying for that test." Sarah pulled a stick of gum out of her gym shorts, cramming it in her mouth. She talked while she chewed, bovine fashion. "It's just, like, you're never around. I've been hanging with Dad and Tiff, and—"

For the first time in the conversation, Gwen brightened. "And what? They're not as much fun as I am?"

Sarah shrugged. "I guess." She scuffed the toe of her sneaker against the floor. "They're just so busy talking about the wedding and all. It sounds like a drag."

The palms of Gwen's hands banged against the keys.

CHAPTER 15

"Your friend Leila is something else."

Rolling her shoulders after a tense lesson, Gwen looked at Adam. And waited for him to ask if Leila was available.

He laughed. "I think I've met her maybe once, and she calls up, leaves a message like we're old friends or something. She's got guts."

She also looked pretty hot, according to most men, in tight pants and short skirts. Adam didn't happen to mention it.

"You're coming?" As she asked, she felt a touch of heat light up her cheeks. "I mean, to dinner tomorrow?"

"I wouldn't miss it." Next to her on the piano bench, where he'd parked himself halfway through the lesson, Adam wrapped an arm around her. He felt toastier than a hot muffin on a cold morning. "But *you* should've asked me, Gwen. I would've said yes even faster."

Hard to imagine. According to Leila, he'd called her back about fifteen seconds after she hung up.

She couldn't figure him out. He focused most of his time with her on teaching and listening, but she could still feel the touch of his lips on her cheek, the caress of his hands when he'd massaged her shoulders. She shivered, then felt his arm tighten around her.

"Cold?"

Not exactly. "Just thinking."

"Me, too." Oh? "You played well tonight."

"Thanks. I squeezed in some extra practice last night, and by the end I was feeling pretty good." Wishing she could put an arm around Adam as easily as he did with her, Gwen panicked. And looked at the sheet music.

"Gwen, I—" He paused, his breath warm in her ear. "I think you feel pretty good, too."

His other arm came around her just as his lips brushed the corner of her mouth—and she could've sworn his hand brushed her breast.

Ohhh. No doubt about it. His hand, bold and curious, cupped her breast while his lips began a full frontal assault on her mouth. She could only surrender, lifting her arms to wrap around his neck. Twisted sideways and on the verge of falling off the bench, she laughed nervously. Until his other hand joined the party.

And she'd thought his *neck* massages were good.

Warring within herself, she pulled away, gasping for air. "Don't you—"

"—want to move this to the couch?" He reclaimed her lips, then released them to travel south. "Yeah, unless my bed would be more comfortable."

"The couch is fine." She'd meant to say no. They should stop, right? *Right?* Now, before she— Ooh. "I'd like that."

Standing up and grabbing her hand, he was at the couch in three strides. With one quick tug, she landed on top of him. Her clingy white top—another Leila idea—was dangling from the lamp moments before their shoes tumbled to the floor. Adam's teeth found her bra strap just as his fingers found her—

"Wait." She almost couldn't talk, and she swatted at his Energizer-bunny hands. "I— We shouldn't do this."

His mouth, firmly latched onto her breast, ignored her words. "Mm-hmm."

"No, I mean—" Ohhh. She hadn't felt like this since—

Tucker. The analyst bills alone were going to kill her.

Adam's mouth didn't seem to understand the meaning of the word "no," but his hands quit roving. Gwen didn't know if that was good or bad.

But then he pulled her body tight against his, letting her feel every inch of him. His boyish grin was almost irresistible. Almost. "Clean bill of health. Nothing to worry about."

Despite his reputation, she hadn't even considered it.

Releasing a breath, she realized—again—that she hadn't thought about it with Tucker, either. Great. She'd lectured Sarah about safe sex, in those rare moments her daughter actually listened, but her own mind seemed to cling to a fantasy of innocence.

She shook her head.

"Honest." Adam shifted, pulling Gwen onto her side, facing him. "Why? Do you have any, uh, issues?"

"Issues?" She felt the crease down the middle of her forehead. "I don't think so." She hoped not. Tucker had used a condom. And she hoped not.

Despite the painful lessons she'd learned at Rob's hands, she still acted like a complete idiot around men. Tugging her bra strap back up and rearranging herself, she rose to her feet.

"It's not that." She spied her shirt and retrieved it, pulling it on before she slipped into her black flats. A glance down confirmed that her pants were still fastened. "I've . . . heard a lot about you, Adam. You and other women. It hasn't been like that with the two of us, but—"

He waited while she grappled for the right words. He'd finally treated her like his other students. She just didn't know why.

She shrugged. "I don't know what to say, and I'm not sure what you want." Still lying on his side, he waggled his eyebrows in response. "Besides that. What you want from me."

"The truth?" Finally sitting up, he rubbed his eyes. "Can't say I know exactly. You're a talented pianist, and you're nice. Genuine. I guess I just like you."

"You like a lot of women." She couldn't help the bite of jealousy in her words or the blush that followed.

He shook his head. "Fewer than you think. Women seem to have the impression that my piano lessons get them—" He looked away. "Something else in return." Remembering her own impetus for taking lessons, Gwen's blush deepened. When he hadn't shown any interest, she'd forgotten it. Mostly. Or she would've, if Leila hadn't reminded her so often. "I don't pursue those women. They're all over me."

Poor boy. He looked like he'd suffered.

"It doesn't work that way for me." Watching Adam on the couch, looking rumpled and edible, part of Gwen wished it *did* work that way. "I can't be someone's girl for the day. Or for an hour."

"You wouldn't be. You aren't— Shit." Adam buried his face in his hands. "Just kill me now, all right?"

Just like that, the knot of tension inside of her unraveled, and she laughed. "See you tomorrow night?"

He nodded as she walked out the door.

"Do we hafta?" Sarah's plaintive whine echoed against the hospital walls, and Gwen glanced sharply at the door to Vivian's room, twenty feet down the hall. Shut. Thank God.

Reaching out, she smoothed the hairs sticking straight up on Nick's head and gave Sarah a once-over. Presentable. Not that Vivian would notice any longer, but it somehow comforted Gwen. She was becoming her mother's daughter. The thought didn't send her screaming down the hall the way it once had. The way it had only a few weeks ago.

Nick didn't say anything, but only Gwen's hand on the collar of his T-shirt kept him moving forward.

Sarah stalled in the middle of the hall.

Frowning, Gwen gave her a nudge. "I thought you *wanted* to see your grandmother, Sarah. You kept talking about it."

"I never did." The ever-silent Nick squirmed against Gwen's hold.

"No, you would've had to speak." Seeing her sullen son's startled reaction, she bit her tongue, regretting her words. Nick pushed every button she had, but kids did that. She needed more patience. "I've told you guys. Your grandmother won't be around much longer, and you should see her. To say . . . goodbye."

"But she looks, like, creepy. Old and sick and really bad." Sarah shook her head. "Gran never looked like that."

"She can't help it." If Vivian could, she would've paid big bucks to haul in hairstylists and beauticians from all over town. She was long past caring now. "So be nice. Hold her hand and talk to her, even if she keeps her eyes closed. Give her a kiss on the cheek."

"Gross." For the first time in their life, Sarah and Nick agreed on something.

Stopping, Gwen wagged a finger at them and hissed in a

low tone. They were right outside Vivian's door. "I mean it. Your grandmother loves you two very much. She's dying. For her sake, be nice. Please."

After a brief knock, she opened the door and walked in. Her dad and Mac huddled together on one side of the bed. Vivian appeared to be sleeping.

The two men glanced up, both trying hard to look stoic.

"Gwen." Mac walked over to her, slowly, before holding her in a long hug. Letting go with one arm, he gestured to Sarah and Nick. "Come on, guys. Give a hug to your favorite uncle."

"You're our only uncle." Sarah smirked, looking every inch a fourteen-year-old, but she gave Mac a tentative hug.

Nick stood back, head down, not joining them. Releasing Gwen and Sarah, Mac grabbed the boy in a bear hug. He then ruffled his hair, which drew a squawk. "One of the many perks of being your uncle, kid. No wonder I love this gig."

Surprisingly, Nick smiled. When Gwen nodded at him, though, he drew a blank mask over his face and ducked behind Mac.

Gwen's dad hardly reacted to their presence. She turned to him, watching his sad, impassive face and the gentle grip he kept on Vivian's hand. From time to time, he fingered his wife's wedding ring, too large now for her shrunken fingers and worn on a chain around her neck.

The corporate giant was a changed man.

Gwen remembered the surprise party her dad had thrown, a year ago this Tuesday, for her parents' fortieth wedding anniversary. Busy with his multimillion-dollar business, he'd never been the type to remember a social event without prodding, let alone organize it.

When they cut the cake, he'd toasted Vivian, declaring his love for her—in front of God and everyone, to Gwen's gagging amusement—and hoping for another forty years with her.

They might not even eke out one.

Approaching Vivian's bed, Gwen gazed at her, almost unrecognizable from the woman she'd been a month ago. Her wasted face held an eerie glow, but she seemed at peace. As Gwen grasped Vivian's free hand, her mother's eyelids fluttered a moment, then opened.

"Gwen." Leaning forward, Gwen barely heard the whisper. "I'm so glad . . . you came." Her mother's eyes lit on Sarah and Nick, still tussling with Mac near the foot of the bed. "And Sarah. Nick. Come here, children. Let me see you."

Two pairs of feet shuffled forward at a snail's pace, stubbornly oblivious to Gwen's anxious head movements.

Finally, they reached the bed. Gwen released Vivian's hand and Sarah touched it, smiling as if her face would crack any minute. Nick stood behind Sarah, waiting his turn and looking as if he prayed it never came.

"Hi, Gran." Despite being fourteen, Sarah always came through in the clutch. "It's nice to, uh, see you."

Vivian smiled, closing her eyes a moment, and reached for Sarah's hand with her own bony one. Too slow to avoid it, Sarah smiled back at her grandmother, pretending this wasn't the most awful thing her wicked mother had ever made her do.

Behind Sarah, Nick looked ready to die. Quite possibly before Vivian did.

"Nick, is that you, dear?" Vivian called to him, softly, her pale blue eyes taking one last look at Sarah. "Did your mom drag you here today?"

That got him. "Uh, no, Gran. I, uh, wanted to come."

It had to be one of the longest strings of words Gwen had

heard out of Nick's mouth in six months. Maybe there was hope.

"I wasn't born yesterday, dear." Vivian's eyes held a slight twinkle. Releasing Sarah's hand, which was quickly wiped on the back of the girl's shorts, she touched Nick's. His lips pursed, but he somehow managed not to pull his hand away. "But it seems like only yesterday I held you in my arms for the first time." Sighing, she closed her eyes briefly, then reopened them. "I'll miss you, child. And sweet Sarah. I wanted to watch you two grow up."

Nick's lips quivered. "Y-you can, Gran. Just get well." A stream of tears rolled down his cheeks. "I don't want you to go." Clutching her hand now, Nick squeezed it, heedless of Vivian's fragile state.

"Me either." Sarah's tears, which mirrored the ones on every adult in the room, joined Nick's. "Don't die, Gran. We don't want you to."

Vivian smiled softly but gave a slight shake of her head. "I can't stay much longer. I wish I could." She glanced at Gwen's dad, whose whole body shook. "Help Gwen take care of them, Skip." Her gaze moved to Mac. "And you, too, dear. Children need good men in their lives."

At last—or too soon—Vivian's gaze returned to Gwen, and her voice grew stronger. "You're a good mother, dear. And so talented. I'm proud of you." She looked at Mac before returning to Gwen. "Proud of both of you. We didn't have the relationship I wanted, Gwen, but somehow . . . it was hard raising a daughter who reminded me . . . so much of myself."

Gwen sucked in a deep breath, trying to stop the tears that desperately wanted to fall.

Her mother struggled to reach for her hand. "I'm sorry about Rob, dear." Gwen glanced at Sarah and Nick. Mac had them both in a fake chokehold, trying to distract them from hearing about their less-than-wonderful father. Heedless of the children, Vivian pulled Gwen close. "I've spent time . . . thinking. And talking to Skip. I was wrong about Rob, and . . . you didn't need that. I realize now that you tried. More than he deserved."

"Oh, Mom . . ."

Sobs filled Gwen's throat, choking her. Anguish for her failed marriage, for her mother, for being too stupid and too goddamned stubborn to have talked to Vivian years ago— when they'd still had time. She'd always blamed everything on Vivian, but she should've saved a generous slice of blame for herself.

"Gwen." Her mother's grip loosened, her eyelids flickered. "Your children need a good man in their life. So do you. I hope— I hope you'll find someone as wonderful as Skip . . . has been to me. You deserve to be happy."

"I'm . . . happy, Mom."

Vivian's pale blue eyes opened, gazing sadly at her, then shut. A moment later, her mother's light, steady breathing told them she'd fallen asleep.

Gwen glanced to each side, at Sarah and Nick, who each clung to one of her hands and looked like they'd seen their first scary movie. She turned to her dad and Mac, whose heads were bowed. "I need to stay—stay with you guys and Mom. I was supposed to have a few people over for dinner tonight. I'll call them and cancel."

She looked at her kids again, who had to get out of there. Soon. Before their nails ripped a hole in her skin. "But I'd better take these guys home first."

"Don't, honey." Her dad's somber voice startled her. He'd been silent until now.

Her gaze pleaded with him to understand. "I-I have to, Dad. They won't make it here much longer."

Another glance at Sarah and Nick confirmed it. Both stood wide-eyed in horror at the possibility that they'd have to watch Vivian any longer. They'd been troupers, doing just what she'd asked of them. Doing it for their Gran.

"That's not what I mean, hon." Her dad shook his head. "We've all said our goodbyes." He choked. "Viv could be here another hour or another week. Maybe longer." It didn't look like it. "Take the kids and have your dinner. Mac will keep me company. I promise we'll call if anything happens."

"B-but—" Indecision warring within her, she sputtered. They couldn't fix a lifetime of hurts in a few conversations, and every sentence cut a little more into her mother's stamina. But she should try. She never really had.

"Oh, go ahead, kid." Mac waved a hand even as he wiped his other hand over his wet eyes. "Since you didn't bother inviting *me* to dinner, as usual, I'd rather not have to see your face around here."

"Twerp."

"Lousy cook."

Nick and Sarah, their smiles restored, looked at their mom and uncle, eager to see an older generation's sibling rivalry. Great. Now they'd fight even more and feel justified.

Shaking her head, Gwen grabbed each by the hand. Neither of her kids had allowed much close contact in at least a couple of years, but they clung to her now. She turned to her dad. "You win." She bit her lip, mentally rearranging her schedule so she could spend a big chunk of tomorrow talking to Vivian. "But call me if anything changes. Please. I want to be here."

He nodded, then returned to his silent vigil.

Mac punched her arm on the way out the door.

The guy would never grow up. She smiled. Good.

———

"You make the most stupendous stuffed pork chops this world has ever known."

Gwen couldn't believe Leila had managed that whole sentence with her mouth full, chewing as if her life depended on getting the last morsel down. She wondered—not for the first time—how Leila stayed so slim. The woman ate like a horse.

"It's, uh, nothing. Really." Her not-so-secret recipe: after dropping the kids at friends' houses, she'd made a fast trip to Lunds & Byerlys—better known as Lunds to everyone she knew. They stuffed the pork chops for her and even gave her the baking time and temperature. She wished her favorite grocery store could make the rest of her life so easy.

"You're too modest." Unlike Leila, Jon swallowed before speaking. He even dabbed the corners of his mouth with his napkin. Someone had raised him right—his mom or maybe his deceased wife. "I can't believe they're so juicy."

Adam, who'd been less talkative than Gwen's other dinner companions, added his praise. Gwen felt a blush stealing up her neck and heading for her cheeks.

She also blushed at the smoldering glances Adam had shot her all evening, as if he wanted a replay of last night but with a steamier ending. She liked the attention—or sort of— but it also embarrassed her somehow.

Too polite to say anything, Jon often looked the other way. Leila hadn't done much more than cough. And kick Gwen under the table. And giggle sporadically when no one was saying anything particularly funny.

Leila smirked now, raving again about the pork chops. "I just don't know how you do it."

Then she winked.

Busted. Gwen gave her an innocent look. "I really can't say. The recipe comes from an old friend of the family." As long as Lunds had been in business, it'd been her friend. And her mother's before that.

The thought jarred her, interrupting her unexpected enjoyment of the dinner and her friends—so incongruous with the scene she'd left this afternoon.

Leila brought her back to reality. Leila's reality, at least. "Oh? Which member of the Lund family would your friend be? Maybe I know her. Or him."

"Lund?" Jon wiped his glasses, then settled them back on his nose. "Your friend's name is Lund?"

Riotous laughter ripped through Leila, making Adam stare. Gwen didn't blink. Gazing down at his plate, Jon's fork jabbed his pork chop. Leila didn't notice any of it. "I'm not sure just how *close* they are, but, yes, I'm pretty sure Gwen's friend is a Lund. As in . . . Lunds? Get it?"

Jon kept looking down, apparently fascinated with the food on his plate. Gwen caught Leila's eye, then nodded quickly at Jon. Sobering, Leila touched his forearm. "I was just teasing Gwen. She *is* a great cook, but today she had a little help from her favorite grocery store." She darted a glance at Gwen. "I know you've had a rough day. I didn't mean anything by it."

Gwen waved off her sympathy. "You're right. I didn't have the time or the concentration to do much else this afternoon. Sorry."

Adam grabbed her hand, the tenth time he'd done it in as many minutes. "Everything is great, Gwen, and I can't blame you. Why waste a ton of time in the kitchen when you can buy something like this?"

Why? Because she normally enjoyed cooking. She suspected Adam stocked his freezer with microwave meals.

He also ate out a lot. Leila spotted him all over town—and breathlessly reported every sighting to Gwen.

Jon's head was still down, almost as if he were the one whose mother was dying in a hospital two miles away. Gwen shot another worried glance at Leila.

"Jon? Are you okay?" Leila cooed at him. She didn't flirt with him the way she did with most men she knew. Sometimes Gwen wondered if, maybe, she liked him more than she wanted to admit. "I was just joking. Gwen and I tease each other a lot."

Or Leila teased Gwen, as the case may be.

"Um-hmm." Jon cleaned his glasses again. "I'm sorry. Here I go, spoiling everyone's dinner." He turned to Gwen, looking mortified. "You're a marvelous cook, with or without help. I like to cook, too, but sometimes you just can't pull it all together."

Gwen suspected he wasn't talking about the food.

"I know what you mean." Leila's wine almost came out her nose on a snort. "I sometimes have days when I can't manage much more than takeout Chinese. Or Punch Pizza. Or burgers from Five Guys."

Jon didn't say anything. Taking a cautious sip of wine, Gwen turned to Leila. "I'm familiar with those days of yours. I was under the impression you had, oh, about seven of them a week."

Laughing, Leila waved her hand. "Now you're telling all *my* secrets."

"I don't think it's much of a secret."

One thing she could say for Leila: she never tried to hook a man with false boasts about her domestic skills. She had none, but she more than made up for it in every other way.

Jon looked up again, scanning the faces of his dinner companions. He turned to Gwen, across the table from him.

"You'd think after two years I could deal with it. And Leila told me what you're going through with your mother. I'm so sorry." Gwen didn't need more reminders. "It's just that Annie's last name was Lund. Sometimes I . . ." He trailed off.

Leila spoke in a loud whisper. "Annie was his wife."

"Thanks, Leila." She had that one figured out.

"Oh?" Adam broke from his ardent study of Gwen long enough to glance around the table. "You were married, Jon? What happened? Get divorced?"

Stunned silence greeted his questions. Gwen couldn't blame him, since divorce would be more logical for someone Jon's age. Death happened to old people. People a lot older than Vivian, even. A lot older than sixty-three.

Leila rubbed Jon's arm as she answered Adam. "Jon's wife died. In an accident." Jon's gaze had returned to his plate, but Adam's eyes were wide. When he grimaced at his faux pas, Gwen patted his hand.

According to Leila, Jon had been in the tragic accident, too, a four-car crash on icy roads in late March, almost two and a half years ago. A free spirit, Annie apparently didn't believe in seatbelts. She'd been the only one in all of the cars to die. Jon still blamed himself for not avoiding the accident, for not convincing Annie to wear her seatbelt. And, as everyone around Gwen's table could see, he'd never recovered from her death.

As conversation stoppers went, they'd nailed it.

"Tell us about Annie." Gwen fingered her wine glass, trying to avoid Leila's startled frown.

Jon looked startled, too, but he smiled like someone still in the first blushes of love.

After clearing his throat, he began, his voice quiet at first, then gradually stronger. "We met in college. Young Dems. Annie was the biggest radical in a group full of them, and I—

I guess I just wanted to join something different. They were a far cry from my frat buddies and the other side of the world from the geeks I met in business classes."

Gwen loved stories like this. It could've been her story with Tucker—if she hadn't taken a detour that led to a dead end.

Or maybe Rob and Tucker were both wrong turns. It hadn't taken Rob many years to show his true colors, but Tucker hadn't turned into a man she respected, either.

She wished, for a moment, that she'd been Annie. Cherished. Jon glowed as he offered highlights of the woman she'd been. Annie hadn't surrendered her radical ways with graduation, as most of their friends had. She'd become an artist, painting a world far prettier than the one she knew.

Her last painting, unfinished, had been her vision of the twins she and Jon were expecting when she died. Her ultrasound a week earlier had given them the happy news after years of trying. While Jon raced around buying two of everything, even though she was only eighteen weeks pregnant, Annie had painted.

He kept the unfinished painting in an unfinished corner of the unfinished nursery. Everything about him seemed the same.

Unfinished.

Abruptly, Leila pushed back from the table and started to clear the dishes. To anyone who knew her, that was a neon sign. Leila didn't do housework. Ever.

Gwen got up to help her. After a moment, so did the men.

With the dishes cleared and in the sink, Gwen looked at the makings for chocolate fondue that she'd organized on the counter. It had seemed like such a decadent idea when Leila suggested it late this afternoon. She held her stomach, unable to imagine another bite. But the bananas were that perfect yellow ripeness and Leila was already nibbling at the raspberries. Jon popped a strawberry in his mouth.

Gwen slapped both their hands.

Adam fiddled with her CD player, and strains of her favorite Boz Scaggs album floated out to the kitchen.

Reaching for a banana, she gave up and joined the party. As Leila dumped the chocolate in the fondue pot, the phone rang.

"Gwen?" Mac.

Her voice cracked. "Oh, God. Is she . . . dead?"

"Nope, not yet. But I think we're heading there. Come as soon as you can."

CHAPTER 16

V ivian's hospital room was utterly silent when Gwen reached it after a heart-stopping race to the hospital and a mad dash down several blindingly white hallways. Her own winded breaths thundered in her ears.

Her mother's face—her ashen skin almost transparent now—greeted her. Vivian's eyes were closed. She looked peaceful, as if she'd already died. Gwen's breath caught in her throat, choking her. Thanks to a silly dinner with friends, she'd missed her chance to say goodbye.

Mac stepped forward, shaking his head at Gwen's wide eyes, and spoke in a low voice. "She's resting. Monica was here half an hour ago. She thinks it'll be soon. She told the nurses to clear out."

She rushed to her mother's side, where her dad sat hunched over on a hard wooden chair. When he looked up at Gwen and tried to smile, she put her arm around him. "I'm so sorry, Dad. You guys were so close."

"She loved you and Mac, too, honey." He choked on every third word. "It wasn't always easy for her to show it."

"I didn't make it easy for her. I—" Something broke deep inside of her, and Gwen couldn't finish.

"You were a wonderful daughter, dear." Startled, Gwen quickly gazed at her mother, whose eyelids flickered, then opened. "I love you so much."

"I love you, too." Trying desperately not to cry, Gwen bit her lip. She shook her head, the anguish of more than twenty years flooding through her. "I'm so sorry, Mom. I was pretty awful to you."

"Don't say that." Vivian smiled when Gwen took her hand, squeezing it lightly. "I was a better wife than a mother." She glanced tenderly at Gwen's dad before turning back to Gwen. "But I loved you. You and Mac. My darling children."

On the other side of Vivian's bed, Mac drew closer. Gwen and her brother and dad took turns leaning down to hug and kiss Vivian, trying somehow to keep her with them.

It didn't work.

Vivian gazed at the far corner of the ceiling, a smile lighting her face. She then looked at each of them in turn. "Skip, dear, I'll always love you. Forever, like we said."

His face crumpling, Gwen's dad gave a vigorous nod, trying to make up for the words he couldn't speak.

"And Mac." Vivian smiled weakly, her strength clearly ebbing. "Be a good boy, dear. I love you. Thank you for spending these days and hours with me."

Mac gave her another hug. "Oh, Mom. I wish we had more of them. I don't want to say goodbye. I love you, too."

She nodded before turning to Gwen. "Dear Gwen. I hope you'll know someday how much I loved you. I wanted us to be such good friends." Gwen nodded through the tears she couldn't stop. "I hope you . . . find happiness. I . . . love . . . you."

"I know you do, Mom." Gwen returned a watery smile. "I love you, too. I'll miss you. I want to—"

Vivian's eyelids flickered, then closed for the last time.

———

THEY BURIED VIVIAN ON TUESDAY. The morning of her forty-first wedding anniversary.

Head bowed, Gwen huddled between her dad and Nick in the front pew, her arm stretching across Nick's narrow shoulders to run her hand through Sarah's hair from time to time. Mac sat on Sarah's right side, holding her hand.

Words flowed from the pulpit, but Gwen scarcely heard them. Leila gave the second reading in a bright-red dress of remarkably modest length. She'd told Gwen before the service that Vivian had loved red, and she'd worn it for her. Gwen's dad had nodded his solemn approval.

The church was packed. Relatives, her parents' country-club friends and neighbors, a few dozen of her dad's business acquaintances, several of Gwen's work colleagues, even a few of Mac's friends from Duluth. Monica Lauren sat behind the family in the second row. Gwen shook her head, amazed at the close friendship her family had formed with someone whose first tie to them was cancer, and now death.

From the glances flickering between Mac and Monica earlier at the back of church, though, it looked like Vivian's death might not be Monica's last tie to the family.

Rob had shown up, solo. Maybe Tiffany was too busy planning the wedding. Or too young to attend funerals.

Or maybe even Rob wasn't a big enough asshole to bring her.

He sat a couple of rows back, probably figuring correctly that Gwen's glares outranked the fervent pleas of Sarah and Nick that he sit with the rest of the family. He wasn't Gwen's family. Even for her kids, she wouldn't be that charitable. Not today.

For her kids and her dad, though, she held it together.

She'd ruined her pillowcase with mascara-stained tears the last few nights, but she forbade their appearance today. Her dad, stooped over and shaking, needed her. And Sarah and Nick, brave little soldiers battling their first real experience with death, needed her more than they'd ever admit.

Nick hadn't touched his computer in three days—until this morning, a half hour before they left for the church, when Gwen had found him hunched over the keyboard, his gaze glued to the monitor. For the first time, she'd found the sight of it comforting.

Sarah was tougher to read. A few of her teammates had shown up today, maybe at the chance to skip out of class as much as anything. She'd ignored them, pretending she hadn't seen them waving until Gwen pointed it out to her in the middle of her hundredth hug of the day. Ever since Sarah visited Vivian at the hospital that last time, she hadn't said much. About anything. She spent every spare moment at home in the driveway, the thump-thump-thump-bang of her basketball dribbles and shots nearly driving Gwen insane.

Gwen's fingers had drummed an incessant beat on the piano keys. Ignoring the pieces she was supposed to practice for this Saturday's recital, she played haunting, heartbreaking melodies that resounded with death—or, at least, what Gwen felt when she thought of Vivian's death.

Mac, always the peacemaker, had not only held it together but tried to glue it back together for everyone else. Gwen glanced at him now, his gaze intent on Pastor Dane Jenson, a short, gray-haired, whirling dervish of a man, who'd just stepped behind the lectern to give the homily.

Try as she might, Gwen caught only snatches of words. She closed her eyes and let memories flow as the minister attempted to capture a woman who defied description. And, for most of Gwen's life, understanding. ". . . strong woman who . . . so proud of her children . . . and grandchildren . . . a loving wife . . . loyal friend . . . in peace and eternal rest. Amen."

Amen to that. Pastor Jenson knew Vivian, had known the family for years. And yet—

Tap, tap. She didn't have to turn around. Only Leila would tap a bereaved daughter on the shoulder during her mother's funeral. At least she'd waited until the closing hymn.

Leila had the decency to whisper. "I saw your friend Tucker in the back."

"He's not my friend." Gwen had spotted him, too, when they walked in with the casket. The men in her life had too much gall. Her dad's brows knit together at the whispering, and Gwen twisted to lean closer to Leila. "Could this possibly wait another five minutes? We're almost done."

Leila nodded, but she enjoyed intrigue too much to let it go. She'd already tapped Gwen earlier in the service to point out Rob and, on the other side of church, Adam. She sang a few bars of the closing hymn before whispering again. "Jon Abelard is here, too. He hopes you're doing okay."

Jon had sent flowers and, bless him, the best homemade apple pie she'd had in years. Gwen had told herself she'd gobbled half the pie in one sitting just to figure out how he got his crusts to turn out so well. "Thanks. Maybe he can tell me that *after* the funeral."

Leila nodded and allowed the hymn to end without another word.

Outside the church, Gwen greeted friends and relatives before beginning the long, sad drive to the cemetery. Their relatives and family friends hugged her and Mac but spent most of their time with her dad, who needed it. He needed

Gwen, too, and she'd focus on him as soon as the crowds faded.

Adam hugged her, maybe a little too effusively, but everyone reacted differently to a funeral. Jon approached in his quiet fashion and held her hand for a long moment, his eyes speaking his sadness for her. Somehow, his "words" were just right.

Leila kept her arm wrapped around Gwen whenever someone else wasn't hugging her. She'd been like that all weekend, less witty and wise-cracking than usual—and Gwen would be forever grateful to her friend for that.

After offering Nick and Sarah a quick hug, and Gwen a nervous smile, Rob made a hasty retreat.

Tucker tried to approach several times, but she artfully turned her back on him each time he made it within five feet. Or she hoped it looked artful. From Leila's raised eyebrows, not everyone might agree.

"You'll have to face him someday." Leila's soft words, free of accusation, floated in her ear. "For your own sake, you need to understand what happened."

"I have a pretty fair idea." As she spoke, Gwen glanced around until she spotted Tucker's back. He was headed toward the church parking lot. Thank God.

Leila squeezed her shoulders. "I doubt it. The guy was the love of your life—you said so yourself. And now you won't give him the time of day? He must've had a reason."

Rolling her eyes, Gwen tried to dismiss the ache that still gnawed at her. "Yeah, it's called getting laid. I just wish he'd quit showing up everywhere."

"He can't help showing up in his own restaurant."

"Funny." Leila had invited Gwen to dinner the week before at Tootie Fruitie, Tucker's restaurant in Eden Prairie. Gwen had said yes only because she assumed that he spent most of his time at Melba Toast downtown. She'd assumed wrong. Tucker had shown up a minute after they were seated. Gwen fled, leaving her menu and Leila at the table.

"Gwen, he's obviously not giving up. He came to your office, he's tried calling you a few times, and he showed up today." Leila pointed at Tucker, now climbing into a shiny black sedan. "He's not acting like a guy who just wanted a piece of ass."

Gwen tried to rub the tight knot out of her neck. "So he feels a little guilty. He should. I didn't deserve that."

Leaning closer, Leila whispered in her ear. "No, but you also didn't ask any questions before picking things up with him again. He obviously still means something to you. You're always so cautious, and it wasn't like you."

But enough about Gwen's regrets.

More people approached. It wasn't the right time for this conversation. If Gwen had her choice, it never would be.

She hissed. "I can't believe you're talking about this right now."

"Hey, I'm just trying to get your mind off the funeral." After a final hug and an unsettling look of understanding, Leila spun on her heels and walked over to a group of their mutual neighbors and friends.

Gwen shook her head at her friend's departing back.

———

"How're you holding up, kid?"

Gwen gazed blankly at Mac as she rubbed her feet, painfully sore after too many hours in heels. The burial had been particularly brutal, in more ways than one, and she'd repeatedly yanked her sinking heels out of grass that was soft from yesterday's rainstorm.

Before answering, she shot a quick glance at her dad, stretched out in his recliner with his eyes closed. "Fine, I guess. I'm glad they're all gone. I'm surprised the food held out."

Mac nodded. "No kidding. After watching your friend Leila eat, I thought we should've bought a lot more."

She threw an embroidered sofa pillow at him. "You should talk. At least Leila has a high metabolism. If you'd packed one more stuffed whatever-that-was in your mouth, we'd have to rent a forklift to haul you out of here tomorrow."

"You're leaving . . . tomorrow, Mac?" Her dad's eyes opened, offering a glimpse of the bone-deep sorrow in them. Gwen had heard Mac tell their dad a dozen times that he had to drive back to Duluth early tomorrow morning—he had another trial starting next Monday—but it wasn't the first thing Skip Withers hadn't heard or understood in the last few days.

"Yeah, Dad." Mac tossed the pillow back at Gwen. "I'll come back as soon as I can, but they need me at work. Big trial next week. Defending good against evil." He laughed, trying to draw a smile from their dad. It didn't work. "You know, the usual. Not like that nasty stuff Gwen does for the big guys."

He got the pillow back. In the face.

"I, uh, might not be doing that forever." She flushed, knowing how silly she'd sound to her dad and Mac, taking the LSAT at almost forty. "Or I'd be doing it differently."

"You got a promotion?" Her dad sat up, smiling despite his obvious pain, the way he'd always done if his kids needed encouragement. "That's great, hon."

"Um, not exactly." She glanced at Mac, wishing she'd never mentioned it. Thank goodness her kids were downstairs, playing pool in the rec room. Sarah spent half of her time whining that Gwen would change—and ruin—all of their lives if she went to law school.

Mac stared hard at her. "You didn't quit, did you?" He wagged a finger at her, but he seemed genuinely worried. "Seriously, Gwen, that's exactly what they tell you *not* to do when someone dies. Overreact and quit. Or move. Or whatever."

"I didn't quit." Gwen rushed to reassure her dad, who suddenly looked ill. "Really. I just decided to take the LSAT."

"The LSAT?" Mac's eyes grew wide. "Shit. That's *worse* than quitting. You'll be a damned lawyer!"

It wasn't the reaction she'd expected.

"I don't see you complaining about it." Actually, she'd seen it countless times in his haggard face when he'd raced into town for a quick weekend trip. Even before Vivian had gotten sick. "At least, you've never said anything."

"That's because I'm the strong, silent type." He looked from Gwen to their dad, who didn't seem to grasp what either of his children was saying. When Gwen snorted, Mac gave her a slow smile. "But I guess you're right. I'm tired all the time, but I like what I do. Mostly."

"No wonder you're tired. I can't believe how many trips you made here in the last two months." This time Gwen didn't look at their dad, not wanting to see how he'd reacted to her reminder of Vivian's illness and death.

"It was worth it." Crossing the room, Mac dropped to his knees at the side of their dad's chair. "I wouldn't have missed the time I spent with Mom and you for anything."

At the sight of their dad, who stared straight ahead without blinking, Gwen went to his other side. Leaning over his chair, she hugged him. "Me, too, Dad."

She wished she hadn't wasted so much time avoiding

Vivian. Avoiding the words they both needed to say. She wished she had her back, if only to have a second chance at those final weeks.

Reaching across their dad, Mac rested a hand on her shoulder. "It was pretty hard for you guys, Gwen, but you talked. Finally. We had a family again."

"I guess." She didn't want to think about it. She'd already cried enough in the last week, and she refused to do it now. And sniffles didn't count. "We said everything we had to say. I'm just sorry it took so long. I was such a jerk to her all those years."

She laid her head on her dad's shoulder, wanting the shelter of his comfort as much as to comfort him.

Mac poked her in the arm. "You'll make a great lawyer." Catching her gaze, he grinned. "Because you can really be a jerk sometimes."

She slugged him until he begged for mercy. Then she slugged him again. That's what families were for.

———

"This is nuts, Adam. I can't do it." Gwen breathed into the phone, wincing at Adam's sputtered reaction to her decision not to play in the competition. It was only three days away and she didn't even remotely know the music for it.

She'd spent Wednesday morning at her dad's house, helping him cope with Mac's departure, and was now back home. She'd called Danny at work, asking to take the rest of the week off. He'd readily agreed, probably hoping she'd spend her time cramming for the LSAT.

None of the men in her life wanted her to take it easy.

"Of course you can." Sounding a lot more relaxed than Gwen felt, Adam probably didn't want to push her over the edge a day after her mother's funeral. "You said it yourself—you've spent a lot of time at the piano in the last several days. You'll be fine."

He hadn't heard a word she'd said. "I wasn't playing the pieces for the competition. I haven't touched them in almost a week."

"It'll be good for you. Take your mind off . . . stuff." Adam paused. "But we can skip the pieces we'd planned for the competition. Tell me what you've been playing, and you can do that instead."

Gwen made a mental note not to call anyone else today. With her luck, she'd end up running the PTA, buying and preparing all the food for a neighborhood barbecue, and cleaning Leila's house.

She wasn't up to a struggle with Adam, but she also didn't plan to cave in. Not for at least another day. "I'll think about it." When he started to argue, she cut him off. "That's all I'll do for now. Think. I'll let you know."

She hung up before his reaction could hit her ear.

She'd spent a lifetime not making decisions, or not stopping everyone else from making them for her. Vivian had made them for her, and Rob had made a million awful ones. Her bosses, Leila, even her kids did. At least Leila's decisions were fun. In the last few months, she'd faced too many dilemmas and crises, but at least she'd finally started to make her own decisions.

And she'd screwed up half of them.

Leila said she just needed more practice.

Practice? Lowering herself onto the piano bench, she flexed her fingers and began to play.

SATURDAY DAWNED COLD AND CLEAR, a perfect morning for a sore throat, a backed-up sewer system, a screaming teenage daughter in full tantrum, and a son—who might never see the other side of eleven—unwilling to budge from his room even after she'd promised him banana-chocolate-chip pancakes.

And a piano teacher who would arrive in ten minutes—despite her current ratty bathrobe and hair resembling Einstein's—because he didn't trust her to show up at the piano competition under her own steam.

Gwen considered locking the doors and drawing the blinds.

Knowing Adam, he'd just go next door and get her house key from Leila, who would sell Gwen's soul to practically anyone for the price of a blender drink.

She gave up and headed for the shower.

Two minutes later, she had a head full of shampoo and a daughter still screaming at her. "Mom! That piano guy's here. He's a hottie!"

Perfect. Since Adam and half the neighborhood had now heard Sarah's assessment, Gwen gazed down at the drain, wondering whether she could squeeze through it.

She hummed instead. Loudly. Maybe Adam would go away when she refused to open the bathroom door, even if she was forced to beg for food scraps from anyone within earshot of the second-floor bathroom window.

Sighing, she rinsed, soaped up, rinsed again, and turned off the water. She couldn't avoid him much longer.

Fifteen minutes later, she walked downstairs, her silk paisley skirt swishing against her legs, and pretended she had more dignity than she felt.

Adam whistled at the bottom of the steps, ignoring

Sarah's smirk. "Nice. If the judges are all men, you'll win hands down. Before you start playing."

"I doubt it." But she blushed anyway, stopping only at another fiendish grin from Sarah.

The grin faded and Sarah's whine returned. "Mom, I thought you were going to my volleyball practice. And we have a game on Tuesday, in case you forgot."

"I didn't forget." Gwen glanced into the kitchen, checking to see whether she'd turned off the coffeemaker. "Aren't you the one forgetting things? My piano competition is today. Did you say hi to Adam?" Turning to him, she nodded at Sarah. "This is my charming daughter, Sarah. I think you two met once before." At Greta's wedding reception, moments before Gwen had exited in a fifty-yard dash. "But unless you're a coach or can beat her in basketball, she's a little shy."

He smiled at Sarah, extending his hand to her. "I can dunk, you know."

"No way." Taking his hand, she released it in a nanosecond.

"Way. On the nine-foot hoop at my parents' house."

"That's so lame." Sarah rolled her eyes, then turned back to Gwen. Her lower lip curled. "Dad's gonna be there, ya know. And Tiff. I guess they wanna see me play an' all."

After a week of Sarah's lengthy descriptions of the rock on Tiffany's left hand, Gwen wouldn't have gone to volleyball practice even if she didn't have other plans.

Just a few weeks ago, the possibility of Rob outdoing her with the kids had forced her to attend more volleyball practices and other kids' events than she ordinarily could fit into her schedule. Most parents went only to the games, after all. Now, though, with her vision sharpened by Vivian's death, she looked at Sarah with different eyes. She did want a close relationship with her daughter—something she hadn't had with Vivian.

But she wasn't going to beg for it. And Sarah, Gwen had finally begun to understand, was manipulative as hell.

Sarah needed a man in her life, but her fascination with Rob seemed to ebb and flow with her desire to get something she wanted from Gwen. Thank God Leila had forced Gwen to take a good, hard look at the situation.

Not that she'd ever admit it to Leila, of course.

She grinned at Sarah. "Nice try, kid. You'll have to give me another report on Tiffany's ring." She rolled her eyes for Sarah's benefit. "But I have to play in the competition—I've told you all about it. I'll be home by early afternoon. Maybe Nick will even make an appearance by then." She raised her voice on the last sentence, but no sound came from upstairs.

As usual.

Gwen headed for the front door, Adam trailing her.

"Mom?" Sarah had perfected her tragic wail. "Can I shoot hoops after practice? With Diana and Kelly?"

"Sure, but I thought your dad was coming to practice." She frowned, turning back to Sarah. "Won't he want to take you to lunch afterward?"

Head down, Sarah scuffed the toe of her sneaker on the floor. "Uh, I'm not sure he'll be there."

As she'd suspected. "I guess the update on Tiffany's ring will have to wait." Smiling, Gwen sailed out the door.

Her smile faded at the sight of Adam's car—a clunker of an old VW Beetle with a convertible top. The top hadn't been white in years, and it looked as if someone had poked holes in it with rusty pitchforks. "Should we take my Honda?"

He pulled open the passenger-side door of the VW. It

creaked at the offense. "My car is handy, and you said you loved convertibles. It's a treat for your big day."

She loved *driving* a convertible. Her own convertible. Clinging for dear life to a door with rusty hinges and a broken handle wasn't quite as high on her wish list.

Saying a silent prayer to the patron saint for really stupid ideas, she climbed in. And she hung on as Adam backed up, swung into the street, and careened down the road toward the university—as far as she could tell, all without ever using his brakes.

Twenty minutes later, her face whiter than it had started out and her hair both dry and utterly disheveled, Gwen climbed out of the car with rubbery legs and a firm resolve to take a Lyft home. Adam looked ebullient.

With a hand on her elbow, he steered her across the parking ramp, past a couple of campus buildings, and to the steps leading up to the music building. Finally, he turned her to face him. "Knock 'em dead, Gwen. You can do this."

"I know." Her nerves shook, and a flood of emotions sprang loose from inside of her. Tension from her daily arguments with Sarah. Lingering sadness over Vivian. Stark terror that she'd embarrass herself today. She tried for a pun. "I knocked one dead just last week—my mom."

As they both winced, he led her inside.

CHAPTER 17

"I still can't believe you took second place." After insisting on making a celebration cake for Gwen, and despite Gwen's assurances that frosting came in a can these days, Leila licked the frosting off the beaters. Apparently, Leila's "famous" seven-minute frosting didn't come in a can. Gwen suspected that the rapture on her friend's face had more to do with licking the beaters than anything.

But God knew they needed something to celebrate.

"Thanks for your vote of confidence." Scanning the disaster that Leila had made of Gwen's kitchen, and the dirty pans and bowls in the sink, she wondered why she'd gotten only one lousy cake out of the deal. "I'm sorry I didn't do better, but the six-year-old who won had ten-inch fingers."

"Bummer." Leila bent down to retrieve a gob of frosting that had landed on the floor. On the verge of licking her finger, she caught Gwen's eye and wiped her hands on her designer jeans. "I know you're good, but that competition was a much bigger deal than Adam admitted to you. And you still took second."

"He didn't want to make me nervous." Still picturing the intensity on the faces of the performers—many of whom were at least twenty years younger than her—Gwen shook her head. Several of them had looked as if they'd chewed off all their fingernails, and probably their instructors' fingernails to boot. "And it came out okay."

"No shit." The timer dinged. Leila panicked, throwing mail and magazines off the counter in her frantic search for hot pads. Gwen reached into the drawer next to her and handed Leila a couple. "I mean, second place out of, what, fifty?"

"Sixty-five."

"What does it mean? Do they just give you a certificate and a pat on the head?"

"A certificate, a hundred dollars, and a scholarship to the U's graduate program in music."

"You're kidding. What does the winner get?"

Gwen rolled her eyes. "From the looks of him, he should've gotten a scholarship to preschool." She didn't really care. She'd just wanted to survive the competition, and she had. "More money and a classier certificate, I suppose. I didn't stick around to find out."

"Are you taking the scholarship?"

"No. I just took the money and the certificate. I'd hoped to do well, but I realized in the last few days that I'd rather play piano for myself. It helps me through the rough patches that come my way. I never should've quit." Gwen bent over the cake, catching a whiff of its delicious aroma. Banana. Wow. "I almost forgot. They also gave me a gift certificate for dinner at Melba Toast, one of the sponsors of the competition."

Leila's hands flew up to cover her mouth, leaving white frosting all over it. "Oh, God. He wasn't there, was he?"

"Tucker? No. He's only around for my humiliating moments." Gwen frowned, thinking about the afternoon.

"My dad came. He said Vivian would've been proud of me." She walked over to the sink, mostly to avoid Leila's sharp gaze. "I wish I'd known that a long time ago."

"But you do now. It's better than nothing."

Leila's tongue ran around the outside of her mouth, licking the excess frosting. Gwen could think of a few men who'd appreciate the sight much more than she did. Thankfully, Nick was hiding out in his bedroom and not particularly interested—yet—in what women did with their tongues.

She sighed. "I know. It's just— Vivian and I had a lot of ground to cover in a few short weeks, and I didn't exactly make the most of it."

Waving at the cake in a futile effort to cool it off, Leila eyed the bowl of frosting. Gwen swatted her hand.

She snatched another dollop anyway. "Why do you still call her Vivian?"

"Habit." Wondering the same thing, Gwen chewed on the corner of her lip. "I spent a lifetime calling her that. I had only a few weeks thinking of her as my mom."

"At least you had that, and you still have your dad and Mac. A couple of sweethearts." Leila blew on the cake. After the two margaritas she'd inhaled as a prelude to her culinary efforts, the damn thing probably smelled of tequila. "And Sarah and Nick—at least, what little I see of that kid—must be a comfort."

"Don't even think about it." Gwen stopped Leila as she headed for the refrigerator with the cake in her hands. "Yeah, they're good kids. But like you say, I don't see much of Nick, or even Sarah. Her schedule is all sports, all the time—if she's not playing, she's watching."

"She's fourteen. Last time I checked, that was considered normal." Defeated in her efforts to cool the cake—or eat all the frosting—Leila dragged a stool to the counter and perched on it, watching Gwen clean up the mess she'd just made.

"I know." Gwen used the inside of her wrist to push back a lock of hair that hung in her face. "I was the same way at her age. Right about the age when everything went wrong with Vivian."

"You're not Vivian."

Gwen looked at her friend. "Sometimes she looks at me the way I used to look at Vivian."

"Like I said, she's fourteen. Teenagers have that look patented, or they should. Every kid I knew in school was the same way." Grabbing a dishtowel, Leila stunned Gwen. She was going to help clean up? No. She twisted it a few times and snapped Gwen in the butt. "I'll bet you even did it to your dad, and you adore the guy."

"Maybe." Shrugging, Gwen debated whether to nail Leila with a dish towel. Somehow, Leila would fight back until Gwen had an even bigger disaster of a kitchen to clean. "I just don't want to let history repeat itself. And Nick—I don't know what to do with him."

"Why don't ya just throw me away, like you threw my dad away. Huh?" Nick, the boy who never left his room, found a really lousy time to make an appearance. Gwen hurried over to where he stood, just outside the arched doorway to the kitchen, but he crossed his arms and backed away from her. His whole body shook. "I hate you!"

"You don't understand, Nicky. I didn't— I mean, your dad was the one—" Torn between her need to console Nick and her desire not to be the one to drive a wedge between her kids and Rob, Gwen cut herself off. Instead, she dropped to her knees to hug Nick. He could've been made out of marble. "I would never throw you away. I love you. To the moon and back."

He tugged out of her grasp and fled up the stairs, shouting down at her. "I don't love you! You're a big jerk!"

"If it's helpful, you're not that big." Leila came up behind Gwen and hugged her. "And he'll get over it. I promise."

"For once in your life, Leila, you might be wrong."

———

"I'M NOT sure that playing tennis today was a good idea." After wiping the sweat off her forehead, Gwen glanced at her watch. "The LSAT is next Saturday, and I've hardly read any of the materials."

On the other hand, she and Leila had wolfed down half of Leila's cake in one sitting yesterday. She wouldn't mind working off a few of the thousand or so calories she'd consumed.

Not that they hadn't been worth it.

Picking up a ball at the net, where Gwen was doing the same thing, Adam leaned over it. "You know what they say about all work and no play."

She tapped him lightly with her racquet. "Yeah, yeah. It makes me do better on the LSAT." Returning to the baseline, she turned back to him. "Besides, I didn't see you telling me to play when the competition was coming up."

"That's different. That was important."

"Hmpf." Hands on her hips, she glared at him. "That's your—" She stopped her tirade when he burst out laughing. "Cute. Real cute. The LSAT is important to me, too."

Still at the net, Adam motioned Gwen closer. Judging from the curious looks they were attracting from the players on the next court, it wasn't a bad idea. After an hour of hard volleys, sweat drenched Adam's shirt and made his legs almost glisten. With effort, Gwen returned her gaze to his face. He grinned at her as if he knew the path her mind had taken.

She blushed. "Well, it is, you know."

"I didn't say it wasn't. Important." His racquet lay on top of the net, clicking against hers. "I've just been wondering if law school is more important to you or to someone else—that guy you work with, or maybe your family or something."

He'd sounded almost jealous when Gwen had mentioned Danny and the firm's scholarship. Realizing it, she probably hadn't needed to mention it several times.

She smiled. "Good question. I've let too many people make decisions for me, or force me into them." She tapped his racquet a little harder. "Like entering me in piano competitions. Things like that."

"It was good for you." He grabbed a towel and wiped his face. "And you did well."

"So if I win a fancy ribbon, that makes it all okay?"

Looking down, Adam stubbed the toe of his sneaker against the court, much as Sarah would do. "Hey, I'm sorry I pressured you. It's just—" He halted as if searching for the right words.

"Yes?"

Flushed, he finally met her gaze. "You really *are* good, whether or not you play in competitions or accept a music scholarship. But I, uh, hoped that if you won or placed high, they might offer me a position in the music department." He bit his lip. "It's what I've always wanted."

Everyone had an angle. At least, most of the men who passed through her life seemed to. But she wasn't angry. She was too accustomed to the experience to feel much of anything.

At least Adam was honest about it. "And did they?"

He nodded. "Next semester, but only on a trial basis while one of their tenured faculty is on maternity leave."

Come to think of it, she *did* feel just the tiniest bit angry. Not to mention incredulous. "No offense, but did anyone bother to ask just how much *influence* your teaching had on my performance yesterday? Do they know I've taken lessons from you for only a couple of months?

Startled, Adam flinched. "No. But I—"

"You, you, you." Gwen shook her head. "You probably even *kissed* me so I'd go along with your little plan." She swung her arm wide, encompassing the tennis court. "And played tennis with me. And . . . whatever. You weren't even remotely interested in me before the competition entered the picture."

"That's not fair. Or true." Adam's voice rose, and the couple on the next court stopped playing altogether, lingering at the end of their net closest to Adam and Gwen to catch every word. Adam didn't notice them. "The competition was good for you. And—and I like doing things with you. You're not like my other students."

"Why? More gray hair?" She loved her new hair color and the sassy style, but she somehow never forgot that at least a few strands of silvery-white hair lay underneath it. Leila had helped her turn into a "package," but she hadn't yet fixed all the inner workings. Her soul.

Adam brushed his hand against her hair, then her cheek. "The hair's cute. And you're cute." He waved his hands when her own hand came up, threatening to slap him. "Hey, I don't see why women hate being called cute. It's a good thing."

His eyebrows danced, provoking her first laugh in the last ten minutes.

He laughed, too, before turning serious. "But I also like

talking to you. You're fun, and your sense of humor is wicked." At her raised eyebrows, he nodded. "Yep. That's a good thing, too. But—"

Here it came. The part where he admitted that she looked like a toad. Or his mother. Maybe his grandmother.

"You're too hard on yourself. You've made progress even in the short time I've known you, but you still need to figure out what makes you happy. Being a music professor will make *me* happy. I want the same thing for you."

"Have you been talking to Leila?" At Adam's confused frown, Gwen shrugged. "That's been her daily lecture to me for the past two months. She must've bottled it."

"I have to admit, Leila and I do have at least one thing in common." He tapped her racquet one last time with his. "We both like short skirts."

———

"Welcome back. We missed you." Late Monday morning, in his usual fashion, Danny swung a leg over the side of the chair in Gwen's office. The rest of him slouched against the other side of the chair.

"Why? Did you have to get your own coffee for a change?"

"Smartass." Danny glanced at the file in his hand. "We're all set for the Treadman meeting. The proxies are coming in, and it's looking pretty positive despite all the media crap."

"That's good." Gwen pointed at the file. "Is that for the meeting? Did you want me to put together the script?"

"No need. This is for you. Something to maybe help while you're getting ready for the LSAT. Stuff like that."

To think the man had a degree from Harvard.

She held out her hand, but he clutched the file. Gwen sat

back in her chair. "Will you be giving it to me before Saturday, or am I just supposed to imagine what's inside it?"

It couldn't be much. The file was pretty thin.

"You can look it over later." Danny studied Gwen's desk. She'd cleared it a week ago yesterday, the day after Vivian died. Partly so she wouldn't worry about unfinished work while she took time off and partly to take her mind off everything else in her life. "How are you fixed for work?"

She'd hoped to avoid it this week so she could study for the LSAT. "Fine. Odds and ends. Enough for now."

"And . . . everything's okay?"

Danny made a good pal, and he excelled at both law and happy hour, but Gwen knew he'd taken his own mother's early death hard. He avoided mentioning Vivian's death as much as possible.

"It's fine. I spent some time with my dad, and I took second place in a piano competition on Saturday. What the heck."

"I didn't know you played piano."

"I didn't. Or not for a long time. I'm trying to get back into things again." She didn't elaborate, knowing Danny didn't need a blow-by-blow of everything she'd done—or at least tried to do—in the last few months.

Or her ongoing struggles to make some sense of her life, including whether law was what she wanted to do when she grew up. Her current struggles were a refreshing change, though. Until a few months ago, she'd stopped caring enough to bother trying.

"That's good." Danny glanced at the open door for at least the fourth time in five minutes. "So. Nervous about the LSAT?"

She raised her hands in the air. "Not really. Life goes on. If I bomb, nothing will have changed."

"You won't bomb."

"Probably not." She knew that. She'd been nervous before the piano competition but had done well. Looking back, she'd always done well whenever she'd bothered to make an attempt. Since marrying Rob, and even since divorcing him, she'd forgotten that about herself.

"Look." A little agitated, Danny glanced again at the door. "Claudia's birthday is Friday, and . . ."

"You're hoping I can bake a cake. Not a chance." Crossing her arms, Gwen shook her head. "I can't believe it, Danny. You know I've got the LSAT on Saturday, and I told you I'm tired of everyone stomping all over me. I never figured you'd be one of them."

He actually looked a little sheepish—until he grinned. "Nice work, counselor, but I'm not quite as bad as you think. In fact, I was going to offer to pick up a cake—" He shuddered for effect. "But now I'm afraid you'll just cram it down my throat."

"Not if it's chocolate."

"Chocolate it is, then. I think that works for Claudia, too." He laughed as he dropped the file on Gwen's desk, then pointed at it. "Since you're obviously ready for the LSAT, if not the bar exam, I'm relieved to admit that this isn't about any of that. I'm just not good with this kind of stuff."

Curious, she opened the file. It contained a sympathy card signed by the entire department—including a couple of semi-retired partners whom she'd long suspected didn't even know her name. Danny had also scribbled an invitation to join him, Claudia, and a few other lawyers for a celebration dinner Saturday night after the LSAT.

At Melba Toast.

Her face fell. "I . . . can't do it."

She still couldn't face Tucker, no matter how many pep

talks Leila gave or how many shots of alcohol slid down her throat. When it happened—and it definitely would—it would be on her terms and when she didn't have so many things scrambling her brain. When the hurt of what he'd done had stopped stinging and faded to a dull ache.

She also *really* couldn't explain it to Danny. Too Much Information.

For that matter, she had a few questions about law school. A few things she needed to think through and discuss with someone, but Danny wasn't the right person. In his mind, she'd already finished law school, been admitted to the bar, and started practicing law. At Pembroke and McFarley. In the office next to his.

"No problem." Danny offered the stoic face he always gave to opposing counsel, but his shoulders drooped. He'd been so excited the last few weeks about the LSAT—almost as if he were the one taking it. "Another time?"

She felt like an idiot, but she wouldn't force the group to change their plans, even if their plans revolved around her anticipated victory over the big, bad LSAT. "Sure. But my brother Mac will be in town, and he . . . wants to have dinner."

He'd actually be in Duluth this weekend, still in trial. She'd just fibbed to Danny, her friend and, more importantly, the lawyer known throughout the firm for sensing a lie at a hundred yards. She told herself that Mac *would* be in town— at some point—and would definitely want to have dinner. Also at some point.

It didn't help.

Flushing, she flashed back to the summer, when she'd turned down Ted Harrison's dates with a long string of flimsy excuses. Despite everything she'd done for herself since then, nothing had changed.

"Oh." Danny let her get away with it, but the crease between his eyebrows told her that he knew something was off.

"No." She glanced down for a moment, then looked up to meet his curious gaze. She *had* changed. Maybe not enough to face Tucker yet, but she'd started to grow up. She hoped. "I'm sorry. I do need to spend time with my dad, yes, but the truth is that I just can't go to Melba Toast. Ever." She didn't fill in the blanks. "But I really do want a raincheck. Please?"

"Anything for you." Grinning, Danny stood up. "Even when you don't make a damn bit of sense."

———

"You're still not yourself." Fresh from her weekly massage, Leila positively glowed—and, unfortunately, felt inspired to fix Gwen. Again. "It must be time for another session at the day spa."

It'd been two months since her afternoon at Leila's spa. She didn't have Leila's frivolous streak, but she sometimes wished she could borrow it.

Feet up on her sofa, Gwen hunched over the LSAT preparation materials. The exam was less than two days away. Time to cram.

"Could it wait? I've got the LSAT on Saturday, and work is busy, and Sarah and Nick . . ."

Were spending another evening with their dad. And Tiffany, also known as Miss Perfect to Gwen's kids. Logically, it made all the sense in the world that they liked her. Hell, she was practically a child herself. They could bond with her. Compare puberty notes.

But why did Rob have to marry Tiffany? And why were the kids somehow slipping away from her?

The LSAT book on her lap slammed shut, and Leila hovered over her. Gwen pretended to shudder, pointing at Leila's red stilettos, which tonight found themselves matched with tight green capris and a yellow cropped top.

"Get over it." When Gwen didn't look up, Leila dropped down beside her on the sofa, making the LSAT book bounce in her lap. "Forget about the kids for a minute. You still haven't told me why you're taking the LSAT."

Gwen frowned at her. "To. Get. Into. Law school."

"Duh." Leila waved a hand in the air. "I'm not an idiot—" She glanced down at the front of herself. "Despite how I sometimes dress."

"You said it. I didn't." Gwen covered her smirk with her hand.

Leila laughed. "I couldn't help myself. It's already October, and I can't bear the thought of winter."

"I know. Almost time to store convertibles for the winter. I may not have one anymore, but such a tangible sign that winter is coming still depresses me." Gwen could still picture herself tooling around the lakes in her old convertible on a sunny, early-October day like today. Not having it at all was worse than putting her baby away for the winter.

Leila stuck a gumball in her mouth, chomped a few times, and quickly blew a bubble. "Your choice, kiddo. The way you tell it, you threw away all your trinkets when Rob walked out. Stupid. Throw out the guy, but keep the loot."

"Too late now." She'd questioned her decision a few times over the last two years, but she couldn't look back. She only wished Rob had left her life as completely as her convertible and other loot had.

"You didn't answer my question." Leila stretched the wad of gum a foot out from her mouth. "Why are you going to law school? To be like Mac? Or because Danny tells you to?"

"Those aren't good enough reasons."

"That's my point." Leila popped another bubble. "But I haven't heard any other ones come out of your mouth."

"That's the problem." Giving up, Gwen tossed the LSAT book on the coffee table. She wouldn't read it as long as Leila stayed around, and her friend was practically pitching a tent in Gwen's living room. "When I was with Rob, I stopped doing things for myself. Stopped even *being* myself. Now this opportunity comes along, and I want to take it. Only—"

"Only it doesn't set your butt on fire."

Gwen tried not to picture it. "That's not it, or not exactly." She'd puzzled over it ever since Danny had first broached the idea. Even if she liked the thought of law school, she wasn't sure where it would lead. Should she wait until she knew? "I'd like to help people. Women, especially, and kids. But that's not what I do at my law firm."

"So do something else." Leila snapped her fingers. "Mac works for a nonprofit, doesn't he? Maybe you can do something like that."

She sighed. "And tell my firm 'thanks for the scholarship, but I have to run now'? I don't think it works that way." She lifted her feet, resting them on the LSAT book. "Maybe I should skip law school altogether."

"Right. Run away from another thing. That makes sense." Leila scrunched her nose, then grabbed a sofa pillow and hugged it as she thought. "Maybe for once you *should* run away. Not from law school. From the scholarship."

Gwen looked around the living room, from the faded rug to the worn-out rocking chair to the sofa of a thousand stains. She sometimes wondered how she could bear to sit on it. "If I give up one, I give up the other. I can't afford law school without the scholarship."

"Hmmm." Leila did the same visual inventory of the

room, looking at it as if for the first time. "We'll have to think on this. In the meantime, study up for the test. Keep your options open."

"I wonder how I'll—"

The pillow sailed at Gwen, catching her in the stomach. "You'll do great. And next week we'll do the spa. My treat."

"I'd say thanks, but I hate to encourage you." Gwen threw the pillow back at Leila. "You're just as pushy as everyone else in my life."

"Oh, much more so." Leila flashed a grin. "You love it."

———

"You did it. Congratulations, honey." Skip Withers leaned back in his recliner, puffing on a horribly stinky cigar that Vivian would have forbidden within a hundred yards of their house while she'd been alive.

The leftovers from dinner were already stowed in Dad's refrigerator, and he looked content. At least, more content than he'd been during the two long months that had just passed.

Gwen had dropped by after she finished the LSAT, bearing cartons of Chinese food and two grumbling kids. She'd figured the one made up for the other. Seeing Sarah sprawled on the carpet with music blasting in her ears and Nick groaning over the dinosaur of a computer at the far end of her dad's study, she had her doubts.

"It's not as if the scores have come back, Dad." She smiled at him, wondering whether he'd be shocked if she asked for a cigar. She'd never tried one. "I just finished taking the test. It's not much to celebrate yet."

"Not true." He blew a ring of smoke over his head, watching it float to the ceiling. "You've done something for yourself. That's always a reason to celebrate. It's what . . . your mother would have wanted for you."

A few weeks ago, and certainly a couple of months ago, Gwen would've scoffed out loud at her dad's words. She'd figured Vivian wanted only the country-club life for her, the life she herself had led. The life Gwen had led with Rob.

Now? She didn't know. When it came to Vivian, all of her preconceived notions had been thrown out the window, but she hadn't yet found anything to replace them with. As it turned out, she hadn't known her mother at all.

Reaching for a cigar, she enjoyed her dad's raised eyebrows. He said nothing as he offered her a light. She nearly choked on the first inhale.

"Don't inhale them." He tapped the ashes from the end of his own cigar into an ashtray. "They're not like cigarettes, not that I've ever seen you smoke those, either."

Puff. Choke. "I-I never told you." She cringed. "These smell a lot better than they taste, you know that?"

"It's an acquired taste. Most things are."

She let that comment pass. The conversation could head in too many directions, most of which she wasn't prepared to sit around discussing with her dad.

Her face was probably turning green. An ambulance would soon arrive, and they'd wheel her out of Dad's house under an oxygen tent. Gamely, she kept puffing. Inhaling. And choking.

Her dad's lips twitched.

She moved to the chair next to him, sharing his ashtray. When she tapped her cigar against it, the ashes flew over the edge and onto the table. Her dad chose not to mention that, either. A wise man. Possibly a terrified one.

Finally he spoke, taking both his and Gwen's mind off her struggles to handle a cigar. "I'm sure you'll do well on the

LSAT, hon. Will you go to Minnesota for law school? And work at your same firm?"

"I suppose Minnesota. The other local law schools are private, so they're much more expensive. On the other hand, I could enroll in the evening program at a school like Mitchell-Hamline and work during the day." She played with her cigar, trying not to burn herself. "I'm not sure where I'll work. That's part of the problem."

Her dad tapped his cigar against the ashtray without looking at it—and without spilling a single ash. Amazing. "Isn't your firm giving you a scholarship? I would think you'd automatically stay there. Easy choice."

"Easy for everyone but me." She set her cigar in the ashtray, not willing to die her first time smoking one.

After a minute, her dad snuffed it out.

"Hmmm." He snuffed out his own as well. "Easy choices are nice, but only if they work for you. Why doesn't this one?"

She shrugged. "I'm not sure I want to work there after graduation. I'm not sure what I want to do. But I have two kids to support."

"I could help with the money." Her dad smiled, a little sadly. "You've never asked for any help, honey. After you and Rob divorced— Well, your mother and I always wanted to do something for you and the kids."

"Rob always paid for everything." Remembering her financial dependence on him for so many years, while he'd screwed everyone in sight, still made her sick. "I wanted to make it on my own."

"And you did. Your mother was proud of you, and I am, too." He reached for her hand. "But this is something new. You want to spread your wings. If you want to quit your job while you're in law school, or get one with fewer hours, do it. I'll help you out. I'd be honored."

Gwen shook her head. "I can't, Dad. Sorry. You're too generous, but I still need to make it on my own. It's the only way I'll ever be happy."

"Financial independence doesn't make anyone happy." Her dad squeezed her hand. "It might buy you a few toys or fancy clothes or even a mansion on a lake—" Thus spoke the man who lived in a mansion on a lake. "But you have to find happiness somewhere else." He tapped his heart. "Here."

"It's a start, anyway. I'll figure out the rest as I go along." She clasped her dad's hand in both of hers. "But it's a wonderful offer, and I do appreciate it. It's just—"

"You have to support yourself."

"You got it." She tried not to worry whether her kids had been listening in, but a quick glance told her that they were both absorbed in what they were doing. Whatever it was.

"Fine. Support yourself." The twinkle in her dad's eyes should probably make her suspicious, but this was Dad. Okay, she was suspicious anyway. "But you *do* have a big birthday coming up soon. Is an old man still allowed to buy his daughter a gift, or have you given those up, too?"

"You're not old, but I'm still accepting birthday gifts." She wagged a finger at him. "No mortgage or tuition payments. Maybe something little and cute and fun. You know—a treat."

"Little and cute and fun. I'll see what I can do."

CHAPTER 18

"I'm sick of everyone telling me to get happy. Don't I look happy to you?" Late Tuesday afternoon, Gwen frowned at Leila as they climbed up into side-by-side pedicure chairs.

"Now that you mention it, no." Bending down, Leila rolled the hems of her remarkably loose-fitting slacks up to her knees. "And you're not supposed to frown like that right after a facial. All the lines you lost come right back."

Gwen touched her face. "I didn't lose any lines. She just slathered a bunch of goop on them. Camouflage."

"Whatever." Leila held her thumbs and forefingers together to form a "W," which Sarah did to Gwen on a daily basis. She wondered which one had taught the other. "Speaking of happy, how's Adam? Or has he dumped you now that he got his big dream job?"

"He's still in the picture, I guess." Thinking about it, she wrinkled her nose. She'd cancelled her usual Friday-night piano lesson last week to study for the LSAT, but Adam had stopped by on Sunday afternoon and stayed for a while, shooting hoops with Sarah and Gwen in the driveway.

He'd cleaned Sarah's clock in a short game of one-on-one. Gwen smiled, remembering the dismay on Sarah's face.

"Based on that smile, he *must* be in the picture. At close range?" Leila cackled, and Gwen shot her a withering glance that only increased her friend's laughter.

"Not as close as you'd like, I'm afraid." Gwen exhaled on a sigh as the potent mixture of warm water and a vibrating chair pushed her closer to nirvana. Happiness. For an hour, at least. "We're just friends."

"That's not what it looked like when we had dinner at your house." Adjusting the massage buttons on her chair, Leila leaned back and shimmied against it.

Gwen didn't have a good comeback. That night—the evening Vivian died—Adam had acted as if the sun rose and set over Gwen. His apparent interest had cooled since then. Not completely, but enough to irritate her a little.

Leila leaned down to whisper something to the young woman doing her pedicure—Tiffany again. Gwen's nail tech, Amber, was new to the spa. She had incredible hands and offered sparkly silver polish. And she didn't say much. A triple victory.

Tiffany looked curiously at Gwen. Reaching over, Leila patted Gwen's hand. "I told Tiffany that you're a piano ace, every law school in the country wants you, and gorgeous young men climb all over you. She's probably wondering why you're not happy, too."

"I've had too many lousy men in my life." Gwen tipped her head at Tiffany as she answered Leila. "It's ugly out there."

"Don't I know it." The young woman shook her head. "I work all day, spend half my time on my MBA classes and studying, and most men just want to get laid. I wonder how they ever become successful."

Gwen nodded, marveling at the bright mind in the serious young woman wearing chunky shoes and spandex.

Leila laughed. "They screw the right woman, and everything else falls into place."

"Leila." Gwen rolled her eyes. "Some of them work hard and are nice—like my dad and Mac. Probably most of them. It's just bad luck. I keep running into the jerks of the world."

"There's no such thing as bad luck." Leila leaned back in her chair, closing her eyes. "It's karma. You know—settling scores from past lives." Leila had been spending too much time in the self-help section of Jon's bookstore. "But once you've worked it all out, you'll meet a nice guy. Soon, I hope."

"And live happily ever after." Not in this lifetime. Wiggling her toes in the water, Gwen decided that Leila needed a job. Something to do besides micromanaging Gwen's life.

"It's true." Tiffany brightened as she placed Leila's right foot on the towel, setting the left one back in the water to soak. "I bet you'll find someone nice. I finally did."

Eyes still closed, Leila smiled. "Am I behind on my gossip? Who's the lucky guy?"

"His name is Rob. Rob Stanhope." As her whole face lit up, she didn't notice Leila's white-knuckled grip on the arms of her chair or Gwen's choked gasp. "We're getting married in late spring after I finish my classes."

Dear. Jesus.

Leila recovered first. It wouldn't take much, since Gwen was still choking to death. "Tiffany? I think it's time I made a proper introduction. This is Gwen. Gwen Stanhope."

———

"Of all the women named Tiffany in the world, why did you and Rob have to know the same one?" Two hours later, after finishing their pedicures but cancelling their scheduled manicures, Gwen touched the straw from her second raspberry margarita to her lips, drawing another long sip.

At this rate, she wouldn't be able to drive home. She also wouldn't let Leila drive, since she was matching her sip for sip.

Gwen glanced around the dark bar—Pendulum, which she didn't have to avoid anymore because of Ted—where the presence of a blender and fresh fruit seemed nothing short of a miracle. It was half full on a Tuesday evening, with most of the crowd seated at tables and just a couple of strays, plus Leila and her, at the bar. Leila spent half of her time flirting with the bartender, a man named Jed, and pretending that Gwen hadn't just survived an earthquake.

The only benefit of Pendulum today, besides the surprisingly good margaritas, was that no one she knew from work would stop in here on a Tuesday night. She could practically guarantee it.

She hoped.

But at Pendulum, even on a weeknight, there *were* no guaranties.

After fluttering her fingers at Jed, Leila stared at her own margarita. Mango. "I can't believe it, and I'm so sorry. After seeing Tiffany every week for my nails, I thought I knew everything about her." She whistled, drawing a few looks. As always. "All that time, she just talked about her MBA program. If she mentioned dating a guy, she never said Rob's name. I swear."

"I believe you." Gwen fished a few quarters out of her purse. Time to hit the jukebox. Some loud music might blast through the chills still shaking her. Pushing back her chair, she turned to Leila. "You know what I hate the most?"

"What?"

"Tiffany's a nice young woman. Rob doesn't deserve her."

Leila shook her head. "He didn't deserve you, either."

Maybe not. But it'd take at least one more margarita before she'd believe it.

Gwen walked to the jukebox and inserted the quarters before looking at her choices. She didn't have many. No Eagles, which was both good and bad. After glancing at the song titles and receiving some shouted suggestions from the crowd, she chose Patsy Cline and a few other songs guaranteed to depress the hell out of her. Hugging herself, she stared at the jukebox as "Faded Rose" floated into the air.

"That's one of my favorite songs." The voice behind her wasn't Leila's. Gwen turned, prepared to reject some drunken idiot and whatever pathetic pick-up line he offered next.

Jon Abelard smiled at her. She nearly fainted.

"Patsy's version is nice but so sad. I prefer Willie Nelson. Except for his braids." He pointed at his own shaggy brown hair. Hanging over his collar, it was a little longer than the men at Gwen's law firm wore theirs. "Not that I have much to talk about."

Leila joined them, skimming her fingers through the ends of Jon's hair. "You should've joined us today at the spa. While they were painting our toenails, someone else could've been snipping and primping your hair. Turn you into a real boy toy."

"I think I'm too old to qualify." He looked down, but the dark bar didn't offer a good look at their toes, even though Leila wiggled hers for Jon's benefit. "Besides, maybe I'd rather get my toenails painted. Might be fun."

Pointing at his beat-up loafers, Leila winced. "Don't waste your time. Between those scuffed pieces of leather and the cowboy boots you're so fond of, we've never seen your toes."

"I'll buy some sandals."

"Bad timing. Winter's practically here."

As the two kept bantering, Gwen surreptitiously studied Jon, wondering what twist of fate had brought him downtown and into Pendulum when his bookstore and life were very much in Uptown. She would've left for home after the first margarita if it hadn't been for the bartender's amazing generosity with tequila.

She blurted out her question. "What are you doing here?"

Leila and Jon both stared at her. Leila patted Jon on the arm. "Forgive her. Gwen's only on her second margarita. It might take a couple more before she's nice again."

"She's already pretty nice—for someone who wants to be a lawyer." He smiled, surprising Gwen when dimples appeared. But seriously? Leila must've blabbed about the LSAT to half the people she knew, and she hadn't even gotten her results back yet. "Leila called me. Not that I don't stop by here often—" His eyebrows rose as he scanned the room. "But she asked if I could make a special point of it today. Something about the two of you, a rotten ex-husband, and a bottle of tequila."

She'd pay Leila back for this. The first chance she got.

And she'd never again go to the bathroom without first taking Leila's cell phone away from her.

On the other hand, they now had a ride home. Forty-five minutes, another margarita for the women, and two Cokes for Jon later, they took it.

———

"When do you hear back on the LSAT?" As Danny stuffed the burger in his mouth, the words came out a little garbled.

The lunch crowd at Pendulum was louder than usual, even for a Friday, and Gwen could barely hear him over the noise. She didn't have to read lips, though, to figure out what Danny wanted to talk about. He was single-minded in his devotion to her budding legal career.

Gwen picked at her chef's salad. She should've ordered a burger, since Pendulum was famous for them, but she'd already promised to meet Adam here tonight, and she hadn't been able to refuse when Danny and Claudia asked her to join them for lunch on the spur of the moment. She'd already told Danny she couldn't eat at Melba Toast and didn't want to say no to Pendulum, too, but what were the odds that he'd ask her to lunch *and* want to eat at Pendulum? High, apparently. "I'm not sure. Pretty soon, I suppose."

Claudia, the third member of their old trio, evidently wanted to end her waiflike status. Having already polished off a burger, she munched on fries with a gusto that Gwen could only admire. She also admired Claudia's restraint. Unlike Danny, she didn't mention the LSAT every other minute.

"Which law school do you want to go to?" So much for Claudia's restraint. "Minnesota? Or someplace else?"

"She's not going to Georgetown." Harvard-boy Danny always needled Claudia about Georgetown, her alma mater, to which Claudia usually responded that only one of those schools ever had a decent basketball team. And it wasn't Harvard.

Claudia sniffed. "I didn't mention Georgetown." No, but she'd already left a brochure for it on Gwen's desk. Anonymously, of course, since she wouldn't want to be a pest. Like, say, Danny.

"Anyway, you know she can't go anywhere else." Danny

paused to inhale another large chunk of his burger, swallowing before he spoke again. "Gwen's got two kids."

She also had two good ears and a normal-sized ego, none of which liked being treated as if she weren't there. Not that she needed to be. Apparently, Danny already had her whole life mapped out for her.

Where had he been when she'd been twenty?

Oh, yeah. In sixth or seventh grade.

She ignored him, turning instead to Claudia. "Probably Minnesota, but I haven't decided yet. It depends on—"

Oops. She clamped her mouth shut.

"On what?" Danny and Claudia spoke in unison.

Gwen looked from one to the other. They'd been good friends to her almost since the day she'd started at Pembroke. "Actually . . . money." Head down, she attacked her salad with gusto.

Claudia grabbed the handle of her fork. "What are you talking about? Danny told me about the scholarship. You're all set—whatever you want to do."

She pried her fork back from Claudia, but her appetite had vanished. "I'm not, uh, sure what I want to do."

"That's okay." His burger long gone, Danny moved on to Claudia's fries, earning a slap on his hand. "Apply to a few schools. You can decide later."

"That's what I did." Claudia nodded.

"Yeah, but the good ones were already taken, so you went to Georgetown." When Claudia reached out to swat Danny, he grabbed a handful of fries off her plate. "Harvard didn't want you."

Claudia smiled sadly. "True. I wasn't a weird enough head case for Harvard."

"What? That came later?"

She shoved her plate across the table at Danny, who didn't miss a beat. Or a fry.

"Guys." Their sibling-like bickering could go on for hours, and Gwen needed to get back to work. Her least-favorite client had called that morning, asking her to file an SEC report this afternoon that wasn't due until next Wednesday. She could set her clock by the jerk and his damned rushes.

Her friends quit picking on each other long enough for Claudia to speak. "Danny is right, Gwen. You don't have to decide now, and money's not an issue. The scholarship pays for everything."

"I-I don't think I can accept the scholarship."

"*What?* Are you insane?" Danny practically jumped out of his chair. "It's a free ride. Why wouldn't you take it?"

She drew a deep breath, then let it out slowly. "Because I want to go to law school, but I'm not sure what I want to do with myself when I'm done."

Two pairs of eyes blinked at her.

Danny motioned to the waitress and asked for the check. In dead silence—except for the ongoing wailing from the jukebox—they waited for it to arrive. When it did, Danny waved off the other two and pulled out his wallet. "It's on me." He looked at Claudia. "Gwen just told us she can't afford it, and you need to be saving up for that house you want."

"Right." Claudia snatched the check away from Danny, who snatched it right back. "I'm the senior partner here." She grinned. She beat Danny by one year. "And I think I can still afford lunch."

Gwen opened her purse. "Why don't we split it?"

Two heads turned to her. "No."

When the waitress came back, Danny shoved the check

and a few bills at her, telling her to keep the change. He got up to leave, and Claudia and Gwen followed him out the door.

"That was my treat, since you couldn't join us for dinner last Saturday." Danny's eyebrows rose on a grin. "You probably had a hot date or something."

"Or something." Gwen leaned forward to ward off the windy gusts threatening to blow her down the sidewalk. "It wouldn't have been much of a celebration, anyway, since I'm probably going to turn down the scholarship."

Danny laughed. "Like hell you are. If you go to law school, you're taking it."

"You didn't hear what I said."

"Every single word." He stopped, forcing Claudia and Gwen to pull up short. "Gwen, I told you about my own scholarship. Ted didn't give it to me so I'd work at the firm. No strings; there aren't any on you, either. I changed my mind half a dozen times in law school about what I wanted to do. You probably will, too."

Claudia nodded. "All through high school and college, I told everyone who'd listen that I was going to be an ACLU lawyer. A hotshot First Amendment lawyer saving the world from evil. And you know what? I hated constitutional law with a passion—and every single First Amendment case. By third year of law school, I decided to do the big-dollar deals instead, because they were actually more interesting." She smiled sheepishly. "I guess you can say that I sold out, but I honestly don't think so."

Gwen hunched her shoulders, crossing her arms to keep out the wind, and the three started walking again. "But I might not want to work at Pembroke when I'm done. I might not even want to keep working there while I'm in school. To be honest, I have no idea what I'll do."

"Good." Danny buttoned his suitcoat. "That means you already have half a brain. I worry about the ones who go into it thinking they know everything."

"Sounds like someone I know." Laughing, Claudia dodged Danny's elbow and started running down the street. Patent-leather pumps and all.

———

"It just doesn't feel right." After a light day at work, Gwen leaned back on a bright-yellow Adirondack chair on Leila's patio, sipping a cool lemonade on an unseasonably warm late Friday afternoon. The midday breezes had come and gone. "I mean, Danny said so, but—"

"Stop right there." Curled up on a black wrought-iron loveseat with hot-pink cushions, Leila waved her bottle of Corona at Gwen. "You already said your firm will give you the scholarship no matter what. Babe, life throws enough problems at you. Don't start inventing new ones."

"But—"

"But nothing. You're not being dishonest. Hell—you don't have a dishonest bone in that skinny body of yours. And who knows? You might *want* to work at your firm when you're done with school. You don't know. So take the scholarship, go to law school, and figure it out along the way."

Pressing the bottle to her lips, Leila took a swig and somehow made it look like high tea at the Ritz.

Gwen blew out a long breath. "I suppose you're right." Leila nodded, looking too smug for words. "But should I stay in Minnesota for law school? Or take a chance, go somewhere else, and drag the kids along with me?"

"Tougher question." Leila wrapped her arms around her knees while she thought about it. "All things being equal, I'd say Minnesota. Law school is enough of a disruption, from what little I know. On the other hand, I'm guessing that not many people turn down Harvard."

Gwen's lemonade snorted out of her nose, and she made a wild grab for napkins to wipe up the mess. "Harvard? I'll be lucky to get into Minnesota as it is."

"Who knows? Apply to Minnesota and Mitchell-Hamline, maybe St. Thomas, and a few other schools that ring your bell." Leila shook her finger at Gwen. "It's your turn to get lucky." She grinned slyly. "Speaking of which, what's up with Adam?"

Glancing at her watch, Gwen jumped. "Yikes. I almost forgot. I'm meeting him at seven."

"Tonight?" A frown started at Leila's forehead and worked its way down her face. "Didn't you say you were giving up piano lessons?"

"Competitions. I still plan to keep playing piano." Gwen stood up, then wiped more of her spilled lemonade off of her pants. "I told him I'd take a lesson once in a while, even after he becomes a hotshot university professor." She grinned. "I like jabbing him with that one. Anyway, he said it leaves his Friday evenings free again and asked if I'd spend this one with him."

Leila choked on her beer. "Is it a date? I thought he'd backed away on that."

"Yes. And yes. At least, I think so." Gwen set her half-empty glass on a nearby table. "I mean, I'm not sure what it is. He goes hot and cold all the time."

"Sounds like a date to me." Rubbing her hands together briskly, as if plotting the Great Date of the Century, Leila squealed. "So don't be a prude. Wear something wild."

Gwen rolled her eyes as she headed toward her own yard, calling over her shoulder. "It's not that kind of a date."

Another squeal. "We'll see!"

———

"Wow. You look good."

"Thanks." In the dark lighting of Pendulum, where Gwen had agreed to meet Adam before realizing she'd be practically living here this week, she was surprised that he even saw her in the crowd at the door, let alone what she was wearing.

After Leila's advice, or despite it—she wasn't sure which—she'd changed clothes several times. Ultimately, she'd rejected the "safe" outfit she'd originally picked out in favor of a short skirt and stretchy top, both of which clung to her in ways that made Gwen grateful her kids weren't around when she'd slunk out the door.

Sarah had gone to a friend's house for dinner after volleyball practice. Nick had mumbled something about computer club. She'd spent more time with him recently. He hadn't repeated his shouted words at her, but he also hadn't retracted them. At best, they had a nervous truce. But Mac would be in town next weekend for her birthday. She could badger him again for advice on dealing with boys.

Specifically, boys who lived and breathed computers.

Adam said something she couldn't hear over the music and the raised voices of the crowd, then leaned forward to speak into her ear. In khakis and a snug polo shirt, he looked more than good. And he smelled clean and outdoorsy, like someone she'd like to tumble in bed with—or might, at least, if she had Leila's guts.

She didn't. Worse, the still-fresh memory of her stupidity with Tucker refused to go away no matter how many of Leila's affirmations she chanted—when no one was listening, of course. She'd stopped short of burning sage and rubbing crystals, and cursing him probably wouldn't be sporting of her.

"I said, are you hungry?" Adam's lips pressed against her ear, stirring her thoughts toward hunger of a different kind.

She nodded. "Want to eat here, or just have a drink?" Pendulum had fantastic food—as she ought to know—especially if you loved burgers and weren't picky about grease. She did and she wasn't. Besides, it was too dark in the place to notice. Or almost too dark.

"Here!" Adam shouted as he spotted an empty table and grabbed it, latching onto a chair a split second before a large, cranky-looking man in a tight sportcoat could. Gwen would've offered the chair to the man, afraid that she'd otherwise find him sitting on her.

The man surprised her by nodding, even pulling out the second chair for her. She thanked him, breathed a sigh of relief, and sat down.

Finding a table—and chairs, for bonus points—on a Friday night at Pendulum was a coup to be savored. Maybe even more than the burgers.

A waitress soon found them, and they placed their orders. Using the loud bar as their excuse, maybe, neither spoke until the waitress returned with their drinks.

Gwen could still taste her miniature hangover from Tuesday night's margaritas, so she nursed a Diet Coke. Adam drank some vile dark beer with a name she didn't recognize. At his urging, she tried a sip—and stopped just short of spitting it back in the bottle.

"Did you borrow that skirt from Leila?" The back of his hand trailed casually along her upper arm, making the hairs stand on end. "Are you sure you can wear something that short without a permit?"

She'd probably last flirted fifteen years ago. If then. "You said you liked short skirts. Or was that only on Leila?" A month ago, she'd have been afraid of his answer, afraid he really *would* prefer something—or nothing at all—on Leila.

"I like them just fine on you, too. Not that you need to wear them on my account." He waited until realization dawned on her, and she nearly fell out of her chair. "But I'd probably wait on that until we're out of here."

"At least." She mumbled it, shaking her head when he asked her what she'd said. His grin widened.

Two burgers arrived and slid down their throats in record time. Adam threw a few bills on the table, which was good, because Gwen's nervous hands alternated between ice cubes and sweaty clumps of clay, and she was pretty sure she would've bungled any attempt to reach into her purse to pay.

Outside on the sidewalk, Adam took one of her clammy hands in his. "Wanna come over for a while? Or do you have to get home?"

He'd given her an easy out, but the look in his eyes said he didn't want her to take it. She was pretty rusty on most details of the dating scene, but she knew that look. He wanted her.

She just wasn't sure what *she* wanted.

When Leila had first told her about Adam, she'd signed up for piano lessons partly as an excuse not to go out with Ted—but also wanting what other women all seemed to have. Sex. She hadn't had it in over two years, and what she'd had with Rob during their marriage hadn't counted for much. Then she'd made love again with Tucker. Her first love. Her stupid mistake.

She'd learned that even great sex wasn't always so great. On the other hand, sex with Adam might be worth exploring.

Eight o'clock. After fumbling in her purse for her cell

phone, she dialed the landline at home, which she kept mostly for the kids' schools. No one answered, which was odd. She didn't expect Sarah yet, but Nick should be home by now.

Adam waited patiently, considering the telltale bulge in the front of his slacks that she tried not to stare at.

Feeling sixteen, she looked down at the sidewalk. "I-I'll come over. My car's just down the street. Meet you there?"

"Nope." He tipped up her chin. "Let's drive together and go around the lakes. I'll bring you back downtown for your car."

Five minutes later, they were in his VW Beetle. He had the top up tonight, but he still didn't use the brakes as much she'd like.

Five minutes after that, Gwen's cell phone rang.

"Mom?" Sarah's voice sounded thick. "Could you maybe come right away?" Home? She'd just called there. "I'm at the hospital, and they said you oughta be here."

Gwen's head spun. Whatever it was, at least Sarah was able to function well enough to talk. "Are you okay, honey?"

"I'm a little—" Sarah groaned in obvious pain as voices chattered in the background. "Hurt. But don't worry." Another groan. Even over the phone, Gwen could tell she wasn't faking it. "My jump shot went in."

CHAPTER 19

The girl who never let a sprained ankle or twisted knee slow her down had actually admitted she was hurt? It must be awful.

Her car forgotten for the moment, Gwen let Adam rush her to Kendall South in his rust bucket. He'd barely stopped at the entrance to the emergency room when she flung open the door and ran inside.

Judging from the stares she got, not a lot of people visited patients in short skirts and clingy tops.

Breathless, she hurried to the counter and sputtered out Sarah's name, then was led to the curtained room where a frightened Sarah tried hard to show she wasn't. Between popping bubbles with her gum and raising her eyebrows at Gwen's outfit, she did a decent job.

She couldn't do much to hide the splint on her arm.

"Are you Ms. Stanhope?" A short man in a lab coat, who had sleep-tousled hair and looked about seventeen, glanced from his clipboard to Gwen. "I'm Dr. Edelstein."

Gwen nodded. "Sarah is my daughter. She broke her arm?"

"I'm afraid so. It's a clean break and should mend well, but she won't be doing anything with that arm for six weeks."

Sarah's lower lip stuck out. Mutiny was imminent.

Gwen smiled at the man. "I don't suppose you already mentioned that to her."

"I did as soon as we got the X-rays back." Dr. Edelstein tapped the lit-up screen on the wall. "You might want to mention it again while I start working on the cast. If that's okay."

His beeper went off. Without waiting for Gwen's answer, he sprinted down the hall.

She turned to Sarah, who looked both defiant and miserable as she perched on top of the gurney. Her lower lip trembled. "No way, Mom. I'll miss the rest of volleyball season and the beginning of basketball." Her voice went up an octave. "I won't even make the team!"

Gwen held up her hands. In surrender? "We'll talk to the basketball coach. But what happened? You must've finished practice a few hours ago." Sarah's gaze was glued to the floor. "Weren't you at Diana's house?"

"Didn't I say I'd be?" The words rushed out so fast, Gwen almost didn't catch them. But she knew evasion when she heard it. She'd used it on her own parents often enough as a teenager.

"Yes, you did. Were you in *fact* there?"

"You sound like a lawyer already." Sarah grinned nervously, clearly stalling for time.

"Thanks. Maybe I can skip law school and just take the bar exam." Gwen almost sat on the only chair in the room before remembering her short skirt. "But you didn't answer my question. Let's put it another way. Where were you, and what were you doing?"

Sarah started to raise her splinted arm but quickly

winced at the pain. "I was at Diana's." Her head dropped again. "For a while. Then we went over a couple blocks to Tommy's house to shoot hoops. He and his friends, uh—"

"Don't tell me." Gwen counted off on her fingers. "They're kinda cute, and they think you're the best basketball player they've ever seen—for a girl. And you might've been showing off, just a little, which is when you crunched your arm."

Sarah's eyes widened. "How'd you know?"

"Been there, done that." She smiled at Sarah. "For a dinosaur, I'm pretty hip."

Sarah stared at the floor again. "I guess. Tiff is hip, too—" She shrugged her narrow shoulders. "Sorry. I know you don't like her."

"Actually, I've met her. She's not so bad if you don't count her taste in men." Gwen held up a hand. "Sorry. I know you don't like me saying anything about your dad."

Sarah looked all around the small room before answering. "I called him when I couldn't reach you at first." Wincing, Gwen remembered hearing a faint ringing at Pendulum, a few minutes before she'd left with Adam. Not expecting a call, she'd assumed it was someone else's phone. Adam—

She'd forgotten Adam. Yikes. She'd have to go back to the lobby soon and check in with him. And somehow retrieve her car. So much for a wild encounter on a Friday night.

Somehow, she didn't mind.

"I'm sorry I missed you. I was in a loud restaurant and didn't hear my phone."

Sarah fiddled with the splint on her arm. "Yeah. So I call Dad, and Tiff answers. She, like, tells him to come get me, but he says they already had plans tonight. He told her to make up some lame excuse. I heard him, Mom. He didn't even care."

Her tough daughter looked ready to melt.

Rob. The rotten louse. "Of course he cares, honey. He's just busy sometimes."

"Right." Sarah's head was practically buried in her shirt to avoid Gwen's gaze. From the muffled sound, Gwen suspected a few tears were gathering. "He's never too busy for Tiff. He j-just doesn't like me."

Gwen put her arm around Sarah, careful not to jostle her bad arm, and held her until the shudders eased to a stop. "He'll always be your dad, and he'll always love you. He's just caught up in everything with Tiffany right now." She tipped up Sarah's chin, giving her an arch look. "Just like you might've been with those boys tonight. It's new."

Sarah caught her breath. "Y-you're not gonna do that, too, are you? Find somebody new so you don't care about us so much anymore?"

Not at this rate. Adam was probably long gone by now.

Running a hand through Sarah's hair, Gwen propped one hip against the gurney and inched closer to her daughter. "I'll always care about you exactly the way I do now." She tapped Sarah's nose, much as she had when Sarah had been a little girl. "To the moon and back, just like in that story we always read."

"And you won't find somebody else?"

Gwen shook her head. "I can't promise you that. I hope I *do* find someone, someday, who's right for me. But it won't ever change how I feel about you or Nick." She winked. "When you're not yelling at me, you're not too bad."

"Oh, Mom." Sarah leaned her head against Gwen. "I'm sorry. I just wanted Dad to do stuff with us, like you always do. I guess he's not gonna."

"Sure he will." If Gwen had to drag him through hot coals, she'd make sure of it. She smiled at the thought. "I'll bet you can talk Tiffany into doing things, and he'll see how much fun you're having and want to join in."

"Really?"

Gwen crossed her fingers behind her back, hoping Rob could transform himself into something other than a thoughtless, self-absorbed, total loser for the sake of their kids. "Really."

———

"Nick? Nick!" His bedroom door remained closed, even though Gwen had called his name several times in the last ten minutes. They were already late for the nine-thirty church service. Another minute or two, and they'd be embarrassingly late. "We're leaving!"

Sarah started up the stairs. "I'll get him, Mom."

A little more than thirty-six hours after breaking her arm, Sarah was already running everywhere she could, complaining that her arm either ached or itched, and generally driving Gwen nuts. Fine. Let her handle Nick, too.

His door banged open. Gwen winced, hoping Sarah had used her good arm on it.

"Mom! He's not here!" A little gleeful, Sarah came whooping down the stairs.

Gwen looked up at her. "What do you mean, he's not there?"

"I mean he's not there." Sarah rolled her eyes. "Like, duh. He's. Not. There."

She believed Sarah, but it didn't stop her from running up the stairs. Reaching his room, she peered inside. No Nick. The room was such a mess, she couldn't tell if he'd taken anything, let alone where he'd gone or when he'd left. If he *had* left.

"Sarah." Poking her head out the door, she called down to Sarah, who looked highly pleased at officially being too late for church. "Look in the basement and check the backyard. If Nick's not there, go next door to Leila's and ask if she's seen him this morning."

Gwen tried to remain calm, looking again through Nick's room before searching the bedrooms on the second floor. That done, she breathed a little harder and went downstairs. There weren't many places he could hide.

It also wasn't like Nick to hide, except in his room on the computer. He just didn't consider that hiding.

The front door slammed.

"Nick? Is that you?" She couldn't help the frantic note in her voice, and Leila's deep-breathing exercises weren't cutting it at the moment.

She didn't understand. Nick wasn't a kid who ran around the neighborhood playing with other kids. He also didn't usually drag himself out of bed before nine or even ten on weekends. She couldn't imagine where he could be.

"It's me." Leila's face appeared around the corner in the kitchen, where Gwen gripped her cell phone, wondering whether she should call someone. Rob? The police? The nearest hospital? Distracted, she almost didn't notice Leila's Winnie-the-Pooh pajamas. "Sarah says you can't find Nick. I told her to check out the neighborhood—partly just to burn off some of that excess energy she's got."

Gwen nodded, grim with fear but still hoping Nick would show up. Soon. "Thanks. He hasn't run around the neighborhood in quite a while, though. I don't know where he could be."

"With Rob? Doesn't he like to make secret plans with him just to bug you?" Leila grabbed a glass from the cupboard, then opened the refrigerator and poured herself some juice.

Gwen stared at her friend. With her own nerves jumping, she doubted she could put anything down her own throat and keep it there.

After swallowing the juice in two long gulps, Leila set the glass on the counter. "Now, let's see. Don't you figure he's with Rob? Give him a call."

"Rob's probably with Tiffany."

"No doubt." Leila waved a hand, brushing off Gwen's words. "But you don't care about Tiffany. You're trying to find Nick, and I don't think Sarah's going to find him playing tag or kickball in the street."

Gwen sighed. "You're right."

She dialed. No answer. After leaving a brief message on Rob's cell phone, in which she tried not to sound like she was out of her mind with worry, she hung up.

A moment later, she texted him, too.

"See? They're not home. Probably out doing something with Nick right this minute." Leila opened the refrigerator again, taking out a bagel and popping it in the microwave. "So relax. You've told me that Rob checks his messages all the time. He'll call back. It'll be fine."

"I hope you're right." Gwen appreciated Leila's cool assurance and wished she shared it. Her head pounding with worry, she reached into the cupboard for the bottle of aspirin.

"Have I ever been wrong?" The microwave dinged, and Leila juggled the steaming bagel on her fingertips for a few seconds before dropping it on the floor. Picking it up, she brushed it off and chomped on it.

As she swallowed two aspirin with a splash of water, Gwen pretended not to notice. "You? Wrong?" She paced, her low heels clattering against the tile floor. "Shouldn't I call the police? Just in case?"

"You know as well as I do what they'll tell you." Leila talked around the bagel in her mouth. "He's a kid. He's probably outside playing somewhere. It's a nice, sunny day. The cops won't worry until he's been gone all day."

"But we're talking about Nick. He might—"

Leila pulled the bagel out of her mouth. "Don't even suggest it. Nick is fine. He's probably with Rob, but if he's not, we'll find him. Maybe he went to the store."

"Nick doesn't shop unless it's in a computer store, and the closest one is three miles away. That's too far, even on his bike, not that he ever rides it anymore." Just to be sure, she opened the back hallway door into the garage.

Nick's bike was gone.

She sucked in a breath just as her cell phone rang. She grabbed it off the counter in a heartbeat. "Yes?"

"Gwen?" Rob. "I had to check on a patient. What's up?"

"Is Nick with you?" He wasn't. She knew he wasn't. But she wasn't above praying for a miracle.

"With me? Why would he be?" From the muffled voices in Gwen's ear, it sounded like Rob was covering the phone while he talked to someone else. "Tiffany hasn't heard from him, either." He barked at her. "Why? Have you lost the kid or some damn thing?"

Closing her eyes, Gwen tried to visualize serenity, or at least something other than strangling Rob. It didn't work.

The thought of strangling him felt too good.

"You're one to talk, aren't you?" She steeled herself against his likely reply, knowing that Rob was the king of gaslighting. "Nick's missing, and I'm looking for him. I started with you, even though I should've known you'd have no idea. You never do. You don't give your kids the time of day."

He cursed, which brought more muffled voices in the background, then surprised Gwen by calming down. "Sorry. You're right. I'm not much help, am I?" Gwen nearly fainted at his words. "I didn't help Sarah the other night, and now this. By the way, what did Sarah want? A ride to one of her damned games?"

Gwen winced at the sneer in his voice. "No. A ride to the hospital." Hearing him gasp, she smiled. A point scored for Sarah. "Don't worry. She just broke her arm playing one of her damned games."

"I've told her—"

"As I recall, you once broke your leg playing hockey when you were old enough to know better. How's that different?"

"You know perfectly well. Sarah's a girl." Rob blew out a long-suffering sigh—the sort he'd often used when explaining to her, in the waning days of their marriage, why a man might need to have other "interests" to make himself happy.

It had always made Gwen feel like an idiot. Now it just pissed her off.

"No shit, Sherlock." She turned her head, hoping Sarah wasn't around, either for her language or what she had to say to Rob. It was long overdue.

Leila's fingertips twinkled a cheery wave at her. Despite her worries over Nick and her anger at Rob, Gwen almost burst out laughing.

She heard a click on the line but kept talking, hoping Rob hadn't already hung up on her. It was a favorite tactic of his. "Sarah's a girl—and a tremendous athlete. She loves sports, is incredible at them, and—believe it or not—wishes her dad would notice. And root for her." She blew out her own long-suffering sigh. "So get over your prehistoric attitude, Rob. It's time you got to know your daughter, unless you want her to be the next kid we lose."

Before Rob could respond, a woman's voice interrupted. "Sarah's a good kid, and I can't believe her hook shot. It's—"

"Tiffany?" Gwen's and Rob's voices joined in the question, then Rob snapped a follow-up. "Could you get off the phone, Tiff? Please? I'm talking to Gwen."

High-pitched laughter. "Oh, Gwen and I are old friends." Gwen had to give the girl credit for guts. She'd never admit it to Rob, but she actually found Tiffany fun. Too fun for a prune like him. "And she's right, Rob. You're a little—what'd you call it, Gwen? prehistoric?—when it comes to Sarah. She's growing up before your eyes."

Yeah. One of these days, she'd be as old as Tiffany.

Silence. Then, improbably, Rob laughed. "Okay, okay. Two against one. I'll catch one of her games. Soon."

She'd never heard Rob concede a point so quickly, let alone to a woman. Unbelievable. Either he was still in the first stages of romance or Tiffany had worked a miracle. The toad had lost a few warts.

Just not enough that she'd ever want him back.

"It won't be anytime soon. Sarah has a cast on her arm, and the doctor said she's out of sports for six weeks." Gwen doubted that Rob would be counting down the days. "Right now, we have a son to find."

"Why would he—"

Tiffany cut off Rob's question. "We'll help, Gwen. Just tell us what to do."

———

In late afternoon on the longest day of her life, Gwen flopped back on the sofa, taking a break after six hours of frantic searching that felt more like sixteen. She closed her eyes and wished the nightmare would end. And end happily.

The landline rang. She'd jumped every time her cell phone had rung all day, but for once someone else could pick up the landline. Someone like Leila, who was still eating her out of house and home, claiming that stress did it to her. Of course, having called Adam and Jon to help search, Leila probably figured she'd done enough. The two men had taken off together three hours ago in Adam's clunker of a convertible, checking out nearby malls and computer stores.

Rob and Tiffany were driving around south Minneapolis, checking in periodically by cell phone. Despite her broken arm, Sarah and a small posse of friends were searching by bike. Neighbors and friends had been alerted, and many were helping. The police had come and gone, promising to return if Gwen hadn't heard anything by evening.

Evening. It wasn't yet four o'clock, and she'd already chewed off all of her fingernails.

The phone kept ringing. Apparently, Leila couldn't eat, drink, and answer phones at the same time. Gwen reached for the portable phone she'd moved to the coffee table.

Let it be Nick. Please. "Hello?"

"I think I've found the perfect birthday gift for you." Her dad chuckled into the phone. "You said you wanted something little and cute and fun. I even wrote that down." He paused. "Okay, it's not always fun, but at least it'll arrive before the big day."

"Oh, Dad." She hadn't called him, not wanting to worry him so soon after Vivian's death. He didn't need more trauma. "I'm not in the mood for presents today. Or surprises."

"Really? It's a good one."

She had to tell him. Either that, or he'd stay on the phone, joking with her while someone else tried to call with news. "Dad, it's—"

"I know, I know. It's far too generous of me. But I always did like to spoil my little girl, even if she's all grown up now." He dropped his voice to a conspiratorial whisper. "You've got to see it. Could you come over? Right away?"

Gwen shook her head. He *did* spoil her—but always on his schedule.

She hated telling him no, but Nick took priority. Finding him meant absolutely everything. "Sorry, Dad. I can't. Nick is—"

"—with me right now." His voice dropped even lower. "He's a little upset, and he doesn't know I called."

Speechless, Gwen nearly dropped the phone.

"Happy birthday, hon. Hope you like your present."

A tear rolled down her cheek. "I do, Dad. It's your best ever. Thanks. I'll be right over."

———

"What are you doin' here?" Cornered in the den of his grandfather's home—where, according to Gwen's dad, Nick had been working on the old computer for the last half hour—Nick gave Gwen a baleful look, then glared at his grandfather. "I told ya not to tell her."

Gwen's dad shrugged. "Sorry, champ. She's your mom, and she missed you. I couldn't do that to my favorite daughter."

Breathless from her frantic drive to her dad's house, Gwen's knees still shook from tension that refused to ease even with the news of Nick's safety.

"But you could do it to me." They could probably land a jumbo jet on Nick's protruding lower lip. He hung his head, peeking through his bangs at Gwen's dad. "I thought you liked me."

The older man put his arm around Nick, who squirmed. "There's no one I like better than you. But your mom feels the same way. I'll bet she's been worried sick."

Sick didn't begin to cover it. She still felt the nausea that had churned her stomach half the morning and all afternoon. Even knowing that Nick was safe, terror choked her. Seeing his bitter anger, the defiance that lit his eyes, she felt helpless. Would her lifelong estrangement with Vivian repeat itself with her son, ending only on someone's deathbed?

God, she couldn't let it happen again.

Taking a step toward the pair, she stopped when Nick thrust out an angry hand. "No way. All she cares about is Sarah. She likes Sarah a whole lot better 'n me. She probably didn't even know I was gone."

"Nick, that's not—"

Gwen's dad waved a hand, cutting her off. He bent down, hands on his knees, and looked Nick in the eye. "You know, you're probably right."

"*What?*" Her heart in her throat, Gwen nearly collapsed.

Nick looked a little startled. "I-I am?"

"She probably wants to get rid of you. Get you out of the house. For good." Her dad turned slightly, catching her eye long enough to wink. She didn't see the humor. Turning back to Nick, he shook his head. "And I'll bet you can guess why."

Nick looked like he'd just taken a bullet to the stomach. "N-no." His brow furrowed as he thought. "Is it 'cause I don't play basketball like Sarah?"

Utterly somber, Gwen's dad shook his head. "No. Try again."

Looking for all the world like the saddest boy in it, Nick stared at the floor. His shoulders shook, and Gwen doubted the wisdom of her dad's teasing, or whatever form of torture he was using on Nick. She took another step toward her son, but her dad again waved her away.

"I-I don't know." Nick positively drooped.

Putting both his arms around Nick, Gwen's dad hugged him tightly, then let go. He tipped the boy's chin up, again looking him in the eye. "It's because of your computer."

Good grief. She'd never forgive her dad.

Anger blazed in Nick's eyes as his tiny chin thrust out. "Yeah, she hates it. An' she hates me. She's just a big jerk. She never lets me use my computer."

Gwen couldn't help rolling her eyes, but fortunately Nick didn't see it. Her dad did, and he frowned at her.

As he did, Nick tore from his arms and started running from the room.

"Nick! Stop!" Two words from his grandfather halted a pair of feet that never obeyed a paragraph of commands from Gwen. "Come back here, my boy. You have it all wrong."

Gwen stared at Nick, silently willing him to turn around and hear what his grandfather had to say—whatever the hell that might be. She pressed a hand against her stomach, waves of nausea now twisting in her gut.

Nick turned around, but he didn't move. Gwen's dad went to him, motioning to Gwen to follow.

At Nick's defiant look, she stayed where she was.

Reaching Nick, her dad spoke again. "She's just jealous." *Huh?* "You see, even though your mom is really smart, she doesn't understand a thing about computers." Her dad should talk. For a guy who ran a huge electronics company, he couldn't even be bothered to keep a decent computer in his own house. "She wishes you'd teach her, but I don't think she has the guts to ask. You're quite a whiz at them, after all, and that might intimidate your mom."

The slightest dash of hope flickered in Nick's eyes as he stared at his grandfather. "Really?"

"Really. But I'll also bet you've never told her, like you told me, what you've been doing on your computer."

Oh, God. Did she want to know? Was it illegal?

Her dad frowned at her, as if he knew what she was thinking, before turning back to Nick. "You were telling me all about how you're using—what did you say? computer-aided design?—as part of that university group decoding something or other to help science find solutions to—" Her dad looked as mystified as Gwen felt, but Nick nodded. "I'm not sure I understand. But have you explained this to your mom?"

"She thinks I just play silly games on my computer. Like, all day long."

He didn't? What *was* he doing on his computer?

Her dad shook his head. "If she thinks that, it's only because you didn't explain. How would she know? Go ahead. Ask her what she thinks."

It wasn't quite how Gwen would've handled the situation, but maybe her dad knew a thing or two about boys, even if he didn't know much more than she did about computer-aided design. Except that he probably did. Much more.

But Nick's defiant look had vanished, replaced by a tremulous smile.

"Is— Is that right, Mom? You want to know about the work I do on my computer?"

She nodded. "Absolutely. And I'd love to have you show me a few things. I can never figure out Word."

"Aw, Mom." Nick rolled his eyes. "No wonder. Everybody uses Google Docs or other programs so you can share files, but maybe your law firm doesn't know any better. An' there's some cool stuff on the Internet I could show you. Even junk about law school."

"I'd really like that."

From the look on Nick's face, she suspected he couldn't understand why she'd go to law school without someone putting a gun to her head. Just like she couldn't understand why he sat in his room on a sunny day, for hours on end, playing with a computer—or *working* on it, as the case may be, solving all the problems of the world.

Maybe they could figure out both riddles. Together.

Gwen held out her arms. After hesitating a moment, Nick rushed into them. She had her son back. "You don't need to be like Sarah, honey." She glanced up at her dad, who looked unduly smug. "For one thing, then I'd have *two* kids with broken arms."

Her dad and Nick groaned at the same time. They sure stuck together. She smiled, liking the thought. "Besides, you're going to be busy. It sounds like your grandfather needs computer help, too. Maybe you can talk him into getting a new computer and teach him a few things."

Her dad's eyebrows rose. Served him right.

But no good deed went unpunished. "Good idea, and I have another one." Her dad joined Nick and Gwen, putting his arm around Nick's shoulders. "Maybe I should get a puppy, too. Now that— Well, with your grandmother gone, I'm going to be a little lonely. If I got a puppy, I don't suppose you'd be willing to help me take care of it, would you?"

"You mean it?" Nick practically leaped in the air.

"I sure do." Her dad smiled at his grandson. "I'm going to need all the help I can get."

Biting her lip, Gwen looked away. Her dad knew as well as anyone about her holy terror when it came to dogs. She couldn't believe he'd get one, even though she'd felt his heartache when he mentioned Vivian.

"Don't worry." Her dad ruffled her hair as if she were eleven years old, too. "The puppy will go in the basement whenever you come by. My favorite daughter isn't going to give me any excuses for not visiting. Often."

"Deal." She hugged him. She wasn't sure if the puppy was more for her dad or Nick, but she liked the return of a sparkle to her dad's eyes.

"And Gwen?"

"Yes?"

"Now that I've found Nick, does this mean I don't have to buy you a birthday gift?"

He'd found Nick but promised to get a dog. From her point of view, they almost cancelled each other out.

"No way. Start shopping."

Her dad saluted her. "Aye-aye. As you wish."

CHAPTER 20

"Any special plans for your birthday? The big four-oh?"

Washing her blue Mini Cooper in the driveway, Leila bent down with the scrub brush to attack the chrome on the wheels, almost losing her bikini top in the process.

Why she was wearing a bikini top in mid-October, Gwen had no idea.

Mimicking Leila's usual behavior, she pulled up a lawn chair and sat down to watch her friend work. She could've sold tickets.

Her birthday was this Saturday—and here it was, already Wednesday evening. Three months ago, she'd wished her fortieth birthday would never come. Now, she didn't dread it so much. What the hell. She might even get a few presents.

She could handle it.

She took a sip of her Diet Coke. "No plans. Turning forty isn't such a big deal."

"Of course it is." Her tongue peeking out of one corner of her mouth as she scrubbed, Leila was a study in concentration. "You've weathered a lot of storms in the last few months. I'm proud of you."

"Right." Gwen swirled the ice in her glass. "I'll agree

with the storms, but I'm not sure how well I've weathered them. Most of the time, I got soaked."

Grabbing the hose, Leila rinsed the tire and moved on to the next one. She looked a little too triumphant considering that the chrome was still pretty muddy. Gwen decided not to point it out to her. She wasn't the one with the hose.

"You know, they actually have drive-through car washes these days." Gwen grinned, trying to look helpful. "I'm not sure I remember the last time I saw someone do this."

Leila ignored her comment. "You really need to stop bashing yourself all the time. You've done well. Really well. You're okay with Rob—"

"Hardly." Tiffany had become a good buffer, to Gwen's unending surprise, and Rob had started making amends with both Sarah and Nick as soon as she'd brought Nick home on Sunday, safe and sound. But he was still Rob. She pitied Tiffany.

"Fine. You'll never be thrilled with him, but that's not the point. You're figuring out how to deal with him."

That was true. She'd also realized, after all these years, that she'd never been all that thrilled with Rob. She wouldn't mind having all the wasted years back, but at least she had Sarah and Nick, and she wouldn't give them up for anything.

Life with her kids was, all of a sudden, good. More laid up than she liked with her arm in the cast, Sarah hung out in Nick's room for the computer "classes" that Nick was giving Gwen. Nick was so proud of himself, he even trudged along —okay, once—when Gwen and Sarah walked around Lake Harriet.

Leila interrupted Gwen's happy reverie. "What about Tucker? Have you talked to him yet?"

"No, but maybe I'll break down and do it someday." She gave the matchmaking Leila a warning look. "Not today or tomorrow, but someday. I've had so many other things to deal with, the whole disaster with him doesn't faze me as much anymore."

"That's good." The smile Leila gave her was sweet. Sweet and cunning. "But what's happening with Adam? Since Friday was a bust, do you guys have another date lined up?"

"No." Gwen closed her eyes, remembering how eager she'd been for something to finally happen with Adam. The moment Sarah called from the emergency room, he'd disappeared from her mind even as they drove together to the hospital. That told her everything she needed to know. "The truth is, I think we're going to turn out to be just pals. And I think I'll like it that way."

"Why?" Having finished her assault on the last tire, Leila stood up and stretched. "I thought you liked him. And God knows he's cute."

"He also plays a wicked game of tennis." Gwen laughed at the puzzled look on her friend's face. "I know. Adam is good looking and nice—and he kisses like nobody's business. He's also thirty-one. I think I'd rather be with someone closer to my own age."

It wasn't really his age. After jumping in bed with Tucker, she'd discovered—too late—that she wanted more from sex than a hot body. Yes, she'd waited too long to resume her life, but she could wait a little longer for a man who felt right. She was worth it.

Leila gave her car a final rinse. "Have someone your own age if you want, but until he arrives on the scene, you can still have fun with Adam. He likes you."

"And I like him." Gwen shook her head, not knowing how to explain. She hadn't explained it too well to Adam, either, when they'd spoken Sunday after she found Nick. "The chemistry can be pretty hot when we're together. It's just—I don't know—I'd rather have him as a friend. Or even a younger brother."

"You already have a younger brother, and you have plenty of friends." Leila aimed the hose at Gwen, threatening to soak her. Knowing she wouldn't, Gwen didn't blink. "You don't get hot chemistry every day of the week. I'd take it and run."

"But I'm not you." Being Leila would be exhausting. "You told me I had to take baby steps. I took a lot of them, and you were right. But now that I'm finally growing up, I guess I just want to be me."

Leila smiled. And turned the hose on Gwen full force.

Soaking wet, Gwen leaped up and ran after her, yelling like a banshee until she reached Leila and the hose. They struggled for control of the hose until both had water streaming from their eyes and down every inch of their clothes and skin.

"What was that for?" Throwing the hose on the ground, Gwen marched to the outside faucet and turned it off.

Leila didn't stop her. "You said you were growing up. I didn't want it to happen too fast."

———

A RINGING PHONE jarred her awake. Opening one eyelid, Gwen peered at the clock on her nightstand. Seven. Only Mac would call her at this hour on a Saturday morning. Even on her birthday.

Her dad was too polite, and Leila would still be asleep.

Not bothering with a hello, she picked up the phone and pressed it to her ear. "I'm old, Mac. Too old to talk to anyone this early in the morning. Especially to pesky little brothers."

Silence. Then he cleared his throat.

"Do you take calls from pesky dads?" Her dad's husky voice rumbled over the phone, ending on a chuckle.

Great. He'd spent too much time around Mac lately. She liked the way her dad used to be. This version was a little pesky.

"I prefer them at a later hour. Like, say, after seven."

"Thank goodness. It's seven-oh-two." Another chuckle.

"What's up, Dad? Or did you dial a wrong number?"

Before answering, he burst into an off-key rendition of "Happy Birthday." Then he laughed again. "You'll be pleased to know I've found it. After a lengthy search, I followed your instructions to the letter. 'Little and cute and fun.' Your exact words. So I bought it."

She barely remembered the conversation, but if "little and cute and fun" referred to a puppy, she'd strangle him. With the puppy's leash. "And you called me at seven in the morning to tell me this because—"

Laughing, her dad sounded inordinately pleased with himself. Fine. She would've been pleased, too, if he'd let her sleep a little later on her birthday. Maybe until seven-thirty.

"It's a surprise." Her dad whispered into the phone as if he wanted to keep others from finding out the surprise. She wanted to tell him not to worry. No one else would be awake at this hour. "And I can't wait another minute to give it to you. I'll be right over."

He hung up before she could tell him to stop, reset his alarm, and go back to sleep. She rolled out of bed, glaring at the sunshine peeking in through the blinds.

At least her dad was happy. But thanks to him and his lousy good humor, her own day had started too early and was heading downhill fast.

Ten minutes later, when she'd barely had time to slip on sweatpants and a T-shirt and run a brush through her hair, a horn honked in the driveway. Perfect. It wasn't enough that her dad had to wake her at dawn. Now he wanted to piss off the whole neighborhood.

"I'm coming!" Grumbling all the way, Gwen stomped down the stairs, even though the kids would probably wake up and the intended target of her grousing—her dad—was outside. Honking the horn again.

As she swung open the front door, her jaw dropped. Her knees almost dropped right along with it, but she grabbed the doorframe for support.

He'd bought her a convertible. And not just any convertible.

A restored, lemon-yellow MG Midget. With a huge blue bow on the hood. Except for the bow, the tiny convertible was exactly the classic British sports car she'd coveted all through high school and well into college. She didn't think she'd ever confessed her secret desire to her dad—or certainly not in the last twenty years. Before that? No more than a hundred times, tops.

Little and cute and fun? Her dad wasn't kidding.

He gave one more short tap on the horn, then extricated himself from behind the wheel. His grin was as wide as the car.

A door slammed. Then another. As she stepped out her front door, Gwen whirled to hear Leila's "holy shit!" and saw a blurred vision of slippers and a short nightie that vanished almost as quickly. Hearing footsteps behind her, Gwen turned, holding out a hand for Sarah, who rubbed the sleep out of her eyes. "Wha's going on, Mom? Who's—"

Sarah's jaw dropped, too.

But she didn't miss a beat. "For me?"

"Not in this lifetime, sweetie." After giving Sarah a quick

squeeze, she ran down the steps and into her dad's arms. "Oh, Dad. I can't believe it."

His grin faded. "Your mother and I spent hours planning this. She . . . wanted so much to be here, to see the look on your face when we gave it to you."

"Well, she's getting a front-row seat from heaven." Leila, in a shirt and jeans she'd thrown on and—in her obvious haste—only zipped up halfway, came up behind them. Whistling, she ran an admiring hand along the side of the car. "You've got great taste, Mr. Withers."

"Skip." He moved back to the MG. "Nice to see you again, Leila." Gesturing at Gwen, he called her over to the car before turning back to Leila. "And thanks for the compliment, but Gwen picked out the car, right down to the year: 1976. She probably just thought my memory had faded over the last twenty-five years." He smiled, opening the driver's door for Gwen. "But I couldn't forget this little baby. I'm a big fan of cars myself."

"Me, too." Leila nodded enthusiastically. "You know, my birthday's just around the corner . . ."

Gwen climbed in, running her hands over the steering wheel and fingering the stick shift. "Dad. I absolutely love it, but you shouldn't have. It's so expensive. I mean, we talked about this. I'm supposed to be supporting myself."

Sarah jumped in. "Then can I have it?"

Leila put a restraining hand on Sarah's shoulder. "Over my dead body, squirt. Didn't I mention my birthday? We could call it an early gift."

"Early is right." Gwen shook her finger at Leila. "Aren't we talking June?"

"Details, details." Smiling, Leila climbed into the passenger side of the two-seater.

"Sorry, Leila." Gwen's dad then turned to Sarah, ruffling

her hair. "And you, young lady, are not even old enough for a learner's permit." He tipped his head at Gwen. "Tough luck, kid. You're stuck with it. All you said was no mortgage or tuition payments. I didn't hear anything about cute little convertibles."

As she stumbled over a response, he shrugged. "Your mother and I both wanted you to have it. After she . . . died, and you said you wanted little and cute and fun, I knew the MG we'd been looking for would be perfect. They don't get much smaller than this."

Reaching down, he rubbed his kneecaps for effect.
"But I . . ."

All her life, she'd wanted this car. It just didn't feel right taking it. After spending so many years being taken care of, she wanted to stand on her own two feet.

"Take it for a spin, honey. If it's too much for your birthday, consider it an early law school graduation gift." Crouched next to the driver's door, he pointed up at the bright, cloudless sky. A morning chill still hung in the air, but they'd predicted a high in the seventies. "There won't be many more fall days like this one. If you drive it and still want me to take it back . . ."

The keys dangled from his fingers. Snatching them away from him, Gwen inserted the key in the ignition, thrilled at the rumble of the finely tuned engine.

Not being a fool, her dad stepped away from the MG and motioned to Sarah, who was giggling with Leila on the passenger side, to do the same. As the car backed up a few inches, her dad frowned. "Don't you want to put the top back up? Or I could grab a jacket for you—"

The tires squealed as she rounded the turn into the street and took off.

———

"WHAT?" The wind roared in her ears and through her hair, wreaking havoc with her early-morning attempt to make it look halfway presentable. After tooling around the lakes for twenty minutes before hitting the open highway, her hair didn't stand a chance.

She loved it. She felt alive, free, and happy.

She also couldn't hear a word Leila said.

Leila tried again, this time shouting. "I said, he's gotta be the coolest dad on the planet. What a gift! You're not going to return it, are you?" She grabbed Gwen's shoulder as they zipped around a sharp turn. "You'd be crazy!"

"I'm not *that* crazy." Glancing at Leila, Gwen smiled before returning her gaze to the road. "I've been thinking about it. Maybe I can support myself and still let my dad spoil me once in a while. I guess you've taught me well."

"Thank God for that." Leila peered at the old-fashioned clock on the dashboard. "Is that thing right? It's not even eight o'clock yet?" Gwen nodded. "No wonder I feel so awful."

"Sorry. I guess my dad was a little excited."

Leila ran a hand through her hair, which somehow managed to look even better now than when they'd begun their wild ride. Another reason to hate the woman. "Half the neighborhood must be speculating over their morning coffee about how that dratted Leila is ruining sweet, kind little Gwen."

"I doubt it." Reaching out, Gwen patted Leila's leg. "Most of the men are too busy wondering how they're going to get a ride in this thing."

"Funny."

"And everyone loves you. Even if you *do* spend most of

your time and energy trying to ruin me." She smiled sweetly at Leila a split second before taking another hairpin turn.

Leila squealed. "At least I'm not trying to *kill* you."

"Don't worry." Gwen slowed for a light that went from yellow to red. "I won't take too many chances." She adjusted the rearview mirror, then turned to Leila and winked. "Not with my new car."

———

"I TOLD you I didn't want to make a big deal out of my birthday." Hands on her hips, Gwen released a frustrated sigh as she glared at her brother and dad. "At least tell me where we're going."

"It's a surprise." Her dad took her hand and tugged her toward the front door of her house. Nick and Sarah were already outside, waiting in their grandfather's silver Lexus. Mac had generously offered to drive Gwen's new convertible.

Declining, she'd perhaps been less than gracious.

"You're full of surprises today." At the last minute, she tossed her keys to Mac, who'd spent the last half hour drooling over her MG, and climbed in the passenger side. "Okay, okay. I guess I've had enough practice behind the wheel."

After four or five hours spent giving everyone she knew— and a few people she really didn't—a ride in the convertible, she could be nice to Mac. Just this once. After all, he'd offered to let her drive his beat-up Jeep.

Mac had almost as much trouble bending his tall, lanky frame into the tiny convertible as their dad had experienced. Youth, and a lifelong disregard for his limbs, helped.

After their dad drove away in his Lexus, Gwen turned to

Mac. "So spill. What's the big surprise? Where are we going?"

Mac didn't speak as his gaze and hands roamed all over the dashboard. He looked like a kid with his first bike.

Much like Gwen had looked at seven-thirty this morning.

He finally started the car and backed down the driveway before answering. "Nothing too fancy. Dad wanted to try this place, and I guess he just likes his surprises." He grinned at her. "Like this Midget. What a beauty."

A few minutes later, Mac pulled onto the entrance ramp for 35W, heading downtown. Gwen groaned, hating the thought of some sixteen-year-old boy offering to valet park. Not a chance.

Mac must've guessed her thoughts. "Don't worry. I'll even spring for parking, and not valet. What the heck—it's your birthday."

"Big spender." She closed her eyes and leaned back, a little awkwardly. Whoever had restored this MG had fixated on using headrests like the originals. Unfortunately. "Knowing you, I hope I'm not paying for dinner."

"Taken care of."

They listened to the radio without further comment the rest of the way downtown. Just as Gwen felt herself start to doze, Mac screeched to a halt. "Oops. Almost missed it, since the main door is around the corner on Nicollet. Here, I'll let you out and go park."

Considering the heels she wore, Gwen wasn't about to say no. "Thanks. I'll—" As she started to open the door, she recognized the side door to the restaurant. And froze.

He'd brought her to Melba Toast.

She stammered. "C-can't we go somewhere else? I hate this place."

Shaking his head, Mac grimaced. "Sorry. We've got the

whole thing set up, and I think everyone's already here." Then he frowned. "But I don't get it. Dad asked Leila, and she said it's a great place."

Damn it. And on her birthday, no less. No wonder the traitor had asked about Tucker the other day. That rotten, scheming—

"Hi guys!" The object of her wrath materialized out of nowhere. Opening the door for Gwen, Leila took her arm. "Come on. The gang's all here."

Gwen climbed out but left the door open as she debated what to do. How to end this disaster. "I can't believe you did this to me. On my birthday."

Slamming the passenger door, Leila clucked. "Is that any way to talk to your best friend? Really." Pressing her hand over her heart, she pretended to look crushed. "After all the things I've done for you."

Gwen wrinkled her nose. "Like this?"

Mac picked that moment to pull away from the curb. Gwen shouted at him to stop. He accelerated.

"This is mostly your dad's fault." Leila faked her best helpless look. "Or should I have told him why you'd rather avoid this place?"

"Funny. You could've said I hate the food."

"But you don't. And I never lie—or at least no more than absolutely necessary." She grinned. "Besides, you told me you were ready to deal with Tucker."

Groaning, Gwen shook her head. "*Someday*, Leila. I said someday. And it sure won't be in front of my family."

"Fine. Then do it right here." She looked behind Gwen, smiling brightly at someone. "Hi—I think we've met." As Gwen turned to see Tucker, Leila blithely ignored the horrified look on her face. "And I know you know Gwen. Shoot. I should really get back to our table, but maybe you guys want to talk."

"No, we—"

Leila shushed her, then turned back to Tucker. "It's her birthday. Be nice for a change." With that, she whirled and hurried inside the restaurant, leaving Gwen and Tucker alone on the sidewalk.

Knowing Leila, she'd quickly find a spot inside by one of the darkened windows just to watch the fireworks.

"Gwen." Tucker took her hand, holding it for a moment before she pulled it out of his grasp. "I'm sorry about what happened." He looked to each side. "But this probably isn't the best place to talk about it."

"I doubt that any place would be good." All the hurt, the disappointment—the shame—came flooding back, and Gwen stared down at her feet.

At least she was wearing cute shoes.

"Maybe. Maybe not." Tucker didn't say another word until she looked back up at him. "I won't try to tell you I'm separated, or getting a divorce, or even unhappy. I love my wife. She's— Well, she's great. And we've got a beautiful baby girl."

He had a *child*? A baby? Gwen felt herself go numb.

"Am I supposed to congratulate you?" She snapped. "That's rich. Don't hold your breath."

"That's not what I meant." His hand grasped her bare forearm, but the sizzle she'd always felt when they touched didn't happen. She stared at his hand until he released her. "What I meant was—"

When he didn't continue, she crossed her arms and tapped her toe on the sidewalk. "Yes?"

He shoved his hands in his pockets. "I'm not sure *what* I meant that day. I have to admit—part of me has always been angry. You dumped me without even bothering to explain. Just like that." He snapped his finger. "I'd been saving up for an engagement ring."

"You never mentioned marriage." She didn't know whether it would've affected anything, but . . . it might've? Pressing her lips together, she ached for the disappointment he must've felt. Looking at his face now, she suspected it had never really gone away.

He shrugged. "I didn't figure I could. Girls from Edina want a better life than I could afford. And your mom—"

"Please." She held up a hand to stop him. "Don't go there. Not that you're wrong about her, but I'm the one who made the mistake. Not Vivian."

He waited as a group of young people wandered by, peering into the restaurant windows before continuing down the street.

Nodding, he jabbed his thumb at the departing group. "We weren't much older than they are, you know? A long time ago. I just wished we could've talked."

Gwen looked everywhere but at him. "I know. I was a jerk. I never had any willpower when it came to you, and I figured I'd never be able to leave."

"Yeah." Tucker waited until she returned his gaze. "We spent most of our time horizontal. That's— I guess that's the real reason I let things happen. Here, in my old condo, which my wife isn't exactly a fan of, even though I honestly kept it for occasional late nights and a few key employees who sometimes need a place to crash." He nodded up at the second-floor window. "But I've always wanted to know, I guess, if it would be the same."

She knew the feeling but wasn't sure she wanted to know his conclusion. "And was it?"

Whistling, he nodded. "Oh, yeah. I almost didn't tell you

—tell you I was married. After finally having you back, I wanted to keep you there."

"I'm glad you told me." She rolled her eyes. "Too late for me to do anything about it, but at least you did."

His smile was a little sadder this time. "At a minimum, I owed you that. I'm sorry. This time I'm the jerk. To you *and* my wife."

"I guess it's your turn." Holding out her hand, she waited until he shook it. "I suppose we both wanted something we couldn't have—or at least can't have anymore. And I'm not sure where it leaves us. Friends? Acquaintances?" She laughed awkwardly. "I know tonight won't be the last time I visit one of your restaurants. The food is too good to pass up."

"Maybe someday we *could* be friends again. That'd be . . . nice." He tipped his head at the window, where Leila's nose was pressed against the glass. "But I'm keeping you from your party. Let me take you inside."

———

". . . Happy birthday, dear Gw-e-en . . ."

Gazing around the large table at the dozen or so people singing loudly and without a shred of musical talent, Gwen smiled. Turning forty was turning out not to be so bad.

Tucker and a few waiters joined the group for the song, then disappeared into the crowd. Back to work.

She'd expected her family and Leila. Dad smiled at her, Sarah stared at a cute teenage boy at the next table, and Nick looked like an eleven-year-old who'd rather be eating at McDonald's. Mac had slipped into his chair halfway through the song, shrugging as if he'd had trouble finding a parking spot.

No one believed it.

The other guests were a surprise, but a nice one. Monica Lauren leaned close to Mac, whispering something in his ear that made him smile. Leila had brought her friend—and now Gwen's friend—Jon, who'd given her a silly birthday card and an utterly ridiculous pair of fuzzy dice for her new rearview mirror.

Her favorite co-workers—Danny and Claudia—completed the group. Leila must've somehow conspired with Gwen's secretary to invite them.

Seated between her dad and Jon, Gwen leaned over, kissing her dad's cheek. "Thanks, Dad. I guess I owe you one."

His arm came around her shoulders. "Anything for my baby girl. You have to let me spoil you every so often. I'd forgotten how good it felt."

He'd spoil her whether she liked it or not. "Deal."

On her other side, Jon tapped her arm, then pointed at the fuzzy turquoise-and-yellow dice. "Now that your new car has all the right accessories, I hope you'll be offering rides."

He looked hesitant but much happier than he'd been when they first met.

"It takes more than a cheap pair of dice to get a ride in my car." She grinned at him. "More like chocolate."

He slapped his forehead. "If I hadn't eaten those M&Ms on the way over, I'd be all set. But Leila's driving made me too nervous."

"Having ridden with her more often than I'd care to think about, I'll have to forgive you. Even if that's my favorite chocolate and you were—" She shuddered, even though her lips twitched. "A complete cad to eat them. Think nothing of it."

"You're becoming as dramatic as Leila." He nodded at Leila, on the other side of him, but she was engrossed in conversation with Danny. "It must come from driving with her so often."

"I'll try to avoid it from now on."

"Good." He glanced around the table, then leaned closer. "Maybe you could take a drive with me sometime? On a date?"

It wasn't her first surprise of the day—not by a mile—but he could've knocked her over with a feather. Mute, Gwen stared at Jon, her mouth open in surprise.

She kind of liked the idea. Jon, a man who hadn't been sure he ever wanted to date again. A man who loved good books—and made a life out of selling them—and baked pies and bought goofy gifts and spoke intelligently about everything from opera to gas grills.

Maybe he'd even like the Eagles.

But it'd be okay if he didn't.

In her silence, Jon's face started to fall, and she scrambled to recover. "I'd like that a lot." She laughed when he looked doubtful. "I mean, as long as you let me drive my car. I have a really cool pair of dice, you know."

"So I've heard." He drew closer, so close that she wondered if he planned to kiss her cheek. Instead, his voice dropped lower. "I like doing things with you, Gwen Stanhope. And the talks we've had."

"The ones where Leila interrupted every five seconds?"

"Even those." He smiled a little tentatively. "But . . . I was hoping we could take things a little slow at first. It's just—"

Nodding, she rested her hand on his, linking them. "Slow sounds pretty good to me." Leaning toward him, she grinned. "Except when I'm driving my convertible."

A NOTE FROM MARY

Thank you for reading **Driving with the Top Down**! Turning 40 shouldn't be that big of a deal, but Gwen Stanhope inspired me to *make* it a big deal. Similarly, my own love of Eagles music inspired Gwen to love the Eagles, too. (Especially Glenn Frey, because . . . Glenn Frey.) Funny how that works! As luck would have it, I also managed to throw in a few references to Minneapolis bands I love. By the way, I will note that I wrote the first drafts of this book several years ago, long before I was taking my own music lessons (although it's guitar for me and piano for Gwen). So apologies in advance to my fabulous guitar teachers, Ryan Smith and Mark Wade, if they read about Gwen's adventures with her piano teacher, Adam, and maybe want to throw up. The things I write! Ha ha!

If you enjoyed this book, I would really appreciate it if you could leave a review wherever you buy or talk about books. Whether super short or longer, all reviews are good, and they help other readers discover my books. Thank you so much!

I also love to hear from my readers! Please stay in touch by signing up for my newsletter. You can also connect with me on Facebook, Twitter, Instagram, or through my website. For links, check out my bio on the next page.

Happy reading!

Mary

ABOUT THE AUTHOR

Mary Strand practiced law in a large Minneapolis firm until the day she set aside her pointy-toed shoes (or most of them) and escaped the world of mergers and acquisitions to write novels. The first manuscript she wrote, *Cooper's Folly*, a romantic comedy, won RWA's Golden Heart award and was her debut novel. Her love of Jane Austen prompted her four-book YA series, The Bennet Sisters.

Mary lives on a lake in Minneapolis with her family, too many Converse Chucks, and a stuffed monkey named Philip. When not writing books or songs, she lives for sports, travel, rocking out on guitar, dancing (badly), and ill-advised adventures (including dancing) that offer a high probability of injury to herself and others. She writes YA, romantic comedy, and women's fiction novels.

Driving with the Top Down is the second novel in The Pendulum Trilogy.

You can find Mary at www.marystrand.com, follow her on Twitter or Instagram, or "like" her on Facebook.

ALSO BY MARY STRAND

Cooper's Folly

THE BENNET SISTERS

Book 1 - *Pride, Prejudice, and Push-ups Bras*

Book 2 - *Being Mary Bennet Blows*

Book 3 - *Cat Bennet, Queen of Nothing*

Book 4 - *Livin' La Vida Bennet*

The Bennet Sisters four-book set

THE PENDULUM TRILOGY

Book 1 - *Sunsets on Catfish Bar*

Book 2 - *Driving with the Top Down*

Book 3 - *Seemingly Perfect* - COMING SOON